The GRACES

Also By Siobhan MacGowan

The Trial of Lotta Rae

The
GRACES

SIOBHAN
MACGOWAN

WELBECK

First published in 2023 by Welbeck Fiction Limited,
an imprint of Welbeck Publishing Group
Offices in: London – 20 Mortimer Street, London W1T 3JW &
Sydney – Level 17, 207 Kent St, Sydney NSW 2000 Australia
www.welbeckpublishing.com

The lines from 'On Raglan Road' by Patrick Kavanagh are reprinted from
Collected Poems, edited by Antoinette Quinn (Allen Lane, 2004), by kind
permission of the Trustees of the Estate of the late Katherine B. Kavanagh,
through the Jonathan Williams Literary Agency.

'Rare Ould Times' by Pete St. John is reprinted by kind
permission of Emma Music/Celtic Songs.

A CIP catalogue record for this book is available from the British Library

Hardback ISBN: 978-1-78739-733-0
Trade paperback ISBN: 978-1-80279-322-2
Ebook ISBN: 978-1-78739-734-7

Printed and bound by CPI Group (UK) Ltd., Croydon, CR0 4YY

10 9 8 7 6 5 4 3 2 1

To the Dubliner who raised me on songs and stories.

My beloved father.

Grá go deo

'On Raglan Road on an autumn day I met her first and knew
That her dark hair would weave a snare that I might one day rue;
I saw the danger, yet I walked along the enchanted way,
And I said, let grief be a fallen leaf at the dawning of the day.'
                    – 'On Raglan Road', Patrick Kavanagh.

'Raised on songs and stories, heroes of renown
The passing tales and glories that once was Dublin town
The hallowed halls and houses, the haunting children's rhymes
That once was Dublin city in the Rare Ould Times.'
                    – 'Rare Ould Times', Pete St. John.

1

Mount St Kilian Abbey, Dublin, 1918

High in the monastery, in the stillness of his chamber, Brother Thomas placed a candle upon the arched window's deep stone sill. He cast an eye on the late August sun setting now on the Tallaght Hills and Mount Seskin beyond. His eye moved downhill to the chapel roof, the cloisters, the sweep of grounds, before coming to rest on the saplings, the oaks, the monastery woodland. There, in the scant light, he followed the flicker of flames, a steady, solemn procession of candlelight weaving through the trees. Bound for the bell tower. They had come.

Disturbed by a knocking, he turned at the whine of the heavy wooden door.

'Brother Thomas.' It was Dominic, the new postulant, still being versed in the ways of the monastery. 'There is a Father Sheridan asking to see you. Shall I show him in?'

Brother Thomas frowned in surprise. He had not seen Father Sheridan for many a year. He wondered at this unexpected visit.

'Yes, of course. Please. Show him in.'

The boy disappeared from the door, Father Sheridan appearing soon in his place.

'Thomas.' Father Sheridan greeted Thomas warmly. 'It's good to see you after all this time.'

'And you, Declan.' They clasped hands, Brother Thomas studying his old acquaintance. He remembered when last he had seen him. The three years that had passed had changed Father Sheridan only slightly. He was stouter, his once-greying hair whiter. But his skin was still fresh, his expression as ever warm. They held eyes for a moment before Father Sheridan spoke.

'It's been too long, Thomas. We have not seen each other since . . .'

He did not finish but Brother Thomas nodded. 'Please,' Brother Thomas said, gesturing to two chairs by the small fire in the hearth; the night on the cusp of autumn was chill in the stony vastness of the monastery. 'Sit.'

Father Sheridan stepped across the room, the pine floorboards creaking beneath his feet. Brother Thomas watched him take in the surroundings he had once known so well, the thick, ochre walls, the blood reds and gold gilding of the painted icons, the graceful and sorrowful face of the statuette Madonna. 'How have you been?' Father Sheridan asked of his host. 'You look well. You serve as a champion for monastic life.'

Brother Thomas smiled. 'I am well. And you?'

'The students are keeping me busy.' Seeming lost in thought, Father Sheridan passed the chairs at the hearth to wander to the window. He stood silently for a moment, looking out. 'So they have come. On this, the third anniversary of her passing.'

Brother Thomas stood silent behind him. Every year on this night, as the sun set, they came. Came to pay homage to the one they called the Rose.

Father Sheridan mused. 'Her pilgrims. Come to walk the Way of the Rose. For what she saw came to be.' He turned slowly from the window. 'It seemed fitting that I come tonight, as it is of her we must speak.'

Brother Thomas observed the priest. 'You wish to speak to me of Rosaleen Moore?'

'Yes.' Brother Thomas said nothing, but gestured again to the chairs by the fire. Father Sheridan sat, Brother Thomas taking a seat to face him. 'You know I saw her?' Father Sheridan said. 'Shortly before she died.'

Brother Thomas turned to the fire. 'I did not.'

'When she was dying she called for me. She was a woman haunted. And now I too am haunted. Haunted by what she told me. Of herself.' He paused. 'Of the Abbot.'

Brother Thomas looked up as the priest fell silent.

'It seems the Abbot haunts us all,' Father Sheridan said at last, casting his eyes over the chamber. 'He, the confessor. He who for so long heard the sins of others, now condemned to a cell to pay for his own. When I think of the many hours I spent talking to him in this very room. Of the many years I knew him. And then to learn what he did. Still, I cannot conceive of it.'

Brother Thomas turned again to the fire as Father Sheridan went on, 'I always believed him a good man.'

'He was a good man,' Brother Thomas said softly.

'It is because of the Abbot I come to you now,' Father Sheridan said. 'Because of him that I must tell you what Rosaleen spoke of that night on her deathbed. What she told me I could hardly believe. I am not sure I believe it now. That is why I must speak to you of it.' His eyes moved as if remembering. 'I can still see her so pale, so frail against the pillows as she struggled to speak, yet so desperate to be heard, to make her peace.' He lowered his eyes to gaze upon the flames. 'I see her. I hear her still.'

Eccles Street, Dublin, August 1915

Now I am to die, Father, I find my heart returning to when I was born. I was born to a winter wind – the wild wind that howled around the Clare hills far, far from here. I hear it whispering to me now at the window. It carried me into this world, now it comes to carry me away.

I hope it lets me fly, over every place I have loved. Over the burst of broad Dublin streets so alive, every alleyway and arch, the great, rushing Liffey. But I have a deep fear. That it will sweep me away to the blue Dublin mountains. And, there, will set me down. By the monastery, in the woodland. At the bell tower.

You will come to know why I fear it, Father. Perhaps the bell tower strikes fear in your own heart for what has happened there. And it is of what happened there that I must speak. That of which I must cleanse my soul.

But more, more than for my own soul, I care for the soul of another: the Abbot's. I cannot rest knowing what he has confessed.

I learned of his confession in these weeks past. And that is why I called for you. For now, at my dying, I must tell the truth. A truth so terrible I could never speak it before. But, first, you must hear how it all came to be. What trouble brought me here to the city. The greater, much greater trouble that found me here.

Perhaps I need not fear. Perhaps the wind will be kind. Perhaps it will carry me home. Take me from these streets back to the hills of Clare. Take me back as I will take you now, Father – for I want you to understand where it all began. And what gift or curse I was born with.

The wind rattled the old cottage windows as my mother birthed me. My aunts Cot and Bridie were with her in the loft room, my uncles pacing, sucking on their pipes in the kitchen below. My father had died while my mother yet carried me, so it was to that cottage, her own birthplace, that she had returned for her labour, and it was there that I grew. By night my dressmaker aunts would sew under paraffin lamps in the parlour, by day sink their fists into cavernous bowls on the kitchen table to knead the bread dough. My mother had nimble fingers for sewing but no hand for baking and Aunt Cot would chase her away for fear her very nearness would sink the bread. But Aunt Cot would lift me on to the chair at the table and hold the knife with me to cut the cross into the round dough. 'To break it more easily once it's baked,' she said. 'To give

5

thanks to Our Lord,' Aunt Bridie would counter as Aunt Cot raised her eyes to the heavens.

Aunt Bridie tried to instil in me some religion but became disgusted and ashamed of my heathen ways as I grew. She admonished me for running to the fields to escape the evening rosary, for paying no attention at Mass and certainly no heed to her little sermons at home. To her mind, I did not show enough reverence for Father Byrne when he came to call. Later I would suffer the consequences of her wariness of me but when still a child I was happily unaware of the seeds I was sowing.

In our home, the kitchen was the biggest room, with its stone floor and wide hearth and a hefty hook for pots over the roaring fire. I slept with my mother, often rising early to catch Aunt Bridie on the loft stairs, arranging her red flannel petticoat, Uncle Pat like a white ghost in his long johns folding away the settle bed in the kitchen below. We women would help my uncles Mikey and Pat work the small farm; I scattered chicken feed in the yard, always insisting I could carry the too-heavy pails of frothy, warm milk. My favourite task was to help harness the horse to the trap before we went on our way to fetch water from the crossroads pump, or to Nance Darcy's post office and grocery on the road to town. It was there the men collected their tobacco, the women their messages and gossip and always a bag of lemon sweets or toffee for me.

Once the cottage had housed my grandfather and grandmother and their seven children. With my grandparents dead, there remained only five siblings there.

Aunt Ellen lived married in Dublin, but they'd had another brother – Joey. Joey was spoken of only in whispers. As if his name might cut their tongues, leave them wounded.

They said my grandmother had the sight. They would talk of the night of the face at the window, how, sitting at the kitchen hearth, Grandma had seen her cousin, Willy, appear at the window, his face aglow from the fire, lighting his smile in the darkness. She had gone to seek him in the yard, calling for him, but he was not there. There was no need for Grandma to be told he was dead. She knew it before his father brought her the news, before the priest announced it at the altar. Mammy, my aunts and uncles talked of that often. But it was only rare nights by the fire, in solemn whispers, they would talk of Joey. Of the night Grandma had awoken drenched, shouting Joey's name. Overtaken by fear for him, she had rushed to make sure he was safe in his bed. He, a young, strong lad of seventeen had laughed at her, telling her to away from the room and let him rest.

It was two days later it happened. My uncles would help with the threshing at neighbouring farms, and it was one such summer afternoon. All the men around were bending, gathering the straw so nobody saw what happened. But my uncles looked up at an ungodly screaming. Joey must have stepped out before the thresher's monstrous blade, become caught in it. They never spoke of what they saw then, only of how all the men came running, how my uncles had chased with Joey's bloodied body into the farm's kitchen, desperately trying to revive his weakening heart. But he was gone. They would talk of how my grandmother fled to the fields, wailing, when they brought her the news. How for hours they could not coax her back inside, the cows chewing dumbly as they looked upon her, numb to human pain.

My grandmother had the sight. They said she had been touched by the Graces. A gift. Yet Aunt Bridie soon said mine was not a gift but a curse. That no good could come of a girl like me.

I was born with a sense, Father.

2

It came upon me softly, the seeing. When I was young, I knew no different. Did not know that many times I could sense what others could not. It began simply. Oftentimes, our neighbours would gather in the kitchen to chat, laugh and swap gossip. Sometimes Aunt Cot would take up the accordion and we would beat out the rhythm and sing.

Long before Billy, a lad from a neighbouring farm, and I became sweethearts I would take secret glances at him, thinking the others could feel it too: the stab in his gut as he watched our friends growing ever more merry, waving their whiskeys or stout to the music. It was only later, on the long summer nights as we held hands in the sweet hay-scented fields that I looked into his deep sorrow-filled eyes and listened to his whispers of how he had watched his father die from drink.

With Nance Darcy, the postmistress, too, I would see her smile as her husband talked, but sit far from him. I could sense the resentment through her pores, and knew she believed he had done her wrong. Only years later did the women tell me she blamed him for an argument that had seen their son leave them to live far away.

The trouble was, I was young. So young, and innocent of my difference, I would say what I saw.

'He is sorry,' I said to Nance Darcy by the kitchen fire one evening, touching her hand. 'Please be kind to him.'

'What are you saying, child?' Her voice sharp, she quickly glanced around to see if others had heard. I could sense her shame and wondered what I had said wrong.

'Is our Rosaleen at her sorcery again?' Uncle Mikey said, laughing. 'Come away, you little tyke, and don't be tormenting our friends.'

My aunts and uncles paid little mind to my early utterings, Mammy seeming to accept it with a soft knowing. But Aunt Bridie would stare, her eyes hard and black.

'There's devilment in that child,' I heard her say once to Uncle Mikey. 'Something wrong, some dark trickery in her.'

'Don't be raving,' Uncle Mikey said. 'She's only like her grandmother and just a wean. Leave the child alone.'

It was Uncle Mikey told me my name meant Little Rose. Sometimes he would call me that as he lifted me on to his knee, I pulling at his braces, loving the smell of pipe smoke on his jacket. He told me too that one of our poets, James Clarence Mangan, had written a love song to our country, had named her 'Dark Rosaleen': 'My own Rosaleen! 'Tis you shall have the golden throne. 'Tis you shall reign, and reign alone.' The poet had given Ireland the disguise of a woman, for our country was unfree, and we had been forbidden to utter our love for her.

As he recited the poem, I would picture myself sitting high upon that golden throne, waving my hand over our streams and rivers, mountains and hills, granting to them the freedom he talked of. But I thought little of it, for to me I had freedom. Freedom to run in the fields, to lift my face, my arms to the wind I revelled in, that I felt stir my blood as it blew from the hills. But as I grew amongst those hills so grew another stirring. My sense within. The seeing.

I was fifteen when I first saw the shadow. Uncle Pat had always been such a strong man, tall and broad. Those days he was as he'd ever been, ready with a smile, a joke on his lips, pushing up the peak of his cap to give me a wink. Yet I felt it. A darkness around him. As if a sinister stranger stalked him.

I did not know then what the shadow meant. I only knew it was nothing kind. So, every morning, as he readied himself to work the farm, fearing for him what had befallen Joey, I begged him, 'Please, please, Uncle Pat, don't work today.'

But he would just grin and shoo me away. 'Go on out of that,' he'd say, giving me a pinch on my cheek. As the days passed and nothing befell Uncle Pat on the farm, I tried to persuade the others that Uncle Pat should see the doctor. That I was sure something ailed him. But they only tried to placate me.

'Your Uncle Pat is as hardy as any bull,' Aunt Cot said, the others murmuring their agreement.

It was months later the sickness showed itself. The falter in his walk, a shortness in his breath, a grey pall on his cheeks. Often his pipe had made him cough but now that cough was racking, his voice hoarse. It was then, at last, he visited the town doctor. Uncle Pat had a tumour in his throat – we heard later that the doctor was able to feel it with his fingers – and Dr Hogan feared the worst, that the cancer had spread to his lungs.

There was nothing could be done. Within weeks, Uncle Pat had taken to the bed in the loft room. He could not speak, he could not swallow. Dr Hogan made him up a mix of morphine, cocaine and gin for the pain, while Aunt Cot swore a poultice of dock root would soothe him. Aunt Bridie went to our local healer, Maggie Devlin, who vowed Uncle Pat could be cured by spreading a salve of dough and lard on his neck, and this Aunt Bridie took to doing daily. They kept me downstairs, away from Uncle Pat so I was spared his suffering, but I could feel the sickness seeping through the thick lime walls.

I could feel, too, Aunt Bridie's growing suspicion and hostility towards me. It was almost as if she blamed me for Uncle Pat's illness. As if by my knowing I had wished it upon him.

Our friends and neighbours were gathered in the parlour, saying the rosary the night he died. I knelt with them, willing him to live, but I knew from Aunt Cot's face as she slowly descended the stairs that it was over. Those same friends and neighbours stayed close as we waked him for two days in the parlour, kept vigil over his coffin. As Nance Darcy came to clasp Aunt Bridie's hand, I saw Aunt Bridie's sharp look at me, heard her say, 'We'd better all mind Rosaleen's black eye.'

I think that Uncle Pat's death played its part in what came to be. For it marked for me the end of carefree days, of childhood. No longer did I wear my sense lightly but as if I carried a great weight. Why could I see what others could not? Why should I be shown another's fate if there was nothing to be done? I would sit for hours in the hay barn and wonder. More than wonder, I would fear. Fear I had been chosen to act.

From that time on, my aunts and uncle talked of me in grave tones to Mammy, when I was out of sight. Coming from the yard through the kitchen door one evening, I heard them at the fire, their voices hushed.

'It's not right or natural,' Aunt Bridie was saying.

'How can you say that when our own mother had the sight?' Mammy said, trying to defend me.

'It's not the same,' Aunt Bridie said. 'Our mother was a God-fearing woman touched by the Graces, a God-given gift. Rosaleen has no fear of God, she has all the air of a heathen. She's far from graced.'

'Don't be saying that about my daughter,' Mammy hissed at her, while Uncle Mikey just sighed.

'Stop with your nonsense, Bridie,' he said. 'My only fear is for the child. Her tongue is too free, she's too quick to reveal what she sees. I worry it will bring trouble upon her.'

'Trouble upon us all,' Aunt Bridie said sternly.

On that she was right.

3

I was twenty-one when first trouble found me, in the year of 1910. Billy and I were now sweethearts and had been courting nearly three years. His father dead, he had inherited the family farm and so was in a position to ask me to be his wife. He had not yet made his formal proposal but it was understood between us. In the meantime I was content helping my aunts with their dressmaking and mending for the village and town beyond. I was happy. I believed I knew what lay before me. It seemed in that way at least, my sense had deserted me. For then came Nora.

Nora Culhane lived in the village. She was near my own age, but it had long been rumoured how Rory Kane, a much older, married man was around her and she around him. Over the post office counter, Nance Darcy whispered of it to Mammy, my aunts and any who might be there. All would shake their heads at it, but on meeting the man on the street with his wife, Deirdre, not a word of it would be spoken. It was only when we were on our way that knowing looks were exchanged. Aunt Cot would say, 'Poor Deirdre,' and nothing more.

Yet I felt Nora herself maligned. Although I would always make sure to smile if meeting her on the street, most would snub her – as if she and she alone were to blame, the betrayal of Deirdre all her doing. As if Rory himself had no hand in it.

'What would any man do?' Aunt Bridie said one evening at the kitchen fire. 'When a girl offers herself up, makes herself a temptress. Flaunts herself as she does.'

My mother was kinder; I knew she felt for Nora. 'She's only young, Bridie. She hardly knows what she's doing. He's older, a married man, he should know better.'

But Aunt Bridie just scoffed, while Aunt Cot held her tongue to keep the peace, Uncle Mikey the same.

It was high summer, the hay brought in, when Billy and his mother hosted a gathering at their farm for all who had helped with the harvest. Billy's mother and I had set up the tables in the yard, preparing them with bread, cheeses and hams, and bottles of beer and orange. I was standing with my neighbours, chatting in the fierce July sun when I spied Nora standing mute and alone in the shadow of the hay barn, looking lost, her thoughts far away. It was only a slight movement but I noticed her touching her stomach as if it were something strange to her. At first I thought she might feel sickly in the summer sun, but then it struck me. I needed no special sense. If they only looked, any with eyes could see.

I made my way over to her, passing some remark about the sun being a demon. I offered her a sip of my orange but she shook her head, keeping her eyes lowered, seeming reluctant to talk. But I persisted. I wanted her to know she had a friend if she wished for one.

'Are you all right, Nora?' I said. 'Are you well?'

'I'm well enough.' Her voice was gruff. 'Though most here would wish I wasn't.'

She had raised what I would not dare, so I took my chance.

'Don't mind them. Don't mind what people say.'

'So you've heard the talk?' She looked up, searching my face. 'They chatter as loud as monkeys, you'd think those flapping on their tongues would hear. But look at them.' She nodded over to where Rory and Deirdre stood laughing with others. 'Look at her. She's deaf and blind to it. It's as if they are the most devoted couple in the world. When all the time he tells me if only he could he'd be rid of her. That he wants only me. But they blame me. Everyone blames me.'

Her tongue was bitter but I could hear the pain on it. I touched her arm.

'Would you not leave him, Nora? Let him be and find another. Look at him. He is as old and gnarled as knotted oak.'

She laughed but instantly grew serious. 'I can't. Not now.' Her voice was hushed, I could barely hear. She touched her stomach, unawares.

'Why?' I said softly. 'Because you are carrying?'

She stared at me, panic in her eyes. 'You know? How do you know? Who else knows? Tell me.'

'No one.' I spoke quickly, wanting to reassure her. 'I've heard no talk of it. I only guessed, that's all.'

She looked at me closely. 'They say you see things. Can you see now what I must do? Have you the answer to it?'

No, I had no answer to that. 'Does *he* know?' I asked instead.

She nodded. 'Yes. And he says there is a way.'

'A way to do what?'

'To rid myself of it.' She whispered to me. 'He has Maggie Devlin helping.'

Maggie Devlin. She who had assured Aunt Bridie that her salve would save Uncle Pat. Who had a potion for every ill.

'She is making up a remedy for a price,' Nora went on. 'One that will cause me to lose the baby naturally. That will see it gone.'

I felt suddenly unsettled. *Will see it gone.* I glanced up at the sun, its glare upon the blade of a scythe leaning up against the hay barn. And something in the harsh, relentless light on the metal stirred within me a dread. Filled me with a sickly foreboding.

* * *

Over the following days I let Uncle Mikey travel alone on the trap, walking by myself to the post office to allow me to pass Maggie Devlin's cottage. I'd stare at the array of coloured bottles and strange dolls gathered inside her window. Peering through the net curtains, sometimes I would see the shadow of her moving within.

The dread stayed with me, creeping through me, until I could keep silent no more. On Uncle Mikey's next trip to the village I joined him, so I could visit Nora. Alone, I went to the house on the main street and knocked on Nora's door. After her mother called her to the step, Nora barely had time to greet me before I spoke.

'Nora, you say you know I see things. Sense things. Well, I am telling you now, I sense something dark around you. Something malign. I feel it from Maggie Devlin. I feel it deep in my stomach, in my very blood.'

She stared at me, looked back through the doorway to make sure her mother was gone. 'What could be more malign than what I carry now?' she whispered. 'Don't you realise what will happen to me? My mother would not be able to stand the shame. If Maggie Devlin doesn't help me, I'll be sent away to the nuns, kept a prisoner in one of their homes for fallen women. I couldn't bear it. I'd rather take my chances with Maggie Devlin and her cures.'

'And what if she offers you not a cure, but a curse?' I urged. 'I feel her as a vulture, Nora, see a swarm of black birds gathering around you. I'm begging you, stay away!'

But she would not listen. She did not want to hear. Those nights those fearful black birds would swoop on me with cruel cries, clawing me in my dreams, waking me. One night, woken again by their screeches, lying silently by my sleeping mother, I settled it in my mind. I had sensed the shadow that had stalked Uncle Pat. I sensed it now around Nora. I might not have been able to save Uncle Pat, but with Nora there was a chance. I would not be found wanting.

* * *

The next morning I walked the mile of hedgerows to Maggie Devlin's cottage. I hesitated at the sight of it, shadowed by trees, its walls sunken in the ditch, but I forced myself on through the small, whining gate.

Answering my knock, she greeted me with a look of suspicion. Grey hair knotted at her neck, she wiped her hands down the long bibbed apron that covered her black dress.

'Well?' She blocked the door to keep me from peering in. 'What is it you want?'

'I want to come in, Maggie.' I tried not to falter. 'I want to talk to you.'

She frowned, as if she were going to chase me away. But it seemed curiosity got the better of her and she stood aside to let me enter. Inside the dark kitchen, the long table was set with colourful bottles and bowls, a hearth lined with trinkets and curios. She did not offer me a seat and I did not take one.

'It's about Nora. Nora Culhane.' I spoke as firmly as my nerves would allow. 'I know what you are doing for her.'

Shock sparked in her eyes, although she tried to disguise it. She spoke roughly.

'You would be wise not to talk of such things. What do you know of Nora Culhane?' Her eyes were hard. 'And what do you know of me?'

I kept my voice firm. 'I know you are concocting a potion for her. One you say will relieve her of her trouble. I fear it will not.'

She gave a caustic laugh, then said, 'I don't say I am doing anything for the girl. It is you who is saying it. If I were to provide a remedy for any girl in trouble, I would know very well what to do, I am greatly practised in it. But now you think you know better. I suppose you have had one of your visions. They say you are a strange one. It seems they are right.'

'What is in the potion?' My voice was urgent now. 'Please. Tell me.'

She shook her head as if bemused by me. Then, as if to humour me, she crossed to the dresser, taking down two clay pots.

'My ingredients are no secret.' She carried the pots to the table. 'If you ever find yourself in trouble, young Rosaleen, I would make a mixture of plants and herbs that have been used and trusted for years. Ones well known to every healer.' She placed the pots on the table for me to see. In one were small lilac flowers on long stalks, in the other a green fringed plant.

'A blend of pennyroyal from the ditch, and fringed rue – we call it herb of grace. If taken for ten days by any woman in a delicate condition she can be sure she will be cured. That would be an end to it.' She grew impatient then. 'Now begone and don't bother me any more.' She waved me from the kitchen. 'And mind your tongue. Don't go talking of Nora Culhane and don't go talking of me.'

4

I was tormented. Consumed by the shadow I sensed around Nora, driven by a need to do for her what I had been unable to do for Uncle Pat. When I visited the post office, sometimes Rory Kane would be there. I would watch him, trying to stem my urge to speak. One such day, I could hold my tongue no longer. I loitered in the yard until he was done with his business, then stopped him at the door with a touch on his arm. He turned to smile at me.

'Well, young Rosaleen, what can I do for you?'

My heart beat like a panicked bird in my chest. His courtesy only made worse what I must say.

'Rory, please don't be vexed, but I know,' I whispered. 'I know about you and Nora Culhane. I know of her trouble.'

His smile fled. He stared as if he wanted to beat me. 'Go away, you little witch.' His face was stricken. 'And take your evil thoughts, your poisonous words with you.'

He made off down the yard, but I ran behind him, grabbing his arm. 'Rory, please. Nora is in danger. From Maggie Devlin and her potions. I can feel it.'

Enraged, he shook off my arm.

'Get off me!' he spat. 'You are touched, not right in the head, they all say it. I don't know of any potion or anything about Nora Culhane, so mind your mouth. You are a wicked girl with a wicked tongue.'

With that he was gone, and I could only watch him go. The venom in his voice felled me like a blow. That others whispered of me, thought me mad. Called me *wicked*. Once home, I sat in the kitchen, watching Mammy sew, trying to soothe my wounded feelings with her gentle presence. But before long, Aunt Cot came from the yard, telling me 'that one' – Nora – was asking for me, below, at the gate. I walked to the end of the laneway in dread. I knew what was awaiting me.

'What did you say to Rory?' she hissed at me, even before I'd reached her. 'He is raging at me for telling you about my condition. I told him I did not, that it was you that guessed it, but he doesn't believe me. Now he is so angry he will hardly speak to me. From now on, stay *away* from me and away from him. I have started the potion, and there is *nothing* you can do to stop me. Keep your ramblings from now on to yourself. I want rid of this, and rid of *you*.'

She turned and charged away while I stood crushed at the gate. I leaned against it, defeated. It seemed now there was nothing I could do.

* * *

Five days later at Sunday Mass, I sat in the middle pews with my mother and aunts – Uncle Mikey stood at the back of the church so he could slip out for a smoke. I watched Maggie Devlin slide into a pew across the aisle, with not a look at me. I searched for Nora but she was not there, although her mother and father sat nearby. Rory Kane sat with his wife in a front pew, just before Father Byrne at the altar.

After Mass, the sun high, all gathered to chat in the churchyard. With Nora not there I could not help but worry over her. I crossed to where Mrs Culhane stood chatting with others, and asked after Nora.

'She is a little poorly,' Mrs Culhane said pleasantly. 'A strange thing, perhaps a summer cold. She will be right soon, I'm sure.' She smiled.

I stared at her. *No.* Every nerve suddenly taut, I felt a heady rush of panic. Nora was ill. Nora was taking the potion. That day, travelling home in the trap, I said not a word to Mammy or the others, so lost I was to my fear. That night I dreamt again of the clawing, screeching, black birds.

I knew I could not afford to wait. Next afternoon I took the trip to town with Uncle Mikey so I could call on Dr Hogan who had looked after Uncle Pat. Dr Hogan was a kind man, and I knew I could trust him.

As I sat before him in his surgery, nervously talking of someone I did not name, a girl who found herself in trouble, he leaned forward to interrupt me.

'Rosaleen.' His eyes were concerned. 'Is it you?'

'No, no,' I said, alarmed, managing to assure him it was not myself I talked of but one from a neighbouring town. I could see I had convinced him and he settled back to listen. 'This girl has told me she is going to take a potion,' I said. 'A mixture of pennyroyal and fringed rue to relieve her of her trouble. But I have heard that such a concoction can be dangerous. Am I right?'

Dr Hogan nodded. 'Yes. These so-called remedies can be hazardous. I know of that mix you describe and a large amount of it could be toxic. In some cases, lethal. It poisons the liver, you see. Please, go back to your friend and advise her very strongly against taking any such potion.'

I now had confirmation of my fears. The following day I walked the three miles to the village, back to Nora's house on main street and knocked at the door. Mrs Culhane answered, smiling at me on the step.

'Mrs Culhane,' I said, even before she greeted me. 'Please tell me, how is Nora?'

She stepped back to let me into the hallway and spoke in a low voice.

'She is upstairs in bed. Still not well. I think it is a cold and her stomach is upset. I've had to leave a bucket by her side. And she is clammy. I was thinking I might call for the doctor today.'

I could contain myself no longer. My voice was hushed but hasty. 'Mrs Culhane, Nora is sick because she is taking one of Maggie Devlin's potions. Please forgive me, but she is taking it to rid herself of a child. She is carrying, Mrs Culhane, and I know, just know, that the potion is poisoning her. I fear she will die. Please,

Mrs Culhane, go to her, tell her you know. Make her stop taking it.'

In a second, all the blood had left her face. She stared at me wildly for the longest moment. Then a scream escaped her. 'What are you saying, you wicked, wicked girl?'

She grabbed me by the shoulders as I cried out in protest, and hurled me over the step on to the street.

'Get out!' Her voice was a screech. 'Get out and away from my door with your devil's tongue! You are raving! *Evil.*'

I stumbled on to the street, dumbfounded, then, as the door slammed, looked around at the crowd who had stopped to stare, some coming from their shops to see what the commotion was. I yelped and turned to run from their stares, run for the safety of home.

But my home was not safe from the trouble I had caused. The whole parish was alive with it now. Rumours about what Rosaleen Moore, with her unholy visions and unruly tongue, had said to Mrs Culhane.

'I can't walk in the street for the shame of it,' Aunt Bridie raged at me after she had been accosted in the village by those eager to gossip while feigning concern about me. 'What in God's name did you say to Mrs Culhane? Did you tell her about her daughter's carryings-on? Did you do that to interfere, like you always do, in other people's business? You bring disgrace on us all.'

Mammy lambasted Aunt Bridie, trying instead to coax from me what had happened but I could not betray Nora's secret. I cared little what Aunt Bridie thought of me, I

26

only cared for what had befallen Nora, what might befall her yet. Unable to keep away, I would walk to the village and brave whatever stares as I haunted Nora's house like a ghost, gazing at the upstairs windows, desperate to gain some sight of her. At Mass I could hear those behind in the pews whispering of me, all afterwards huddling in the yard, fixing me with wary eyes, moving away when I passed. Rory Kane, always at Mass with his wife, had terror in his eyes. Terror of what I might already have told Mrs Culhane. Of what I yet might tell. Billy quizzed me constantly on what had me so troubled when we went out walking, but I could not tell him and it created a silence between us. His mother hardly knew what to say to me.

For two weeks or more I went on in this way until one early September night, as the evenings began to draw in and the first of the autumn winds blew up outside, a rap came to the kitchen door. Aunt Cot answered it to find Nora's father, Mr Culhane, there. His face was harrowed.

'Please,' he said, looking around the kitchen door to where I sat at the hearth. 'Rosaleen. Can she come? Nora is asking for her.'

I leapt from the seat, not even waiting for Aunt Cot or any to answer, and climbed into Mr Culhane's trap in the yard. Mr Culhane said little, so intent he was on driving the horse on, but when he did turn to me his eyes were moist.

'She is ill, Rosaleen,' he said. 'Gravely ill.'

When I arrived in their kitchen, Mrs Culhane looked up from the table but did not acknowledge me. Mr Culhane led me up the stairs to the loft room where Nora lay. There was a stench in the room even though the window was open. Instinctively I put my hand to my nose and mouth, then lowered it, not wanting to show I was nauseated.

Mr Culhane left us alone and Nora turned her head on the pillow as I drew closer.

'Rosaleen,' she said weakly.

Her white nightdress looked drenched with sweat and she was shivering. I took a knitted bed-jacket from the chair and put it around her shoulders as she struggled to sit up.

'Don't,' I said, fixing the jacket. 'Lie back.'

She lay back on the pillow, took some breaths. 'You were right,' she said at last. 'Maggie Devlin has done for me.'

'Did you keep taking the potion?' I asked. 'Is that what has happened?'

Nora shook her head, still breathless. 'No. After you told Mammy about the potion she stopped me taking it. She went to Maggie Devlin, demanded to know what was in it, what remedy there was for it. She didn't want to go to Dr Hogan; she couldn't stand the shame. Maggie Devlin told her it was not the potion that was to blame but the baby within me. Refusing to come out. That was what was poisoning me. That she needed to get the baby out of me.'

I looked at Nora, in horror. 'What did she do?'

Nora turned her face as if she could not bear the memory. 'She came with a bag of steel wires. She went at me with them. The *pain* – oh, Rosaleen.' She let out a sob, turning back to me. 'I'm savaged with sores. Blood and pus.'

Mrs Culhane came in then, her eyes lowered. I could tell she still felt aggrieved or embarrassed at what had passed between us. She gave me a curt nod, saying to Nora, 'I'll just change your dressings, pet.'

I turned to leave the room but as Mrs Culhane lifted Nora's nightdress I caught a glimpse of a seeping wound, festering, red and crusty. The stench was overpowering.

Outside on the tiny landing, I waited for Mrs Culhane. I whispered to her on the stairs, 'What does Dr Hogan say?'

She could hardly look at me. 'He is soothing her wounds with ointments but there is nothing else he can do. She is raw with infection, inside and out.'

She went down the stairs then, and I heard Nora calling to me.

'Rosaleen!'

Again at her bedside, I gripped her hand as she looked up at me to speak. 'I called you here tonight because you warned me of this. You told me this would happen. So, I want you to tell me now. I beg you to be honest. Mammy will not tell me. Nor will my father or Dr Hogan.' Her eyes were pleading. 'Am I going to *die*, Rosaleen?'

But I could not tell her. Tell her of the shadow, like a deep ebony cloak hanging from her shoulders. Perched like my nightmares' screeching black birds in every corner of the room. No. I could not tell her what I saw.

5

Nora breathed her last within days. Her funeral Mass was crowded, a horde travelling to the village church from town, many coming, I knew, merely to gawp, for the scandal was mighty. The Culhanes said that Nora had died of appendicitis. But none believed it, for Nora had all but disappeared for weeks, and whispers had come from Monica who worked at the pharmacy. She said that Mrs Culhane had been collecting iodine and bromine ointments, treatments for wounds and sores. When Maggie Devlin did not show her face at the funeral the gossipers concluded quickly that the wounds and sores had been inflicted by her devil's tools, of which all knew but none talked. It was not long before Rory Kane's name was on every tongue too.

Nor was it long before Deirdre Kane heard of it. Aunt Bridie said you could hear her screeches over every roof in the village as she beat him at their doorway, threw him out into the yard. No one knew for how long she would banish him. Only that he had taken a room at the inn, cutting a sorry sight now.

With all the trouble, I did everything I could to avoid the village but I could not avoid Mass. When I walked through the churchyard all drew back, with wan smiles to Mammy but none to me. I felt myself reviled. But more than that, feared. I could sense it. Almost smell it. The villagers' fear of what Rosaleen Moore might see. Of what she might say. Aunt Bridie bit at me, saying word was that Mrs Culhane had cast me from the house that day because I had told her that Nora was going to die. That my dark eye had foreseen it. That afterwards I had haunted the house like a banshee keening outside her window, waiting for her to be taken.

Even Billy started to act differently towards me. I sensed him distant when we met, and whenever I suggested a walk or a trip on the trap to town he would always make the excuse that he had farm duties, even though it was autumn and there was not as much to tend to. I saw him less and less until it seemed I saw him no more. Whenever I met his mother on the road, she would lower her eyes with hardly a greeting. I knew she had counselled Billy to sever his ties with me. I was not the wife she wanted for her son.

I was distraught. All the village was condemning me, Billy now lost to me. It was torture to meet him on the road, watch him barely raise his eyes as if I were a stranger. My heart was sick and sore. Mammy tried to soothe me, tell me that the whisperers would soon tire of their tales.

But as autumn turned to winter the rumours were still rife and Father Byrne preached from the altar one Sunday of the dangers of malicious gossip. I withered in the pew, wondering if he meant the gossip surrounding me, or the Culhanes. Whichever it was, I soon learned he had me in his sights.

One afternoon, when Mammy was with Aunt Cot and Uncle Mikey in town, I was alone in the kitchen. I was startled by the shadow of Father Byrne blocking the low winter sun through the kitchen doorway. Aunt Bridie was behind him. He trod softly to where I sat at the hearth, the two of them smiling strangely.

'Rosaleen,' Father Byrne greeted me softly. He scraped a chair across the stone floor, sitting to face me. 'Your aunt has asked me to talk to you.' He observed me in an odd, kindly way for a moment, then reached to take my hands. 'My dear, it is said in the village that you saw what would become of young Nora Culhane. That you *see* many things. Perhaps things that should not be seen, that you should not talk of. That you told Mrs Culhane that Nora was going to die.'

'I did *not* tell her that,' I said, eyes on his hands as they clutched mine.

'Nevertheless,' he went on, 'you cannot deny this strange sight I talk of. You must understand that this *seeing* is not, as some might say, a gift from God, but a pagan practice, a heathen thing. And so I ask that you pray with me. Let us pray together to purge you of these unholy visions. We must ask God to cleanse you of them.'

He fixed me with a stare, bringing his face close to mine, the waft of his hair oil sickening me. 'Now,

Rosaleen, we will petition the Lord.' He squeezed my hands as he closed his eyes.

Aunt Bridie stood behind his chair, closing her own eyes, clasping her hands. I stared dismayed at the two of them and tried to pull away my hands, but Father Byrne only gripped one of them tighter, releasing the other to press my forehead. I felt his sweaty palm on my brow, watched his thin lips move as he began to mutter breathily.

'O Lord, we call on you, beseech you to hear us. Bless us with your presence now and fill this child with your goodness. Cleanse her tongue of ungodly words, her mind of evil imaginings, her soul of every depravity. Let her leave behind the devil's dark work and take your hand to walk with you in the light.'

Aunt Bridie was fervently whispering with him. 'Hear us, O Lord, hear us.'

I sat rigid in my chair. My stomach knotted at the words, I began to heave. *Ungodly. Evil. Depravity. The devil's dark work.* A sob like a wave rose through me, bursting from deep within my gut as Father Byrne, eyes still closed, nodded, smiling at it, as if my anguish was a welcome thing. It spurred him on.

'O Lord, we thank you, for we feel the Holy Ghost here amongst us. The Holy Spirit stirs within your poor, misguided daughter. Heal her, Lord, with your divine touch. Wash her clean of sin. Cleanse her, Lord, that she may receive you and become a vessel for your immaculate being.'

'Cleanse her, Lord, we beseech you,' Aunt Bridie muttered mournfully.

I started to weep loudly, my limbs shaking. Wretched, I looked at the two of them, desperate for them to stop. But still their eyes were closed, Father Byrne continuing to smile.

'Lord, we give you thanks, for you have heard us.' He opened his eyes, his voice hoarse. 'Good, good.' Lowering his hand from my head, he gripped both my own hands again. 'God is cleansing you through your tears, Rosaleen.'

Aunt Bridie's eyes were open too. 'Thanks be to God.'

Father Byrne made the sign of the cross on my forehead, then stood. 'Don't worry,' he whispered to me. 'I will keep you in my prayers.'

As Aunt Bridie walked him to the door, thanking him, I scrambled up and fled to the parlour, turning the hefty iron key in the lock. I knew Aunt Bridie would come to find me and I could not bear to see her. Soon enough, I heard her beyond the door, calling to me.

'Go away!' I screeched as she continued to call. 'Go away!' I threw myself against the door, pounded and kicked it. 'Get away from me!'

At last, I heard her steps start down the passageway. 'And there's the devil coming out!' she shouted.

I stayed there in the parlour, curled up on the couch, until I heard the horse and trap roll into the yard. I rose quickly, waiting at the door for my mother to come. At last, she called to me through the locked door. Hastily, I unlocked it, and threw myself into her arms.

'Hush now, hush,' she said as she led me back to the couch, trying to comfort me as I told her, through sobs, what had happened. She was shocked, had no idea that Aunt Bridie had intended to fetch the priest. Livid with her sister, she sat stroking my head as I wept.

'I'm hated, Mammy, an outcast,' I cried. 'Everyone in the village thinks I'm a witch.'

She smiled, still stroking my head, lifting my face to look into my eyes.

'You're no witch, my love, but special,' she said. She held my cheek in her hand. 'When you were born your eyes were as deep as a river. Only a baby, you would gaze at all around you and I knew you could *see*. I knew then your grandmother had been reborn. That you too had been touched by the Graces.'

My heart plummeted. They were words I did not want to hear. For they stirred in me the disquiet I'd felt ever since Uncle Pat had died. That whatever gift I had was but a burden. To hear myself called special only made that burden heavier. For if I was special I was alone.

'I can't stay here, Mammy, I can't,' I sobbed as she held me tightly.

As evening fell, Aunt Cot and Uncle Mikey came with tea, bread and cheese for us; Aunt Bridie kept out of sight. The four of us sat up, talking late into the night, and before I lay down in bed to fretful sleep it was decided: I was to go away, to stay with Aunt Ellen in Dublin.

I had pictured my life unfolding so differently. But whatever I imagined of Dublin, even with every gift

35

of seeing I had, I could never have imagined what was to come.

* * *

Brother Thomas slowly stoked the fire, listening as Father Sheridan spoke.

'I talked to Rosaleen of her home in Clare when I first I met her, the following year. Afterwards, she would come to light candles in the church. She told me she loved the peaceful atmosphere and the scent of the wax, and that she lit them for her family and in memory of her uncle, but she never told me what trouble had brought her to Dublin.' He glanced at Brother Thomas. 'Did she tell you?'

Brother Thomas shook his head, eyes still settled on the fire. 'No. She never spoke of it.'

Father Sheridan shifted in his chair, Brother Thomas hearing the questions in his voice. 'She tried to explain it that night. But still I find it hard to make sense of. For if I am to believe what she told me – and if her gift was true – what I cannot fathom is why she could not *see* the disaster before her.'

6

My heart was in turmoil. To leave Mammy and home was a wrench but it was also a relief to be escaping the suffocation of the village, the streets I could no longer walk without reproach. Leaving Billy pained me too, but I would no longer have to suffer his hard face and cold eyes – and people said he was courting Peg Healy now. Mammy tried to comfort me, said that Aunt Ellen would be pleased to have me to help in her busy house and that I would surely find a new sweetheart. I might soon be happy there. On the day I left Clare, the wind travelled with me. It greeted me like a welcoming friend as it rushed from the sweep of Dublin's blue mountains, carrying with it the power and scent of the sea, whipping away the paleness the long train ride had brought to my cheeks, almost robbing me of my hat as I stepped on to the grand forecourt of Kingsbridge Station. I gaped at the vastness. Even on that January morning the city seemed blessed by sunlight, so broad and bright. The hollers of the jarveys touting for business, and of their unruly horses trotting on the cobbles around me, were deafening.

At last I spied Uncle Noel on the forecourt, his face lit up at the sight of me, hand raised in a friendly wave.

Even though I had met Uncle Noel only seldom, a face I recognised amongst this swarm of strangers was a happy sight. He greeted me warmly, relieving me of my carpet bags, waving down a jaunting car. As we crossed the bridge over the River Liffey, I could hardly hear him for the noise of the traffic and the jarvey shouting to other drivers he knew, but, once we were on the quays, Uncle Noel pointed over the river to the giant gates of the Guinness brewery with its great smoking chimneys.

'That's where I work!' Uncle Noel shouted to me. 'In the offices. I promise I don't spend all day sampling the product!'

I gazed in awe at the sprawling building, at the glistening river running alongside us, its arching bridges. We soon turned from the Liffey on to the broadest of thoroughfares which seemed to stretch ever onwards, disappearing into the sky.

'Sackville Street,' Uncle Noel shouted again. 'Dublin's jewel. One of the widest streets in all Europe.'

I gazed around me. At the monuments rising from the heart of the thoroughfare, the elaborate ironwork of the lamps surrounding them. At the grand hotels, the verandas, the colourful canopies over each and every kind of shop, the bustle of passers-by on the street. I turned my head to follow a motor car: never had I seen one before. I felt thrilled, yet lost and heartsore, all at the same time.

At the top of Sackville Street, we travelled up a quieter, short hill road, crossing another louder road of carriages and bicycles, before turning into a more tranquil street. A few doors along, my uncle shouted to halt the jarvey.

'Here we are, Rosaleen.' He smiled. 'Home.'

Eccles Street. The first time I saw it I thought it the finest I'd ever seen. A terrace of tall, red-brick Georgian houses with wide steps within railings, doors of every colour. Once out of the jaunting car, Uncle Noel led me up a set of steps to his own blue door with an ornate brass knocker. My aunt must have heard my uncle turn his key, for she was in the hall to greet us.

'Ah, there you are.' Her voice was jovial; she stood with hands on her hips. 'Been causing trouble down there in the Holy Land? You're better up here then, amongst us sinners.' She laughed, a big hearty laugh.

Aunt Ellen was just as I remembered her. A stout woman, as hearty as her laugh, with a broad bosom. My slighter, more gentle uncle faded beside her, but seemed to delight in her, happy to do her bidding. A Dubliner by birth, he had met my aunt at a regatta on the Shannon in Clare.

Aunt Ellen ran a boarding house that, after our tiny Clare cottage, I thought a palace. To begin with, I felt tiny and timid within it. A parlour and dining room stood one each side of the hallway, where there was a staircase that led down to the basement kitchen and another that climbed three floors. The dining room was kept for the boarders, the parlour being my aunt and uncle's private room, with two armchairs by the elegant sash window, a grand mirror which reflected the sun, and the dining table which was always polished and smelling of beeswax.

But I quickly grew easy in my aunt and uncle's company, even if Aunt Ellen's ways in particular at first sometimes shocked me. In the parlour was also a sideboard always topped with a jar of fresh celery for Aunt Ellen to nibble, and where she kept an old winning hand at bridge, a rare perfect hand in a brown envelope. I'd hear her victorious cheers as she played bridge with the neighbours and boarders at the dining table, gambling shamelessly both on cards and horses, often asking Uncle Noel to place a bet for her. I had never seen a woman playing cards so wantonly for money or betting on horses in the country. And she was a keen gin drinker, which she kept no secret either. Perhaps many a woman drank in Clare, hidden behind closed doors, maybe even hidden from their husbands, but never with such abandon. Aunt Ellen had no care who saw her and I soon came to understand that, there in Dublin, no one did care. I was to learn that things were very different here in the city.

My aunt had no intention of letting me be idle. 'You'll earn your keep easily here,' she said. 'Plenty to do in the running of the house. I'm delighted to have you.'

And so, glad of my new surroundings, relieved to be rescued from gossip and prying eyes, I set to work with Aunt Ellen and her maid Mary on the many chores: the endless cleaning, turning down the boarders' beds, setting the dining-room tables for the lodgers' breakfasts and dinners, and carrying up plates from the kitchen.

I grew fond of Mary. She would allow me into her loft bedroom to look out from the window over, it seemed, all of Dublin: the blue mountains beyond, the church spires rising against the sky, the screeching gulls that flew in from the sea, perching and pecking on the roofs.

I took my breakfast with Aunt Ellen and Uncle Noel in the parlour but I would often spy the boarders in the dining room. My aunt would whisper to me of them: of the womanising of Jolly Jack, a cooper, his nails blackened from crafting wooden casks and barrels. Of the fussy ways of one she called Tidy Tony, a tailor, and Harry, a coachmaker, rumoured once to be a dentist before he broke a man's jaw. Another, Mossy, was a lamplighter, who every evening at dusk put his torch to the streetlights of Dublin.

'He's always moaning now,' my aunt said over breakfast, 'about the electric lights they've put on O'Connell Bridge and that are springing up everywhere. He says they're the work of the devil, that they have a wizard's wick. There'll be plenty won't want any electric devilry lighting up their business, if you believe what Mossy has to say. Ask him about the priest he once spotted caught short in an alley.'

The poor, unfortunate boarders sometimes suffered at my aunt's tongue, but there was one for whom she had a great deal of time: Lorcan. Lorcan Mulhern. I have many regrets, Father. But I can never regret meeting Lorcan. No matter what came of it.

*   *   *

I had met him in passing on the landing and the stairs, nodded a shy greeting before ever we spoke, but I knew him to be a favourite of my aunt's, for she would swoop on him and bully him into playing bridge with her in the parlour. I would hear them laughing from within as I passed. My aunt told me he worked in the Round Room at the Rotundo, the Roto, at the top of Sackville Street, an electric theatre showing moving pictures, which I thought so exotic. He was tall, older than me, but not yet thirty, with thick dark hair. Before we spoke, I had already noticed his smile that brought a dimple to his cheeks, a warmth to his eyes. One morning I was helping Mary clear the boarders' breakfast dishes, passing with them through the hallway, when I met him at the foot of the stairs, ready to battle the weather in his hat and coat. He stopped before me.

'Rosaleen?' There was a question in his voice. 'Miss Moore,' he went on, as if unsure how to address me. He tipped his hat, with a dimpled smile. 'Good morning to you.'

'Good morning,' I replied, a little disconcerted at his eyes so intent upon me. I tried to sound confident. 'And, please, it's just Rosaleen.'

He smiled again. 'And I'm Lorcan. It's a pleasure. A real pleasure to meet you.'

I was somewhat surprised at the enthusiasm in his voice. I was not sure why it should be such a pleasure.

'Your aunt has told me much about you,' he went on. I looked at him, uncertain what she might have said, but it was clear from his manner that whatever he had heard had pleased him. His eyes were so warm as he looked upon me. But even though I was drawn to that warmth, the scrutiny there also disturbed me.

'Please forgive me,' he continued, 'but she told me of what might be called your special gifts. I find that most interesting. And I know others who would find it very interesting too.'

He tried to hold my eyes, but I looked away as my stomach gripped. Since coming to Dublin I had relished my anonymity. Neither my aunt nor my uncle ever mentioned the trouble that had brought me to Dublin, or my unwelcome gift. Only once my aunt had joked, 'If you foresee Jolly Jack scarpering without paying up, be sure to tell me.' That she should have talked to this stranger of something so personal baffled and vexed me.

I was shaken and the dishes in my hand were growing heavy. I was going to say something as politely as I could and go on my way, when he said eagerly, 'I have friends – good friends, who live on this very street, just a few doors up – we meet often to discuss such things as your aunt talked of. I wonder, would you be interested in joining us one evening?'

His look was earnest as he waited for my reply. I would have been cross at the intrusion but for his obvious sincerity. Because of it I was slow to refuse. I found a way to delay it.

'Yes, perhaps,' I said. 'But I should talk to my aunt first.'

'Of course.' He smiled again. 'Well, let me know whenever you've decided. I would be only too delighted to escort you there.' He tipped his hat once more, and was gone.

During the afternoon, as I helped Mary with the chores, I found myself unsettled by the encounter. I had felt happy and safe in my aunt's house, as if I could start anew. Now it was as if my past had travelled from Clare to find me. On many evenings in my room I had lain on my bed and imagined what my life might become here in Dublin. I had imagined finding a suitor. Perhaps I might obtain a post as an assistant in the one of the fashionable stores in Sackville Street, once I'd found my feet here. That seemed like a dream to me. I had envisioned the stylish folk I might encounter. The new friends I might make. But so far I'd had little opportunity to meet people beyond my aunt's house. Even so, I had no wish to be introduced to any to talk about my 'gift' – if gift it was, for the burden I felt it, the trouble it had caused. I did not want to be a subject of interest, a feast for prying eyes.

That evening, I went to Aunt Ellen in the parlour where she sat alone in the armchair, reading by the light of the oil lamp. I told her what Lorcan had proposed, unable to keep the accusation from my voice.

'Ah,' she said, placing her book on her lap. 'I thought that might happen. So he wants you to meet his friends. I'm sorry, Rosaleen; perhaps I should have held my tongue. But Lorcan has such an interest in those kinds of things. People that have . . . abilities such as yours. I thought maybe you might like to meet people of a similar mind. That it might be good for you. Perhaps it was wrong of me.'

I softened at her contrition. I was curious.

'Well, who are they?' I asked. 'What do you know of them?'

'Very little,' Aunt Ellen said. 'I know the woman of the house, Mairéad Kinsella, but only in passing. But, to be honest, from what Lorcan tells me, they sound a strange lot. Perhaps you'd be better to keep away.'

But my aunt's words only piqued my curiosity. The following days, as I went about my chores, I'd spy Lorcan coming and going. He'd always greet me with a smile, but not another word about his invitation. That he did not pester me made me feel less under siege and more favourable towards him. And he had seemed so sincere.

Finding myself intrigued by these people that my aunt thought strange, I began to feel braver. At last, one morning, I stopped Lorcan as he left the dining room.

'Lorcan.' I smiled at him. 'Thank you for your invitation. I would be delighted to meet your friends.'

7

The house lay past the Dominican convent, at the higher end of Eccles Street, near the grand steps and pillars of the Mater Hospital. I shivered at the cold of the evening air, as Lorcan nodded to the proud building.

'The Mater Misericordiae,' he said, smiling down at me. 'The Miserable Mother.' At my baffled expression, he explained. 'It's run by the nuns, the Sisters of Mercy, and *misericordiae* is Latin for mercy – but also pathos, so it's often taken to mean misery. My own father was a patient there, so I call it the Pater Misericordiae. The Miserable Father.'

He winked at me and I blushed but could not help smiling. Lorcan had such an easy way about him it was impossible not to warm to him. At a Georgian red-brick house identical to my aunt's, we climbed the steps to a yellow door. Lorcan rapped loudly on the brass knocker. The door drew back.

'Lorcan!' A man greeted us. He was much older than Lorcan, perhaps fifty, with hair speckled grey and a pleasant face. 'Well, as you can see the lady of the house has me, as usual, acting as doorman.' His playful eyes settled on me. 'And you have brought us a guest. Delightful!'

He stood aside to let us pass into the hallway, and I found a staircase climbing before us, two rooms to either side: the very same design as my aunt's house. The man led us into the room to the left. 'Into the parlour with you!' he said jovially.

I looked about the room in wonder. The oil lamps were turned down low; many candles were alight on the mahogany sideboard and set on coffee tables before plush couches and chairs. Velvet ottomans were scattered about the elaborate Turkish rug and there was the scent of something sweet – oils burning over a candle some-where. Although the house itself was much the same as my aunt's, it felt a world away. There were some people sitting on the couches but my eye was immediately drawn to a striking woman seated on an ottoman by the draped window. Her dark hair was loose aside from a beaded comb; it fell over the shoulders of the rich red kaftan she wore. Spying us, she smiled and rose immediately. As she moved towards us, arms extended, I could see she was older than Lorcan but likely still shy of forty. In all my days, I had never seen anyone like her.

'Lorcan.' She greeted him fondly, then looked at me, her piercing eyes as dark as her hair. 'And this, I'm sure, is Rosaleen.' She took my hands in hers. 'I am so pleased to meet you.' Her manner was warm but her eyes intense, searching mine as if to find something. Taken aback both at her appearance and her intensity, I forgot to speak.

'This is Mairéad,' Lorcan said to me, 'our mistress and leader.'

'Lorcan!' she chided him, laughing. 'Don't pay him any mind, Rosaleen. There are no mistresses or masters here. Each soul here is as precious as the next. None above any other. We are as one. One great, universal soul.'

I flushed, hardly understanding, not knowing what to say. I remained speechless as, still holding my hand, she turned to the others seated around us.

'Everyone,' she announced. 'This is Rosaleen. Rosaleen Moore. At last, Lorcan has brought her to meet us.'

The men and women on the couches looked up at me as Mairéad started to make the introductions. She led me first to a man with greying hair at his temples, so long-limbed his legs stretched out from the couch far before him. I was struck by his height as he stood, bowing his head to me.

'This is Dr Gerard Mallon,' Mairéad said. 'Gerard is a renowned homeopath with a very successful practice in the charming village of Tallaght.'

I had no notion what a homeopath was, but tried to make sure to look as if I did.

'Charmed,' he said, towering over me as I shook his hand. His stature and refined tone of voice made me think him distinguished.

Mairéad gestured to the couple who'd been sitting beside Dr Mallon. 'And this is Mr and Mrs Armstrong. Bernard and Frances – fondly known to us as Ciss.' She smiled at the woman. 'Bernard and Ciss are our neighbours and dear friends.'

Bernard Armstrong, I immediately sensed, was a genial man. I felt a little more at ease as I stood before him. With his sparse, greying hair, I guessed him some twenty years older than his wife, who appeared forty or a little more. Bernard stood to shake my hand; he had an English accent.

'Most delighted to meet you,' he said.

His wife, a slight woman with doe eyes, remained mute. It was clear to me she was greatly anxious. Her mouth twitched as she smiled and her hands were fiddling on her lap. Her nervousness, in some strange way, almost settled my own nerves. As if I wanted to reassure her.

Mairéad led me to a woman sitting alone on another couch.

'And this is Noreen Ducey,' Mairéad said. 'Noreen lives just beyond the canal in Rathmines. So, not a neighbour but another dear friend.'

Noreen appeared to be about the same age as Ciss, and seemed to me severe. A plain woman with a broad face and pinched lips, ash-brown hair tightly pinned, she did not smile but gave me a brisk nod, extending her hand to shake mine for only a moment. I felt unwelcome.

'And my husband, Fergus. Gus,' Mairéad said as the pleasant man who'd greeted us at the door arrived at her side.

'Yes, penance for her past sins,' he said cordially. Mairéad hit him playfully on the arm. I smiled at him, grateful for his warmth after Noreen's chilly stare.

Gus left us to answer another knock at the front door and Mairéad ushered me to sit on one of the ottomans by a coffee table before the couches. Standing above me, she opened her arms wide at the sight of a new arrival. I turned to see.

'And Conor O'Lochlainn,' Mairéad said. 'Dear Conor. Conor, please come and meet our new friend, Rosaleen.'

Conor. When first I met him he seemed to me little more than a boy. I guessed him younger than me for sure. He was lean and lanky, shaking off the cold from his coat, cheeks nipped by the frosty air. They became even more ruddy on his introduction to me. With an eager but embarrassed smile, he held out a long-fingered hand.

'So pleased to meet you,' he said, shaking my hand. His palm felt clammy and I could tell he was anxious, keen to please, as he turned to Mairéad. 'So sorry I'm late. I was delayed in the library, then walked from St Stephen's Green.'

'Ah, a night stroll along Sackville Street, stopping off at the Monto, Conor?' Gus said amiably as Conor reddened even further.

Lorcan, sitting on an ottoman by my side, grinned at me. 'The Monto, Montgomery Street, just behind the Gresham Hotel, full of kip-houses.' He saw my confusion. 'Brothels,' he explained. 'Biggest roaming ground in Europe for ladies of the night, so they say. Does a brisk trade with all the Brit soldiers from the Royal Barracks. Best not to walk there at night, Rosaleen.'

'Plenty of Irish availing of it too, Lorcan,' Gus said.

I stared, shocked that the grand Gresham Hotel my uncle had shown me from the jaunting car could veil such vice. This city truly was a world apart from Clare. Not only was there such debauchery little more than a street away but all those gathered here were talking about it openly. And before Mairéad, in front of we women. I'm sure I was gaping.

'Don't be teasing Conor and don't be scaring poor Rosaleen,' Mairéad said. She turned to me. 'Conor is a neighbour of Dr Mallon – Gerard – out in the Tallaght Hills. He lives beside the monastery, the beautiful Mount St Kilian Abbey. He's studying Classics here in the city at the University College.'

'Yes, naughty Catholic, not welcome at Trinity,' Gus teased. Mairéad shook a scolding finger at him.

'Well, now you're making me feel bad,' Bernard Armstrong joked from the couch. 'Because I'm a naughty Protestant, like the gang at Trinity.'

'Don't worry, I like the Prods,' Gus said.

'Why's that?' Lorcan, beside me, said.

'Did the world a favour,' Gus said. 'Translated the Bible from Latin so all could understand it, rescued it from the priests' hands and put it into the people's. Did away with the middle man.'

'But I know it's not as simple as that here,' Bernard said. 'Ireland and Irish Catholics have so long been downtrodden by the British that their religion is almost tantamount to their nationality.'

I looked at him, surprised at this criticism of his own countrymen.

Mairéad raised her hands. 'Whichever or whatever. Catholic. Protestant. Hindu. Sikh. Jew. We don't recognise such fabrications, such man-made labels here. Simply cloaks we wear. Cloaks that conceal our natural form and hide the truth. That we are all born from the one universal energy, draw from the one breath of life.'

I gazed up at Mairéad, taken by what she said. These were words I thought I understood. I had little time, myself, for the squabbles of religion, the nonsense of whether the Almighty favoured the ornate Catholic naves or stark pews of a Protestant church. Although I did not have her fluency, I had often had much the same thoughts. The quarrels struck me as saying more about the nature of people rather than the nature of the Almighty. To say this, though, in Clare would be outrageous.

Mairéad sat down on a chair at the draped window and addressed me. 'You must be curious about us, Rosaleen, so let me tell you a little about us. We are followers of the German medic, Dr Franz Mesmer, and so are known as mesmerists. As such, we recognise the life force that powers body and mind. We believe that life force runs like a stream within us. That any obstruction to its flow brings about disharmony in our being and causes illness.

'We are sometimes known as magnetisers. For we use our hands, the magnetism of our own life force, to draw free the blocked stream in a suffering soul. Our own small group here like to call the source of that life force within us the Spring. Like a beautiful spring of mountain water from which every river flows. We revere that natural power, all that is natural and only that which is natural. And we believe there are some beings so perfectly attuned to the life force, to unseen powers within and without, that they can see and do what others less evolved cannot.' Her eyes settled on me. 'We believe you might be one of those beings.'

In the still of that moment I could feel every eye upon me, just as had happened in Clare. Except these eyes did not look upon me with dread. These eyes did not malign me. They looked upon me as if I were not something to be reviled, but to be revered.

In that moment I did not know which I feared more.

8

I thought much about Mairéad later that night as I undressed. As I rolled the stockings from my feet I thought of her feather-light steps. I mused on her deep eyes, and the kindness I had seen there. And her grace. Her beauty. Unpinning my hair at the dressing-table mirror, I was unsure if what I saw there pleased me. My features seemed too impish, not noble like Mairéad's. Where once I might have fancied my face had a country bloom, now my cheeks appeared too ruddy, unlike her even tones. My hair, though, was dark like hers. My mother had always been proud of our family's blue-black hair, claiming our ancestors to be the long ago Spanish sailors from the Armada who'd been shipwrecked off the Atlantic coast. But tonight my hair felt like straw. I brushed it over and over to make it shine like Mairéad's.

Yet, even with my shortcomings, Mairéad had seemed captivated by me. I was both surprised and gratified at that thought as I settled into bed, thinking on those I had met that night. Dr Gerard Mallon, so refined, as if possessing knowledge that allowed him walk taller and surer than any other. The amiable Bernard Armstrong and his nervous wife for whom I'd felt an instant compassion.

Gus, so witty and warm, and Conor, so shy I'd felt an urge to protect him. There had been only one I could not say I liked: the severe woman, Noreen Ducey. After her cold greeting, later she had tried to smile at me, but I'd felt that smile hollow like a winter sun. One that shines brightly but holds little warmth.

Every other person I had found welcoming, and I had enjoyed their banter. After Mairéad had said her piece, as if sensing she must tread lightly, afterwards she had simply asked how I was settling in Dublin and of my home in Clare. Only as I left did she whisper to me at the door, 'You are touched by the *aisling*. You are blessed.'

Not understanding what she meant, on our walk home I asked Lorcan.

'The *aisling*,' Lorcan said. 'The Irish word for vision. And if you don't mind me saying so, Miss Rosaleen, you yourself are a vision tonight.'

I knew he was teasing but I could not help but feel pleasure. Although I had dreamed of meeting stylish people, I had never imagined my own neighbours would be so exotic. My earlier doubts about them were replaced with a happy glow. And it had been good to hear strangers call my gift blessed just as my mother would, as if it were a thing to be cherished rather than condemned. It soothed some of the hurt I had carried with me from Clare. I felt it as a balm as I lay down to sleep that night.

But it was not only Mairéad who had charmed me. It was from that night on that I felt a leap in my stomach at the thought of Lorcan. I would find myself looking out for him, making it my business to know what time he left for the Roto, what time he might be expected home, which was often near eleven, after the last picture. Even though I was usually tired after my day's chores I would stay up to greet him, pretending I had always been a late sleeper, and we would sit together in the parlour. Lorcan would pour himself a whiskey and I'd take a nip of it in my hot milk. Eager for conversation, I asked him one night to tell me more about his friends as I sipped.

'Well, Mairéad, you'll be unsurprised to learn, is an actress, and Gus is a stage manager,' he said, sitting on the couch opposite me. 'They work in many of the theatres in town. It was on one of their tours abroad that they came across mesmerism and now they're firm disciples. Mairéad, I think, more so than Gus. Gerard Mallon studied homeopathy in Germany and came across mesmerism there. He already knew Mairéad and Gus, so they started to meet.'

'What about Conor?' I asked. 'He seems so young.'

'Ah, Conor. He's a dote, isn't he? He met Mairéad at a recital at the university and I think he was enchanted.' He looked down at his glass, thinking. 'He always seems a little lost, to me, somehow. I think that's why he comes to the meetings.'

'And Noreen?' The severe woman's face clouded my mind, although I tried to keep my tone even-handed.

Lorcan laughed. 'Aha! Noxious Noreen!' His face lit up. 'Don't pretend you liked her – you didn't! Go on, admit it!'

I started to laugh also but feared being too candid.

'Don't worry, only a saint like Mairéad could possibly find a place in her heart for her,' he said, grinning. 'I think our Noreen has taken quite a fancy to Mairéad. She saw her initially at one of her performances and then became a frequent audience member. She is a devotee now of mesmerism. Possibly because she is a devotee of Mairéad!'

Looking at me, he raised his eyebrows. I looked back at him quizzically.

'They are great friends?' I asked.

He laughed again. 'From Mairéad's point of view. Perhaps a little more than that from Noreen's.'

I didn't understand, but did not press the point. I wanted him to think me as shrewd as he seemed to be.

'And Bernard Armstrong, as you've probably gathered, came from England. London. He's retired now but he came to set up a company and met Ciss here.' He looked down at his glass again. 'Mairéad has been so kind to Ciss. She suffers greatly with her nerves. We're practising mesmerism upon her and Gerard Mallon is treating her with his remedies.' He looked up. 'They have a child, you know? Amy. Only seven years old.'

Again, my eyes were questioning. The Armstrongs seemed a little old to have a child so young. He took my meaning.

'Amy is fostered by them. The illegitimate offspring of some aristocrat – the poor mother paid off, the gentleman paying for the service of ridding himself of the nuisance.'

I was shocked and it must have shown. 'It's a common practice,' Lorcan said. 'Rife all over Dublin. But Bernard and Ciss didn't take the child for the money. They were unable to have a child themselves and desperately wanted one. And now she is theirs.'

'And you?' It was to this question I most wanted to know the answer. 'How did you come to join the mesmerists?'

He swilled the whiskey in his glass. 'I often met Mairéad, in passing, on the street. She seemed like such a kind, gentle soul and I was curious when she spoke of mesmerism with such passion. I was drawn to her. She is quite spellbinding, don't you think so?' He looked at me, his eyes smiling.

I did think so. I felt that same draw myself. Yet, to hear *him* speak of it. Aware of a spike in my chest, I quickly recognised it as jealousy. I tried to dismiss it, thinking it ridiculous that I could be jealous over some-one I had only recently met. But I will admit, it was not only my enchantment with Mairéad but my desire to spend more time with Lorcan that enticed me back to the mesmerists.

* * *

The next time Lorcan took me to Mairéad's I sat by him on the ottomans at the coffee table, Conor beside us, while Gerard Mallon, the Armstrongs and Gus sat on the couches. The lamp was low where Mairéad was seated at the window, Noreen leaning forward from another couch to speak.

'This is a dangerous time for us.' Her eyes and voice were stern. 'We must beware. Science is now meddling with nature to an enormous degree. Every day, the medics are concocting poisons in their laboratories that they claim will cure us but in fact will only destroy the natural balance within our own bodies. All we need to heal us lies within our bodies and the natural world. And it is vital we make people understand the root of disease. That it is brought about solely by a spiritual – mental or emotional – disturbance within us. That disturbance in itself is due to our not being allied with nature, an obstruction of the Spring. We must make people see that by aligning ourselves truly with the Spring we can restore that balance.'

I stared at her as she spoke. I thought of Uncle Pat and the cruel disease that had ravaged him. It did not seem to me that the ravaging had been caused by his being no ally of nature. He who had worked to the command of the rising and setting sun in the lush green fields all his life. I thought too of how Maggie Devlin's natural cures could not save him. But neither could Dr Hogan's science.

Mairéad leaned forward to speak. 'Yes, I believe that disease is often the work of a dis*eased* mind. A mind not at *ease*. If all were to know of the beauty of the Spring, perhaps then their minds and souls would be healed. Perhaps then there would be no more disease to cure.'

I softened under her voice, like it was a balm or a lullaby, but I thought again of Uncle Pat, incredulous at the notion that simply an uneasy mind could have caused that plague which had wasted the flesh from his bones, made of him a breathing skeleton.

When Mairéad spoke with such heart, though, it was beguiling. Perhaps she was right about science. It had not helped Uncle Pat and had no remedy for Nora's infection either. But then, Maggie Devlin had made a concoction for Nora from the very natural ingredients that Mairéad and the others seemed to revere. Ingredients that were natural, and therefore, they would say 'pure'. But I had learned they were pure, all right. Pure poison.

Yet I found myself wanting to believe what Mairéad said. I began to wonder if the problem with Maggie's potion had been Maggie herself. That she had been a bad practitioner. That she was not privy to the same knowledge as Mairéad and these obviously cultured people. Mairéad was so worldly yet other-worldly. It was possible she held secrets I could not know.

'What do you think, Rosaleen?' Mairéad asked, smiling.

I froze at her attention. I so wanted to please her. I sensed Mairéad, more than any other, fixated on my gifts. I realised the burden I'd felt that gift to be, my worry of what trouble it might bring, had faded. In its place, a fresh fear. I was frightened I might not be the girl Mairéad thought me. That I would disappoint.

I glanced at Conor. He was smiling at me encouragingly, willing me on. In that second I recognised him as a kindred spirit. Earlier I had noticed he stuttered when he was called upon to speak. Now I realised the two of us were both drawn to the bright star of Mairéad, and both feared we might not be worthy.

At last, I managed some words as close as I could to the truth.

'I do not know,' I said. 'But I am willing to learn.'

Mairéad was still smiling. 'And that is all we ask,' she said. 'An open mind, an open spirit. And perhaps it is not only you, but we, that will learn. Perhaps you have much to teach us.'

Under such scrutiny I felt every sense she so prized in me seize. With much expected of me it seemed all I could offer was fear. That same fear I could feel pulsating from Ciss Armstrong. I watched her that evening as she sat mute, cleaving to her husband, her eyes moving rapidly, at last coming to stare dully into the distance as Bernard's hands enfolded hers.

It would be on Ciss that I first saw them practise.

9

Lorcan had told me there was going to be a healing. On the appointed evening I was nervous at the prospect, but also excited. Excited, too, at being close by Lorcan's side as we walked to Mairéad's. Gus greeted us on the steps but before I could utter a word he put his finger to his lips, gently signalling me to hush. Lorcan nodding to me, I thrilled at his hand on my back as we slipped quietly down the hall. Entering the parlour I saw the lamps lit low, candles flickering on the sideboard and upon the coffee tables. From the couches, Gerard and Conor raised their eyes in silent greeting but Noreen, eyes closed, seemed lost to a faraway world. Mairéad was seated on a chair at the draped window, her back straight, poise elegant. Her eyes, too, were closed, her face serene, and she had her palms upturned gracefully on her lap.

Lorcan whispered to me. 'She is readying herself.'

I nodded, glancing at Bernard's nervous face as he sat alone on the couch, without Ciss. Shocked, I saw Ciss seated on a rigid chair in the middle of the room, another empty chair before her. She appeared so exposed there, this woman who seemed to hide herself in corners, loath to leave her husband's side. Her own eyes were closed, but tightly, her forehead in a frown, hands fidgeting in her lap. She was stiff and clearly ill at ease. I tensed at her anxiety as Lorcan led me past her to sit beside Bernard. I attempted to give this suffering husband a comforting look, lightly touching his hand. He gave me a grateful smile.

Gus, now the only one standing, softly closed the parlour door and Noreen rose. She moved around the room, lowering the lamplight even further until the room was dim. With just candlelight flickering on the walls, I heard what I thought was a tiny pleading yelp from Ciss in her lonely chair and Bernard went to stand, to go to his wife, but Noreen stopped him. She shook her head and he sat again.

Noreen stayed standing and in the deathly silence of the room my eyes were drawn past her to the window at a low humming sound. Almost a moan. Mairéad had begun to sway gently in the chair, gradually coming to rise as if lifted by an invisible hand. She opened her eyes and even in the low light I could see her gaze distant and glazed. Slowly she crossed the room to where Ciss sat and slipped on to the chair before her. She mirrored Ciss's straight pose, her knees almost touching hers. Noreen beckoned to the rest of us and, at Lorcan's gesture, I followed him and the others, watching them form a circle around Mairéad and Ciss. I took my place beside Lorcan.

Looking down at Ciss I could see a tremble in her hands, her lip, as if she were going to cry. But Mairéad only reached down and arranged Ciss's hands in her lap so her palms were upturned. Mairéad sat back then and closed her eyes. She lifted her own upturned palms to the ceiling and leaned back her head to look heavenwards. She began to hum again.

'*Mmmmmmmm* . . .' Her voice sounded strange. The tone deeper than I had ever heard it. She breathed heavily into her stomach.

'*Mmmmmmmmmmm* . . .' As she intoned, the others too lifted their palms heavenwards, leaning back their own heads and beginning to hum. Lorcan touched my shoulder, bidding me to do the same. I watched him take up the pose then mimicked him, uncertainly raising my palms and leaning back my head but did not close my eyes. The humming grew louder until it thickened to a dense, deafening drone.

'*Come*, come . . .'

At Mairéad's guttural voice, I stole a look down. Everyone still had their head leaned backwards so could not see me. Mairéad was chanting, bidding, beckoning.

'*Come*, come . . .'

'Come, *come* . . .' Each started to chant but not in unison. Staggered words and incantations swarmed in the air. Breathy whispers, moans, commands. I watched in amazement. Most before me were stolid, but Noreen started to sway.

Suddenly, Mairéad swept her arms downwards, and leaned in close to Ciss, raising and lowering her palms, finally bringing them to rest inches over Ciss's. Mairéad made a throaty moan.

'*Come, come . . .*'

'*Come, come . . .*' A swirling of moaning, chanting, surrounded me. My eyes, suddenly heavy, started to close as the sounds seemed to carry me away, and I began to sway. In the swirling, moaning, chanting, I was sure I could hear another sound, the lightest tinkle of crystals as if ringing in the air around me. Faint at first, they grew louder, louder.

All at once, Mairéad's voice cut through the chants, bringing an instant silence. I snapped open my eyes. It was not the voice I knew, but fervid, as if being drawn from every crevice of her being.

'*We stand ready now, O Spring. We are willing channels. Ready to serve as conductors of our all-powerful energy. Let the strength of our life force act upon the life force of our sister's. Let it restore her being to health and harmony.*'

'*Restore her being to health and harmony . . .*' The others took up the cry. '*Restore her being to health and harmony . . .*' No longer were the chants staggered but sounded in a heady, rhythmic unison. I looked to see if there was anything that could explain the chiming of crystals I had heard, but there was nothing.

Mairéad lifted her palms to pass them before Ciss's face and over her head, the others lowering their own palms to hover over the two women. Noreen started to roll her head and moan. Although alarmed, I lowered my own palms, the chants no longer pleas but commands:

'*Restore her being to health and harmony . . . Restore her being to health and harmony . . .*' Louder. Ever louder.

I could see Ciss furiously fidgeting in the chair, wringing her hands in her lap. Her eyes still closed, but tightly, her forehead deeply furrowed. In her swaying, Noreen must have opened her eyes. Shock bolted through me as her screech rang out:

'You must keep your palms open on your lap! So the force travels into you!' She bellowed over Ciss. 'And you must believe! You must *believe*!'

Stunned I watched Ciss flinch then gasp, shielding her mouth and eyes. I knew she was trying to stem her tears. The sight of her so fragile made me brave. I stepped out from the circle just as Bernard hurried to put his arms around Ciss's shoulders. I crouched down before Ciss and gently took her hand from her face. She let me hold it, looking down upon me with welling eyes.

I had only known her to be silent. Now, her words, at last come, were rushed. 'I have no peace, no rest.' Her voice was pleading. 'My head is swamped by a black mist, my stomach gripped by an icy fist. I am trying to see through eyes that are two dark tunnels in a mind no more solid than a rolling sea.'

Noreen made a furious sound, storming past Bernard as he gripped his wife's shoulders. 'You are hindering our healing power,' she spat at Ciss. 'You are blocking the Spring. It's your own fault. You won't let the healing come.'

Mairéad raised her hands in dismay. 'Please,' she said. 'This is not our way. Our way is only one of kindness and understanding. We will stop now.'

It was clear Mairéad was both distressed and angry at Noreen's outburst. I got up from Ciss's side, Lorcan turning to look at me with raised eyebrows. Gerard and Gus both appeared disturbed. I could see Conor was greatly upset.

At Mairéad's recrimination, Noreen sidled like a whipped dog to sulk on a corner chair. I observed her hurt eyes as she glanced over at Mairéad, as if looking to her mistress for a sign she was forgiven. Noreen was clearly a formidable woman, but it seemed Mairéad could tame her. In that moment the strangest thought came to me. I would have believed Noreen in love with Mairéad, if such a thing were possible.

Bernard helped Ciss from the chair, leading her to sit on a couch. She lifted her watery eyes and attempted to give me a weak smile. I tried to send her every kindness I could with my own.

Gerard went to stand over Ciss, his hand on her shoulder, bending as he spoke. 'I will give you some more remedy to help you rest tonight.'

She smiled up at him gratefully while my heart welled with sorrow for her. That night, Father, I did not truly understand the terror she felt. But in time I would come to understand only too well.

I was disturbed though by her anguish. The healing had reminded me in part of the cleansing I had suffered under Father Byrne. But I blamed Noreen for upsetting Ciss and Ciss's own anxieties rather than the ceremony. For I had felt something amongst them in that room. Had heard, I was certain, a ringing like the bells of angels in the air. Before Noreen's outburst, I believed I had been witnessing something magical.

10

Once I'd helped set the fires and cleared the breakfast dishes with Mary, I'd throw off my apron, and my aunt would release me to join Lorcan on his regular stroll, before he reported for duty at the Roto matinee. At the end of Eccles Street I'd glow as he took my hand to cross the busy road to Temple Street, there to pass beneath the gleaming white spire of St George's. We'd skip over the sweeping crossroads at the Roto, running in between the rumbling carriages, looking out for the tram, and amble the length of Sackville Street. In the bracing gusts of wind from the sea and mountains, in the sparkle of that early spring sunshine, Dublin and my senses sprang alive. All about us seemed friendly faces, men tipping their boaters or caps, women smiling from beneath their hats, others with flushed cheeks, too busy to mind us, almost tripping in their rush along the bustling street.

On our first stroll I'd stopped at the grand Gresham Hotel, peering down the passageway to the Monto, trying in trepidation to spy a 'lady of the night'. Lorcan only laughed.

'Come on,' he said, tugging my arm. 'Otherwise they might try to recruit you!'

I hit his shoulder at the notion I'd be deemed suitable for such an occupation and he arched his elbow so I could slip my arm through his. Always we'd stop beneath the canopies and spectacular five storeys of Clerys department store where I'd gaze at the colourful array of cloaks, dresses and hats in the vast, sheeny windows. We'd leaf through the books outside the bookshops, passing the milliner's, the draper's and tea, wine and spirit merchants. I loved the constant traffic of the horses and rattle of the trams as we scurried behind them, crossing to the shade afforded by the stately columns of the General Post Office.

We'd linger beneath the soaring Nelson's Pillar to watch the barefoot boys playing mouth organs, men winding barrel organs and shawled women and girls selling fish, fruit and flowers. Lorcan would throw down a farthing or buy me a posy.

'There,' he said the first time, folding my hands around the posy. 'Flowers for you, my Black Rose. To mirror the bloom in your cheeks.'

'Why *black* rose?' I asked him. But he just smiled and continued to walk.

As we wandered away from the filthy children in their ragged clothes I lamented their sorry state.

'They're children from the tenements,' Lorcan said. 'Where there are fifty, eighty people in one house, one tap outside between them. The finery of this street masks the shame of the slums. But believe it or not, things are supposed to be better for children nowadays. The Liberals have brought in new laws to protect them.

The children are meant to be at school in the morning and not show their faces to sell here on the streets until later. I don't know how many obey it.'

Always, we'd come to rest at the mighty O'Connell statue at the end of Sackville Street, overlooking the swell of the Liffey, and O'Connell Bridge.

'Daniel O'Connell,' Lorcan said the first morning as we sat on the steps, amongst the pecking gulls and pigeons. 'The Liberator.' He threw down some crumbs to the birds from the bag of buns we'd bought. He looked at my inquisitive face. I'd heard of Daniel O'Connell as a great man who'd died some forty years before I was born. But I had not paid attention. I was curious now.

Lorcan answered my silent question. 'You know how through history we Catholics could not hold land, or civil or military positions or seats in Parliament?' I shook my head. I'd known some of it but not all. He went on. 'Well, we couldn't inherit property either or practise our religion. We couldn't vote in elections and if a Protestant wanted his Catholic neighbour's property or land he could take it.'

This I knew. Uncle Mikey had often talked about the dispossession of houses, businesses and land. How in our own village and town, many Protestant houses and shops had once belonged to our Catholic neighbours but had been stolen from them. The Protestant families had simply taken them.

Lorcan went on. 'So, Daniel O'Connell is called the Liberator because he brought, at last, full Catholic emancipation. And all by peaceful means. By his time, nearly a hundred years ago, Catholics were permitted to vote but could not take a seat in Parliament. He stood in a by-election and won but was not allowed become an MP. So, there was an outcry and the Brits were afraid of rebellion. He was allowed to take his seat and it paved the way for full emancipation. He was a great man.' Lorcan looked up at the statue above us. 'And he fought for the abolition of slavery too.'

I looked up also at the bronze, cloaked man, his face broad and kind, hand to his breast. Four mammoth winged figures – Victories, Lorcan told me – faced out from each corner of the plinth he stood on.

'There's the Maid of Erin standing beside every man and woman in Ireland,' Lorcan said, nodding to a figure at the front of the crowd that was carved on the plinth between the great man and the winged Victories. 'There's plenty who don't call this street Sackville, after some duke, but O'Connell Street. That is its rightful name.'

It was one of those mornings on Sackville Street that I was revisited by my sight. I stood with Lorcan by the horses and hansom cabs lining the middle of the thoroughfare, the trams rolling before and behind us. I was aware of a woman and a small boy at our back, preparing to cross the road on the other side. A gust of wind blew up, and from the corner of my eye I saw the woman distracted for a moment, releasing the child's hand to secure her hat. Hearing the rattle of the tram behind me, I felt my hackles rise. I glanced at the little boy, saw him suddenly surrounded by a black plume and, in those seconds, knew what he was going to do. Speedily, I turned to grab him just as he stepped out on the road, the tram hurtling past. The woman screamed, the boy wailing from fright and my rough handling. The child was delivered safely into the arms of his mother; she was overcome.

'Oh, thank you, thank you,' she panted. 'Oh my God, when I think of what could have happened. When I *think* of it.'

Flustered, she seemed desperate to repay me, while I assured her there was no need. Lorcan and I helped the woman and boy across the road, and as the woman went on her way, fussing about the child, Lorcan held my eyes.

'Well, there we have it, Miss Rosaleen. You sensed what I did not. What I *could* not. And there is evidence of your gifts.'

I tried to make little of it. I was glad of his attention but not upon whatever gift I had. It also made me more aware my gift was unwitting. Not a thing I could call upon, but something that visited me. It seemed only to flee when I was too mindful of it.

We went on our way across the rolling Liffey, looking at the Guinness barges packed with casks from St James's Gate. Lorcan leaned on the bridge, nodding down to the smoking funnels of the brewery.

'I call it the *Vati*can.' He turned to me, smiling. 'For it truly is a holy place.'

'Well, does that make Uncle Noel the pope?' I joked.

Smiling, I took his arm again. At Trinity College, Lorcan rescued me from being trampled by the hordes of book-laden laughing students flooding from the gates on to Grafton Street. Escaping them, we passed under the grand stone Fusiliers' Arch of St Stephen's Green to look upon the lake that lay like smooth glass before us. We laughed at the waddle of the ducks and took in the exotic trees and the delicate spring buds before turning for home.

Once, we went home by way of Bewley's Oriental Café. The smell of roasted coffee wafted on to the street, and we followed it in and took a seat in a luxurious wooden booth, Lorcan ordering two cups of this drink I thought so sophisticated. As I put the cup to my lips, I was startled, wincing at the sour taste.

'Delicious,' I said wryly. Lorcan laughed loudly.

'You hate it! Come on.' Leaving his own cup, he took my hand, pulling me from the booth. 'I'll take you somewhere else.'

It was back on Sackville Street that morning that he first took me to Wynn's Hotel. His beloved place. There, they knew Lorcan well. The concierge greeted him, and from the foyer he called into the bar to men that saluted him. Women were not allowed sit in the bar, so we made our way to the lounge where I saw a large group of women seated at white-clothed tables in plush chairs. The women smiled up at Lorcan, greeting him, glancing at me curiously.

I wondered at them too. For, many times as I sat with Lorcan at our own white-clothed table, I'd see these women in plain skirts, suits and pale blouses come and go from the bar, seeming to have fetched some of the men who followed behind them to join the women at their table. Their conversation was avid but hushed. As if they did not want to be overheard. Lorcan never made any comment on it, would pass some words with them but never join them while I accompanied him. He would always bid them farewell, though, when we were leaving.

He did not introduce me to his friends and I some-how knew not to quiz him. But I did not worry. For I loved those mornings with Lorcan. I loved the nip of the spring air, the shimmering Dublin sunshine. I was begin-ning to love, it seemed, every paving, every cobblestone of the city.

I was beginning to love him.

*   *   *

Brother Thomas gazed upon the flames as Father Sheridan spoke.

'She was weak. But her face lit up when she talked of that spring of 1911. When she talked of him.' He looked into the fire. 'I knew Lorcan well. I met him first with Conor at a college awards ceremony in the University Church. That was how I met Rosaleen too. Afterwards, she would often come alone to light candles. It was then

I came to talk to her of home.' He paused. 'Did you know him? Know Lorcan?'

Brother Thomas reached to stoke the fire. 'Yes, I knew him slightly.'

Father Sheridan nodded. 'She did not live to see what would become of him. But I learned later that night that she had already seen what his fate would be.'

11

At home, in Eccles Street, my aunt had cause to call upon the doctor. Poor Uncle Noel lay in bed with a bad cold and, coming down the stairs, in the hallway I saw the tall, fair-haired doctor as he talked to my aunt.

'Thankfully, his chest is only mildly affected,' he said. 'I can hear no signs of infection and we must try to fend any off – we'd have little means to treat it should it set in. He ought to be all right if you keep him warm and in bed.'

My aunt, looking relieved, thanked him, turning to where I stood at the foot of the stairs.

'Ah, Dr Lydon,' she said. 'This is my niece, Rosaleen. She's been living here with us these past months. Rosaleen, come and meet the doctor.'

I absorbed his pleasant face as I walked to shake his hand. He had an affable manner and appeared no more than forty.

'A pleasure to meet you,' he said. 'I am your neighbour; my dispensary is just a few doors up. I'm sure we'll cross paths again if you intend to stay amongst us in Eccles Street?'

I did, indeed, intend to stay on Eccles Street, for familiar now with my new companions, those bright spring days were filled with fun. To my delight, Mairéad and Gus, as well as Gerard, owned motor cars and when I'd finished my afternoon chores, turning down the beds and preparing the tables for the boarders' evening meal, we would take trips to the sea at Kingstown.

At first I'd been petrified by Mairéad and Gus's shining green motor car, like a hooded wagon with white wheels. I'd been terrified at its speed, the wind rushing in through the open sides. I wondered at Mairéad and Gus embracing such machines when they'd professed disapproval of anything unnatural. Motor cars seemed to me the most unnatural things in the world. But I soon became thrilled by our rides. As Gus drove, Lorcan and I would push and pull each other like children in the back seat, as we hurtled around corners. I was overjoyed when he joined us, for he was more often working. He'd nudge me at Noreen sitting stiff with fear beside us and I'd giggle. Gerard travelled in his more sedate black motor car with Conor, the Armstrongs and their little girl, Amy. Yes, Amy, Father. I see you flinch. But I knew Amy well.

We'd meet in Kingstown harbour, Amy racing from Gerard's motor car to greet us.

'Conor!'

She adored Conor. He'd pick her up as Lorcan ruffled her honey-red curls, and I'd kiss her pink, excited cheek. When Conor put her down, she'd go scampering towards the ice-cream stand, us chasing behind her.

Grabbing the wafer we'd buy in her small fist, she'd dash to show Ciss her treat.

'Mammy, Mammy,' she'd screech and I could see a spark of life in Ciss's eyes, a soothing of her spirits. The healing effect her child had on her.

There, on the promenade, we'd stand to watch the big ships mooring, the small boats out sailing. It was in the pavilion I first tasted a cockle, Amy shrieking with glee as I instantly spat the slimy thing out into my hand.

It was on those seaside visits I learned more about what had drawn my newfound friends to mesmerism. As we strolled along the pier that seemed to stretch for ever into the sea, we'd engage in intimate conversation. Gerard had no doubt of the power of our practice. He explained that his own path of homeopathy helped the body to heal itself just as mesmerism did. He considered his medicine the true medicine and himself nothing less than a doctor. Noreen never chose to stroll with me, but when we sat to rest on the pier she would often deliver furious tirades on modern medicine.

'If only people would open their eyes,' she'd say. 'It's so clear what's going on. These so-called doctors and scientists forming a clique to give themselves the monopoly on health. Taking people's power over their own health away from them. And taking their money too. It's a travesty.'

Those times, Bernard would merely give a quiet and appeasing smile and gently move Ciss and Amy along to a more peaceful vista. I did not think him a true believer, as such. It was more that he was desperate to find a remedy for Ciss's crushing anxiety. Ciss herself seemed too disorientated to be sure of anything. I knew Lorcan was neither faithful nor a sceptic. On the precious days he strolled with us or the many evenings we shared nightcaps at home, I gleaned from him that he was more interested, perhaps fascinated by the practice, rather than a believer. Whatever drew him to mesmerism, I was only glad that it had brought us together.

Mairéad, though, was like a guiding angel amongst us. A devout believer in the might of mesmerism, the benevolence of the universe. Often she would say to me, 'The universe is inherently good, Rosaleen. It wants only our well-being.'

I could not help but think of every sorrow and trouble in the world and wonder why the universe would not deliver its goodness to all, but there was something about Mairéad herself which seemed so intrinsically good that her words touched me. I could see Gus felt the same. His devotion to mesmerism might not be as strong as his wife's but his devotion to her was palpable.

One day on the pier, I had let the others walk on, staying back to gaze upon the beautiful blue hills beyond, closing my eyes to revel in the rousing sea wind, when I opened them, startled at a voice in my ear.

'I can see you feel its power.' Mairéad's voice was soft. 'The power of the wind, the sea. This is the force I'm talking of, Rosaleen. The force within us as powerful as an ocean.'

She smiled, then walked away down the pier while I mused on what she'd said. I felt the power of the wind, for sure. And it was true. It was often as if I harnessed that power as it soared through me. Always it had seemed to lift me, my very soul, as if I could fly, as if I could do anything. Perhaps that was what I had always felt. What Mairéad talked of. My own power within.

One day on the promenade, I noticed Conor lingering behind, leaning on the railings, staring at the waves. I watched him for a moment, before going to stand beside him. He turned to smile, then turned back to gaze again upon the sea. I leaned with him on the railings.

'Are you happy, Conor?' I asked gently. I found the question slipping from me. It was a thing I had often wondered, for I sensed something in him so alone.

'I am on days like these,' he said, turning to me, again with a smile, 'when I'm with you and the others.' He was quiet for a moment. 'I've always felt an outsider. Before, at school, now at university. An interloper somehow. It was only ever at home I felt comfortable. With my mother and father and my brother, Rían.' He smiled. 'I hope you meet him someday. He has always taken care of me.' He looked up to where the others walked. 'But here with them also, I feel I belong.'

I nodded and we stood, looking out together, in a quiet and warm understanding. For I felt just as he did. No longer did I feel an outcast. Here with Conor and the others, it seemed I finally belonged.

That day was the first time I heard the name of Rían O'Lochlainn, Father. It would not be the last. And I will tell you now too of the first time I set eyes on the monastery. And the Abbot.

12

Gerard had invited us to his home, where he practised, in the Tallaght Hills, a grand old house, an avenue of trees winding to the door. Amy had been there many times before and, when I arrived in the car with Lorcan, Noreen, Mairéad and Gus, we found the Armstrongs there before us, with Amy acting as mistress of the house.

'Look!' she exclaimed in the hallway. 'Look at the flowers up there!' We gazed up at the floral etchings in the high ceilings as she ran about our legs, leaping on the chaise longue by the stairs and pulling Lorcan into the drawing room where she tugged on the luxurious drapes at the tall windows.

'Don't swing out of the curtains, darling,' Ciss urged.

'No, because you'll look too much like the monkey you are!' Lorcan teased. Amy shrieked with laughter.

Conor, who lived with his family nearby, met with us there. Amy screeched when she saw him, running to jump into his arms. He picked her up, swinging her.

'Conor, Mammy said we had to wait for you,' Amy said breathlessly. 'But can we go now? Can we go and walk in the woods?'

It is so hard to think of now. But we walked with her in the monastery woodland. Amy loved it there. As we took the short stroll to the abbey and stepped through its ornate wrought-iron gates, I remember being struck by its beauty: the sweeping grounds, the arched cloisters and the chapel high on the hill. The grand monastery, every stone as if steeped in silence and peace. The regal windows seemed to cast a serene eye down upon us.

Amy ran ahead on the path to the woodland.

'Careful, darling,' Ciss called after her. 'Mind the branches and the roots beneath your feet.'

But Amy paid her no mind, so Conor chased after her to keep watch.

Noreen was treading the uneven ground nervously, hanging on to Mairéad's arm while Mairéad raised her face to deeply breathe in the air. I was revelling too in the earthy scent, the twigs crunching underfoot reminding me of home.

Lorcan ran in front of me to a small wooden bridge.

'Madam, allow me to escort you over.' He bowed before me.

'Why, thank you, kind sir,' I said, holding my hand out daintily. He took it and led me over the brook, the water rippling over the rocks below.

Conor had caught Amy before she ran over the bridge and took her hand. She was still protesting, demanding she be allowed to run as we pushed deeper into the woodland. To where the bell tower stood.

There it was, before us. A high arch of engraved stone rose to form a pointed roof, ivy creeping at its foot. Within it hung a heavy, bronze bell dulled by the weather, attached to the tower by hefty metal. Amy obviously delighted in it; released from Conor's grasp, she jumped up, stretching out her arms to try to reach the cord.

'Can I ring it this time, Mammy? Please.'

'You know we can't ring it, my darling,' Ciss said.

'No,' Bernard said. He whispered in Amy's ear, 'We might disturb the monks.'

Amy's eyes grew wide and wary, staring through the gaps in the trees to the monastery as Bernard went on. 'If we frighten the Abbot, he might come out and scold us. And we can't have that.'

'Too late.' We turned at a voice and the crunch of wood and earth behind us. 'He's here.'

And there, on the far side of the bridge, I saw him. The day was warm, and his hood was pushed back on to his shoulders; his black habit was tied with a long knotted cord, dressed with a simple cross. He smiled as he strolled across the bridge towards us. A man of older years, his hair was sparse and white.

'Good afternoon, Father Abbot,' Gerard said as he reached us. 'I hope you don't mind us taking advantage of this fine weather for a stroll in your beautiful grounds.'

'Not at all,' the Abbot said. 'You are most welcome. And I hope you will forgive my intrusion but I spotted you from my study window.' He looked around at us all.

'Well, Gerard and Conor, my neighbours, I know, but I've not yet had the pleasure of meeting your friends.'

Gerard began the introductions, the Abbot nodding with a gracious smile. As I shook his hand, I met his eyes, which seemed to me kind.

At last, Gerard came to Amy who was standing, staring in awe at the Abbot.

'And this young lady is . . .?' the Abbot enquired.

'Amy,' Ciss said, bending down to her. 'Amy, say hello to the Father Abbot.'

Amy, clearly overwhelmed, bit her lip, remaining mute. The Abbot laughed.

'I have struck you dumb,' he said. 'If only I had the same power over my brothers when they are called on to observe silence. Well, Amy, it is my very great pleasure to meet you.'

As he bent to shake Amy's limp hand, she gave a curtsey. We all laughed.

'Ah, such courtesy,' the Abbot said. 'I wish I could always inspire such respect.'

'Father Abbot.' Amy had found courage through our laughter. 'May I ring the bell? Daddy says I'm not allowed for it might frighten you.'

We all laughed again, the Abbot smiling. 'Indeed you may,' he said. 'I am not so easily frightened.'

Amy allowed him to take her hand in his. Together, they stepped to the bell tower and he lifted her in his arms. Eagerly, she grasped the cord, trying to ring the bell but her strike was too weak.

'Let me.' Conor stepped forward to aid her.

Beside the Abbot and Amy, Conor gripped the cord and struck the bell. It rang out over the woods, a scattering of birds fleeing from the trees, screeching above us. Amy squealed with delight.

'Now me, now me!' she called to Conor, with outstretched hand. Conor covered her hand with his, and, at their strike, the bell rang out again, its deep boom and echo seeming to shudder through every leaf. The Abbot held Amy's eyes and smiled.

'There, little one,' he said. 'Now, whenever you come again, you may ring the bell. And I will know it is you calling to me.'

* * *

I will know it is you calling to me. Brother Thomas met Father Sheridan's eyes. The words hung heavy in the deep silence, at last broken by a knocking at the door.

'Brother Thomas.' Dominic, the postulant, appeared there. 'Forgive me, but a Mrs Quinn from Henrietta Street has just left this gift for you, below. She wanted me to give it to you with her great thanks for the kindness you recently showed her family.'

Brother Thomas looked at the leafy potted plant in Dominic's hand, rising to take it from him.

'Yes, I remember Mrs Quinn. That is very kind of her. Thank you, Dominic.'

Dominic nodded, taking his leave as Brother Thomas crossed the room, placing the pot on the mahogany table beneath the Madonna near the window. He glanced out. He could see candlelight between the trees, the pilgrims still there. He arranged the plant, stroking its leaves. From behind him, Father Sheridan spoke.

'Your kindness is well known, Thomas. Your work in the tenements, with the poor. I hear your praises everywhere on my travels. You truly live a life of service.'

Brother Thomas remained looking at the plant. 'It's nothing. What does it cost me? I, who live this comfortable life here amongst my brothers.'

'Still, they say you are tireless. The Abbot would be proud of you.'

Make me proud, Thomas. Brother Thomas still gazed upon the plant. He was visited by a vision of the Abbot's face the morning they had taken him away. They had allowed the Abbot time to say his goodbyes. The Abbot had circled the great hall, gripping each of the brothers' hands, heartbreak etched on every face. Heartbreak on Thomas's own.

The Abbot had reached him. He'd looked into Thomas's eyes, placed a hand on his shoulder. 'Make me proud, Thomas,' he'd said.

13

From that time Mairéad had spoken to me of the power of the wind being one with the power within, I had sat on my bed, listening to the force of it outside my window. I imagined it gusting through me, rousing that blessed place within: the Spring. She had told me to breathe the wind in deep, deep into what she called my solar plexus, named such because it radiated like the sun. Day after day, doing as she bid, I felt something stir. As if my core were strengthening like a muscle. A sun spreading from my naval to warm my chest. Soon that inner sun allowed me to walk taller. Prouder. I was not shamed, huddled and hidden as I had been in Clare.

I was determined to truly harness, nurture that power. To share with others its gift. Every night in my room, I would close my eyes, summoning the Spring, feeling it surge from my stomach into my spine, travelling through to my fingertips, my toes. I subsumed myself in it. I began to think of myself as a vessel.

At each healing I grew more confident. It was for the most part women who attended our sessions, men, perhaps, too proud to confess to any weakness. They came with vague symptoms such as dizziness, weakness or fatigue, and some I sensed anxious like Ciss. While most would sit under our hands quietly, seeming visited by a genuine peace, others would moan and roll their heads and I would delight in their fervour. That the power of our union was allowing the Spring to work through us.

I know Mairéad noticed the change in me for she said, 'I think you have truly come to us now. Now, you understand. You are embracing your full power.'

It was on a fresh April evening in Mairéad's parlour that Gerard brought us a guest. Only Bernard and Ciss absent, I sat beside Lorcan, looking up as Gerard escorted the woman into the room. A woman quite clearly wealthy in her tailored suit, with extravagant feathers in her Merry Widow hat, but she was nervous. That was plain to see.

'Friends,' Gerard said. 'Please let me introduce you to Mrs Madeleine Fitzpatrick. Madeleine is my patient and I have brought her here tonight for I feel, together, we might be of service to her.'

I rose from my ottoman as Mairéad stepped forward to offer the woman a seat.

'Please,' I said, 'let me take your hat.' I smiled, trying to put her at her ease.

She sat to unpin her hat, and I went to hang it in the hall. When I returned, Gerard and the others were discussing her ailment. It seemed she had been suffering from an indeterminable malaise, headaches, some nausea, for which no doctor could find a cause.

I had an immediate sense: I felt no threat of illness, but stirring in my gut was a deep loneliness – the strangest sensation, for loneliness was far from my own feelings. I suspected it visited me because it dwelled within her. I wondered if this was the root of her ailment, but I said nothing.

At last, discussion done, with the light of the April evening, Noreen drew the drapes and put a taper to the oil lamps, while Mairéad sat quietly, deeply breathing, readying herself. We sat in silence until Mairéad started to hum, then we all rose as she stepped, as if led, to the chair before the woman in the middle of the room. Quietly we formed a circle around them, Mairéad gently turning the woman's palms open on her lap.

'Mmmmmm . . .' Mairéad raised her face and palms heavenwards and started again to hum.

'Mmmmmmm . . .' As we hummed in unison, I leaned back my head, closing my eyes, summoning the power from my core, willing it to radiate from me. Being lulled by the soft humming, again I heard the gentle chimes of crystals, angel bells over Mairéad's breathy, deep voice:

'We come together, strong and present in the power of the Spring. May our power awaken our sister's own. Restore her being to harmony.'

'Restore her being to harmony . . . Restore her being to harmony . . .' I was chanting with the others, swaying to the rhythm, when I was suddenly stricken by a blinding bolt behind my eyes. I heard no gentle chimes now, felt no peaceful flow but a terror. Dark flashes. A fierce rumbling which I tried to identify, quickly hearing it as the thunder of horses' hooves. Fast, faster, too fast. Then a stumble. A flash of sunlight, a glare through glass. Friendly laughter ripped through with screams, a terrible tumbling, within what I guessed instantly was a darkened carriage. An upturning of people, an upturning of the world. I opened my eyes hastily.

'Please.' Quickly I stepped from the circle to crouch down before the woman, Mairéad looking dazed, shocked from her trance, the others staring down at me. 'Tell me, do you possess a carriage?'

The woman looked startled. 'Yes. Yes, of course. But why?' Her eyes were confused, searching mine.

'I sense danger, great danger,' I said. 'On a sunlit day. In the company of friends in a carriage. There will be an accident. People will be hurt. I implore you to be careful. Have you any trips planned with friends?'

She looked bemused then spoke. 'Yes.' Her voice was faltering. 'Not in our own carriage but we are to be collected by friends. We are accompanying them to an Easter tea at the Viceregal Lodge in the Phoenix Park on Saturday. Are you telling me this will be dangerous?'

'Yes,' I said. 'There is great danger. You must not go. Not in a carriage.'

She shook her head in disbelief. 'But my husband will insist upon it. It would be unthinkable to refuse the Viceroy's invitation. And he will insist we travel with our friends as planned; he would see no reason not to. I cannot do what you ask.'

Still, I urged her to heed me, while the others looked on. At last, Lorcan took my arm to help me rise.

'Our Rose has special gifts,' he said. 'Please listen to what she says.'

The woman looked flustered. Gerard stepped forward to touch her shoulder. 'Come, Madeleine,' he said. 'I will take you home. But I ask you to think on what our friend has said. Speak to your husband and your friends. Tell them. Warn them.'

'I cannot,' she said, rising, her face dismayed. 'They would think me mad.'

The evening deemed over, the woman left with Gerard. Mairéad looked at me thoughtfully, Lorcan standing over me as I sat wearily on the couch.

'How sure are you of what you saw?' he asked me.

'Very,' I said. 'Very sure.'

*   *   *

And so it began, Father. That was the start of all that came after, of what I came to be. For what happened after that encounter became the talk of all Dublin, the word on every tongue.

Madeleine Fitzpatrick did speak to her husband. But he did not believe her. Even as she grew hysterical, begged him not to ride in the carriage that Saturday, he would not heed her. She disobeyed his orders not to speak such nonsense to their friends and warned them, but they too dismissed her. Madeleine did not have to refuse to travel as her husband insisted she stay at home, saying she was obviously unwell and that he would make her excuses.

She clung to her husband's coat that Saturday as the carriage rolled into the courtyard. When at last it drove away, she roamed the echoing rooms of the house, waiting for the news she was sure would come. When the doorbell clanged, she pushed aside the maid to open the door herself. And there stood the police on the steps. They were sorry to inform her that there had been an accident in the Phoenix Park. The carriage in which her husband had been travelling had overturned, the horse thought suddenly struck lame by a stray rock. There were casualties. Her husband and his companions had been taken to the Mater Hospital. All were injured, but none seriously. The police escorted her to the hospital, for her husband was asking for her.

When Gerard brought us the news in Eccles Street, Mairéad and the others sat in shocked silence, then gazed upon me. I saw Lorcan smile quietly but I was distressed by the accounts of the injuries.

'None were hurt badly,' Lorcan said to comfort me. 'Who knows what might have happened had Mrs Fitzpatrick gone. Perhaps you saved her.'

Noreen seemed to care little for anybody's welfare, only sat excitedly on the edge of the chair, her eyes alight. 'Now all will believe,' she said.

It was from that day, Father. From that day they called me the Rose.

* * *

Brother Thomas looked up from the fire. 'So it was Lorcan. Lorcan who first called her the Rose.'

Father Sheridan nodded. 'She weakened when she spoke of it. Of the time she became the Rose. I thought she should rest, so I touched her shoulder lightly, preparing to leave, but she begged me to stay.

'"Stay, Father," she said. "Stay for the Abbot. And the sake of my mortal soul."'

14

Madeleine Fitzpatrick spoke to all her friends of me. As did her husband, Raymond and his travelling companions from that ill-fated day. Raymond had suffered concussion but, like his companions, no lasting harm; all of them moved in high and fashionable society. Raymond, known to be a man of reason, could not speak highly enough of me and my gift and all were enthralled. The visitors to Mairéad's parlour and our meetings became manifold; Noreen was delighted; Mairéad and Gus acted as gracious hosts.

I could feel Madeleine in awe of me, not only for what I had foreseen but for securing her husband's attention. He was a charming man but I gathered from Madeleine's conversation and my own sense that his eye wandered; often he had left her alone, his mind set on the prize of status rather than the happiness of his wife. Surely this was the root of her loneliness. But now, all had changed. Always by her side in Mairéad's parlour, he relished being the topic of conversation amongst the high-ranking guests, his wife the one who had borne the extraordinary tidings.

At first I was overwhelmed by the melee in the parlour and only wanted to hide, but Lorcan would gently lead me from my refuge in the dining room to mingle with the visitors.

'Don't hide away,' he said. 'At least let them see you. Otherwise, we will never be rid of them!'

Lorcan, though, was not impressed by all who graced the parlour. I saw him frown at some of the men in their finery, friends of the Fitzpatricks, and looked to him for an explanation.

'Bastions of British rule.' His voice was surly. 'A crowd from Dublin Castle. Well, it seems a young Irish country lass has impressed them. That's a wonder in itself.' He looked at me then in the oddest way. 'Perhaps it could be useful.'

I had no idea what he meant, just found myself swept away by a crowd of breathy women, the men hovering, curious, behind them. Some of the women beseeched me to lay my hands upon them, reveal what I saw.

Noreen, although basking in the attention, snapped at them. 'This is not a fairground. And she is no fortune teller. She is guided by a greater force and will tell you only what that greater power wishes you to know.' She treated me now with a kind of reluctant reverence.

Those nights, I would catch sight of Conor in the corner, and knew him to be as overwhelmed as I was. I would send him sympathy with my eyes, he returning the same to me. Ciss would join him in the shadows, Bernard by her side, and I knew she could not abide the commotion. But Gerard strode amongst our guests a man at ease, answering to enquiries of his remedies and practice. I would always seek out Lorcan when snared by an excited gaggle, see him sometimes looking on from across the room.

That he now called me his Rose brought me the greatest pleasure. But his eyes across that room, or when he spoke that name, troubled me. It was if I were something untouchable. Something sacred. A special little sister of whom he was so proud. I did not want him to think of me as a little sister. Or untouchable. I wanted him to think of me as a woman.

*   *   *

Often now, we were invited to dine at the Fitzpatricks', and would go to their fine house by the sea in Dalkey, the grand dining room holding a long white-clothed table set with candelabras and elaborate floral centre-pieces, seating twelve people, often more. It was clear the Fitzpatricks wanted to show me off to their friends. Lorcan always refused the invitation; Bernard often reluctantly declined due to Ciss's nerves. Conor would make excuses of college work but I knew him too timid to attend, so it would be Mairéad and Gus, Noreen, Gerard and I that would go to these gatherings.

Being from much the same background as our hosts, Gerard, Mairéad and Gus settled easily into the company, making polite and witty conversation. Noreen, however, was prickly and on edge.

'Stuck-up snobs,' she'd whisper to me. 'Think they're a cut above us.'

She insisted on coming, though. It seemed anywhere that Mairéad led, she would follow.

I was greatly intimidated by these dinners at first, bemused by the array of setting plates and cutlery, not knowing for sure which plate or knife or fork to use. There were place names at the table, and at the first meal I was thankful that Mairéad had been seated beside me.

'This one.' She nodded to the outside knife with the strange shape I had not seen before. 'It's for fish.' She smiled at me as I picked it up. 'Don't worry, I'll teach you,' she whispered.

And teach me she did. In her dining room in Eccles Street she explained to me the finer points of table manners, and settings and which glasses were used for which drink. 'And this one for the liqueur,' she said, holding up a tiny glass. 'Although by the time you get to that, no one cares as they're all too squiffy.'

I gained confidence through Mairéad's guidance and was soon very much at ease with the Fitzpatricks. Sometimes, before Mairéad performed, the Fitzpatricks, their friends and I would dine at the grand Shelbourne Hotel, spectacular with its electric lighting, then stroll by St Stephen's Green, crossing a bustling Grafton Street to the Gaiety Theatre where Mairéad, inside, prepared for her role. When not working, Mairéad and Gus would join us in the audience and we'd screech with laughter at the actors' antics on our many visits to see Gilbert and

Sullivan's operettas. At other times just Mairéad, Gus and I would go to the Abbey Theatre which Mairéad considered a cultural jewel founded as it was by the poet and playwright William Butler Yeats and the folklorist and writer Lady Gregory. It was a stage on which she was eager to act, and we would peer down upon it through our opera glasses from the balcony. I enjoyed these enacted tales of Ireland, the characters often reminding me of Clare and home, at times making me homesick. In my letters to Mammy I'd tell her of these outings and how I had worn the dress Aunt Cot had made me for my first dinner at the Fitzpatricks'. Soon, though, I was spending my wages on dresses available to buy ready-made from Clerys. Mammy would reply, delighted to hear of the merriment. Even though Lorcan was not there I greatly enjoyed these occasions full of mirth with my new companions.

'You need no lessons in social etiquette,' Mairéad said to me one evening in the Gaiety's foyer. 'You are already charming. Already have the Graces.' She smiled.

I had told Mairéad about my grandmother said to have been touched by the Graces. That my mother thought the same of me. I smiled in return at her play on the word.

'And I see in you something else,' she said.

She told me then of the three Graces in Greek mythology, the daughters of Zeus: Aglaea, personifying radiance, Euphrosyne, joy, and Thalia, flowering.

'You personify all of these now,' she said, touching my face. 'For you are radiant, joyful and truly blooming.'

* * *

Each healing evening now brought women, sometimes men, from all over Dublin. Noreen was delighted.

'This is what we wanted,' she said to us before we began one evening, as three women in the parlour awaited their turn to sit under our hands. 'For all to believe. To know the truth as we do.'

I looked over at the women. 'What is it that ails them?' I asked Gerard.

'A general malaise,' Gerard said. 'It is of no matter that we identify the illness specifically. The Spring within them will act. Will restore their balance.'

That evening as one of the women took her place in the middle of the room, as Mairéad readied herself and we sat in silence, I was aware of the eyes of the other visitors not upon Mairéad as they would usually be, but upon me. I swelled a little at their obvious admiration but tried to focus on my core, to awaken the Spring.

At last, Mairéad, silent and ready, came to sit before the woman in the healing chair, and we gathered around her. I watched Mairéad lower her palms down over the woman's, then, at her humming, closed my eyes.

'*We stand ready in your power, O Spring. We stand ready in your power . . .*' Mairéad began the chant.

'*We stand ready in your power . . .*' I chanted it with
the others, my fingertips tingling as I lowered my own
hands, circling them above the woman's head. Swaying
at the chanting and the humming, I grew heady, the
ringing of the crystals in my ears, lights flashing in the
darkness of my closed eyes. These lights did not alarm
me – I had now seen them many times while healing –
but I was dazzled and delighted, spellbound by their
bright colours, as they swirled like a kaleidoscope upon
my closed lids.

I suddenly heard a laugh beneath me. At this, I opened
my eyes to see the strangest contortions on the face of
the woman below. Her mouth was twitching and twist-
ing, her shoulders jerking. As she swayed and moaned,
Mairéad leaned back her head with a joyful expression
on her face, Noreen beginning to laugh along with the
woman. I felt the oddest sensation of laughter rising
also within me. With them, I laughed, the woman's face
a picture of ecstasy. Noreen swayed more and more
feverishly until she fell sideways as if swooning and
Gerard caught her, holding her by the shoulders.

'She is going into raptures. The Spring is acting within
her,' Gerard said, looking at the woman we were healing, and at this I felt euphoric, a manic laughter swelling
within me.

All at once the woman's face changed from joy to
pain. She lifted her palms from beneath Mairéad's, her
shoulders still jerking, but she was crying now, a violent
crying. The sound filled the suddenly hushed room.

I was stunned, but Mairéad looked up from her chair and urged us to remain silent. She waved her hands gently before the woman's face, then drew them back towards her own chest.

'The power of the Spring in each one of us draws on your own like a tide. Lets it flow free over any obstacle,' Mairéad said softly. 'You are released from all that ails you. Be at peace now. Be relieved.'

The woman's crying quietened, grew softer, softer until, at last, her head fell forward and she was still. Mairéad lowered her arms like wings settling at her side. 'The Spring flows free,' Mairéad said. 'It is done.'

The woman's head was still bowed. At last she lifted her face and smiled gently upon us.

'I felt it.' She spoke with a quiet joy. 'I felt every ill within me released.'

Noreen, dazed, looked down upon her. 'And now you must take this message to all,' she said hoarsely. 'Let all know of the Spring. The gifts that are there for them to receive.'

'Yes,' the woman said. 'Thank you.' Her words were directed to me.

I shook my head, not wishing her to think it was I alone had caused the transformation within her. But as our circle gently disbanded and she stood to walk to the couch, she whispered to me, 'I felt the power. I felt it from *you*.'

* * *

More and more people came. More and more people told me that they had felt my presence above all, a strong energy radiating from my palms. That it was the passing of my hands that had lulled them into a trance or aroused in them such exhilaration.

'No,' I said at first. 'It was not just me but the power of our union. The power of the Spring acting within us all.' But they would shake their heads with a smile and say no, it was me.

Back at my aunt's, I would sit on my bed and unfurl my hands to gaze upon them. I knew my gift of sight to be true. For I had been born with it. But now it seemed I really had harnessed the power of the Spring. That truly I had become a vessel.

That I held the power of healing in my hands.

15

One evening, as I made my way down the hallway to attend a healing, I was stopped by my aunt's voice calling from the parlour, where she was taking tea with the visiting Dr Lydon. They both looked up from the table as I stood in the parlour doorway.

'Where are you off to?' Aunt Ellen said. 'Up to that house again? The only time I ever see you now is when you're doing your chores. Don't you think you are spending a little too much time up there? And what are you all doing anyway? Dr Lydon tells me there's all sorts of funny business going on in that house.'

I flushed as Dr Lydon looked up at me.

'Yes. I think you should be careful, Rosaleen,' he said. His eyes were concerned. 'I know of these mesmerists and I know that they are carrying out all sorts of strange, so-called healing rituals in that house. Practices that are dangerous. Dangerous to the genuinely ill.'

I felt the heat of embarrassment and anger. How dare he? What could he understand of the power both sacred and natural within us? He who meddled with nature. Who with his pills and potions tried to be master of it? I was affronted by the insult to my friends. To myself.

'We have a doctor amongst us.' My voice was stiff. 'Dr Gerard Mallon of Tallaght.'

Dr Lydon shook his head, his face darkening. 'He is no doctor but a shyster. A charlatan. No man of science but of snake oil. That is exactly why these people are so dangerous. Proclaiming themselves to be something they are not. I beg you, please, take care.'

But I was ripe with indignation.

* * *

It was in late May that Mairéad suggested we should leave the noise and fuss of the city and spend the warm evening in Gerard's house in the coolness of the Tallaght Hills. She was quiet as we travelled in the motor car and I sensed she had much on her mind. In Gerard's grand drawing room, Amy sat on the floor, leafing through a picture book kept for his patients' children. Conor sat beside her, pointing to the ducks and quacking, as Gerard served refreshments. I was laughing at Conor's antics when Mairéad whispered to me to come away. Alone with me in the dining room, Mairéad sat before me at the table, covering my hands with hers.

She spoke softly. 'Rosaleen, I wanted us to come here tonight, to the peace of the hills, for I have something important I must say.' She took a breath and looked at me intently. 'I am stepping aside. From now on, I want you to lead the healings.'

I stared at her, stunned. For what seemed an age I couldn't speak, then said at last, 'No. I cannot do that. Our meetings belong to you.'

She shook her head. 'No. The blessings of the Spring, and so the meetings, do not belong to me, but to every one of us. And those blessings have chosen to reveal themselves through you. And it is you, now, those who come to us seek. It is you they wish to guide them.'

I shook my head, vigorously. 'No. I would not know what to do.'

She smiled. 'You do know what to do.' Her voice was gentle. 'You have watched me long enough. And besides, you do not need to know what to do. Just let the Spring act within you. As it surely already does.'

Too shocked, I said nothing else, just followed her silently through to the drawing room. She stood in the centre of the room, the others lounging with tea or wine, Amy sipping lemonade. She was still looking at her picture book with Conor, seated now on his lap. Lorcan looked up at me from the couch, plainly curious, Gerard, Ciss and Bernard sitting around him. Noreen sat near Gus, who stood at the window.

'Friends, dear friends.' Mairéad pulled me to her side, taking my hand. 'I have something of the greatest importance I must share with you. From this night on we will have a new guide. It will not be me but our own Rosaleen, our Rose, who will lead the healings. In this I am bowing to the clear signs of the universe.'

I looked around at everybody, both desperate for and nervous of their reaction. Amy was oblivious to anything but her book, but Conor beside her smiled. He was clearly pleased for me. Bernard and Ciss also smiled at me softly; I could see I had their blessing. But beside them I saw Gerard's jaw clench, his eyes lowered. He was plainly riled. And Gus, too. Although I could see this had come as no shock to him and he remained impassive, he averted his eyes when I looked to him and I knew he felt a chagrin at his wife's displacement. It was Noreen, though, who made her displeasure felt.

'No!' She sprang to the edge of her chair, her face stricken. 'No. The meetings belong to you, they are yours,' she cried to Mairéad.

'They are *not* mine,' Mairéad said firmly, 'but belong to us all. And surely it is clear to you all that Rosaleen has been chosen by a higher power to lead. That she was sent to us. That she is special.'

She smiled at me as I wondered at her graciousness. In that moment I wanted to tell her that it was not I but she who was special. So selfless. I gripped her hand, anxious at what had been thrust upon me. I looked at Lorcan, wanting his reaction most of all. He was gazing at me. Gazing at me with pride in his eyes. As if I was indeed special.

* * *

The bright days and long evenings brought a constant rush of visitors to Mairéad's parlour, those who were eager to join our discussions, say they had seen the Rose, had sat under her hands.

Now leading the healings, I did as Mairéad had counselled. I did not follow her way but allowed myself to be guided purely by the Spring within.

At the healings, I would prepare myself just as Mairéad had, gather the others to stand around me in a circle, but would sit in deep silence. In that silence I would gently open the palms of the woman, sometimes man, before me and close my eyes.

Rise within me . . . I intoned silently to the Spring. *Rise within me and stir within this woman your gift of healing. Rise.* I intoned stronger. *Rise* . . .

My eyes still closed, I would feel the warmth swell within me. Leaning back my head, I would open my chest to the force until I felt it subsume me. I willed that warmth to travel into my arms, my hands, my fingers, gently leaning in to pass my hands over the palms before me, over the man or woman's head, cupping their temples.

I would hum, hearing the others hum around me, in that humming hear the crystals ring, see the dancing lights before my lids. Again, I willed every warmth to travel from my palms into the sufferer's tortured skull, to ease them, soothe them, heal them. Within the heady humming I fell silent and burned with the heat between us.

Hearing a weeping, a moaning, or a joyful cry from the healing chair I would stay deathly still until I had felt every warmth pass from my body into that body before me. I would hear the moans, the cries, the laughter surrounding me. I would feel that same rapture rise within me, open my eyes to the man or woman limp before me, spent. At last, elated, they would raise their head, whisper to me:

'*Thank you, thank you . . .*'

Dazed, they would almost stumble as Gus escorted them from the house, and Mairéad would come to touch my shoulder in delight at the healing that had just taken place. Lorcan the same. I would search his eyes and, as well as admiration, I was sure I saw love there. I was certain of it. And basked in it. I no longer minded that he so obviously thought me special for I felt him, like the others, falling under my spell. Sometimes I would catch him watching me closely, seeming deep in thought, and the light in his eye told me it would not be long now. Not long before we became one.

Those evenings Bernard would pat the couch beside him for me to come, Ciss, even in her anxiety, managing a smile. It was Ciss, above all, who I wished I could heal. With Gerard's remedies having little effect, I had carried out a healing on her. On that night as I sat before her, I did not close my eyes as I normally would. In the intense silence between us, as I cupped her temples, I looked deep into her eyes. Willed into her mind and soul every peace I felt within mine.

Feel, feel, feel it, I intoned silently, *feel it.*

I closed my eyes, then, passing my palms over her head and face, cupped her cheeks. With all the energy in my body, I tried to draw each ravaged nerve from hers. I was so lost in my task that, at first, I did not hear it. But then grew aware of a soft mew, a whine. I felt two hands clutch mine.

I opened my eyes to see Ciss's forehead pressed against my palms, her hands travelling up my arms to grip them. Her whine gave way to racking sobs, her shoulders shuddering. I was still until her shudders eased, the only sound in the room now again her soft mewing. I moved closer to touch her cheek gently. She lifted her face to mine. Her eyes were no longer dead but alive with tears, her brow unfurrowed. Her body seemed soft and spent.

'Thank you,' Ciss whispered to me as Bernard bent to grip her shoulders. Her pupils were deep and wide. 'Thank you.'

In the great hush I heard Mairéad speak. 'It is released.'

* * *

For a short time, I was overjoyed, but whatever release I had brought about in Ciss did not last. Soon she was jittery and nervous, withdrawn again, her eyes dull. Noreen, who had been unable to hide her rancour at my displacing Mairéad, now could hardly hide her delight. It was clear my failure meant more to her than Ciss's recovery.

While the others were disappointed at Ciss's relapse, I sensed resentment also from Gerard. I suspected he believed that if anyone other than Mairéad were to lead the healings it should be him. After all, he was a man of medicine. Of standing. And although Gus attempted to hide his pique at his wife's standing down, I knew it perturbed him.

One evening, disturbed by the acrimony I felt surrounding me, discouraged by Ciss once more unwell, I expressed my doubts to Mairéad that the others would ever accept me. But Mairéad was firm.

'You must lead us,' she said. 'You affected Ciss in a way that no one else could. I am sure she just needs further healing.' She looked at me intently. 'You have the power, Rosaleen.'

* * *

Brother Thomas crossed again to the window. The night had drawn in, the candles glowing in the dark of the woodland. He pulled open the window to breathe in the dying summer air, listening to the sweet hum of song, evening prayer, rising from the chapel beneath. On the sill, the candle's flame flickered in the breeze. He closed the window.

'The power.' Father Sheridan spoke as Brother Thomas turned back to him. 'The Abbot wielded a power too. The power of his habit. Bestowing on him the authority of God. Just, I suppose, as mine. But he had another power. Over those who loved him. That love, it seems, leaving us blind to any fault. Making us believe him to be someone he was not.'

Brother Thomas returned to his seat at the fireside. He recalled his days as a postulant. How he had sat with the Abbot in his study beneath the dark oak beams, at the mahogany desk before the vast arched, latticed windows, amongst the sweet scent of beeswax candles.

'We are all flawed.' The Abbot spoke gently to Thomas at his side. 'The Rule of St Benedict teaches us that. And we will only know real peace when we truly accept those flaws. In others. In ourselves. When we see ourselves and others not as we would have them be, but as we and they truly are. The imperfect human. The fragile human. There is beauty in that.'

Thomas's eyes had followed him as he'd risen from the desk to stand at the window, looking out over the great oak beyond. The Abbot had spoken quietly.

'And knowing that, accepting our differences, our weaknesses, we must be minded then on mercy. Mercy rather than culpability. Mercy rather than justice.'

Father Sheridan interrupted Thomas's thoughts. 'Have you ever been to the jail? To visit him?'

Brother Thomas looked back to the fire. 'No. He asked me not to come. He said he did not wish me to see him in that place.'

Father Sheridan nodded. 'It is a sorry sight. He is not the man he once was. But then, it seems, he was never what we thought him. Perhaps the blame lies with us. Perhaps we idolised him. Made of him not only something he was not. But something he could never be.'

16

Those summer months were heady. On Lorcan's days off, he and I would often cool ourselves on the banks of the Liffey, stroll in the green of Phoenix Park, or take a jaunting car to the Strawberry Beds where women would sell us the juicy fruit from their baskets.

'Here.' Lorcan would bend to put a strawberry on my tongue, only to pop it into his own mouth. I'd hit him and we'd laugh as we walked arm in arm along the hedgerows.

There were parties, too, those summer nights. With the Fitzpatricks, their friends and Mairéad and Gus's flamboyant theatre crowd. I remember the fun when Mairéad and her fellow actresses sported the new harum-scarum pants from Clerys that were causing such a stir in the city. The outrage at women wearing trousers. We howled as Mairéad and the others paraded in them across the parlour and I gasped as Mairéad collapsed on a chair, swinging her legs high to cross them.

'No need to avert your eyes,' she called, gaily. 'Nothing to see here!' She laughed as the men reddened and Madeleine Fitzpatrick's friends gaped.

I watched Noreen that night. Watched her watching Mairéad. Her face was a mix of adoration and ire. And now I understood it. Understood what Lorcan had tried to tell me of Noreen and Mairéad when we had first met. One night at Mairéad's when only a few party stragglers remained, I was passing the parlour, intending to enter to bid Mairéad farewell, when I heard Mairéad and Noreen talking. It was obvious they were alone and speaking of me so I stopped in the hallway to listen.

'It's not the same,' Noreen was saying. 'Her way. She has made it all about her. With the silences. She gives us no chance to intone, to chant, to summon the Spring. I do not feel it as I once felt it with you. I wish you would take your place to lead us again, Mairéad.'

I could hear Mairéad's voice soft in reply. 'I understand, Noreen. I understand that change is difficult. But each of us has our own way of communing with the Spring and Rosaleen's way, I believe, is powerful. Are we not seeing the results before our eyes? And, so importantly, how our word is now spreading, how many people are coming to believe. And that is what we have always wanted.'

Noreen was quiet. 'That's true,' she said eventually. There was another silence before Mairéad spoke again.

'Noreen,' she said gently. 'I know why you feel as you do. I so dearly value your loyalty and support. I value your love.'

'But you do not return it,' Noreen said quietly.

'Not in the way you would like me to. I do love you, though, as a friend. A dear friend. You know that.'

I stood stunned in the hallway. I had felt it. Sensed that Noreen's feeling for Mairéad went beyond mere friendship. That she was in love with her. But I truly had not thought such a thing possible. For a while I reeled with it. Would find my eyes following Noreen every time she was around Mairéad, fascinated by her. Dublin was teaching me of a world I could never have suspected in Clare.

Those party nights Lorcan was present I would see him again watching me in that strange, close way, often as the Fitzpatricks' friends, the men from Dublin Castle, approached me to ask to sit under my hands. I both worried over it and revelled in it. Worried, for I knew these men of the Crown vexed Lorcan; revelled because I was sure he watched me in the same way Noreen watched Mairéad. I was not fooled by these men, knew some only saw me as an amusement, a part of a curious parlour game. But I would humour them. Would wave my hands over them, declaring, 'There. I have transformed you from a brute to a man most charming,' as everybody laughed.

Others amongst them, though, were serious. I felt them enthralled. And I knew some feared me. What I might see. And well they might. For, amongst the Fitzpatrick's friends, I could sense unfaithful hearts, wives abiding with their husbands purely for status or money, envious of the other wives' place in society. And with the actors I saw jealousies too, their coveting of others' roles, successes, beaus. With one man I knew it was no woman who occupied his thoughts but the man at his side. This did not shock me now as it once would.

And all the time Lorcan watched. When I caught his eye he smiled. You may think that with my gift I should have been able to sense what was in Lorcan's heart. But it seemed I could not. Those nights were so intoxicating, my own feelings for him so overpowering, it was as if they made me impervious to his. And more.

Sweet, shy Conor would attend these parties with newfound friends. It seemed now he was at the heart of such a glittering set he was judged no longer an out-sider but a desirable companion. Even though I was pleased for him, I was worried that he was becoming surrounded by false friends, who were stepping on him to reach social heights. I took him aside.

'I'm glad you have found companionship, Conor,' I said quietly. 'But take care. These people may not truly be your friends; they may simply be using you as a way to others.'

He smiled at me. 'I know. Don't worry. They've ignored me so long, I'm enjoying watching them fight for my attention. I know only too well who my true friends are. You and the others.'

I should have heeded my own advice. Should have seen the fawning over me for the slimy simpering it was. Should have stood solid, rooted to the earth, not been swayed by the acclamations, the adulation.

But, little by little, I was becoming swollen with it, Father. One night as I swept down the hallway, wrapped in a silk shawl that Mairéad had lent me for a dinner with her theatre friends, Aunt Ellen said from the stairs, 'Ah, Rosaleen, mind. If you let your head be turned any more by that fancy crowd, soon it won't fit through the doorway.'

But I ignored her. For I was full of a vanity that seeped and burst through my veins, driving out not only any supernatural but all natural sense. It would make me deaf to any voice but that which echoed my own. Blind. And that is why I could not sense what was in Lorcan's heart, why I could not see what horror lay before me.

There then came something that should have made me doubt. But it only made me more sure.

*   *   *

The wife of one of the Fitzpatricks' friends, Emma Rainsford, had asked for a private appointment with us. She was pale as she entered the parlour that afternoon, hair rolled thickly under her hat, in summer dress and white lace gloves for the heat. She looked perturbed at us all gathered there, anxiously eyeing the men. Flushing, she glanced at me pleadingly. I took her message.

'Do you wish to speak only with me?' I asked.

Reddening, she nodded. 'Yes, please. You and perhaps the other women.' She looked to Gus, Bernard, Gerard and Conor. Lorcan was not present. 'Forgive me.'

Gus gestured to the other men, Conor compliant, Bernard looking slightly concerned at leaving Ciss alone, Gerard affronted, and they exited to the dining room. Mairéad asked Emma Rainsford to sit. She did so, nervously, unpinning her hat, laying it on her lap. She sat silently fidgeting with it, so I leaned forward gently.

'Now, Mrs Rainsford. Emma. Please. Tell us what is troubling you. And how we might help.'

She spoke falteringly. Without the shadow of her hat, I could see on the corner of her mouth a small but unsightly sore.

'It's something of the most personal nature,' she said. 'The most mortifying thing. I have been struck by an affliction I have told no one of. Not even my husband.' She glanced again at her hat. 'Especially not my husband.'

I could see everyone was as puzzled as I, before she went on. 'You will notice this sore near my lips.' She lifted her hand to her mouth, barely touching it. 'It is so ugly and the reason I am so disturbed by it, is that I have just such a sore –' she hesitated before lowering her eyes to her lap – 'below. In an intimate place.'

Her eyes were pained, apprehensive as she raised them to gauge our reaction. Mairéad gazed at her sympathetically; Ciss looked distressed; Noreen sat stiffer than ever. I nodded calmly to inspire her confidence.

'I've been making sure to dissuade my husband's attentions, so he doesn't know,' she continued. 'But I have been feeling unwell, and I am worried what these sores might be and if more will come. I have been too

118

embarrassed to go to any doctor. I've come here in the hope that you might rid me of them.' She looked at me directly. 'That you might heal me.'

Again, I nodded at her, hoping to comfort her with my eyes. I went to sit by her, taking her hat, laying it beside her on the couch. I covered her gloved hand with mine.

'There's no need to worry,' I said. 'We will help you. The force within you is the cure for all and any ills. Please, take off your gloves and come and sit on the healing chair.'

Noreen rose, drawing the drapes to rid the room of the afternoon sun, and Mairéad led Emma to the two chairs in the middle of the room where she fumbled to remove her gloves. Normally, Ciss would be judged too unwell, her power too weak to assist any healing, but we were so few in number, I signalled to her to join Mairéad and Noreen in the circle. As I sat before Emma, she raised her eyes nervously to mine.

'We will work now to heal you,' I said softly. 'Please, lay your palms open on your lap and close your eyes. Calm and open your mind. Let it become ready and willing to receive the healing.'

Emma did as I bid, closing her eyes, opening her palms on her lap.

'Let us be silent now,' I said.

I closed my eyes to prepare myself. Silently, I summoned the Spring to come, rise within me. I heard the crystals ring. This time, though, at the edges of my mind I heard a hum. A humming coming from within, growing more forceful, louder, until I knew I must release it, beginning to sway to its sound and rhythm. Around me I could hear the others humming, humming too, louder and louder, until the air was thick with the drone. The lights danced before my eyelids, the crystals rang. In waves I felt the Spring warm me as it flowed up through my stomach, into my heart, my arms, hands and fingertips, causing them to tingle. Ready, I opened my eyes, placing my charged palms before the sore on Emma's mouth, the others lowering their palms over us.

I moved my palms down to Emma's own so the heat might pass from my hands into hers. I fixed my eyes on my hands, willing my energy into her palms. Closing my eyes, I bowed my head. The others continued to hum, to moan, to make exclamations of joy as I communed with the Spring in deep silence. It felt both as if time had stood still during that silence and as if a great age had passed as, at last, I opened my eyes and lifted my hands. At first, I was unsure. Could not be certain what I was seeing. The room was dim but I thought I could see a rise, a swelling on Emma's left palm.

I looked up. 'Noreen, please draw back the drapes.'

Noreen, still in a daze from the healing, looked puzzled, but did as I asked, an instant sunlight flooding the room. As Emma stirred, adjusting her eyes to the light, I looked again at her upturned palm. There, near the thumb, was a swelling, a rough, brown patch as if suddenly sprung there. I was sure it had not been there before. As I stared, Noreen, returned, cried out in excitement –

'Look!' She tugged at Mairéad, reached over me to touch Ciss. 'A rash, a swelling. The sickness. It is drawn out! Look! *Look!*'

Mairéad and Ciss leaned in closely to look, Ciss gasping, Mairéad murmuring in astonishment.

Quickly I spoke to Emma, who looked bewildered at the sudden fuss. I took her hand and lifted it. 'Emma, this rash – this swelling – was it there before?'

She looked down at it, dismayed. 'No. At least, I don't think so. I have been wearing my gloves all day but I'm sure it wasn't there this morning. Oh, my God, does this mean the sickness is getting worse?'

'No, *no*.' Noreen spoke quickly. 'It is well known that a rash is a sign of sickness being purged. That is what it is. It is the sickness leaving your body. It has been *drawn out*.'

I spoke to Emma softly, trying to be calm, although calm was far from what I felt. I touched her unmarked hand. 'Will you let us call Gerard? Dr Mallon? We do not need to tell him the nature of your ailment but he might be able to confirm for us what we are seeing. Will you agree?'

Emma, still bewildered, nodded as Mairéad went to fetch Gerard. He came with her hastily into the room. Mairéad had clearly informed him what had occurred.

Forgoing all formalities, he bent to Emma. 'Please may I see?'

Again, she nodded as he lifted her palm to him. He studied it.

'And this rash was not present before?' he asked.

'I don't know,' Emma said. 'I don't think so.'

Once more, he studied the affected skin.

'Yes, indeed,' he said at last. 'I would vouch that is the sickness being flushed from the blood.' He smiled at Emma. 'All should be well now.'

Noreen wanted to call the rest of the men immediately back into the room to proclaim this marvel but Mairéad stopped her, saying Emma was still in need of her privacy. Flustered, overcome, Emma did not stay with us long, but thanked us over and over. She gazed at me, her eyes deep with gratitude.

'And you're certain this rash on my hand will disappear?' she asked me as she stood and I helped her with her hat.

Noreen rushed to answer before I could speak. 'The rash will disappear. The sores too. For the sickness is flushed from your blood now. Be sure of it.'

I smiled at Emma. 'Dr Mallon has confirmed the cure, so we can be assured. Until the rash fades you can wear gloves. So it will be easy to conceal.'

* * *

At last, when Emma, so greatly relieved, departed, Gus, Bernard and Conor returned to the parlour.

Bernard immediately joined Ciss on the couch, who whispered breathily to him of what had occurred. He stole admiring glances at me, smiling and shaking his head in wonder. Conor standing over them, listening to Ciss, gazed at me in awe.

'Rosaleen.' Conor stepped forward, throwing his arms around me, hugging me tightly. Overwhelmed, I hugged him back.

Without divulging the whereabouts of Emma's more intimate sore, Mairéad told Gus what had happened in his absence. Even Gus, nowadays slower to praise me, seemed happy with this news. He looked at me with some regard. Gerard, also usually less willing to applaud me, looked pleased. He had, at least, been called on to confirm the healing and I suspected he felt his standing as a doctor had been respected and restored. Noreen was trilling, so excited, she lost sight of her antipathy towards me.

I felt dazed but delighted. The women who had sat under me before had displayed such vague symptoms. I had often secretly wondered if they were truly sick in body or if it was a sickness of the spirit that had brought them. But now. Now, a physical manifestation had appeared before my eyes.

Now I had solid evidence of healing. By my hands.

17

Alone with Lorcan in my aunt's parlour later, without revealing the full nature of Emma's affliction, I told him of the healing. He crossed from his own chair at the window to mine and took my hands.

'Rosaleen.' He looked upon me so lovingly. No, there was no doubt now. I could see the love in his eyes. 'My Rose. You are so truly blessed. You are our Airmid. Our Celtic goddess of healing.'

My heart sprang alive at his words. He thought me a goddess. A Celtic goddess. I swelled with contentment, pride and happiness. I had come into my full power. I was a renowned, now proven, healer. I had found my place in this world. And soon the man I so desired would be mine. He held my eyes a moment before returning to his chair.

'Rosaleen.' His voice was graver now. 'Tomorrow morning after you finish your work I want you to come with me. I want to take you somewhere. I need to talk to you.'

I nodded. I smiled. I was overjoyed. It was time now. He was going to declare himself. And I was ready.

*   *   *

The next morning I rushed through my chores, paying them hardly any attention. I was a little resentful of them now. Beginning to feel them beneath me. I no longer wanted to sully my hands with dirt for I believed them not made for scrubbing, but far greater things. No matter. Once the work was done, this day was going to bring me the greatest joy.

By eleven, Lorcan and I were strolling on Sackville Street, the sun high in the sky, the sea and mountain breeze as heady as my feelings. I linked his arm happily, and he smiled down at me, poked my straw boater, and I poked his hat in return. We laughed. As we reached the end of Sackville Street, I expected we would cross the Liffey, perhaps to walk to St Stephen's Green, to sit by the lake, a perfect location for us to talk in peace.

I was shocked, then, when he turned to lead me though the railings of Wynn's Hotel. I did not think it a suitable place for us to talk, always brimming with people he knew. Men and women who, even if they did not join us, would salute us and be an interruption. Also, I was somewhat jealous of these nameless men and women. I sensed they knew a part of Lorcan that I did not and I resented it. This morning he escorted me into the lounge as he often had before, saw me to a table and asked me to wait.

As he went back to the foyer I looked over at the group of women gathered at a nearby table. They were in conversation but one or two looked up, sent me watery smiles. I sent my own. At last, Lorcan returned, three men at his side. They were older than he and wore no jackets but waistcoats and shirts with sleeve garters. Lorcan smiled down at me.

'Here she is,' he said. 'Our Black Rose.'

Confused I looked to Lorcan for an explanation, but one of the men, shorter than Lorcan, with oiled dark hair and darker moustache, spoke.

'Miss Moore?' he said. 'Very pleased to meet you.' He extended his hand, which, looking again to a nodding Lorcan, I took and shook. 'My name is Jim Reddan,' the man continued. 'And these are my comrades, Michael Cahalan and Patrick Mulvihill. Would you mind if we sat?'

I shook my head, bemused, and the four sat down at the table, Lorcan beside me. He placed an encouraging hand on mine before withdrawing it.

'Miss Moore,' Jim Reddan began. 'Rosaleen, if I may, for I feel as if I know you. Your fame has spread throughout the city and Lorcan talks of you so highly and constantly. It is a great pleasure to meet you at last.'

I was somewhat appeased at the mention of Lorcan talking of me constantly. I smiled.

Jim Reddan went on. 'Rosaleen, you have charmed, it seems, all of Dublin. Everybody you have met. And it is easy to see why. You have even captured the attention of those at Dublin Castle. Captivated many of them, by all accounts.'

He was silent for a moment, holding my eyes as if I should take meaning from his words. But I did not understand. I shook my head slightly.

Jim Reddan leaned forward. 'We believe that your influence with those at Dublin Castle could be of great advantage to us.' Again, he was silent before going on. 'Do you know who we are, Rosaleen?'

I shook my head. Jim Reddan looked to Lorcan. Lorcan turned to me and touched my hand.

'Rosaleen, these are my friends. My very good friends, my comrades. I might even call them my brothers, for we are a brotherhood.'

I shrank at Lorcan's words as the realisation began to grow. A brotherhood. I knew of a brotherhood. *The* Brotherhood. Everyone in Ireland did. A secret sect who swore oaths of silence. The Irish Republican Brotherhood. Fenians. Uncle Mikey had told me tales of their stacks of dynamite which had lit up London. And Lorcan was one of them.

'The *IRB*?' I whispered to Lorcan as he nodded. 'And you are part of this?' I stared at him, incredulous, my voice rising. 'And what is it you want me to do?'

'Rosaleen.' Lorcan took my hand again, his eyes desperate. 'You have the ear of those men at Dublin Castle. You know things about their wives, things that could be used against them. Many of the men are enchanted by you; you could get closer to them now. Lure them into spilling their secrets to you. Information we can use.'

I could feel my face reddening, rage springing within me. 'For what?' I spat. 'Information for what?'

'So many things,' Lorcan said. 'You could tell them that your gift allows you to sense their worries. Coax them into talking to you about their troubles and trials at work. Who knows what information on their operations you might garner? The more you beguile them, the closer you get, the more they might be willing to tell you. Rosaleen, you could help us so much.'

I tore my hand away from his and stood. I looked down at the men whose eyes were now cast downwards, obviously realising I was lost to their cause.

'So you want me to prostitute myself!' I hissed at Lorcan. I could see the women at the nearby table, glancing up at my hysterical voice. 'Like a lady of the night at the Monto. Well, Lorcan, you warned me I might be recruited. It seems you were right.'

I turned, nearly tripping in my rush for the lounge door, running into the foyer and out on to Sackville Street. Blindly I ran along it, hearing the racing footsteps of Lorcan behind me.

'Rosaleen!' he called after me. 'Stop, please stop!'

I shouted at him as I stormed on. 'I cannot believe that you wanted to use me like that! That you would cheapen me so.'

He caught up with me and grabbed my arm, turning me to him.

'Cheapen you?' he railed. '*Cheapen?* It is because I hold you in the highest esteem that I wanted to award you what I consider the greatest honour. The most noble of tasks. To take your place in the fight for Irish freedom.'

'To be your *Black Rose*.' My voice was almost calm now, so thick it was with tears. 'What is that? What does it mean?'

'The Black Rose.' His voice was soft now, his own eyes welling at the fire of our fight. 'Róisín Dubh. The beloved woman. Ireland, Rosaleen. The name we used for Ireland when we could only whisper it. The adored Rose. The cruelty of her chains. It is the most beautiful name I can bestow upon you.'

* * *

I left him there in the street. He did not try to follow me and I ran home and unhindered to my room and curled up on my bed. His Black Rose. Róisín Dubh. Like Uncle Mikey's 'Dark Rosaleen'. I tried to be glad of it, being one he considered so beautiful, but my heart was raw. That morning I had left the house so full of sun. So certain that Lorcan would declare his love. I hid my eyes from the perverse sunshine through my window now. There was no place for it in my heart, only darkness.

18

I avoided Lorcan those next days. I did not see him that evening, did not wait up for him as I normally would and, the following morning, busied myself with chores upstairs, beyond reach at the time we would usually stroll together. It was my feelings being so in turmoil that probably caused me to act as I did with Dr Lydon when he came calling on my aunt the afternoon after my sorry encounter with the Brotherhood.

I was in Aunt Ellen's parlour, dusting the sideboard and freshening her celery in the jar, when the two of them came in to take tea there, Mary carrying a tray behind them.

'Perhaps Rosaleen will join us in a cup?' Dr Lydon said to my aunt as Mary set down the tray on the table. I sensed he offered this pleasantry to placate me after our last tense meeting when he had criticised my friends.

'No, thank you,' I said, more tersely than I should. My spirits were still low, my mood tetchy.

'No, indeed. No time to be drinking tea. There's my winning bridge hand to be dusted,' Aunt Ellen said, referring to her rare perfect hand stowed in the sideboard.

Dr Lydon laughed and I smiled, the tension somewhat broken. I was polishing the mirror, letting them get on with their chatter about the neighbours, the warm weather and the health of Dr Lydon's mother, when Aunt Ellen leapt up.

'What am I thinking?' she said. 'I have some gorgeous seed cake in the kitchen. I'll fetch it now.'

When she'd gone I glanced at Dr Lydon's reflection in the mirror. He was observing me. 'How are you, Rosaleen? You're still visiting your friends here in Eccles Street?' he asked.

His tone was amiable enough but I was irritated at the question. I could sense the rebuke beneath it. 'Yes, indeed,' I said. 'In fact, we are getting on rather well up there.'

'Oh, yes?' he said. 'How so?'

In my chest, I felt a swell of pride. I would not divulge myself as the leader of the healings but I intended to let him know now how wrong he was to belittle us. I flicked my duster along the ornaments on the mantlepiece. 'We have recently had a great success in our healing. A lady who had been feeling unwell, afflicted by unsightly sores, had the sickness flushed from her blood.'

'Flushed from her blood?' I glanced in the mirror to see his frown. 'What on earth do you mean?'

I lowered my eyes again. 'As we were healing her a rash sprang up on her hand. A swelling where there had been none before. A clear sign of the body ridding itself of the sickness.'

He made a sound of incredulity. 'A clear sign of no such thing.' I heard him stand behind me and turned to face him as he went on, 'What in heaven's name makes you think it means that? So now she has developed a swelling, a rash as well as the sores? Where are these sores? Which parts of her body?'

I reddened, lowering my eyes.

'Near her lip,' I said.

I tried to stop the flush, but could feel my face burning.

'And elsewhere?' he asked. He glanced to the door, watching for my aunt before he turned to me again. 'And *elsewhere*?' he repeated.

I felt myself stiffen. Mortified into silence.

'Rosaleen. This is very important. Am I to take it from your silence that the lady in question also had a sore or sores in a private, most intimate place?'

My face now was blazing red. It was enough of an answer.

'Rosaleen, we have very little time, but let me say that if that is indeed the case it is vital that this woman sees a doctor – a qualified doctor – straight away.' Even though I refused to raise my eyes I sensed him looking directly at me. He softened his tone, speaking more kindly. 'I understand why she might be reluctant to visit a doctor, the embarrassment she might feel, but her symptoms suggest she could be suffering from a very serious illness and far from any rash being a sign of the sickness subsiding, it is far more likely a sign of the sickness progressing. If my suspicions are right, the good news is that there is treatment she can receive but it must be timely—'

At the sound of the door opening and my aunt returning he broke off. Grateful for the interruption I nodded to them both and hurried with my duster from the room.

* * *

There was no meeting or healing arranged for that night but, glad of the chance to avoid Lorcan who might return, between pictures, to the house, I went later that afternoon to Mairéad's, hoping to speak to her of my encounter with Dr Lydon. My luck was in, for not only did I find herself and Gus there but also the ever-devoted Noreen, and Gerard who had called as he was in town.

When I entered the parlour Mairéad saw I was unsettled and sat me down with her at the window, the others gathering close to listen. As I told them of my conversation with Dr Lydon, Mairéad and Gus listened carefully, while Gerard, standing above us, looked sceptical. Noreen made a scoffing sound.

'Don't mind that quack,' she snapped. 'He only wants the business. Only wants to fill the poor woman full of his pills and potions. He doesn't want to believe that any other than he can cure sickness. It would put paid to his profession.'

Mairéad looked up to Gerard for guidance.

'Noreen is right,' Gerard said. 'Dr Lydon, like all in his profession, has a closed mind. I assure you, that a rash is a sign of sickness being purged from the body. That is a well-known fact.'

Mairéad looked at me. 'Did the doctor say what he thought the sickness was?'

I shook my head. 'Only that the treatment must be timely. And that they have the means to treat it.'

'Oh, of course, they do,' Noreen jeered. 'And there you are. Only his pills will do. The arrogance. He thinks his cures more powerful than nature's own.'

Mairéad spoke to me softly, taking my hand in hers. 'The rash did only appear after your healing. It *must* have been that that drew it out. Why would it suddenly appear unless it was the healing had drawn it? It is the only thing that makes sense.'

'I take it, though, the room was dim?' Gus said. 'Could it have gone unseen before?'

For a moment, I wondered if his question was genuine or if he was taking the opportunity to undermine me, still irritated at the displacement of his wife, but he seemed sincere.

Mairéad shook her head. 'One of us would have noticed it.'

'That's right,' Noreen said. 'The rash was not there; it only came under our hands. Did we not all witness the same thing?'

Mairéad nodded, Gerard also. And I did not doubt it. Had I not felt the stir of the Spring within me? Did others not feel from me its force? Who was Dr Lydon that he believed his man-made cures more powerful than nature's own? He and his like, any who did not recognise what gifts were there for them to receive, were fools. Blind fools.

*   *   *

At last, I could avoid Lorcan no longer. He would not allow it. Days after our row he waited for me in the hall so that, descending the stairs, I could not escape him.

'Rosaleen.' He touched my arm as I reached the bottom stair. I lowered my eyes, would not look at him but he gripped my arm tighter.

'I am sorry,' he said. 'So sorry. I should have talked to you first, before I took you to meet the others. Should have explained myself better. Found out how you might feel.'

'You explained yourself very well,' I said coldly. 'You made it quite clear what you wanted me to do.'

He dropped my arm and lifted my chin. Still I would not look at him.

'I would *never* want you to do anything you did not wish to,' he said earnestly. 'I am so sorry. I misread the situation. I truly did believe I was only showing you the greatest respect by asking you what I did. I realise now I was wrong. And I want us to be just as we were before: the greatest of friends. Please, Rosaleen.'

The greatest of friends. I balked at it. He and I both knew we were so much more than that. But I would allow him his charade. I decided to grant him the benefit of the doubt. Even though I could hardly countenance it, perhaps he really had thought it an honour to ask me to play the coquette with other men. But still it rankled. I nodded though and raised my eyes to see him smile. I attempted one in return.

'There,' he said. 'The smile of my Rose. My beautiful Rose.'

* * *

My heart was torn. As much as I resented Lorcan for his perverse request, I loved him in equal measure. I could not deny it. It was these conflicting thoughts that occupied me next morning, Mary and I busy with chores in the dining room, when a knock came to the front door. My aunt, already in the hallway, answered it.

'Rosaleen,' I heard her call, 'Dr Lydon is here to see you.'

My stomach seized. I did not want to face him. I dreaded the questions I was sure he had come to ask. Like a sloth I made my way to the hallway where Dr Lydon stood.

'Rosaleen,' he said pleasantly. 'Good morning.' He eyed the parlour. 'May I have a word?'

Lamely, I nodded, passing my curious aunt as we made our way into the parlour. He removed his hat but did not sit. Nor did I.

'I won't stay,' he said. 'I hope you don't mind but I wanted to enquire after the lady we talked of recently. Did you have an opportunity to speak to her?'

I mouthed the lie I had prepared on the way into the room. 'Yes,' I said.

'And has she seen a doctor?'

'Yes, I believe she has.'

He studied me. I could feel my cheeks reddening under his gaze. It was clear he did not believe me. His voice was soft but firm.

'Rosaleen, I would not normally divulge any information on a potential case, but, in this instance, I feel it is imperative. I fear the condition this lady may be suffering from is syphilis, a cruel, painful, potentially lethal disease. We have only very recently found the means to treat it. We have a drug now, the magic bullet. If this woman should suffer so needlessly in this day and age it would be a travesty. I beg you, if you have not, to speak to her as a matter of urgency.'

His words felt an attack. Cruel. Painful. Lethal. *But it is cured,* I countered in my mind, *it is cured.* I steadied my gaze to face him.

'I have spoken to her, as I said, Doctor. And thank you for your time.'

I started towards the parlour door. He looked at me almost sadly, before leaving.

'Take care, Rosaleen,' he said.

* * *

Pride and pique had kept me from confiding in Lorcan the doubts that Dr Lydon was casting on our healing.

Pride also caused me to keep it from Bernard, Ciss and Conor. I did not want any not already informed to know. It was for that reason that when next at Mairéad's, I took her, Gus, Gerard and Noreen aside to speak to them out of earshot of the others. I told them what Dr Lydon had said.

Gus whistled. 'Syphilis. So, Mr Rainsford's been a naughty boy then.'

I thought of what Lorcan might say if he were listening. Doubtless, he would wish me to use that information against Edward Rainsford.

'Even if it is syphilis, what matter?' Mairéad said. 'The healing has occurred nonetheless.'

'And I have my own remedy for syphilis,' Gerard said. 'If the healing should need a boost.'

'Should we tell her, though?' Gus asked. 'What the doctor has said?'

'No!' Noreen spat. 'He'll only want to drug her. Pour poison into her body and undo all our good work.'

Mairéad nodded and turned to Gus. 'If we tell Emma what Dr Lydon has said it would only unsettle her. Upset her marriage. Gus, have a private word with her husband. Ask him to come to us discreetly for healing. Or, if it is his wish, to see a doctor. But with Emma her healing has begun. If needs be she can come to us again.'

Gus had no chance to speak to Edward Rainsford, for we did not see him or Emma at any more of our summer parties, and I heard no whispers of them either. I took this as a sign that all was well. And I was fired with belief that if Emma were to go to a doctor she would be poisoned, that the natural healing that was occurring within her body would be thwarted.

Yes, Father, it should have made me doubt. But instead I would go to my room and raise my hands to gaze upon them as if they were anointed. I thought on this gift of healing just as I had thought on my gift of sight when a child. I had felt, then, that gift was a burden. But now, thinking on this fresh gift, I felt it not a burden but a calling. As if I had been summoned to serve. Ordained.

Chosen.

* * *

'Chosen.' Father Sheridan fell silent for a moment. 'To believe yourself chosen is a dangerous thing. Even more so, when others believe it of you. Believers will consider that they commit with impunity any act in the chosen one's name.'

Brother Thomas glanced at Father Sheridan. He thought of the prophets throughout the ages. Those who had believed themselves chosen. Christ surely amongst them. He thought of each prophet's disciples and their zeal. Was Father Sheridan referring to, or, in fact, blind to the acts committed in Christ's name? Those who proclaimed themselves Christians but wielded a cross not of love, but of fear. Fear of hell, yes. But more: fear of being human. Created by those disciples who demanded humanity be immaculate, where Christ had surely only preached tolerance. He thought of the Abbot's words: *'The imperfect human. The fragile human. There is beauty in that.'*

Christ's tolerance, love of our imperfect humanity. The Abbot's. Father Sheridan was a good man. But Brother Thomas thought of the patriarchs of the Church. The love of power that had overtaken the power of love. Throughout every dwelling in Ireland the reign of the priest, ruling with a whip. Flogging those who would sin. Those who would dare be flawed. He thought of the hidden homes, only whispered of. Fallen women cast there to pay the price of their sin, their tainted children punished for their sinful mothers.

Father Sheridan disturbed his thoughts. 'But you, yourself, were in a way chosen, Thomas.'

Brother Thomas looked at him, not understanding.

'By the Abbot when he made you the confessor in his place.' Father Sheridan's eyes settled upon him. 'It was a great honour. How highly he must have thought of you.'

Brother Thomas recalled that morning in the Abbot's study. The morning they had come for him. In a matter of hours the Abbot would leave. The summer sun had streamed through the latticed window, made diamond patterns on the desk as the Abbot stood before Thomas, laid his hand on his shoulder.

'And now, my last act.' The Abbot had looked into his eyes, a deep smile in his own. 'I decree that at your final vows you will become the confessor.'

Standing still and silent, they had shared a look of deep understanding. Each knowing the words they did not speak.

Brother Thomas turned from the memory to stare into the fire.

19

Madeleine Fitzpatrick brought surprising news to Eccles Street in the last, hot days of June. One afternoon she burst into Mairéad's parlour where I sat with Mairéad and Noreen, so giddy she could hardly speak. I laughed with Mairéad while Noreen looked irritated at Madeleine's fast-tripping tongue. Eventually she managed her announcement. It seemed with the coronation of King George in England, he and his wife Queen Mary intended to visit Dublin the very next week. The King and Queen would attend a garden party in their honour at the Viceregal's Lodge in Phoenix Park, and Madeleine and Raymond had been invited.

'And the best news,' Madeleine almost sang, 'is that I may bring a guest.' She turned to me. 'And I could think of no one better than you. One I may owe my life to, and surely Dublin's most fascinating resident.'

I laughed at being described so, but with false modesty. I was growing accustomed to being referred to in such terms. Even so, I was concerned that Mairéad might be offended at being passed over in my favour, Noreen the same. But Mairéad was, as always, gracious, looking delighted for me, while Noreen, I sensed, was caught between resentment at my eclipsing Mairéad, and glorying in the fact that we mesmerists were being recognised.

As Madeleine trilled at Noreen, and Mairéad called to Gus to fetch the champagne they had stored away for special occasions, I took the opportunity their excitement brought to think about the invitation. They had not asked me if I would accept, they had merely assumed I would. My mind turned immediately to Lorcan. He would be outraged by this, I knew. I must think carefully on it. Since our argument Lorcan had done all he could to make amends. In the late afternoon, between pictures, he would come and find me, either finishing setting places in my aunt's dining room, or at Mairéad's. If I was at Mairéad's he would make time to say hello to me there before he reported for evening duty. He was doing everything in his power to remedy the wrong he'd done. Yet I still felt the greatest slight. God forgive me, Father, I wanted to hurt him. Hurt him in return.

As the champagne was poured, looking at Gus's face, I saw a glimmer of resentment at his pinched mouth, in the way he so lovingly and attentively poured his wife's glass as if to assure her that the honour bestowed upon me belonged also to her. But I still had not given my answer. As we all rose our glasses to clink them, I spoke.

'I would be delighted to accept.'

* * *

143

Later, our inner set's planned meeting was full of talk of the royal event. Madeleine had already left when Gerard arrived in the car with Conor. Conor, of course, was thrilled, shrieked when he heard it, and even started to look through the afternoon dresses that Mairéad had laid on the couch in case there were any amongst them I would care to wear.

'This one, Rosaleen!' Conor called, parading with a white lace frock up against him as we laughed mightily.

I could tell that Gerard, a royalist, and staunch believer in the union between Britain and Ireland, was peeved at my invitation. There was nowhere he would rather be than in such august company, that of the King and Queen, no less. But he tried his best to appear gracious. Bernard and Ciss, genuinely happy for me, were smiling, and Ciss was, unusually, circling the room chatting, the news seeming to bring her at least a little cheer. We were still enjoying the revelry and celebratory drinks when I looked around to see Lorcan at the parlour doorway. I knew him to be working that evening but he had obviously called, as he often did, to see me.

He looked puzzled at us all in the midst of celebration, the dresses strewn on the couch.

'What's all this?' he said to no one in particular.

Mairéad crossed the room to him. 'The most wonderful thing,' she said, taking his arms. 'The King and Queen are arriving here in Dublin next week and our own Rosaleen has been invited to a party they will attend. Can you believe it?'

I lowered my eyes, but not before I saw his clenched jaw and dark stare. I heard his words.

'No, I cannot. I cannot believe it.' A hush fell in the room as all gauged Lorcan's mood. I could feel him look at me. 'And you are going?' he said.

I glanced at him for only a second but it was enough to nearly be felled by his glare. Noreen answered for me.

'Of course she is going!' she said. 'The mesmerists granted an audience with the King and Queen! Think of the recognition that will bring us. It is the most excellent news.'

I could not bring myself to raise my eyes. But I heard him utter the harshest sound. I knew he was turning to leave and quickly I looked up as he reached the parlour door.

'Lorcan!' I made towards him, called after him, but he was gone. I heard the front door bang.

Limply, I turned back to the parlour. At the window, I saw Gus raise his eyebrows as Mairéad looked quietly at me. Bernard, Ciss and Conor seemed shocked, Conor coming to touch my arm. I smiled weakly up at him. Gerard shook his head in disapproval while Noreen could not help the slightest of thin-lipped smiles. I sank down on to the couch, amongst the dresses, as if I'd been punched.

At last, Mairéad spoke. 'I think the reason he's upset . . .' she began.

'I know why,' I said.

*   *   *

Later, I waited up for him. I sat without lamplight in the boarders' dining room, knowing if he saw it or my aunt's parlour lit he might pass them by. I heard the front door open just after eleven o'clock and watched him in the hallway, opening the door to the dark parlour and entering. After taking a breath, mustering courage I followed him in. He was sitting by the light of one lamp at the window, a whiskey in his hand. I approached him softly, sat opposite him. He was silent, would not look at me.

'I'm sorry, Lorcan,' I said at last. 'I will not go. Of course I will not go.'

Afraid to meet his eyes earlier, I searched them intently now, desperate for his response. He fired me a dark look. 'You won't go,' he said. 'What does that matter now? The fact is that you wanted to go. That you said you would. That's enough.'

I shook my head, wanting to assuage him, but he railed at me.

'It's not only that you would slight me so, that you obviously care so little for my convictions, but that I can't understand it. How you of all people would consider going to the Viceregal Lodge to preen and bow. These city people can hide from it. But you, a country girl, must know. You *do* know. How they seized our homes, confiscated our land. For centuries we were nothing but slaves for the British landlords. How, during the famine, the aristocracy evicted bereaved, starving people, every day thousands of people, while they themselves dined on lobster soup. You must *know*.'

I shook my head hopelessly. Of course I knew. The great famine was decades before I was born but the memory of it lingered like famished grey ghosts around the western shore: the devastation of the barren lands and deserted homesteads, the dispossessed and starving fled on the coffin ships to America. Uncle Mikey would not call it the famine, but the hunger. He said it could be no famine, for it was known that there was enough food to feed the starving, but the landlords had exported grain and livestock under military escort to England. My young head had been filled with horror at what the survivors had witnessed. Desperate people stealing filthy sods of turf from barns, devouring them. I knew too of the brutality of the evictions, the bereft stripped of their homes, left to die in the ditches. I thought of Uncle Mikey and his poem of love for Ireland: 'My own Rosaleen! 'Tis you shall have the golden throne. 'Tis you shall reign, and reign alone.' Our country unfree. It had been so much a part of my life, it seemed I had formed an acceptance of it. And here in Dublin it was easy to forget the long struggle. The city felt a world removed.

Lorcan's voice was quiet now. 'The British fight for land. But we are fighting for home.'

We fell silent. Finally, I leaned forward to touch his hand.

'I'm sorry. I should never have thought of going.'

He moved his hand beyond reach. 'But you did.'

* * *

Feigning illness, I did not attend that garden party. And I did not witness the arrival of the King and Queen, the state procession from Kingstown along the thronged Dublin streets in the near tropical heat. I know Mairéad, Gus and Noreen were amongst the crowds, enjoying the pageantry, as were Ciss and Bernard, Bernard carrying a gleeful Amy on his shoulders. My aunt was curious, and she and Uncle Noel watched the parade as it entered Dublin Castle. Aunt Ellen said that most were jovial and cheering. Uncle Noel, though, showed me a protesting Nationalist leaflet that had been thrust into his hand, observing wryly that any protests had been swiftly dealt with. He told me that Dublin Corporation had refused to issue a welcome, and James Connolly, the influential socialist leader, had urged all to shun the visit. Uncle Noel said it was just as good that any dissenters stayed away because Dublin was like a tinderbox. In this heat, it could explode. I heard that Gerard celebrated mightily that day in town while Conor, indifferent, stayed in the hills. It seemed Dublin was a city torn. But Lorcan was on the streets that day.

I was to learn that soon to my cost.

20

The summer heat finally yielding to more normal, soft, Dublin rain, Mairéad decided she would host a last summer party. As well as the usual company, the Fitzpatricks, their friends and the theatre crowd, Mairéad was ecstatic when she received word that the poet and Abbey playwright she admired so, William Butler Yeats, had expressed interest in attending as he had heard much of me and would like to meet me.

'William Butler Yeats,' Aunt Ellen said, as she helped arrange my hair at the dressing table on the night of the party. 'They say he's a strange one. No doubt he'll fit in nicely with your friends up there.'

Lorcan and I had been estranged since our argument, the silence growing denser between us by the day. It hurt me so much. His absence like a death to me, I tried in every way I could to restore the easy camaraderie we'd once enjoyed. Our rift, begun with his misstep with the Brotherhood, had been widened by my retaliation and no matter how I tried to heal it, it seemed I could not. Sometimes he might laugh at one of my anxious quips but I felt his laughter forced. The evening of the party he was polite enough, waiting to escort me to

Mairéad's, but his politeness only marked his distance. Inwardly I despaired.

At Mairéad's the parlour glowed with softly burning candles, low-lit lamps, the cushions well plumped, tables laden with hors d'oeuvres. Gus circled with drinks and Noreen with trays of food. Gerard, Conor, all our posse were there, even Ciss, who it seemed had braved such a large gathering for Mairéad's sake. Conor, flushed with champagne, greeted us in the hallway.

'Mairéad is even more spellbinding tonight,' he said cheerily. 'On a mission to impress.'

I tried to return his cheer but my heart was sore for, as soon as we entered the parlour, his duty done, Lorcan left my side.

I saw Mairéad by the window, talking to a man as long-limbed as Gerard, with round spectacles, curls around his forehead. His attire fine, he wore a knee-length deep green jacket with black velvet lapel, and cravat. Mairéad was laughing with him when she caught my eye.

'Rosaleen,' she called, 'please come and meet William.'

As I made my way over, William turned to me with a look of curiosity.

'So, this is the famous Rosaleen,' he said as I reached his side. 'You really are the talk of all Dublin.' He looked directly at me as if he knew me well, saying softly, '"My own Rosaleen! O, there was lightning in my blood, Red lighten'd thro' my blood. My Dark Rosaleen!"'

I looked at him in wonder as he recited the poem I'd heard so often on Uncle Mikey's knee. With Lorcan like a stranger to me, I suddenly yearned for the warmth of my uncle, the comfort of home. William raised his hand, gesturing to another man, sturdy and dark in looks, in simpler attire.

'Mr Pearse, come immediately!' he called. 'Come and meet the most famous and most charming Miss Rosaleen Moore.'

The man came over. His eyes were earnest and even as they smiled I gleaned a great sensitivity in them. Almost a sadness. 'This is Mr Padraig Pearse,' William said. 'A fellow poet and playwright.'

Padraig continued to smile. 'Yes, my pen strikes by night. But by day I'm a schoolteacher.'

'Not simply a schoolteacher,' Mairéad said, 'but master of your own school. And it is well known you are a wonderful one. Not driving children by the whip but leading them by their hearts, opening their minds to learning.'

'Thank you.' Padraig turned from Mairéad, again to me. 'So you are the Rose. Róisín.' He sounded my name in Irish. I remembered, wounded, when Lorcan had done so. 'I am delighted and most honoured to meet you.'

William teased him. 'Padraig might not be a harsh master, but where he is strict is in that we should all speak Irish. They teach through Irish at his school, *as Gaeilge*, as well as English. He'll beat you savagely with a stick if you don't comply.'

'Don't mind him,' Padraig said. 'William is just as fierce a champion of Irish culture. Well evidenced through his writings and his founding of our own national theatre. But it's true our native tongue is the *grá mo chroí*.'

I looked at him, not comprehending. 'The love of my heart,' William said beside me.

Grá mo chroí. To me that sounded beautiful. I stole a glance at Lorcan, who was engaged in avid conversation with two women, one older than the other. The younger one I recognised from Wynn's Hotel. My heart's pain must have reached my eyes. It was a look that did not pass the poet by.

'Perhaps the lady has a love of her own,' William said softly.

I flushed at his shrewd remark, suddenly feeling stripped under his gaze. I was used to having such insights, but was uneasy at being the subject of one. I was relieved when Noreen approached us, eager to be introduced to the company. As introductions were made, I slipped away, meeting Gerard.

'I see you've been introduced to the poet,' he said drily.

I nodded, looking again to where Lorcan was still talking to the women. The younger one was neat and short, with a robust air. Her ash-brown hair was rolled up but not too fussy, her dress elegant enough but simple. The older woman was more striking. In a more elaborate dress than her companion, she was tall, her stature impressive. Her hair high in voluminous rolls, her face cut a strong profile.

'Who are those women Lorcan is talking to?' I asked Gerard.

He looked to where they stood. 'I don't know the younger one, but the older one is the famous Countess Markievicz.'

'Countess?'

'She's married to some class of a Polish count. They all arrived together, her, the poet and the schoolteacher, Pearse. Fancy themselves leaders of some kind of cultural revolution. Saviours of Irish heritage and tongue. Fenians, the lot of them.'

Fenians. And therefore, captivating to Lorcan. Occupied with the women that were so absorbing Lorcan, I wandered near, attempting to make myself inconspicuous in the background so I could study the Countess. She really was a striking woman. From this vantage, I could see her features were as noble as her title suggested. She caught my eye, smiling at me. Sending a wan smile in return, I waited for a lull in their conversation before purposely passing by and brushing against Lorcan. He turned, the two women continuing their chat, Lorcan's attention at last on me.

I edged him away. 'Who are your friends?' I whispered to him.

It seemed his enthusiasm caused him to forget what silence there had been between us. I tried to ignore the light in his eyes as he talked.

'That's the Countess Markievicz. Constance,' he said, gazing at her. 'Originally a Gore-Booth from Lissadell in Sligo. From a family of landlords but her grandfather and father were great philanthropists, fed the hungry during the famine and much more. She's inherited their heart, is a true revolutionary, outspoken on rights for workers and the poor. She joined the suffragettes in London and founded the Fianna Éireann here.' He lowered his voice. 'Training boys to fight for their country. And a Gael clan for young girls too. I met her with the Inghínídhe na hÉireann protesting on the day of the King's visit. She was arrested. Isn't she magnificent?'

I stared at the woman. She was indeed formidable and I realised, with a crushed heart, everything Lorcan admired.

'What is the Inghínídhe na hÉireann?' I asked.

He looked at me. 'Women nationalists. Rebels. The Daughters of Ireland.'

The Daughters of Ireland. My heart tightened as I asked, 'And who is her friend?'

I was loath to hear the answer. Or look at his bashful face as he replied.

'That's Saoirse Ryan. She was born Sarah but she took an Irish name. *Saoirse.* Meaning freedom. She is one of the Daughters of Ireland. She was arrested that day with Constance.'

He said no more but his unspoken words sounded with wretched clarity in my head: *And she is magnificent too.*

* * *

I was called on that night to lay hands upon our honoured guest, William. To tell him what I might see. He had especially requested it.

'Don't be nervous,' Mairéad whispered to me as Noreen turned down the lamps and readied the room. 'William is a true believer in the spiritual realm. He will be a receptive soul.'

The lamps and candles flickering with a soft golden light, William sat in a chair in the middle of the room. All gathered around, in deep, watchful silence. Never before had I attempted to summon my gift of sight but there was something in the man's essence to which I felt attuned. I stood before him, breathed peace deeply into my core. Somehow, even in that crowded room, the respect, the reverence, the hush was so intense it almost heightened my senses. Senses that had been deadened by noisy accolades were, in that moment, awoken. Perhaps it was my own heart so tortured over Lorcan that allowed me so effortlessly to read his. Or perhaps it was his own soul, so trusting. Whichever it was, as I held my palms over his head, I felt our connection was strong.

I was intuited to lower my palms to his heart, feeling from him the greatest longing. A yearning. A yearning such I as felt for Lorcan. It was so forceful it nearly buckled me, compelled me to speak. I leaned in close to him, whispered so others could not hear.

'Perhaps the gentleman has a love of his own.'

He flinched as I echoed the words he had spoken to me, then looked at me with a soft nod and smiled. For a moment he was quiet, then turned, his voice husky as he beckoned his companion.

'Padraig, come take a seat. Sit under the Irish Rose. She has the gift.'

Padraig tried to dismiss the invitation but William rose to escort him to the chair before me. Padraig's reluctance was clear, but as he sat so ill at ease beneath my palms, his fingers twitching nervously, eyes tightly closed, it was almost that reluctance, that unease, that allowed me to read him so clearly. I could sense in him a turbulence. An antipathy. An abhorrence so profound, of what I did not know. Beneath the skin of that sensitive, gentle man I felt the turmoil of his soul. I saw a flame: a flame that burned so bright within that heart. But that night I did not tell him all I had seen. For I saw, too, that flame would rise. Rise and soar, until he was consumed by fire.

I was heartsick. Disturbed by the onslaught of that vision, broken over Lorcan, I wanted to leave. With the onset of excited chatter, I looked towards the parlour door and the way to freedom as those gathered for the healing dispersed. Bidding no goodbyes, I slipped into the hallway, intending to retrieve my stole from the coat stand and go. And it was there I saw him: standing tall in the dining-room doorway, at Conor's side, a man older than he with the deepest of eyes and dark looks, who smiled at me in the most curious way. It was there I met Rían O'Lochlainn for the first time.

I have yet to tell you my greatest shame, Father. That was still to come. But for what I did to Rían O'Lochlainn – for that too, I feel the deepest shame.

21

Rían O'Lochlainn had attended the party that night solely for the sake of his brother. His only and much younger brother, Conor – ten years between them – who had worried him so greatly throughout their lives. Born late to their mother, Conor had been withdrawn, sensitive as a child, always shying away from the world, while Rían had been the opposite. He himself relished the attractions of the wider world and he worried that Conor lacked companionship. So when Conor had first told him of his newfound friends in Eccles Street he'd been surprised and pleased, only to be appalled as Conor later confided in him his new companions' strange practices: they were *mesmerists*. To Rían, a solicitor in his father's firm, a man of law and logic, their teachings were anathema. He saw his brother as vulnerable, easy prey for these shysters to feed on. But any attempt to persuade him so had failed. Conor had stood steadfast, committed to his friends.

So when Conor had excitedly issued Rían an invitation to a party hosted in Eccles Street, where, apparently, a distinguished guest, a well-known poet, would be present, he had taken the opportunity to see for himself what types Conor was mixing with.

He had not anticipated there would be an assortment of people. He had expected a bohemian bunch but the parlour was heaving with all manner of folk, high-ranking officials amongst them. Conor had introduced him to his friends with great enthusiasm. It had been Mairéad and her husband Gus who'd been more as he'd imagined. Theatrical types: Mairéad with kohled eyes and dramatic attire. He'd smiled a little to himself, but had liked them both.

Under the lamp's low light, he'd been settled on a couch, chatting to a Mrs Fitzpatrick, when first he'd spied her. Talking to the bespectacled fellow, the poet, at the window. Her back to him, her dress was of pale blue with a white lace sash, a ribbon trailing the nape of her neck beneath a high pile of the blackest hair, studded with a pearl comb. She'd turned from the poet and he'd seen her in profile. A neat face, almost elfin nose. Dark looks. He'd felt a stirring. Of curiosity. Interest. Mrs Fitzpatrick having turned to another guest, he'd looked to Conor, who was talking to his friend Noreen nearby. He'd beckoned him.

'Who is that?' he'd whispered to Conor. 'Talking to the poet?'

Conor's face had lit up with pleasure. 'That's who I was telling you about. Rosaleen. Our Rosaleen. The Rose.'

So this was the Rose. Conor never stopped talking of her. Apparently she was graced with magical gifts, a mystical vision. Whereas before such a claim would have caused Rían to balk, now it only added to his interest.

'I'll introduce you,' Conor said, 'when she is free.'

Conor had been urged away by another friend, Ciss, who was seemingly feeling faint. Rían took advantage of Conor's absence to observe this beauty, the Rose. She was hovering close to the wall, watching, it seemed, some fellow in conversation with two women. Rían grew more curious. The way she was looking at this man – with great intent, almost a hunger in her eyes – she looked like a hunter lurking in the shadows, as if she were going to spring upon her quarry. And so she had. She'd brushed by the man, he was sure, deliberately. He'd watched the two of them talk, her expression taut. As the man had left her side, she'd wandered, her mind clearly a world away.

With Conor detained by his friend, Ciss, the night had passed with no introduction to this captivating woman. He'd been pleased, then, when all had been called on to gather around the Rose and the poet, where Rían could feast on her, study her in fullness. Mistress of the room now, her manner was one of poise and strength as she stood over what they called the healing chair. He was eager to hear what she had to say, wanted to hear her voice, so he was disappointed when she'd bent to whisper to the man.

It was only when one they called Padraig had been summoned to the chair that she spoke. She stood in deep silence, her palms passing over him until finally, she opened her eyes and said simply, 'You have a soul of fire.'

At last he had heard her voice. Somehow the sound of it moved him. Her words, though simple, felt not hollow but full with meaning. As the man rose to touch her shoulder, everyone once more starting to chat and mingle, he'd felt a sudden desperation not to lose her again in this crowd.

Alarmed, he saw her eyes wander to the parlour door. He was afraid she would go without being introduced to him. He'd searched about for Conor, luckily spying him in the brighter light of the hallway. That was good. If she were going to leave she would have to pass him by there. He went to Conor, pulling him aside.

'Conor, please introduce me to your friend now. I fear she might go before we have a chance to meet.'

And it was then she had stepped into the hallway.

Conor smiled. 'And here she is: Rosaleen. Rosaleen, I'd like you to meet someone. Please let me introduce you to my brother, Rían.'

* * *

I could see this man, Conor's brother, gazing upon me with what appeared intent curiosity. It did not disturb me. I was well used to being looked at in such a way. But at that moment it irritated me. My heart was too sick to entertain idle chatter, I wanted only to leave. But Rían took my hand, lifted it to kiss it.

'I am delighted to make your acquaintance,' he said.

I was taken aback at this old-fashioned show. Mairéad and I and many of her theatrical friends had often mocked this type of gallantry. I had not encountered it before in sincerity. In politeness I was about to nod graciously, plead fatigue, make my apologies and leave when I heard Lorcan's voice behind me, coming from the parlour into the hallway. I knew he was talking to Mairéad for I could hear her laughter. And then it struck me. I'd had to endure the torment of watching Lorcan all evening in the thrall of other women. Let him now see me in the company of another, attentive man. Perhaps that would rouse something in him.

I acted immediately. 'And I am most delighted to meet you.' My voice was louder than it need be, happier than I felt.

The man, Rían, looked slightly puzzled, but pleased, his eyes smiling. It was evident he was charmed by me. Although I did not look I was still able to hear Lorcan's voice further down the hallway, so went on, 'We knew Conor had a brother and now, at last, he brings you to meet us. Tell me, Rían, what do you think of our little gathering?'

He laughed. 'Well, first of all it is not little. And I think it fine. Perhaps the present company the finest thing about it.'

I laughed loudly, again, more loudly than I needed to. I could not resist glancing down the hallway in the direction of Lorcan's voice. There he was, still talking to Mairéad but looking over curiously to where I stood with this stranger. It spurred me on.

'Your brother is most charming,' I said to Conor, who was looking happy at our banter.

'Not charming,' Rían said. 'Simply truthful. Please tell me you are not going to leave. Not now, when we have just made our acquaintance. Perhaps you'll do me the honour of joining me in a glass of champagne?'

I glanced again at Lorcan, still observing us, then looked up at Rían. 'Yes, indeed I shall.' He offered me his arm and I was delighted to take it, knowing Lorcan would see as we crossed the hallway back into the parlour.

For the remainder of the night, I sat with Rían upon the couch, letting the melee go on around us, always watchful for Lorcan. I saw him enter the parlour, looking about him and spying us there. Quickly I turned my full attention again to Rían, as he talked of his home with his parents and Conor, his legal work, and asked much about me. Even as I spoke of my mother and family in Clare, truly, my thoughts were far from them: they were only settled on whereabouts Lorcan stood and how he might feel watching me so captivated by this man. At last, when Rían rose to offer me his arm and asked if he might escort me home, I accepted gratefully, making sure to bid a goodbye to all, so Lorcan would notice. With only a fleeting glance, I waved at him, a nonchalance I hoped would sting.

As I walked with Rían down Eccles Street, I was swollen with satisfaction at Lorcan's irked expression at our departure. When Rían left me at the door, with another kiss to my hand, I knew his question before he asked it. And knew what my answer would be.

'May I see you again?' he asked.
'Indeed you may,' I said.

* * *

Rían had not been fooled that night. As he'd been introduced to this vision in the hallway, he'd noticed something forced in her voice, her laugh too loud, tone too elated. She'd paid him no heed all evening; he had envisaged having to work harder to harvest such interest. He had noticed the fellow with whom she'd seemed so occupied enter the hallway, and guessed instantly at the reason for her gusto. She was hoping to capture this man's attention.

But Rían had not allowed this knowledge to thwart him. He had no notion what lay between the Rose and this man but, whatever it was, there was clearly a rift. That was fortunate. It afforded him an opportunity.

He would take it.

22

Since our rift, my morning strolls with Lorcan were no more. But that morning after the party he came to find me where I was sweeping under the stairs. He leaned against the banister.

'Who was the man you were talking to last night?' His tone was casual but he was unable keep the ire from his voice. 'The one who walked you home.'

I was gleeful, but made sure to seem as if I were fully concentrating on my brush. My voice was airy.

'Oh, that is Rían. Conor's brother. Did you not meet him?'

He shook his head. 'No. I wasn't introduced.'

'That's a shame.' I looked attentively at a spot on the floor. 'He really is the most entertaining man. So witty. Don't worry, you'll meet him. I believe he's going to call on me.'

He was silent and I knew my blow had landed. Lorcan was accustomed to receiving my full attention. Even with our estrangement, that an interloper might come and steal my affections, replace him in my regard, I knew would unsettle him. This was my aim: that he would endure the threat of losing me to another.

Perhaps it would awaken him to the tender feelings I was certain lay in his heart.

'I see,' he said. His tone was also airy but as false as mine, I knew. 'That's good. I will have the chance to meet him, then.'

I did not look up as he turned to walk briskly to the front door and away. But I let a smile creep across my lips.

*   *   *

On the afternoon Rían called for me I was disappointed that Lorcan was not at home; he had already left for the Roto matinee. However, I intended to make a great fuss around Rían's visit, later to my aunt, in Lorcan's earshot. And I was genuinely excited, for Rían was taking me to afternoon tea at the grand Gresham Hotel.

As we strolled to Sackville Street, I could tell my companion was greatly nervous, making supreme efforts to seem at ease through his chatter of the weather and his tram journey, while I was perfectly calm. He took my arm to escort me into the hotel's lavish lobby, and, in the lounge, pulled out my chair for me to sit, something Lorcan never did. From the white-clothed table, Rían raised his hand to the waiter, ordering our tea.

He was gallant, lifting any cake or delicate sandwich I requested with prongs from the tiered tray, while he hardly ate a thing himself, so intent was he on conversation.

'I was enchanted the other evening,' he said, 'watching your reading of the poet and his friend. Tell me, how long have you had such a gift?'

'As long as I can remember,' I said, cutting a lemon tartlet with my fork.

'And Conor tells me you have yet another gift. The gift of healing.'

'Yes.' My voice was listless. I'd long been swollen, sated with praise. I had become bored of the constant fawning. I was bored at Rían's praise of me now. I could see he was fascinated by me just like so many others. I did not want his fascination. I wanted the easy companion-ship, the familiarity and bond I had shared with Lorcan.

'And what do you see when you look upon me?' he asked, with a smile. 'Can you see the secrets of my heart?'

I looked upon him. The raptures of his heart he wore upon his face, in the light in his eyes, the glow of his cheeks. It seemed Lorcan had been right. I had another gift. To bewitch and beguile.

'I see a man who knows what he wants,' I said.

He flushed then, and it took me aback. I truly had him in my thrall. For a moment I liked it. It made me feel powerful, where I had felt so powerless with Lorcan.

'I believe you are right,' he said at last, lifting the pot to pour me more tea, clearly for distraction.

Later, as he walked me up Eccles Street, feeling the beginning of an autumn nip in the air, I felt deflated. The chill only reminded me of the winter I had first walked these streets with Lorcan, and I was eager now to reach home. Rían was nice enough but staid. I had no interest in him and no heart to continue with this dalliance. As we climbed the steps to the front door and I turned my key, I had already decided to gently decline any further meeting. I was turning to bid him goodbye when I became conscious of a shadow in the hallway. It was Lorcan, standing there, looking at us.

My cheeks flared. 'You're home,' I said to him.

'Between pictures.' He stepped to the door. 'And this must be . . .?'

'Rían.' Rían extended his hand. 'Rían O'Lochlainn, Conor's brother.'

'Of course.' Lorcan extended his own hand but his discomfort was clear. 'I'm Lorcan Mulhern.'

They shook hands but each eyed the other glumly. The friction was all too clear. My heart instantly lifted, all earlier resolutions to have done with Rían forgotten.

I would see this man again.

* * *

After his encounter with Rían on the doorstep, Lorcan became more attentive, the unbearable silence between us now broken. Although we did not enjoy the same ease in each other's company, no longer took our morning strolls or late-night drinks in the parlour, Lorcan's tone when we spoke was more kind now, and I felt a well of the deepest emotion between us, so many words left unsaid. I had almost changed my mind about making use of Rían to lure Lorcan, but when Gerard invited all of us to tea in his house, with Rían being his neighbour, I could not help but mention to Conor that perhaps he would ask Gerard if he might bring his brother. I could not resist the notion that seeing Rían again might rouse Lorcan, draw him out. Bring to the surface all that lay unspoken between us.

That day, Conor and Rían were already seated in Gerard's parlour when I arrived in the car with Mairéad, Gus, Lorcan and Noreen. Rían stood up immediately and greeted us amiably, glancing at me in a marked way. I greeted him warmly in return, all too aware of Lorcan watching. Lorcan did not speak, only nodded brusquely at Rían, Rían the same.

Conor said cheerfully, 'You've just missed Amy. Ciss felt too poorly to come, but Bernard's taken Amy to the woods. She wanted me to go but I thought I'd better stay, seeing as my brother is our esteemed guest today.'

As Rían smiled modestly, I felt Lorcan stiffen beside me. Beginning to take our seats, I delighted in Lorcan cupping my elbow, leading me to join him on a couch away from Rían and Conor on the far side of the room. Noreen, Mairéad and Gus sat on a couch beneath the window, Gerard on an armchair, signalling to his housekeeper to leave the well-laden tray on the coffee table before him.

As Gerard poured tea he began to talk about a boy, Joseph, we had treated recently for epilepsy. He had been suffering a spate of fits and his mother had been distraught as her despairing husband had wanted their child committed to the asylum. In Mairéad's parlour I had passed my hands over the poor boy's red-rimmed eyes, his frail, fatigued body. It seemed his fits now had stopped.

'So, there you have it,' Gerard said, placing the full tea cups on the table for each of us to take. 'The boy at last has some ease. It seems the combination of Rosaleen's healing and my remedy have had the desired effect.'

I was thrilled to hear of Joseph's recovery. I nodded graciously at Gerard's mention of his remedy playing its part. I knew it was important to feed his self-esteem.

'It could just be respite, though,' Gus said, taking a cup from Mairéad's hand. 'Doesn't that happen? That sometimes the fits stop only to return?'

I had come to expect Gus's disparaging remarks. His attempts to make little of my successes. But Mairéad turned to reprimand him. '*Gus,*' she said, while I saw Noreen smile. I knew she drew pleasure from Gus's naysaying.

'If his fits return we will do another healing,' I said simply. I looked to Gerard. 'And Gerard will boost the healing with his remedy. We will keep him well.'

Gerard nodded. I no longer concerned myself with their sniping, their petty jealousies. I was concentrated only on my gift of healing. It was that which was paramount. Lorcan spoke beside me.

'You were so wonderful with Joseph,' he said to me. 'So kind. And caring. I swear I could feel the warmth, the healing flowing from you.'

Turning to him, I was elated at his words. I heard Rían's voice from across the room.

'I would like to have seen it,' he said. 'Perhaps you would permit me to attend one of your healings.'

'They're private.' At Lorcan's terse voice, I was jubilant.

Mairéad shook her head at Lorcan, then turned to Rían. 'Of *course* you would be welcome, Rían,' she said to him. 'We embrace any who want to join us.'

'Thank you,' Rían said to Mairéad. I felt Lorcan rigid beside me. The crackle in the air.

Whether or not Gerard felt the friction, he introduced another subject.

'Well, I would like to know what everybody thinks of the memorial to Parnell going up on Sackville Street in a few weeks,' he said. 'I, for one, could do without it.'

Inwardly, I squirmed. This would do nothing to soothe Lorcan. I had heard my aunt and uncle talking about the memorial to Charles Stewart Parnell, who had died twenty years before. Parnell was an MP who had campaigned for land reform in Ireland, to put an end to the rack rents, the excessive rents that tenants had to pay the British and Protestant landlords; he had campaigned for the tenants' right to own land. *The land of Ireland for the people of Ireland.*

I could sense Lorcan about to speak but Rían answered Gerard first.

'Why do you say that? I liked Parnell. I think he did this country a great service with the land reforms. And I am a firm believer, like him, in Home Rule.'

'Hah!' Gerard scoffed. 'We have the land reforms he wanted now. So forget about his ideas of Home Rule. Let our union with Britain stay as it is. I am quite content with the status quo.'

I could feel Lorcan's body tense.

'But if we're granted Home Rule we stay in the Union,' Rían said. 'We'll simply have our own Irish Parliament, but still be within the United Kingdom.'

Lorcan interjected. 'I cannot agree with you, Gerard; I admire Parnell greatly,' he said. 'But neither can I agree with you, Rían. I'm afraid Parnell's Parliamentary Party and Home Rule bills did not go far enough. *The land of Ireland for the people of Ireland.* Yes, that is what I want. We ourselves: *sinn féin.* A completely independent Ireland. A proud and free nation.'

'Hah.' Gerard scoffed again. 'A pipedream.'

Rían spoke, his tone measured. 'But Home Rule is a compromise. In that way we each get a little of what we want.'

'There can be no compromise on freedom,' Lorcan said curtly.

'Anyway, the Ulster Unionists will never accept either Home Rule or independence,' said Gerard. 'The British plantation of Ulster saw to that. They're of a mainly Protestant tradition and ethos and so loyal to Britain. No. They'll certainly never accept your so-called freedom, Lorcan.'

'And some of us will accept nothing less,' Lorcan replied.

I was reeling with the conversation. I certainly did not share Gerard's allegiance to the Crown, but neither was I alive, like Lorcan, with a passion for a wholly independent Irish nation. I found myself drawn to Rían's more balanced argument. But that caused me discomfort, for I felt disloyal to Lorcan. I was struggling within, when the mood in the room was all at once altered by a sudden burst of energy as Amy rushed in from the hall.

Glad of the interruption, my spirits lifted as I watched her run to Conor on the couch, tugging his arm frantically, her voice fraught.

'Conor, Conor, Daddy took me to the bell tower. I wanted to ring the bell to call the Abbot but Daddy wouldn't let me.'

She climbed on to Conor's lap, burying her head in the crook of his arm. Conor smiled up at the shamed Bernard following behind her.

'I'm sorry, perhaps I should have let her ring it,' Bernard said. 'But I really didn't want to cause a disturbance.'

Amy looked up from Conor's arm, her face a livid red. 'But the Abbot *said* we could.'

Rían leaned over Conor to speak to her. I could see him charmed by the child.

'Well,' he said to her. 'I happen to know the Abbot well. And the next time you go to the monastery perhaps you will let me accompany you. And we can ring the bell together. Would you like that?'

Amy stared at Rían, then looked triumphant at her poor father. She turned back to Rían, her words breathy. 'Do you promise?'

'I promise,' he said.

* * *

Still I see her joyful face. Always, I see her face.

23

With Lorcan's attention restored to me, and his clear displeasure at my dalliance with Rían, my hope grew. Once more, in the evenings, I'd wait for his return from the Roto, taking a nightcap with him in my aunt's parlour. I could tell he was pleased too at our renewed warmth and those nights became my greatest pleasure. But those weeks also brought a flurry of notes from Rían. As Conor handed them to me in Mairéad's parlour, he eyed me curiously, plainly intrigued by the situation between myself and his brother. Sending notes by return, I gently declined the invitations as if I were only seeking a postponement while, in truth, I had no intention of meeting with Rían again. I wanted no hindrance to what I felt now blossoming between myself and Lorcan and my heart craved only him.

As the unveiling of Parnell's monument neared, I was intent on attending, determined to show Lorcan that even if my convictions did not match his, I shared his love for our land and was proud of my country and countrymen.

It was 1 October, a bright autumn Sunday, and my spirits were high. I knew Lorcan planned to cross to the ceremony from the nearby Roto, and my intent was to meet him there. My aunt and uncle also attending, I walked with them to the sweeping crossroads at the top of Sackville Street.

'Some in this city still don't like Parnell,' Uncle Noel said as we walked. 'Not only because they thought he was an agitator but because of that tricky business with Kitty O'Shea.'

'Yes,' Aunt Ellen said, laughing. 'What with the monument going up at the top of Sackville Street they're saying that Parnell the two-eyed adulterer will be staring down at Nelson, the one-eyed adulterer on his column. But my goodness, he had charisma. Those eyes, ducky!'

I was not prepared for the multitudes that greeted us. It seemed thousands upon thousands of people spilled all the way down from the Roto to O'Connell Bridge and far beyond. I despaired. I had little chance of finding Lorcan in this crush. I could hear the banging of drums, music somewhere, as I looked to the man addressing the crowds from the veiled monument's plinth, grave eyes, white-haired and moustached. In the noise it was hard to hear him.

'John Redmond,' Uncle Noel shouted down to me. 'Parnell's successor in the Irish Parliamentary Party.'

I was trying to listen but was surprised to see a large group of men and women near the monument, raising their fists and jeering at Redmond.

'Why are they heckling him?' I asked Uncle Noel.

'They're Fenians,' he shouted. 'They don't think the Parliamentary Party are going far enough with Home Rule. They want nothing but our own Irish nation.'

At last the mammoth cloth was drawn down, revealing the monument to cheers. There Parnell stood, sculpted in bronze, a magnificent gold harp behind him, the towering stone pillar topped with a great, burning copper flame. My uncle bent close to my ear.

'The eternal flame. A fire that will never be quenched. The hunger for freedom.'

Freedom. I thought again of Lorcan. Searching for him once more, I spied Mairéad and Gus standing at the corner bookshop. Hoping they might have seen Lorcan, I tugged Uncle Noel's arm to tell him I was going, then pushed through the hordes to join them.

'There you are!' Mairéad said, taking my arm. 'Isn't it exciting? Look over there.' She pointed across the street to Findlater's grocery. 'Under the banner. It's the Inghínídhe na hÉireann. The Daughters of Ireland. The Countess might be with them.'

My heart plummeted. The Daughters of Ireland. Wherever Lorcan was, he would surely seek them out.

Mairéad's eyes grew mischievous. 'You know the Daughters of Ireland were founded by Maud Gonne? She who it's said our poet, William, is sick with love for? Unrequited apparently. He cast her in his play as Cathleen Ni Houlihan, a woman symbolising Ireland, calling for all men that love her to sacrifice their blood for her. So romantic. It's said that every poem he writes is for her. His Maud.'

So, it was she, his Maud, who I'd sensed like the force of lightning in his heart that night. *Sick with love.*

Yes, I knew that feeling well. Behind me, the speeches over, people were climbing the plinth, raising their fists in celebration, cheers going up around us. I strained to make myself heard.

'Have you seen Lorcan?' I asked Mairéad.

'No. No chance in this crowd. We're going to walk back now. Do you want to come with us?'

I shook my head. 'No, I want to see if I can find Lorcan.'

Although the ceremony had come to an end, the crowds showed no sign of dispersing. But I would not give up on my search for Lorcan. I looked all about the monument, down through the masses to the bridge and up around the Roto at the crossroads. It seemed I sought him in every doorway and corner, but for the longest time I would not simply look before me. At what lay plainly before my eyes. I did not want to accept where I would surely find him. At last I did look. And find him I did. Across the street, standing there amongst them: those spirited women with earnest eyes and purposeful frames, their faces resolute as they hoisted their banner high: the Inghínídhe na hÉireann.

* * *

At home I waited for him. I had not gone to him on the street, but had walked dismally back to my aunt's. Knowing he had no work that evening, there, in the parlour, I waited, listening hopefully each time I heard the front door open, my heart deflating at the other boarders' voices greeting my aunt. I waited for him until the clock chimed midnight. I waited but he did not come.

* * *

Early next morning, I looked into the dining room, hoping to see him at breakfast, joyful as I saw him at the table. Busying myself with something unnecessary in the hallway, I waited for him to finish. At last, he appeared in the dining-room doorway. I had prepared what I would say.

'Lorcan!' I ambushed him at the foot of the stairs. 'Shall we walk this morning? I want to see the Parnell monument again. In the morning light, without the crowds. Will you come?'

I'd carefully rehearsed my words for I wanted him to know I had been at the ceremony. That I cared for the monument every bit as much as he. He did not look pleased, however, but startled.

'I . . .' He hesitated. 'I can't. Not this morning. I have an appointment.'

In the many months of our acquaintance I had never before known him to have a morning appointment. His time had always seemed free for me. My annoyance at his refusal caused me to be bold.

'With whom?' I asked.

He flushed, turning as if he wanted to go on his way upstairs. He did not answer the question.

'I'm working tonight,' he said, 'but I'll meet you in the parlour later.' His eyes were soft. 'We can talk then.'

I had no choice but to nod and release him, my eyes following him up the stairs. My sense was still alive, Father, it did not desert me. But it was telling me what I did not want to hear. So I would not listen.

* * *

That night in the parlour we talked. But I recognised a difference in him. His words were kind, his tone as gentle, as amiable as before, but I detected him distant, his mind elsewhere. I tried to coax him back to me with words I knew would please him.

'I was so proud to see the Parnell monument unveiled,' I said. 'There's no denying he was a great man.'

'Yes, indeed,' he said. 'It was a wonderful day.'

But far from drawing him closer to me, as he gave the slightest of smiles, I perceived his mind wander further away. Far away, to something beyond me. To somewhere I could not reach.

Each morning now, he would take his breakfast early, often slipping away before I had seen him. Even trying to deny it, I became sure that he was purposely avoiding me. I did not see him at Mairéad's for now he spent his free evenings elsewhere. He no longer attended our healing or discussion nights.

'Where the hell is Lorcan?' Gus said to us all one evening. 'Has he been spirited away?'

That very evening, Conor had brought me yet another note from Rían, which I held uninterested in my hand. Gus's words made me flinch.

Still, I waited those nights for Lorcan in my aunt's parlour, but, at last, when I heard him in the hallway, he would just peer around the door to softly bid me good night, pleading tiredness and going immediately to bed.

My heart was sick and sore. One morning, finding him gone again, I could bear it no more. I determined to walk the streets of Dublin to find him. I would look first in his beloved Wynn's Hotel. The fire within me made me brave as I pulled open the door of the smoky bar, seeing men leaning there but no Lorcan amongst them. I went through the grand doors to the lounge, where we had so often sat, but there was no sign of him. That first morning I did not find him. Nor the second. But the third morning I did.

The third morning I saw what I had seen in my tortured mind many times. Saw them there together. I saw her seated opposite him at a white-clothed table, a cigarette in her hand. She was laughing across at him. I saw him lean into her, wipe a crumb of cake from her lips. Saw her catch his hand and kiss his fingertips. He took her hand to kiss hers back. I watched him kiss the hand of Saoirse Ryan.

His Daughter of Ireland.

24

I fled from the lounge door before they could see me, stumbled somehow back to my aunt's. In my room, I fell on to my bed, my heart full of sorrow. I raged against him. He who had made me believe he cared. Against she, she who had stolen him from me. Stolen what was surely mine. I sat digging my nails into my palms, crying until my eyes were stinging and sore and I could cry no more. And then I determined what I would do.

At my dressing table, I took two sheets of my flowered notepaper from my drawer. Sitting, I wrote an invitation. It was Mairéad's birthday in just five days and to celebrate she had requested an intimate soirée, more cosy than our large summer parties. I had been greatly anticipating this gathering, imagining it to be perhaps the night that Lorcan and I would at last become one. Finishing my note to Rían, I dabbed it with lavender scent. As I walked down Eccles Street to catch the afternoon post, I now pictured the night in quite a different way.

* * *

Those next days it was I who avoided Lorcan. It was no trouble, for he was hardly ever at home. I knew, though, that he had accepted Mairéad's invitation to her soirée, since I had quizzed her on it. I waited eagerly for the night to arrive.

The night finally come, in my room Aunt Ellen helped me to dress. I asked her of Lorcan's whereabouts and it seemed he was not in the house. I took great care with my appearance. For the occasion, I had bought a crimson beaded gown and satin buttoned evening gloves from Clerys. Aunt Ellen fixed a matching ruby band and feather in my hair.

Promptly, at eight o'clock I heard the doorbell ring, then the voices of Mary and Rían below in the hallway. The soirée was to begin at seven o'clock but I had deliberately asked that Rían call for me late, as I wanted to make sure all were there – that *Lorcan* was there – when I made my entrance. Walking down the stairs to greet Rían, I saw his eyes widen in pleasure. As I stepped into the hallway he took my gloved hand and kissed it.

'You look radiant,' he said.

'Thank you.' My eyes met his and held them. His own lit up.

He lifted my stole from Mary's hands to wrap it around my shoulders, and, bidding her and my aunt goodbye, we stepped on to Eccles Street. Linking my arm as we walked in the cold October air, he rushed to talk.

'It's so good to see you again,' he said. 'It's been far too long. I feared this night might never come.'

'And it is good to see you.' I smiled up at him as we reached Mairéad's steps. I could see a chink of golden light through the drapes, music drifting on to the street. We climbed the steps together, and Rían knocked at the door. Gus, flushed, pulled it open.

'Thank God, at last!' he gasped. 'You must come in and save me from my wife. She is insisting that I dance!'

We laughed as Gus ushered us in, the drink making him more amiable towards me. He took my stole and waved us towards the parlour where Mairéad's theatre tunes were playing loudly on the gramophone. Mairéad called us immediately from the window, waving a champagne flute.

'Rosaleen! Now here is a woman who knows how to dance!'

Quickly, I searched the room. Conor rose from the couch to greet us, clearly delighted to see me with his brother. Noreen sat nearby, looking stiff in her finery, a glass in her hand. Gerard was settled beside Madeleine Fitzpatrick while her husband chatted with Bernard and Ciss. Ciss had clearly braved the party for Mairéad but was making herself small on the couch. But my eyes were only fixed on one: Lorcan. Lorcan sitting on an ottoman by Mairéad's treasured tall fern plant. His eyes rose to meet mine. Rose from the companion seated at his side. Saoirse.

Shock soared through me. I had not expected this. Somehow I had not thought that he would bring her here. On a night amongst our closest friends, a place where we had shared so much. I had brought Rían merely to punish Lorcan. As Lorcan's eyes held mine, my heart gripped. But in an instant I had recovered myself. Searing pain was replaced by a pride that straightened my spine. I strode over to Mairéad at the window, smiling widely.

'Indeed I do know how to dance!' I called. My voice was bright, so bright.

I reached for Mairéad's hands, pulling her into the middle of the room, swinging her wildly. Laughing, she caught my arm, leading me to the sideboard to fetch a drink. As she poured me wine, Mairéad called over to Rían where he stood with Conor.

'And Rían. What will you have?'

Rían joined us, requesting wine also, as I picked cheese cubes from delicate dishes. I could sense Lorcan's eyes upon me, so I smiled up at Rían, sipping my drink, and turned to laugh at a quip of Mairéad's. Mairéad touched my shoulder, whispered into my ear.

'Do you know Lorcan's friend? Saoirse?'

I flushed. I had never told Mairéad, or anyone, of my feelings for Lorcan but she was an intuitive woman. I was sure it was no secret to her. She looked at me, her eyes concerned. 'Really, I should introduce you,' she said, intimating she had no wish to.

Too late. I felt another hand on my shoulder. I turned to see Lorcan, his eyes soft as he looked down upon me.

'Rosaleen.' His voice was gentle. 'May I introduce you to my companion? This is Saoirse Ryan. And Saoirse,' he turned to her, 'this is my good friend, Rosaleen Moore.'

His *good friend*. She smiled at me.

'Of course I know you,' she said. 'Know of you. You are the Rose. The famous Rose. I was not introduced to you at the last party here. There were so many people. But I am very glad to meet you now.'

She held out her hand, plain, ungloved, and suddenly I felt foolish in my satin finery. Ridiculous. Had I hoped somehow to impress Lorcan? When it was clear he was taken with this solid, earthy creature, her plain way of talking, her direct stare. I hated in that moment that she seemed so pleasant. I had wanted to find her charmless. I took her hand.

'And I am pleased to meet you.' My heart flared at the lie.

Lorcan smiled at us both. Mairéad, watching my eyes, clearly wanted to end this torture for me.

'Well,' Mairéad said, 'Saoirse, you really should come and talk to my husband. Perhaps you can persuade him to take his foot from the grave and shake it!'

Saoirse and Lorcan laughed. Together. They laughed together. I stood stunned for a moment as I watched them. Their eyes locking. Watched them still as they were led away by Mairéad, unaware of anyone or anything else around me until I felt a gentle touch on my arm. Rían.

'And perhaps you would care to dance with me,' he said.

* * *

The evening passed like some carnival of horrors. Thank God it was a gathering of our closer crowd, otherwise I would have had to contend with everybody clamouring for my, *the Rose's*, attention, and I had no heart for that. Still, I played the jolly reveller masking the dark creature beneath. I did everything possible to show myself unaffected, so greatly charmed by Rían. And, indeed, he seemed to charm all there. He had already met most at the last party and chatted to everyone easily while I stood smiling, wholly uninterested, beside him. In truth, instead of this show of resilience I yearned for the softness and sweetness of Conor. I longed to collapse into his arms and cry, rather than endure the trial of laughing in the company of his brother.

I stole glances at Lorcan to see if my being with Rían was affecting him at all. But always I found him deep in conversation with his companion. I felt sickened by the small intimacies between them. Her touching his arm as she smiled up into his eyes, he responding with warmth. I watched them laugh. Talk with hardly a silence between them. When he leaned to kiss her cheek, I could bear it no more. I excused myself from chatter with Rían and Gerard and escaped to the dining room. It was cool and quiet, at last peaceful. I sank into a chair at the table, thankful to finally have time to think, be alone with my genuine feelings. I was staring blindly ahead when I heard the door creaking open. I looked around, tormented at the thought of having once again to pretend. But my heart leapt. It was Lorcan.

'Ah, there you are,' he said. 'I noticed you gone. I hope you're feeling all right?'

Flustered, I was caught between delight that he had noticed my absence and not wishing to show any weakness before him. My reply was emphatic. 'Yes. Yes, of course I am all right. It's just so hot in the parlour. I wanted to cool down.'

'It's certainly hot in there.' He laughed. 'Mairéad is on fire.'

I laughed, then lowered my eyes as he came to pull out a chair and sit beside me at the table. I was affected by his closeness. He was quiet for a moment.

'I'm glad you've finally met Saoirse,' he said at last. 'I've been wanting to introduce her to you.' He paused. 'Tell me, what do you think of her? Your opinion is important to me.'

I kept my eyes on the table. 'She is . . .' I fell silent before continuing. 'A surprise.'

My eyes were still lowered but I could sense his confusion. 'A surprise? In that she is someone you would not expect her to be? Or . . .'

I raised my eyes to hold his. 'A surprise in that I knew nothing about her. Why did you not tell me about her before?'

'I . . .' He lowered his own eyes. 'I wanted to tell you. But—'

'Did you think I would not be pleased?' I interrupted.

187

'No, it was just that . . .' Still, he would not look at me. 'She and I had only just started to meet. I wanted to make sure it was . . .'

'A serious thing?' I finished for him. 'And is it?'

He flushed. 'I like her very much.'

'You like her very much.' My voice was tight. 'And admire her?'

'Yes.' Even though his head was bowed I could see his face. A face that could not help but show pleasure. 'I do.'

'And me?' My voice was rising. 'Do you not admire me?'

He looked up quickly. His eyes, shocked, finally met mine.

'Why, yes, of course. Of *course* I admire you. You know I do.'

'But not enough.' I stood abruptly. 'And you have not enough respect for me to tell me you are dallying with another woman.'

He shook his head as if baffled. 'I am not dallying. And why would not telling you of Saoirse be showing you disrespect? You are here with Rían. I don't—'

'Oh, don't pretend you don't understand.' My voice was shrill. 'I went out with Rían only once before and when I did, you did not like it.' My eyes burned into him. 'Admit that to me now.'

He looked away, his voice quiet. 'It's true that—'

'Yes, it's true.' I stared down at him. 'True that you did not want him calling on me. Is that not so?'

He was silent, then spoke slowly. 'Perhaps that is true. I was used to it being just we two at your aunt's. Perhaps I did resent him, saw him as an interloper. That was wrong of me. But I was protective of you.'

'Protective?' I nearly screeched it. 'As if I were a child? Don't try to pretend it was that. You *know* what was between us.'

He shook his head, desperately. 'I don't—'

My tongue – my heart – was on fire. With emotions too great now to hide. 'You *know* what I felt for you, Lorcan. That's why you didn't tell me about Saoirse. Don't deny it. At least have the courage to admit that to me now.'

Still he shook his head, as if searching for words while I glared at him. At last, faltering, he spoke. 'I did suspect that you—'

'You did not suspect. You *knew*!' I shouted. 'And you had not enough courtesy or courage to tell me before you brought her here. Here to this house. This house where we have shared so much. I thought you many things Lorcan. But I never thought you a *coward*!'

He stood to touch my arm, as if to soothe me, but it only made me more furious.

'Don't touch me!' I tore my arm away. 'You knew how I felt. Worse, much worse, you led me to believe you felt it too, only to humiliate me by flaunting another woman before me. Get out, Lorcan, get away from me. Go back to the woman you so admire. Go back to your precious Daughter of Ireland.'

Lorcan looked dismayed, as if unsure what to do. As if he wanted to touch me again, but thought better of it. He made slowly for the door. As he reached it, I called to him.

'Lorcan.'

He looked around. I straightened my back.

'I am a daughter of Ireland, too.'

* * *

When, at last, I returned to the smoky, hot parlour, both music and spirits were still high. I was grateful for that, for, once my temper had cooled, I'd been afraid that my tirade might have been overheard. It seemed I had, at least, escaped that shame. Still stinging from our confrontation, I looked at Lorcan seated beside Saoirse on a couch. He appeared somewhat subdued but she was chatting happily, clearly oblivious to what had passed between us. Aware of my entrance, he looked at me, attempting to hold my eyes, but I looked away. Mairéad rushed towards me, begging me again to dance, but I shook my head.

'I have a headache. Too much wine and too many of your favourite tunes,' I said, in an effort to be jovial. 'I think I'll go.'

As Mairéad tried to persuade me to stay, I noticed Rían standing nearby, watching me. He came to my side.

'Shall I walk you home now?' he said.

I nodded blankly. I had no desire for his company, only wanted to walk in the cool air by myself. But it was easier to agree. He would insist and I had no stomach for a new battle. Without another look at Lorcan, just a smile and a wave to the others, I walked with Rían from the house.

* * *

Once Rían had seen Rosaleen safely to her door, he had returned to Mairéad's to collect Conor. They had hailed a cab and travelled home together. His parents already asleep, after helping his brother, far too merry from wine, to bed, he had gone to the drawing room and sat nursing a whiskey in the stillness. He'd leaned his head back in the armchair, thinking over the night.

He had heard them. Rosaleen and that man, Mulhern. When he had found Rosaleen missing, he had gone to find her. He had stood to listen as he heard voices coming from the dining room. *Her* voice. Anguished. Enraged. He had heard the pain. The certain signs of love in that voice.

Distressed, he now sipped his whiskey. But he had heard, too, Mulhern's denial of her. He had worried these past weeks what might be between them, but now he knew this man did not love this woman. Was fond of her, surely. Protective towards her like a sister. Yes, he knew now that this man was no threat to him. For she could not hope to have him. And Mulhern had denied her so totally, she would know it. She would need comfort. Solace.

And he, Rían, would supply it.

25

Those days afterwards hurt and anger burned like bile in my throat. My stomach in shreds, I could hardly do my chores. I was constantly on edge, afraid of encountering Lorcan, running to hide if I saw him, managing to avoid him in this way for over a week. Aunt Ellen, noticing my mood, asked me what was wrong, but I was able to fend her off, pleading a vague ailment, and for a short while she was satisfied. However, I could not evade her questioning for long. One morning, she called me into the parlour.

'What's going on with you and Lorcan?' She studied me as I stood over her at the table. 'I've noticed a coolness between you. And now he says he is leaving. Have you had some sort of row?'

My bones turned to ice. I could not bear to see Lorcan but neither could I bear the thought of him gone.

'Where is he going?' I said weakly.

'To another boarding house. Apparently one where many of his friends from Wynn's board. But he has friends enough here. What's happened?'

I shook my head in denial. 'It has nothing to do with me.' I wanted to escape to think. Aunt Ellen did not believe me, that was clear. But she just shook her own head and let me go, realising I was not going to enlighten her.

I wanted to run to him immediately. Beg him to stay. Implore him to forget every word I had uttered, forget we had ever argued. Persuade him that we could again be friends, enjoy the easy companionship we'd once shared. But even as I imagined it, I knew it could never be. We could not be friends. Too much had been said.

On the morning he was readying to leave, I hovered in the hallway, watching for him on the stairway. I knew my aunt and uncle would come to bid him farewell, and I was desperate for a chance to speak with him alone. I had no notion what I would say. Only knew I must say something. At last, through the banister I saw him dragging his suitcase down the stairs.

'Lorcan.' I clutched the spindles, whispering up to him, but my aunt and uncle were upon us.

'So you're off,' Aunt Ellen said as he stepped into the hallway. 'Well, we're sorry to see you go. You've been one of my more tolerable guests. Who am I to thrash at bridge now?'

He smiled, holding Aunt Ellen's eyes fondly, taking Uncle Noel's hand to shake it. He glanced at me. My eyes pleaded with him for a moment alone.

'And I'll miss all of you,' he said. 'I'll miss your cheating, Ellen.'

They all laughed, Aunt Ellen slapping his arm, ushering him towards the door as I followed quickly. On the doorstep, my aunt eyed me, then turned to signal to my uncle that they should withdraw.

'Good luck,' she said to Lorcan, Uncle Noel patting his shoulder before they went inside.

I stood speechless at the door, staring at him a few steps below. I could not find the words. At last, I asked, 'Will I see you again at Mairéad's?'

Even before I asked, I realised it was a hopeless plea. Already he'd drifted away. I knew him lost to us.

He smiled up at me, his eyes sad. 'We'll see each other again. I know it.'

In that moment I doubted it. As I stood and watched him walk away down Eccles Street I feared I might never see him again.

I would come to see Lorcan again, Father. But when I did, nothing would be the same. I would be changed. All would be changed.

* * *

My heart was heavy and sore. Many mornings I would wander Sackville Street, linger sometimes near the Roto, both afraid I would see Lorcan and afraid I would not. At Mairéad's, whenever the others quizzed me on why he had left my aunt's, I'd brush away their questions, saying I knew no more than they. Only Mairéad guessed something of what had passed.

'You'll find another,' she said softly to me.

At first, my spirits too low to perform healings, I would plead fatigue, asking Mairéad to lead. My sorrow robbed me of every power. But as days became weeks, there sprang from that sorrow an anger. A fierce anger with a power all its own. Now, I felt that Lorcan had made little of me. Had played me for a fool. After drawing me close had cast me aside as if I were nothing.

Wounded pride consumed me, my heart inflamed as if stung. I stiffened my spine, held myself tall, walked with a spiked dignity. How dare Lorcan treat me so? I who was *the Rose*. I began to attend Madeleine Fitzpatrick's dinners again, accept theatre invitations. Once more I led the healings. When laying hands upon the women I absorbed their raptures. Allowed them to lavish me with their praise.

Saturated in self-regard, I paid Madeleine Fitzpatrick little mind when she brought news of Emma Rainsford to Mairéad's parlour. Even when Madeleine breathed what unspeakable condition we had suspected – *syphilis*. It seemed that Emma lay gravely ill at home. That whatever symptoms her husband might have endured had subsided but that Emma had nurses constantly at her side.

'She is in the most terrible state,' Madeleine whispered to us. 'They say she is suffering paralysis, that she can no longer walk and the weeping ulcers on her legs must be dressed daily. She can hardly see or hear and is losing her mind. What a hellish affliction. And the *shame*.'

Afterwards, when I spoke to those who had known about it, Mairéad, Gus, Noreen and Gerard, I blamed no one but Emma for her fate.

'She should have come to us for a further healing,' I said. 'It's clear her faith was not strong enough. She was not open to the healing power of the Spring. And this is the result.'

I told myself Emma had been foolhardy in not consulting us again. And I told myself Lorcan was a fool. He who could not see what every other saw. I'd sit at my dressing table and stare at my reflection. I would allow no mere man to enslave my mind. Not I, the Rose. And that is why, Father, why I could not see what was to come. I was blind to all but my own sanctitude. I whispered into the mirror a mantra: *Chosen. Anointed. Special.*

* * *

One evening, Conor brought me another note from Rían. I smiled at it in my hand. If Lorcan would not bend to my will, Rían would. His devotion to me I would apply like a balm to my wounded pride. I looked at Conor, my dear gentle Conor. Those days, it seemed only his gentleness was able to penetrate my hauteur. But I did not let it hinder my plans for his brother.

I spoke sweetly. 'Take this message back. I would be delighted to see him.'

From that day I saw Rían often. He took me again to tea at the Gresham, in a jaunting car to St Stephen's

Green, even escorting me to shop at Clerys. He seemed so proud to be by my side as we passed the ferns in the grand hall, climbing the sweeping staircase to the galleries, insisting that I pick out a hat. As I modelled it before the attentive assistant, Rían glowed and I knew he was truly in my thrall. But I held myself beyond reach, for my attentions were far from sincere.

Some evenings he accompanied Conor to Mairéad's, feigning interest in our discussions so that he might see me.

'Tell me, Rían,' Mairéad said, one evening in her parlour, 'you are a lawyer, so a man of reason. Do you see any merit in our belief? That we can align ourselves with an inner force, draw upon its power to heal?'

He smiled. 'I am a man of reason, of evidence, it's true. Perhaps I just have not yet witnessed such a healing. Something I might rectify soon by attending one of your healing evenings.'

Noreen spoke scathingly. 'But you, a man of evidence, as you call it, align yourself then with the doctors and scientists and their unnatural medicines and potions. So arrogant they think they hold more answers than our own natural world. To their shame they refuse to accept that if they work with Mother Earth she will cure all ills.'

'I align myself with no one,' Rían said. 'I hope I am my own man. And I am open to discussion. Debate. Just as we are doing here.'

'But you are not a believer,' Noreen said.

'Belief implies faith,' Rían said. 'Faith does not require evidence. It exists with little or none. Whereas it is true I would require evidence. So, no, I am not a believer.'

Noreen huffed while I smiled.

'But also faith, belief, can grow from evidence,' I said. 'And all of us here have witnessed that inner force acting on others in this very room.'

He smiled at me. 'Then who am I to disagree? I would hardly be a match for such a power. No more than I would be a match for the power of your argument.'

He was, indeed, a charming man. I watched him with the others, how even with his faithless ways he seemed to charm Noreen. He was respectful to Gerard, and greatly kind to Ciss and that warmed me. But still he did not stir my heart.

One afternoon he and Conor invited us all to their home for tea. Close to Gerard's in the Tallaght Hills, the house was stately, set in secluded grounds and lush gardens. Their mother greeted us when we arrived. A fair-haired woman, refined but friendly and warm. She asked the maid to serve us tea in the drawing room but left us to our chat, allowing Rían and Conor to be our hosts. The drawing room was beautiful and grand, the maid setting down the service on a coffee table before the baroque couches as Amy crawled over Ciss's lap.

'Can I pour it, Mammy?' she said eagerly, reaching for the pot.

'No, darling,' Ciss said hurriedly. 'The pot is far too heavy and hot. You might burn yourself.'

'Here.' Rían rose from his armchair, going to sit by Amy. 'Take my arm. We'll pour together.'

He placed his hand on the silver pot's handle, gesturing for her to place her hand on his arm. She giggled in delight as with each poured cup her hand rose with his.

'You see, Mammy, I can do it,' Amy said gleefully.

'Indeed you can,' Rían said. 'But you must always have an assistant. Someone to do your bidding.'

After our feast of scones and cake, Amy leapt up from the couch and tugged Rían's arm.

'Can we go to the monastery now, Rían?' she said earnestly. 'Remember you promised you'd take me?'

'I do remember,' he said, smiling. 'And I would be delighted to accompany you.'

'And Conor too,' Amy said, running to him.

The others declaring themselves too sated to stroll, I rose to join the three, assuring an anxious Ciss that Amy would be safe. At the Abbey's elaborate iron gates, before taking the woodland path I glanced uphill at some brothers with baskets, picking berries from bushes by the chapel.

'They have their own vegetable garden,' Rían said. 'Much of what they grow they give to the poor. But I'd venture they're picking winter berries now, to make themselves some warming grog.'

I laughed. One of the monks up ahead raised his hand, making down the hill towards us. As he lowered his hood I saw it was the Abbot.

'Rían! And Conor,' he called. As he reached us, his eyes settled on Amy. 'And you have brought my little friend to see me again. Well, I am delighted!' Gently he stroked Amy's hair as she smiled up at him. His eyes travelled to me.

'And this is Miss Moore,' Rían said. 'Rosaleen. Rosaleen, this is St Kilian's esteemed Abbot.'

The Abbot laughed, taking my hand to shake it. 'Yes. We met briefly, but were not introduced, on one of your walks before. When I met this most charming creature,' he said, bending to Amy. 'Well, young lady, have you been back since to ring our bell? I have listened out but have not heard it.'

'No, Daddy wouldn't allow me. Can I ring it now?' Amy looked pleadingly at the Abbot.

The Abbot smiled. 'I think we must obey this request. Come.' He caught hold of Amy's hand.

With Rían and Conor I followed Amy and the Abbot down to the path and into the woodland, the winter trees stark now, stripped of their leaves. Rían took my arm to help me over the rickety bridge, the brook rippling over the stones beneath. Once over the bridge, Amy squealed, releasing the Abbot's hand to rush towards the bell tower. The Abbot and Rían followed her while I and Conor stood behind. Amy looked back at us.

'You too,' she called to Conor. 'You come and ring it too.'

Conor laughed. 'I will let my brother have the honour this time,' he called back.

She seemed satisfied with this and the Abbot lifted her in his arms. Rían reached for the cord, Amy's small hands clutching his arm as he drew it back to strike the bell.

As the bell rang out over the woodland, Amy's screech of joy rang out with it. The peal of the bell, her laughter, seemed to stir every bare branch, resound through the sky, echo over the vast lands and hills beyond. Once, twice, three times they struck it, at every strike Amy's laughter only growing louder and more jubilant.

At last, the Abbot turned to place Amy back on the ground. He bent to look into her eyes, speaking softly. 'So, young lady, you have made yourself heard. Now the trees, the hills, the sleeping grass, every bird in the sky knows you are here.'

I will always remember those moments. The Abbot holding Amy's hand. The ringing of the bell through the trees, Amy's laughter ringing out with it. His words to her. I have tried not to think on it. But ever those moments return. Return to haunt me.

* * *

Brother Thomas stared into the fire.

'*Now the trees, the hills, the sleeping grass, every bird in the sky knows you are here*,' Father Sheridan said slowly. 'Just as if, even then, he knew.'

26

The winter it happened, Aunt Ellen received news of a neighbour of whom she'd been greatly fond. A young man, only thirty, with three small children. He had been cutting back the rose bushes for winter when, it appeared, his finger had been pricked by a thorn. I was in the parlour, placing my aunt's celery jar on the sideboard as she lamented the man's demise to the visiting Dr Lydon.

'I can't believe it. That something so simple, so seemingly harmless could cause it,' she said. 'Could cause him to *die*.'

'Sepsis. A blood infection,' Dr Lydon said. 'There was nothing could be done.'

I eyed him from the sideboard. Since our conversations about Emma Rainsford, whom he had rightly suspected to be suffering from syphilis, our encounters, although civil, were cool. That he had surmised correctly did not worry me. It was not the illness but the cure on which we disagreed. My aunt sat shaking her head, then sprang up, seeming to remember herself.

'What am I thinking? Dr Lydon, will you have some tea?'

'Thank you,' he said. 'Yes, that would be nice.'

'I'll fetch Mary,' Aunt Ellen said, seeming flustered as she left the room.

I could only suppose it was the bad news regarding her neighbour that had my aunt so distracted she would not think to send me for tea but, in any case, it left me and Dr Lydon alone in an uncomfortable silence. I could not resist, however, making a jibe. Arranging the celery, I spoke, my voice slow and deliberate. 'It seems then, if our poor neighbour died, that your science does not hold all the answers.'

My back was to him so I could not see his face. 'Not yet,' he said. 'But there is great work going on in the study of bacteria. I am certain that someday soon we will have the means to treat such infection.'

'Perhaps,' I said, my back still to him, 'the answer lies somewhere in nature. In our own natural world. Not in your chemicals.' I turned then to face him. 'The earth offers up its riches.'

He observed me for a moment. 'And also its diseases and disasters.' He shifted at the table. 'Besides, all life is formed from chemicals. All of nature. And many of them toxic. And do not forget, bacteria are natural. Cancer is natural. Earthquakes are natural. The thorn of a rose is natural.' He looked up to meet my eyes. 'Not everything in nature is benign.'

*   *   *

That Christmas I spent in Dublin. I had written to Mammy, asking if I might, and she had given me her blessing. The city felt vibrant, both men and women hurrying along the footpaths with spilling bags and extravagant boxes, urgently hailing cabs in the cold, even the horses seeming spirited, alerted by the icy nip in the air.

I was thrilled when Rían called to take me to the Grand Christmas Bazaar at Switzer's department store. The night was frosty and, afterwards, we stepped out on to Grafton Street, talking of the children's glee at the Fairy Trail and magical windows alight with lanterns and glass balls sparkling by candlelight. It was there in the rush of passers-by, there beneath the street lamp that Rían, his face earnest, drew close to me. There he leant in to kiss me for the first time.

I wish now I had acted differently. Had been kinder. But my reaction was instant. I felt myself recoil. And I saw the look in his eyes. The sting. The hurt. It did not please me, for those two months past I had grown greatly fond of him. He had touched me with his kindness to others and I had come to value the warmth of his companionship. Knowing him a good man, sometimes I tried to stir within myself the same emotion he felt for me. But, even as I tried, I knew. I could not give him what he wanted: my heart.

* * *

They say she descended with the January gloom. The Strangling Angel.

Children all over Dublin were being struck down with fever, but I knew nothing of it until one dull afternoon

at Mairéad's. Mairéad, Noreen and I were in the parlour when we heard a loud banging at the front door.
Mairéad looked at us perplexed as she went to answer,
the sound of Ciss's voice soon filling the hallway. Ciss
clung to Mairéad's arm as she entered the parlour.

'What will I do? What will I *do*?' she was saying over
and over to Mairéad.

'Hush, hush, calm down now, Ciss,' Mairéad said
gently, leading her to a couch, sitting beside her.

'What on earth is wrong?' I said, going to sit the
other side of Ciss, taking her hand.

'It's Amy,' Ciss said with a choke. 'She's not well. She's
listless and won't eat. She tells me her head is hurting. I'm
terrified, oh God, I'm terrified.'

'Of what?' I asked.

'Have you not heard?' Her eyes were wild as she
turned to face me. 'Children all over Dublin have it.
Children on this very street. Girls that Amy has played
with. They call it the Strangling Angel. Diphtheria. Oh,
God.' She clutched her head in her hands.

I caught Mairéad's eye. Both of us suspected Ciss
simply over-anxious as always. Perhaps Amy had a
cold. An ailment that needed bedrest and nursing to
fend off infection but almost certain to pass.

'Don't worry, Ciss, please,' I said. 'Shall we fetch
Gerard and ask him to call on Amy? He'll know what's
wrong.'

Ciss was crying, shaking her head helplessly, her
hands trembling. Mairéad spoke to her softly. 'Perhaps

if you're worried it would be better to call on Dr Lydon. He'll be able to put your mind at rest, I'm sure.'

Noreen scoffed. 'Or see a chance to make some money. I'd keep away from that quack.'

But Mairéad was firm. 'No. Let Dr Lydon see her. Then he can reassure Ciss. Tell her there is no need to fear.'

Mairéad took Ciss to Dr Lydon that very hour. Soon Mairéad returned alone, telling Noreen and me and Gus, who was now there, that Dr Lydon had gone instantly with Ciss to see Amy. Bernard, just home from town, had known nothing of Ciss's visit to us, but promised Mairéad he would bring us news, so when we heard the knock on the front door we assumed it was him. Gus went to answer it. I looked curiously at Mairéad when I did not immediately recognise the male voice in the hall.

The identity of the caller was quickly revealed. We all looked up to see Dr Lydon standing in the parlour doorway. He nodded around the room. 'Good evening,' he said brusquely, refusing a seat when Gus offered him one. I could sense Noreen bristle.

Dr Lydon wasted no time. His voice was urgent as he addressed us. 'I wanted to come and speak to you all as I have news of Amy Armstrong. Normally I would not discuss a patient with anyone but their family but I know you have the greatest influence over Mrs Armstrong. It's too early to be certain, but I'm afraid I suspect that Amy might have contracted diphtheria. A very serious illness. The good news, the very good news, is that we have the means to treat it, an anti-toxin. But it must be administered as soon as possible, as speedy intervention is vital. That is why I have come to ask you to persuade Mrs Armstrong to avail of the medicine. She says she must consult with you first.'

I looked at Mairéad, Gus and Noreen, then back to Dr Lydon.

'And what could happen if Amy does not take it?' I asked.

He looked grave. 'I urge you to not even consider refusing the treatment. For the sake of the child. You would be putting her in serious danger.'

There was a plea in Dr Lydon's eyes. Again, I looked to the others, who were silent. When it was clear we were not going to supply him with an answer, Dr Lydon turned to leave.

'Please,' he said, 'heed my warning.'

Gus escorted him to the door, as we remained staring at each other silently. When Gus returned, Noreen spoke. 'The very thought of giving the child his poison,' she spat. 'You see? He *is* a quack. He's not even sure if it is diphtheria.'

It seemed I suddenly knew what to say.

'It's true,' I said. 'He wasn't sure. But *we* are sure. Sure that his anti-toxin is in fact nothing of the sort. That it, itself, is the toxin. Whereas we can draw on a force completely pure. The Spring. We have that power within us. And whatever ails her, we will heal Amy.'

27

We went immediately to the Armstrongs', only doors away. Bernard anxiously greeted us on the step, leading us into the drawing room, where Ciss sat on the couch, wringing her hands. She leapt up when she saw us.

'Oh, thank God.' She rushed to us and Mairéad placed a reassuring hand on her arm. 'Thank God you've come. You saw the doctor?'

'We saw him,' I said. 'And he told us that he only suspects Amy has diphtheria. That he's not sure.'

'Yes.' Ciss was trembling. 'He said it can be difficult to diagnose, but he strongly suspects it.'

'Well, that's not good enough,' Noreen said. 'A mere suspicion is not a good enough reason to risk poisoning the child. Not when we have a true and pure way to heal.'

Pained, Ciss looked to Bernard, who moved to put his arm around her.

'Rosaleen.' Bernard looked at me earnestly. 'I think we must take our lead from you. Amy is poorly but it does not seem to me so serious. Do you think you can help her?'

My eyes were as earnest as his own. 'I do. I am sure of it.'

The tension lifted from his face. Ciss gave a sob of relief.

'Where is Amy now?' I asked.

'She's in her room,' Ciss said eagerly. 'Shall I take you to her?'

I nodded, letting Bernard and Ciss lead me, Mairéad, Gus and Noreen up the stairs, turning into a room off the landing where only a night-candle was burning. Amy lay curled up in her bed. The others stood around us as I sat at her pillow. The child was fretful.

'Amy, sweetheart,' I said, touching her shoulder. 'Tell me, where is it hurting?'

She squinted as she tried to look at me. 'My head.' Her voice was raspy. 'And my throat. It's so sore.'

Again, this sounded to me perhaps a cold. If her throat was sore, though, that would need care. I smoothed back her curls from her forehead. Her head did feel hot.

'Well, I don't think there can be anything too wrong,' I said in a soothing voice, spying her rag doll on the bed. Lifting it, I wiggled it before her. 'Nothing that Mistress Floppy and I can't fix.'

She smiled up at me weakly as I turned to the others.

'Please,' I said. 'If I could have a little time with Amy alone?'

Ciss looked as if she wanted to stay, but Bernard gently led her away, the others following. As the door closed behind them, the light of the candle caused my shadow to loom large on the wall.

Still holding the rag doll, I whispered to Amy. 'Close your eyes. Mistress Floppy is going to help me make you feel better.'

I laid the doll in her arms, first stroking Amy's hair, then holding my palm over her head, guiding it down to her throat. Closing my eyes, I took deep breaths, aligning my breathing with Amy's. Each breath seemed to fill me deeper and deeper with warmth, lulling me to a place of bliss with the child. I smiled. I felt the purity of the Spring through every pore, and knew Amy could feel it too. At last, with gentle breaths, a motion of my hand to release all that was ill, I opened my eyes to look down at Amy. She was peacefully sleeping.

Downstairs, Ciss was waiting nervously for me in the hall.

'Well?' She hurried to the foot of the stairs as I appeared on the landing. 'How is she now?'

Hearing her, the others came from the drawing room. I smiled at Ciss.

'She is sleeping. No longer fretting. Try not to worry now.' I touched Ciss's arm. 'The healing has begun.'

* * *

Over the following days, news came from the Armstrongs that Amy was much the same but I told them not to be concerned. Gerard had prepared and delivered a remedy and I planned to call with him and the others to perform another healing. On the third day, I was surprised by a visitor. As I cleared breakfast dishes in the dining room with Mary, Aunt Ellen called me to the doorstep. I saw Rían standing there.

He flushed as I approached. I had not seen him since our Christmas visit to Switzer's and I knew he felt shamed by what had happened. I did not want him to feel shamed but neither did I want his attentions. I did not wish to toy with him any more. My fondness for him had made me sincerely glad of his friendship. I wanted to dispel any awkwardness between us, but at the same time discourage any ardour on his part. With this in mind, I greeted him warmly.

'Rían. It is lovely to see you. Please, come in.'

I led him into the parlour, where he nervously removed his hat, laying it on the table as we sat. He could not help but redden as he met my eyes, while I smiled, trying to put him at his ease.

'I hope you had a good Christmas,' he began. 'Mine was tolerable at least.'

I laughed. 'Yes, Conor told me you had to entertain an ancient uncle, your poor mother having to stop him draining the cellar dry.'

'Indeed.' He smiled. 'The joys of family.' He hesitated a moment, glancing down to take a breath. Then lifted his eyes to look at me directly. 'I wanted to apologise to you. For my clumsy and foolish misstep at Christmas. It was unforgivable. And yet, I hope you will forgive it.'

I admired his forthrightness and courage. I spoke quickly to reassure him.

'It's quite all right. Christmas always heightens the emotions. Makes us do and say things we might not, ordinarily. You were caught up in the fever of the season.'

'Yes.' He started to fiddle with the brim of his hat. 'But, still, it should not have happened. The last thing – the very last thing – I would want is to offend you or cause you discomfort. Of this I wanted you to be assured. That I only wish you . . .'

He hesitated again. His assurances were unnecessary. His devotion was all too clear. His next words only sealed it.

'You must think of me as your servant. One only there to do your bidding. I will never again impose my own will on yours. On that, you have my promise.'

I thought of reaching for his hand to show him all was well, but thought better of it. His heart was too raw. Any tenderness from me would only stir and stoke his passion. That would not be in his best interests.

'Don't worry, I am sure of it,' I said, then smiled. 'And now let us get back to the business of being friends. I will fetch you some tea and you will tell me all about your uncle!'

I saw him flinch at my casual mention of friendship, but he smiled in return. Going to find Mary, asking her to bring us the refreshments, I allowed myself a moment in the hallway before facing him again, feeling no little guilt at how I had played so carelessly with his emotions. Now, I only wanted to make of him a true friend. I hoped, in time, he could come to feel the same.

* * *

That afternoon brought yet another visitor: Bernard. He stood on the doorstep, breathless, as if he had run the few houses to my aunt's. He started to speak before I'd reached the door.

'Rosaleen, it's Amy. She has not recovered. In fact, she's worse. Will you come?'

Quickly, I fetched my coat and hurried with Bernard to his house. Ciss was waiting on their doorstep.

'Oh, Rosaleen.' She gripped my arm. 'She is weakening.'

I released my arm and caught her shoulders. 'Don't worry. I'll go to her immediately. Wait down here.'

I took the stairs to Amy's room, opening the door to see the child again fretful in the bed, writhing beneath a rumpled sheet, trying to push it off her.

'Shhhh, shhh.' I tried to soothe her, going to the bed. 'Hush, little thing, you will be all right.'

She did not look up to greet me, only moaned, turning her head to and fro on the pillow, eyes tightly closed. I placed my hand on her forehead, feeling her again hot, noticing a swelling at her throat. And then the thought came to me. *It is tonsillitis.* I had suffered this illness myself as a child, and knew there was no remedy for it but soothing the throat with honey and warm water.

'Open your mouth for me, Amy,' I said to her, softly. 'Let me see inside.'

The child seemed hardly able to hear me, so gently I prised open her mouth, looking to the back of her tongue. Sure enough, there at the sides of her throat were ugly white patches. So I was right. It was tonsillitis and Dr Lydon had been mistaken in his diagnosis. And he so eager to dose the child with his sinister serums. I knew there was no cure for this.

'It's all right, little one,' I whispered. 'Try to sleep now.'

Ciss and Bernard were waiting for me in the hallway. I met them at the foot of the stairs.

'It is tonsillitis,' I said, my voice quiet but firm.

Ciss grabbed my arm. 'Is it dangerous?' Her eyes were panicked.

For a moment I was silent, remembering myself a child suffering the same sickness, Dr Hogan whispering to my mother as they left my bedside:

'It's an infection, so like any infection could spread. But try not to worry. I believe with care she will recover.'

I offered now my own words of comfort. 'Don't worry. We'll give her the care she needs. Dose her with honey and warm water, try to make her drink it. Now I know the precise illness I will ask Gerard to prepare the correct remedy. And I'll gather the others to perform another healing. All will be well.'

28

We planned to meet at the Armstrongs' two evenings later, when Mairéad was not performing and all of us could attend to make the healing as powerful as possible. Gerard had already delivered Bernard and Ciss a remedy for tonsillitis to lay us a solid foundation.

We had a problem, however. Dr Lydon had been making enquiries. He'd called at the Armstrongs', asking after Amy, and they'd had to send him away with assurances that the child was rallying. When he'd asked to see her they'd said she was sleeping and as she had just begun to do so peacefully they did not wish to disturb her. He'd had no choice but to leave.

'I hope we did right in sending him away,' Ciss said, her hands playing anxiously at her mouth when we arrived that evening for the healing. All of us stood in their parlour. Bernard's arm was around Ciss's shoulders.

'Yes. Let's hope we're doing the right thing,' I heard Gus mutter.

'You did absolutely right,' I said firmly, as much to answer Gus as Ciss. I would not allow him to undermine me now. Not when I needed to be in my full power for the healing.

'Yes. Be assured,' Gerard said. 'The medical profession can do nothing for tonsillitis. And my remedy is potent. It will soon come into its full effect. I have more to give her tonight.'

I glanced at Conor. Hovering around Ciss, he looked greatly worried.

'Come,' I said, holding out my hand to him and gesturing to the others. 'Let's go to her now.'

With Conor and the others I climbed the stairs, entering into the dim light of Amy's room. The child had pushed every cover from the bed, and was writhing and groaning. I heard Ciss whimper, and turned to see Conor touching her shoulder to comfort her.

'Don't worry, Ciss, please,' I whispered. 'We're here now.'

The others stood back as I sat at Amy's pillow. Close by her now I could hear she was not groaning but making a ghastly sound. Alarmed, I listened. It was as if she were gasping or choking. *The Strangling Angel.* The words came to my mind but I banished them. Her neck was now hideously swollen. My only fear then was that the infection I'd identified was spreading, taking hold of her body. That I must help her. That *only I* could help her.

'Sweetheart, try to be still,' I whispered to Amy, stroking her arm, as Gerard attempted to lift her head to help her sip his remedy from a vial. She struggled against him, but then too weak, fell limp as again he put the vial to her lips. She could not drink it. Streams ran down her chin, her swallowing was so bad.

I felt greatly distressed but knew I must act. I beckoned the others to come and circle the bed. I looked at them all there. Ciss huddled in Bernard's arms, Conor beside them, eyes pained, while Mairéad tried to nod reassuringly with an air of calm. Gus looked perturbed but Gerard stood steady and stoic, Noreen the same.

The candle flickered on the washstand, casting our shadows on the wall. I fixed on the mellow flame's peace. I breathed that peace in deeply, raising my palms, gesturing to the others to raise their own and breathe with me. Closing my eyes I breathed deeper, hearing each do the same until the room was heavy with the sound. Heavy too with another. Amy's gasps cut through every inhalation.

I would not allow those gasps to sway me. Nor the soft whimpers from Ciss. Only kept my mind clear, a receptacle for the Spring. In and out I breathed, drawing from that well within, letting it subsume me, flow into my arms, through to my palms, the very tips of my fingers. I placed my palms over Amy's throat, willed every warmth into her body.

In, I intoned silently. *Into this child. Your vast treasure, your blessed gift. I will you heal this child. I will you: in.*

But my eyes swiftly opened at a fearsome sound. Amy's racking cough, as if she were choking. She was convulsing in the bed, her chest as if being lifted, then hurled down by an unseen force. Dismayed, I stopped, looking desperately to the others as Ciss cried out, going to run to Amy. Noreen stopped her.

'No!' Noreen said. 'Don't stop. It is the sickness coming out. We are purging her of it. Keep on, Rosaleen, keep on,' she urged, keeping hold of Ciss.

My mind was so greatly disturbed, but I closed my eyes again, trying to find my peace. Urgently I held my palms high, lowering them again to the child, intoning fervently, *Come, come, release every sickness from this child's body. Let it flee. Be gone. Release her from its grip and let her life force flow.*

I intoned it over and over. At first silently, then loudly, the chant fevered on my lips. There was no ringing of crystals now, nor dancing lights. Only a gritty sickness in my gut. Louder and louder I chanted, amidst breathy whispers, moans and a rising chorus of voices: '*Come, come, release every sickness. Be gone, Be gone.*' Noreen was laughing with ecstasy and delight but I could hear the child choking, grisly and guttural, as if she were heaving up her very stomach.

It is the sickness leaving, it is the sickness leaving.

Opening my eyes, I intoned those words now, not a hope, not a plea, but a frantic command. Noreen was still laughing, swaying, waving her palms, the breathy whispers and chants growing louder, ever louder.

Suddenly I was stopped by a horrific sound. A gruesome gurgling, a rattle. It escaped from the child's chest, like a wind's malevolent whine, gathering force, being expelled from her. And then silence.

Is it gone? My mind was awash with confusion. *Is the sickness gone?*

The whispers and chants thickening the air, at last faded, coming to a stop. A deep silence saturated the room. And then a scream. A scream that pierced my very blood. It was Ciss screaming, bending over the bed, clutching Amy's face. Bernard stood behind her, frozen, as if struck and turned to stone. I looked down upon Amy, lying so still. So deathly still.

No. My mind refused to believe what I was seeing. *No.*

And then Bernard was shouting. Sprung alive and screeching to me, to us all, to no one.

'Do something! *Do* something!'

I looked down again upon Amy, went to touch her face. 'Amy!' I called to her, tried to rouse her, gripping her cheeks, moving her face from side to side. 'Amy!' I started to shake her face more forcefully, it only moving limply under my hand. 'Amy, Amy!'

By the bed, Ciss had collapsed to her knees with a savage wail, pushing my hand away from Amy's face, Bernard quickly on his knees behind her, holding her. I looked hopelessly around the room. Conor had fled from the bed, looking stricken in a far corner. Gus, gaping, stood motionless by Mairéad who was whispering, 'Oh, God, no, no. No.' Noreen stood stiff, staring blindly at the still child. Gerard rushed forward, grasping Amy's shoulders.

'Amy!' he cried. 'Amy, wake up!'

'She cannot wake!' Ciss screeched from where she knelt. 'She is gone! *Gone!*'

I felt a surge within me, heard the rising pitch of a terrible moaning, only realising the sound coming from me when Gerard came to shake me.

'Stop, Rosaleen, *stop*.'

I was shocked back to my senses. Ciss was rocking and keening, calling for Amy over and over, her head buried in Amy's tiny chest, Bernard still clinging to Ciss. At last, Conor, eyes tortured, dashed from the shadows, collapsing on his knees by Ciss, holding her heaving shoulders.

'Oh, God, what will we *do*?' Mairéad's voice was pleading. 'What will we do?'

Noreen was roused from her stupor. She turned to Mairéad, her eyes moving rapidly. She moved quickly to Mairéad's side, taking her arm.

'We must think. We must think now.' Noreen's voice was urgent as she signalled to Conor at Ciss's side. 'Conor, get up.' Conor looked at her dazed, then rose as if every limb was lead. Ciss was sobbing, Bernard babbling, stroking Amy's hair, paying no mind to us. 'Everyone,' Noreen gestured to the rest of us. 'We must go downstairs now.'

I was paralysed, could only sit stupefied, staring at Amy. At last, Gerard came to take my arm, helping me rise from the bed. I let him lead me from the room, looking back at the Armstrongs deaf to us, lamenting over their child. Although I could feel him trembling, Gerard guided me down each stair, for I would surely have stumbled. He guided me to sit beside Mairéad and

Gus on a couch in the drawing room, and went to sit on another. Conor sat alone, huddled on a chair.

Noreen stood in the middle of the room. She swallowed as if trying to gather herself, steady her voice. She looked at each of us before speaking. 'The most terrible, most shocking thing has happened,' she said at last. 'But we must be calm now. Regain our senses and think carefully. Very carefully. The child has died.'

'Under my hands!' I mumbled it over and over. 'Under *my* hands.' My whole body, every limb, was shaking. I could hear my voice rising from a mumble to a moan.

'Hush, Rosaleen, be quiet,' Noreen said sharply. 'Think. You said she had an infection, tonsillitis. It is possible that the infection spread just as you said it might. In that case there would be nothing could be done.'

'*No!*' The word escaped me in a rush. 'I must have been wrong. *Wrong!* No spread would have come or been so lethal so quickly. Dr Lydon was right. Amy had diphtheria. And now she has *died*!' I sobbed it, Mairéad trying to pull me close, but I did not want her touch. I could take no comfort.

'If I had known it was diphtheria I could have prepared a different remedy,' Gerard said, his face ashen. 'I was misinformed.'

Gus fired him a vicious glance. 'Oh, for God's sake, Gerard, you think your remedy would have made the difference?' He turned his eye on me. 'We were *all* misinformed.'

'Gus.' Mairéad with a hand on his arm begged him to stop. But I did not care. He was blaming me. Gerard was blaming me. It made no difference. For they were right to blame me. I blamed myself utterly.

'The doctor said it was diphtheria,' said Conor, weakly. 'We should have listened. Not just Rosaleen. *All* of us.'

'And that is why I am afraid.' Gerard spoke lowly, so lowly I hardly heard him. But he had caught the others' attention.

'Afraid of what, Gerard?' Mairéad said.

My mind was too scattered to heed him. But Mairéad reached for my hand, gripped it, urged me to listen. I looked at Gerard through sobs, struggling to grasp his words. He was trying to be stoic but I could hear the tremor in his voice.

'I am afraid we might be in a very precarious position,' he said slowly. 'I have a little knowledge of these things through my practice. I had a very heated discussion with a barrister at a party not so long ago. He was being dismissive of my occupation, my healing methods, and he gave me a warning. Told me I should be very careful when treating children and the advice I gave their parents. Because there are laws I didn't know of that apply to the care of children: that if any parent wilfully withholds adequate medical treatment for their child they are liable to be charged with neglect. His implication was that my treatment would be deemed far from adequate. And I am very much afraid that by ignoring the doctor's advice, Bernard and Ciss will be open to that charge.'

'So, Bernard and Ciss could be charged with neglect?' Gus said. 'That is what you are saying to us, Gerard?'

Gerard glanced down. 'Yes. But not only that.'

'What, then?' Noreen said.

Gerard did not raise his eyes. 'He told me that if the worst – the very worst – were to happen, that if a child were to die as a result of withholding adequate care, the parents would almost certainly be charged with manslaughter.'

I sat stunned with the others. The word swam with all his other words in a mist before me.

'Manslaughter?' Mairéad cried. 'But how can that be? Ciss and Bernard have committed no crime. They were only trying to heal Amy.'

'For God's sake, Gerard,' Gus railed at him. 'If you knew all this, why did you not warn us?'

Gerard's voice was desperate. 'I felt no need to warn you. Never . . . *never* for one moment, not in my wildest imaginings, did I think that Amy would *die*.'

The mention of Amy's name, the brutality of it twinned with *die* made me wretched; an unnatural moan escaped me again. I could hardly absorb what Gerard was saying.

He lifted his eyes, observed us a moment before speaking. 'But we have to ask ourselves . . .' He looked around the room. 'If Bernard and Ciss were to be charged with manslaughter, would we not all also be liable? We who encouraged them in denying medical aid? We, who stood and watched the child failing? *Dying*. Is that not also a crime?'

Everyone was silent, staring at Gerard.

'You're saying that we *all* could be charged with manslaughter?' Noreen said finally, her voice clipped, incredulous.

'I don't know,' Gerard said. 'I don't have enough knowledge of the law. But I am saying that I am almost certain Bernard and Ciss could be charged. And that there is a possibility that we, too, could be seen as culpable.'

No one spoke. Then Noreen went to sit quietly on a chair.

'In that case we must take our next steps very carefully,' she said. 'We must think of the consequences of this. To Bernard, to Ciss. To us all. The worst, the very worst is that we could all be charged with manslaughter. But even if we were not – even if just Bernard and Ciss were charged – think, *think* of our ruination, the scandal. If we report the death now, there'd almost certainly be an inquest and it would become known that the child died under our watch. We would become outcasts in society, condemned as shysters and charlatans. Gerard,' she looked at him intently. 'Your reputation would be in tatters. Your practice finished. Who would attend the doctor that allowed a child to die?'

Gerard flinched but said nothing.

Mairéad, beside me, spoke. 'What are you saying, Noreen?'

'Mairéad.' Noreen turned to her, pleading. 'Your career will be over. Even if you do get work, people will only come to gawk at the actress that killed the child. Gus, it would be the same for you. And our standing as mesmerists will be destroyed. Our mission, our truth will be . . .'

I could listen no more. 'What *truth*?' I cried. 'The truth is that Amy is *dead*. And I killed her!'

'Stop, Rosaleen.' Mairéad gripped my arm. 'You did not kill her. If you did, we all did.'

'Exactly,' Noreen said. 'That is how the world will see it. Even if the law does not. That we killed the child.'

'So, what on earth are you suggesting?' Gus said.

'That we deal with this matter ourselves,' Noreen said. 'Quickly. Quietly. That we involve no one else. No doctors. No police.'

'And what are we to do, exactly?' Gerard asked listlessly.

'I will tell you,' Noreen said.

29

Noreen bid Conor, who stared as if into another world, to go and fetch Bernard and Ciss. I could not bear to look at Ciss as Conor helped her, pale and shaking, into the drawing room, Bernard, ashen, behind them. Conor gently eased Ciss on to a couch, Bernard sitting beside her, enclosing her in his arms. Noreen went to sit on the other side of Ciss, taking her limp hand. She looked at Ciss, eyes deep, as if with care.

'Bernard, Ciss, I must talk to you,' Noreen said. 'The most devastating thing has happened. It has happened here amongst us all. Our dear Amy has died and this is a tragedy for you, for every one of us. But now,' she covered Ciss's hand with her own, 'now we must think of the wider consequences.'

It was clear that Ciss was paying no heed to Noreen, only jerking her head, trying to shake her words away. Noreen grew more insistent.

'People will be cruel, Ciss,' she went on. 'They will say it was at our hands – at *your* hands – that Amy died. They will point at you in the street. They will say there goes the mother that killed her child. They will say that you *let* her die.'

Ciss gave an unearthly wail as Bernard tightened his grip on her.

'I *let* her die!' Ciss started to choke as if she would vomit.

'You mind your tongue,' Bernard hissed at Noreen. 'Or you leave this house.'

I was on my feet. I could not bear Noreen talking to Ciss in such a way. 'Stop, Noreen, stop!' I cried, but Ciss wailed again.

'But it's true,' Ciss choked. 'It's true. They will say I did not love her. Did not love her enough because she was not my natural born child. That I did not care for her as a mother should.'

Bernard caressed her arms. 'Nothing could be further from the truth, my love.'

'It's not true, of course it's not true,' Noreen said. 'But what people will say is not the only thing that concerns us. I must tell you that Gerard has told us something of the law. It seems there are serious repercussions for what has occurred. That in withholding what the authorities would deem adequate medical aid for your child, you could face a charge of neglect.' She paused. 'And by the fact that Amy has died you may face a charge far more serious. A charge of manslaughter.'

Bernard stared stunned at Noreen while Ciss howled. Bernard pulled her close.

'What do you mean?' Bernard said. He looked to Gerard. 'Gerard?'

Gerard nodded slowly. 'I'm afraid it's true. There is a strong probability you would face that charge.'

'And not just you, Bernard.' Noreen glanced meaningfully at the weeping Ciss. 'But Ciss too.'

Bernard was pale. 'That cannot happen.' He shook his head, still staring at his wife now trembling, moaning mindlessly, lost to all reason. 'She would not survive it. No. It cannot happen.'

Noreen touched Bernard's arm. 'That's right. Ciss is too fragile. We must spare her that.'

Bernard's eyes were pained. 'But how?'

'The natural parents,' Noreen said. 'Is there any chance that in the future they could come forward?'

Bernard shook his head. 'Our parentage of Amy is . . . was . . . a full and permanent one. The mother has long disappeared, the father never wanted anything to do with Amy or to receive any word of her. He has paid for the privilege of being rid of her.' His voice broke.

Noreen nodded as if satisfied. 'Then I want you to listen to what I have to say.'

I have relived that night of horror many times. Still, I see Noreen professing distress, gripping Ciss's hand, her voice so soft, so caring as she laid out her plan. Her eyes were wells of sincerity as she implored Bernard to listen, as if what she proposed were solely for Ciss.

'There is a way that we can keep Ciss safe, yet do right by dear, sweet Amy.' Noreen's voice was low as she leaned in towards Bernard. 'A way Amy's name can be saved from becoming fodder for gossiping tongues. We can keep her memory blessed and free from scandal and lay her to rest in peace. In a sacred place. A place that she loved.'

Ciss seemed not to be able to hear, she was still moaning, shaking. But Bernard was listening intently. He shook his head, not comprehending.

'The bell tower,' Noreen whispered fervently. 'Amy's beloved bell tower. I say we take her to the monastery tonight and lay her to rest there in that holy place.'

Bernard recoiled, drawing Ciss closer to him. 'No.' He looked staggered at Noreen. 'No. We *cannot*. We *cannot* do that.'

Noreen still gripped an oblivious Ciss's hand. 'But think,' Noreen went on. 'Your dear child must be laid to rest somewhere. Which is better? Ciss forced to endure endless weeks, months of gruelling questions; the furore and shame of an inquest; the penalty you will both surely pay – all for Amy's name to ever after be sullied and her laid in ground that meant nothing to her, where the curious will come to gawk at her grave? Or that we take her now and lay her in peace in the woodland, amongst the trees, all of nature, in a place she so loved? Which is better?'

Bernard still shook his head but I could see his mind working. He was starting to listen. Ciss must have understood some of it, for she began to moan unmercifully, covering her ears with her hands. Bernard buried his face in her shoulder.

'But how would it be done?' Gus's voice came from beside Mairéad. I turned to stare at him, disbelieving. Was he actually considering such an abominable act?

'It can be done simply,' Noreen said, turning to Gus. 'With the monastery so close to Gerard and Conor's homes. Let Conor, who loved Amy, who she loved so, perform this last act of care for her. He and Gerard can carry her there in Gerard's car. And lay her to rest.'

Gerard sprang back in his chair. 'No!' he cried, while I looked dumbfounded at Conor to see if he had heard or understood. He was staring, eyes wild, at Noreen. Mairéad leaned over the arm of the couch to touch Conor's arm.

'There is some sense in what Noreen is saying,' she said gently. She turned to Gerard. 'To think of our beloved Amy at rest in that tranquil place surrounded by nature. No cold, stark churchyard but in that place she so loved. There is beauty in it.'

I had heard enough. 'No!' I stood. 'Stop with this madness, all of you. Let me go. Let me go now to Dr Lydon and tell him what has happened. I will tell him it was I and I alone that caused this. That I took it upon myself to do the healing, that no one else was present or involved. Please. Let me go to him now.'

Noreen glared at me. 'Do you not realise that he will not believe you?' she said sternly. 'That even if he did it would solve nothing for Bernard and Ciss?'

Gerard looked at me. 'Noreen is right,' he said. 'Bernard and Ciss are the parents, responsible for the child in law. And Dr Lydon had already advised them that Amy needed treatment. They did not supply it, so even if you alone carried out the healing, they would still be culpable.'

'Besides,' Noreen said, 'the truth would come out. Even if the rest of us stayed solid in our story, Ciss would crumble at the onslaught of questioning from Dr Lydon, the police and an inquest. They would find out that we were all here. You'll solve nothing with your heroics.'

'It's true,' Mairéad said, reaching up to touch my arm. I sat down again, numb and defeated.

Noreen turned once more to Gerard. 'So, Gerard. Would you consider doing what I suggest?'

It was too much for Conor. He gave a fierce sob, shielding his eyes with his hands.

'Gerard?' Noreen quizzed again. Gerard was silent.

Ciss's moans grew louder. In an instant she had sprung to her feet and was across the room and out the door. We all looked after her.

'Go with her, Mairéad, please,' Bernard said.

Mairéad quickly followed Ciss as the rest of us turned to Bernard. We needed to hear what he had to say.

'Gerard,' Bernard said at last. 'I think you of all people know that Ciss will not be able to withstand the inquisition and turmoil that will come of this. Her nerves will not stand it. I fear it might be the finish of her. That I might lose her – might lose her too.' His voice caught on a sob.

Gerard observed Bernard for a moment. 'You want me to do as Noreen has proposed?' he asked.

Bernard's throat was thick with anguish. 'I do not want it. I want none of this. And I have no right to ask you to do such a thing. But Ciss – what will become of her?' He started to weep and could speak no more.

Gus looked at Gerard. 'It would seem that Noreen's plan is the only one,' he said quietly.

Gerard said nothing. But, at last, grimly nodded.

'That's right, Gerard,' Noreen whispered.

I stared at Gerard, then at Conor, quiet now, dazed. I could not believe that they truly intended to carry this out.

'Conor,' I said. 'Are you willing to do such a thing?'

His mouth was trembling. 'Perhaps it is what Amy would want. Perhaps it is there in the woods, at the bell tower, where she would wish to be.' His last words were lost to a sob. I was still too numb to comfort him. I hugged myself, trying to stop the great cold I could feel creeping through me.

Gerard remained silent for what seemed an age. Then, finally, he stood.

'Then let us do it.'

* * *

'Did you hear me, Thomas?'

Brother Thomas turned from the spitting wood and flames. He gazed blindly at Father Sheridan.

Father Sheridan spoke again. 'That night, Rosaleen – the Rose – confessed that it was she who killed the child. That it was under her hands that Amy died.'

Brother Thomas sat silent, his mind numb.

Father Sheridan spoke slowly. 'If that is true – if I am to believe that this was not just the raving of a fevered mind – then why, Thomas?' He did not release Brother Thomas's eyes. 'Why did the Abbot lie?'

30

It was near midnight when they carried Amy's small body from the house. Noreen had made a shroud of a blanket, Gerard descending the stairs, holding the gruesome bundle in his arms. I watched them through the open door of the drawing room where I sat stunned. Conor followed Gerard through the hallway and out to Gerard's car. Bernard and Ciss were with Mairéad and the others somewhere in the house, but I only wanted to be left alone. As the front door closed behind Conor, I sat stiff in the silence. Then moaned like an animal. And howled.

It was Conor told me afterwards what had happened. How they had kept watch to be sure there were none about to see, and how Gerard had placed the child's body in the back seat of the car and, in heavy silence, they had travelled towards the hills. At his house, Gerard had collected one large spade, one smaller, and they had driven to the monastery. Not wanting to alert any wakeful brothers, Gerard had turned off the lights of his car as they approached, leaving it a little away from the monastery gates.

When Gerard had given Conor the spades to carry, Conor had retched. The child in Gerard's arms, he had ushered Conor over the steps in the stone wall on to the pathway that led to the woodland. He had handed the child to Conor while he himself climbed. Conor said this time he had not been able to stem the vomit, shaking so violently he had almost dropped her. Gerard, quickly beside him, had taken back the child, gesturing to Conor to pick up the spades.

Together they'd stumbled through the dark woodland, dim light burning up ahead from the monastery. The winter moon had been cold and bright, bright enough to guide their way over the gnarled roots and mud. It had lit the bridge and the brook running loud as a river in the deep silence. It had lit too the path to the bell tower, the moonlight ghostly through the bare branches, casting the bell in an eerie glow.

Gerard had laid the child down amongst a pile of ferns, then stood deathly still as if to compose himself. At last, he had taken up a spade, nodding at Conor to do the same. In the streaming moonlight, there in the shadow of the bell tower they had started to dig. With neither heart nor mind for this grotesque task, Conor said he had no hand for it either. He had never dug in his life, was weak, crying, not wanting to go on; Gerard, agitated with him, had been firm. But Gerard had suddenly let loose his spade, allowing it to thud to the ground.

'I can't do it.' Gerard's eyes had looked crazed in the moon's glare. 'I cannot do it. I am a healer, not a murderer. I cannot – I *will* not – do it.'

Conor had watched in horror as Gerard had turned and staggered away from him, back through the woodland. Conor had opened his mouth to call after him, to beg him to stay, but had quickly regained his senses, realising he could not risk making any sound. Alone now amongst the stark trees, in the chill of the moon and the beginnings of a spitting, icy rain, he'd looked down to the small bundle in its nest of ferns. With an almighty sob, he'd sunk to his knees. He'd taken the bundle in his arms, started to rock with it.

'I'm so sorry, my darling, so sorry.'

He did not know how long he'd sat there with her. Only started becoming aware of his body growing stiff, freezing with cold. As he unwound his numb arms from the blanket, laid it back down, he was stupefied yet certain of one thing. He could not do as he'd been asked. He thought of running, running far from here, never stopping. Far, far away, never to return. But he knew it was hopeless. He was lost. Desolate. Only wanted to lie down by Amy's tiny body and let the bitter night take him, or sleep, sleep never to wake again. He gave in to the desire, nestling into the blanket, resting his head there. And in that moment, that fleeting moment of peace, it came to him. *Rían.*

I did not learn of this, Father, until later. Much later. But it was to Rían his thoughts turned then. Rían would help him. Would know what to do. He must go to him. He must go to his brother.

* * *

Rían, having sat up late with a whiskey, had only just retired when he'd heard his brother outside the bedroom door. Listening to him unsteady, knocking against the hall wall, he'd thought him drunk. He was about to go to him, warn him to be quiet so as not to wake their parents, when the door pushed open and Conor had entered the room.

He'd known immediately that something was wrong. The boy had seemed drunk, yes, but his expression was frenzied. He'd wondered if Conor had been in some sort of fracas. Had some thugs leapt upon him in the street? Quickly, he'd thrown off his blankets.

'Conor.' He'd rushed to take his arm to steady him. 'What in God's name is wrong?'

Conor had fixed him with a ghastly stare, then started to sob, with an almost bestial moaning. He had sunk his head into Rían's shoulder.

'Be quiet, please,' Rían had begged him, worried still he would rouse their parents. He'd led Conor to sit with him on the side of the bed. 'Tell me what's wrong, has someone hurt you?' He'd lifted his brother's chin but Conor would not look at him.

Searching his brother's face, Rían had found no cuts or bruising, but Conor kept whimpering, shaking his head, mumbling words that Rían could neither hear properly nor understand. At last, Conor spoke clearly.

'Come with me, Rían, please.'

Although bewildered, Rían had dressed quickly and followed Conor from the house. He'd wondered where on earth they could be going at this hour of the night. At last he'd realised they were heading towards the monastery. As Conor approached the steps in the stone wall, Rían gripped his arm.

'Why in God's name are we here?' he'd whispered, but Conor remained mute, his eyes imploring Rían's silence.

Rían had watched his brother climb the stone steps over the wall, then did the same. He'd looked up at the monastery in near darkness as they'd trampled over leaves, sticks and mud. Approaching the rushing brook, he'd understood that they were bound for the bell tower. As they'd crossed the bridge, Rían had seen the bell shining in the moonlight and spitting rain, when Conor had abruptly stopped. He'd seemed unwilling to move further. Rían had stared at his brother. Had he lost his senses?

'Conor, for God's sake,' he'd hissed. 'Why have you brought me here?'

Conor had only begun again that strange whimpering, then slowly pointed to the ground. Rían had followed his finger but could see nothing. 'What?' He was agitated now. 'What do you want to show me? Tell me.'

Conor had suddenly fallen to his knees, sobbing, as if reaching for something. Rían had crouched beside him, seeing his brother had lifted something hefty into his arms. Rían had been unable to discern what it was. Some kind of bundle. Under scrutiny it had grown clearer. It seemed like something wrapped in a blanket. Conor's face had been wan and he'd been moaning. Rían had felt a grip of panic but had quickly gathered himself. If his brother had not the wits to enlighten him, if he would not act, Rían must. He would have to examine whatever this was.

He'd eased the bundle, awkward and heavy, from Conor's arms, the wool sodden. Even though loath to do so, he'd started to fumble with the damp blanket which was clinging tightly to its contents. At last, prising it open at one end, blindly he'd pushed his hand through. Fingers touching something stiff, his stomach had turned. He could tell it was something sentient, something once living. An animal, then. His mind had raced. He could not fathom why his brother should bring him on this escapade for the sake of an animal already beyond rescue. Stomach sickening, he'd rolled his hands over it.

'Oh, Christ!' Violently he'd recoiled, leapt back. He'd stared down in horror, shouting, 'There's an arm. An *arm*!'

Conor had whined, a great lamenting whine, bowing his head over the blanket. Rían had knelt back down beside him.

'Who is it? For Christ's sake, Conor, what have you found?'

Conor's voice had been a wail. 'I didn't find it.'

'What do you mean you didn't find it?' Rían had grasped his brother's shoulders, shaken him. Tried to shake him back to sanity. 'Conor, there's a *body* in there. The body surely of a *child*. Who is it? How did it come to be here?'

'It's *Amy*.' Conor had choked up the name. '*Amy*.'

A colossal rush had sounded in Rían's head. Amy? Amy who? His own wits had abandoned him now, he had been unable to take any meaning from Conor's words. *Amy*. Amy *Armstrong*? No. It could not be. It was impossible. He'd shaken his brother's shoulders again.

'Amy *Armstrong*? That is the body of Amy Armstrong?'

'Yes, *yes*.' Conor had been sobbing so hard he was retching. 'And *I* killed her.'

No. *No*. Impossible. None of this was possible. Rían had kept a grip of his brother's shoulders in an attempt to bring him to his senses. He'd stared into Conor's face, but Conor, still sobbing, would not raise his eyes.

'No, Conor, *no*. What you are saying is impossible. Do you hear me? Impossible. So now you will tell me what has happened. You will tell me. Tell me *now*.'

It had seemed, now the horror was revealed, Conor was desperate to release his burden. Rían had frantically tried to comprehend his brother's words as they came quickly, garbled, too difficult to understand. But, at last, through the onslaught of rambling, Rían had heard clearly: *Child ill. Healing. The Rose.*

The Rose.

He'd tightened his grip on Conor's shoulders. 'What are you telling me? You are saying that Rosaleen tried to heal the child and she died?'

Tears had streamed from Conor's eyes, on to his lips as he spoke. 'Rosaleen said she could heal her. The doctor said Amy was too ill, that she needed medicine, but we didn't listen. We *killed* her.'

Waves of shock, nausea had seared through Rían. He'd tried to absorb the words. Rosaleen had attempted a healing and the child had died. And his brother was part of it. He had to think now. *Think.* Must gather his wits and think as a lawyer would. What crime? What crime had been committed here? Murder? No, no, surely not. There had been no intent to kill, only an intent to heal. What, then? Manslaughter? But he could not be sure. This involved a child. Parents and a child. And his every day was spent with matters of conveyancing, he was no expert on criminal law. Even if he had been, he could not think properly now. He could not think as a lawyer, only as a brother. And a lover.

His brother had been involved in what would almost certainly amount to a crime. And Rosaleen. The Rose. *His* Rose. She had been at the head of it. He could only envision the repercussions for Conor. For her. At that moment, what crime had been committed he'd been too confused to know, but of one thing he was sure: what they proposed now was a crime most heinous. To not report the death, but keep it hidden. To attempt to

241

conceal the body. For this was surely why his brother had brought the child here.

'And you are going to bury her?' He'd been incredulous. 'Is this what the Armstrongs want?'

Conor had sobbed. 'In this place that she loved. In this holy place.'

Rían had known what he should do. He should stop this right away. Should take his brother to the police to report the death. What part Conor had played in the child's demise had surely been small. It was more than possible he would be seen as young, an innocent, no more than a naive bystander. And the authorities would look kindly upon him for coming to them. There would be an inquest and Conor would be shown to have had little or no hand in the child's death. He'd been almost certain that would be the case. But what about Rosaleen?

Rosaleen would be ruined. Even if she were not found culpable for the child's death in law, the scandal that would arise from this, attach itself to her, would ensure her a life of shame. She would have to leave Dublin, go far away. It was unthinkable. Rían had released Conor's shoulders.

'Go home, Conor,' he'd said quietly.

Conor had stared at him, eyes wild and welling.

'Go home,' Rían had repeated. 'Don't fret any more. I will take care of this.'

31

That night I stumbled from the Armstrongs', back home to my aunt's. Mairéad had asked Gus to walk with me but I could bear no one by my side. I only wanted to leave that house of horror, and all in it, far behind. The house was in blissful darkness with none to bother me as I staggered up the stairs to my room and sank down on my bed. I did not light the lamp, only lay there. It all seemed a fevered dream. I gripped my arm to wake myself in case I really was asleep, trapped in a nightmare. I dug my nails into my flesh, trying to hurt myself. To feel the pain. Pain I deserved to feel. I had *killed* a child. I had killed *Amy*.

I was so tired. I wanted to sleep and never wake. Still dressed, I buried my head in the crook of my arm. In and out of fretful sleep I drifted, awaking before dawn only to realise again what I had done. The weight of it nearly buried me.

I knew I must leave the house before my aunt and uncle woke. I could not face them, for I would not be able to pretend. They would guess immediately that something was wrong and I would crumble under any inquisition. I left the house in the dress I had slept in and wandered Eccles Street in the dark, until eventually I came to sit on a bench near the Mater Hospital. At last, light breaking, I looked down towards the Armstrongs' door.

I never wanted to pass through that door again. I wanted to run far from it, this street, this city. Yet through that door was the only place I could go. The house both repelled and drew me for it was the only place where I would not have to hide behind a mask. It had been arranged that the others and I would meet there this morning to discuss what next to do. I would be early.

I rose from the bench, feeling a great dread as I trudged towards the Armstrongs' railings. I hesitated as I saw their maid, Kitty, take the steps to the door, unlocking it with a key. Staying back, I let her enter before, at last, I climbed the steps and knocked. Kitty, still in her coat, answered.

'I'd like to see Mr and Mrs Armstrong, please.' Kitty looked at me hesitantly. She was not overly familiar with me, and was obviously taken aback at such an early visitor. As she dithered, Bernard called from the drawing room.

'It's all right, Kitty, let her in.'

Kitty stood aside and, with a deep breath, I stepped into the hall. As Kitty took off her coat, I looked through the drawing-room doorway. Bernard and Ciss were huddled together on the couch, in their clothes of the night before. They had not slept. That was plain from their drawn and deathly pale faces. Ciss started to moan when she saw me, a ghastly sound. She buried her face in Bernard's chest. It was clear she could not bear to look at me.

Bernard was mute, staring at me with a dazed expression. He whispered to Ciss. 'Kitty will bring you some sweet tea, my love.'

He called Kitty in and she hurried to fetch the tea. When she'd left I spoke the only words I could think of.

'I am sorry. So, so sorry.' Each word felt laden with grief but Ciss kept her face turned, Bernard granting me barely a nod. I was offered no seat, but I took one far across the room. We sat in silence until Kitty returned with the tea tray, setting it upon the small table before Bernard.

'Kitty, we will not need you today,' he said to her. 'You can take the day for yourself.' Kitty looked surprised but at Bernard's assured nod, uttered her thanks. We listened to her scurrying in the hall, gathering her hat and coat, and, finally, the front door closing.

Bernard's hand shook as he tried to pour the tea, so I stood quickly to take the pot from him, filling three cups. Ciss would not take the tea at first, but Bernard gently guided the cup to her lips. She took just a sip, then turned her face away. As I sat again, I held my own cup, grateful for its warmth as the silence between us grew colder.

Finally came the sound of the knocker. I leapt to answer it, desperate to escape the room and show myself their willing servant, after all the suffering I had brought upon this house. Mairéad and Gus stood on the steps.

'Oh, Rosaleen.' Mairéad reached for me, burying her head in my shoulder while Gus stood behind her, his expression hard. Numb, I let Mairéad hold me, then walked with her and Gus into the drawing room.

Ciss lifted her eyes at our entrance, then looked away, Bernard giving a slight nod. Mairéad went to Ciss, attempting to embrace her, but Ciss yelped at Mairéad's touch. Clearly wounded, Mairéad crossed to the far side of the room to sit with Gus and myself. At the knocker sounding again, Mairéad rose to answer it, returning with Gerard and Noreen.

'We met on the street,' Noreen said, her words fading at finding us in such deep silence. Gerard went to Ciss, bending to gently touch her shoulder, holding in his hand a vial.

'I have brought you some remedy,' he said softly. 'I will—'

Ciss lashed out with her arm, knocking the vial from his hand. 'I do not *want* your remedy. *Remedy*. What remedy can there be for *this*?' Sobbing, she buried her face in Bernard's chest as he stroked her head tenderly, whispering to her.

Evidently stung but attempting to remain stoic, Gerard picked up the vial and came to sit with the rest of us. Mairéad spoke to him quietly.

'So, we are only waiting on Conor. Did he not come with you, Gerard?'

I looked at Gerard. It was obvious that he was disturbed by the question.

'No,' he answered.

'But last night . . .?' I whispered, leaving the words unspoken. *What happened last night?*

Bernard looked up. It was clear from his face that he also wanted to know the answer to that question. Clear too, that he did not wish his wife to hear it.

'Mairéad,' Bernard said, 'will you go with Ciss to the dining room? Take her tea in there?'

Mairéad nodded. 'Yes, of course.' She went to help Ciss rise but Ciss would not allow it. She stood herself, walking blindly from the room as Mairéad trailed her with her tea cup. When they'd gone, Bernard looked at Gerard.

'Well?' Bernard flinched. It seemed even as he asked the question, he could not bear to hear the answer. 'Did you . . .?'

Gerard, his expression still disturbed, was silent.

'Gerard, what happened?' I said, anxious now. With no sign of Conor, I needed to know he had not come to any harm.

At last, Gerard spoke. 'I couldn't do it.' As we stared at him, he was unable to look at us. 'We took . . . we went to the monastery. To the bell tower. But I left Conor there alone. I'm sorry, so sorry.' His words came in a rush. 'I couldn't *do* it.'

Noreen looked at him, incredulous. 'You left Conor there alone? *Conor?* What in God's name were you thinking? You thought the boy was capable of carrying out a thing like that alone?'

I spat at Noreen. 'Well, it was *you* who suggested it. It was *you* who sent him there.'

'Stop, *stop.*' Bernard stood. He looked aghast at Gerard. 'You're telling me my child is lying out there in the woods, all alone? Lying there, abandoned, like some slaughtered animal?'

'*No.*' Gerard looked earnestly at Bernard. 'I promise you, she is not. I called on Conor this morning.' He hesitated, then lowered his eyes. 'It is done.'

* * *

That morning, once Ciss and Mairéad had returned to the drawing room, Bernard told us what it was that he and Ciss planned to do.

'We are going to London,' he said. 'I have kept a town house all these years and it is there we will go. Away from here. Far away from this . . .' He did not finish. 'I have some affairs I must put in order first but we will go quickly. By the end of the week.'

I knew it was the right thing. Of course they must go. For any hope of sanity. And how else could the disappearance of Amy be explained?

'And if there are questions?' Noreen said.

'I don't think there will be questions,' Bernard said listlessly. 'If we are asked of Amy's whereabouts, we will simply say we have sent her on ahead, with some unspecified cousin. There should be no further questions after that.'

'You should remove the child's clothes, then,' Noreen said quietly. 'And her trunk. So the maid does not see them still there.'

Head on Bernard's shoulder, Ciss started to moan again. He comforted her while he acknowledged Noreen's words dismally. Undoubtedly he had not thought of it, and I wondered at Noreen's cunning, her ability to think so clearly in a time of such great sorrow. I hated her at that moment. Detested her guile. But all too quickly that hate I turned upon myself. How could I judge another after the tragedy I had brought about through my arrogance?

'We have much to do,' Bernard said. 'Much to arrange.'

'And you must let us help you,' Mairéad said softly.

'No!' Ciss spoke suddenly. She rose, her body trembling, but her voice clipped and clear. She looked at each of us, her eyes not dead but with an icy sheen. 'This will be the last time any of you set foot in my house. When you leave today I never want to see any one of you again.'

32

Ciss could despise me no more than I despised myself. I spent long hours at my aunt's, alone in my room, tortured, trying to fathom what I had done. In those dark hours I longed for Clare and the softness of my mother, but I felt I could never go home again, for I could never tell them the truth. There would for ever be the darkest of lies between us, they could never know the deepest part of my heart. With Aunt Ellen so busy, it was possible to avoid her scrutiny, make some show of pretence but I would not be able to do so with my mother.

Noreen had forced us to take a vow. After we had left Bernard and Ciss that morning, we had gone to Mairéad's and sat in her parlour in a dazed silence. Noreen had taken charge. Had made each of us swear that never would we reveal what had taken place in Amy's room that terrible night, nor what had become of her afterwards.

'If the sword falls on one, it falls on us all,' Noreen said. 'We must not betray this vow, or one another.'

I had no interest in her solemn vow. No wish to save myself from the sword: I wanted to let that sword fall, come slay me, punish me. Yet even in my torment I knew this would do no good. The wish for punishment was only to salve my own conscience. It would not bring Amy back. And I knew that by bringing punishment upon myself I would bring it also upon the others. Most of all upon Bernard and Ciss. And that I could not countenance.

And yet I felt a desperation to unburden myself. In the following days, I wandered often to St Stephen's Green, where I had once strolled so happily with Lorcan. And I lingered outside the University Church. Your church, Father. I longed to come and speak to you. You who had always greeted me so kindly, enquired about my home and family whenever you found me lighting candles. I longed to kneel before you, confess what I had done. Have you hold my hand and guide me, soothe me with your counsel.

But I knew if I was to do or say anything it must be within the seal of the confessional. Before you, who had taken your own solemn vow: that you would never reveal what you heard there.

And so, having noted the confession times, one afternoon I found myself seated in the cool, near-empty church with only one other, a man, in the pews, waiting on you. Greatly nervous, I wrung my hands, breathing in the sweet scent of incense and candles, as I stared at the altar, trying to imbue its peace, but that peace could not touch me. My mind was in too much turmoil. I heard the echo of footsteps as a woman left the confessional, the waiting man entering. In that moment I wanted to run.

But I pressed my feet tightly upon the kneeling cushion, my back against the pew, forcing myself to stay.

At last, the rich burgundy curtain was drawn back and the man left the ornate mahogany box. I trembled as I stepped towards it, opening the half-door to the airless, dim enclosure. I knelt, resting my forehead against the wooden hatch, the smell of beeswax comforting me as I waited for it to open. Finally, I heard its slide and looked to see your face shadowed and in profile through the diamond lattice. As we both made the sign of the cross, I took a breath.

'Bless me, Father, for I have sinned. It has been many months since my last confession.'

You bowed your head graciously, your voice warm and kind. 'But you come now to lay down your transgressions before the Lord. Tell me, my daughter.'

Tell you. How could I tell you what I had done? That I had killed a child. That I had been so swollen with pride, I believed sickness not a thing that comes unbidden, part of that very nature I so revered, but almost as if something chosen, over which we had command. I realised now that it was not Dr Lydon who had been arrogant by trying to intervene in nature, outwit it with science, but me by believing myself master of it. By refusing to accept the fragility within nature – our own human nature. Strength we had, yes. But vulnerability, too. I had thought us – myself – all powerful.

My voice was barely a whisper. 'I have been guilty of the sin of pride.'

I watched you gently nod, waiting for me to go on.

'I have . . . I have hurt someone. I have hurt them badly.'

Again, you nodded. 'And is there a chance you might repair this hurt? That you might make amends?'

'I . . .' I felt such great hopelessness inside. 'No, Father,'

You were silent for a moment. 'And yet, in your heart you are truly sorry?'

'I am.' My throat tightened. 'So truly sorry.' Then came the tears. Like a hot spring from my heart, pouring, pouring from my eyes. I did not try to stem them but let them fall. Felt the blessed release of them.

I know you heard me weeping. You spoke softly. 'Then, my child, it seems you already atone through your sorrow. But for your act of penance I ask you to pray thirty days and thirty nights for those you have hurt. That their hurt might be healed. Are you ready to make your act of contrition?'

My heart, opened like a flower by tears, burst to tell you what I had done. But I could not. I had not the courage. Instead, I began to say the words I had known all my life, had learnt at the knee of my mother: 'My God, I am sorry for my sins with all my heart, for choosing to do wrong, and failing to do good . . .' Every word felt hollow on my tongue.

I heard you whisper the Prayer of Absolution: 'By Christ's power given me, I forgive and absolve you from all your sins, in the name of the Father and of the Son and of the Holy Ghost. Amen.'

I rose from my knees, stumbled from the dark of the confessional into the aisle of the church and sank down into a pew. I realised I was now supposed to be forgiven. Forgiven by a God to whom I had hardly given a thought. I had followed my mother's and family's religion all my life, but had never actually considered if I truly believed. I came to light candles in the church for my mother, aunts and uncles and in memory of Uncle Pat. For love of them, not love of God. I did not want God's forgiveness. It was no good to me. I wanted the forgiveness of Bernard and Ciss. Of Amy.

No, it was not God's forgiveness I had sought in that church, Father, but to confess myself to you. To take from you human comfort. To give to you my secret. I had hoped that if you carried it with me, you would make it less heavy. But I was not brave enough to reveal it.

And so it sat still like a cancer on my heart.

* * *

Father Sheridan gazed upon the fire. 'As she lay there on her sickbed, so fragile that night, and recounted to me that confession, I remembered it. For I'd been struck by her weeping and, of course, I knew it was her. But never could I have imagined what it was that she truly meant to confess.'

Brother Thomas lifted his eyes. 'If she had confessed it, what would you have done?'

Father Sheridan stared at the flames. 'Unless she had released me from it, I would have been bound by the seal of the confessional. I would have remained silent.'

Brother Thomas nodded. 'And if she had released you from it?'

'Then the Abbot would never have gone to jail.'

* * *

The knock came at the door only days after Amy died. When Aunt Ellen called me and I saw Dr Lydon in the hallway, I was gripped by dread.

'Good afternoon, Rosaleen,' he said. 'May I speak to you a moment?'

I nodded reluctantly, not taking him, as I would any visitor, to the parlour, but stood with him in the hallway, wishing to make this encounter short. My aunt was hovering curiously, but at my glance left us. I turned back to the doctor.

'Rosaleen,' he said. 'I have been trying to call on the Armstrongs for days, but their maid keeps insisting they are not there. I know Mrs Armstrong does not often venture out, so I find it very curious. I wanted to enquire about Amy's condition. Do you know anything of it?'

I was terrified he would notice the flush I could feel in my face and neck, the tremor in every limb. There could be nothing I feared more than this very question.

'I . . .' I faltered, then thought of what I should say. 'I believe the Armstrongs are planning to move to London. You know Bernard Armstrong came from there originally? It seems some business has called him back. Perhaps they are busy with arrangements.'

Dr Lydon looked at me quizzically.

'Going to London? For good? Well, this is all very sudden.' He paused. 'But what of Amy? How is the child, do you know?'

Such heat rushed through me, I was sure he could feel its burn. The words I spoke next tasted foul. 'I believe she is recovered.'

'Recovered? She is quite well now?' He frowned.

'Yes, I believe so.'

My stomach churned, sickened by the lie on my tongue.

'I see. Well, that is good,' he said uncertainly. 'It would seem I was wrong then. In my diagnosis.'

Mute, I nodded, unable to meet his eyes. I remained silent, desperate for him to leave.

'Well,' he said at last. 'If that is the case, then all is well. Thank you.'

He turned to go, but I had to ask.

'Doctor.' He turned back to me as I went on. 'You said you were unsure if Amy was suffering from diphtheria. How would you know for sure?'

He studied me before speaking. 'In the later stages white blemishes would appear on the back of the throat. Then we would know for sure it was diphtheria. But by then it can often be too late for treatment.'

I nodded again, looking down. I could sense his scrutiny. I wished I had said nothing but I'd had to know. At last, he turned to leave.

'Good day, then,' he said, and was gone.

I shut the door behind him, leaning my head against it. The white blemishes on the back of Amy's throat. Signs, I had thought in my ignorance, of tonsillitis. Now I knew it had been diphtheria for sure. And I had prevented any chance of help until it was too late.

33

Gus brought a summons from Mairéad the afternoon after Dr Lydon's visit. A request that we all meet that night in her parlour, stressing that Gerard should bring Conor, who none of us had seen. That night, with Conor once more amongst us, somehow my heart felt soothed. If I could not have the softness of my mother, I could at least take comfort in the sweetness of Conor. I went to sit by him, taking his hand in mine, only to find it trembling. I searched his eyes which were darting nervously. Even so, he tried to smile at me, as if to assure me he did not blame me for this horror. My heart broke for him. What anguish my deeds had brought him.

Bernard and Ciss, of course, were absent. Mairéad spoke gravely to the rest of us from her chair at the window. Bernard had called to her that morning. It seemed he had learned through Kitty of Dr Lydon's visit to me and what I had told the doctor of Amy.

'Whatever you told Dr Lydon clearly did not satisfy him,' Mairéad said to me. 'I think we are in trouble. He went to Bernard's after he saw you yesterday, asking questions of the maid. Asking her if Amy was in the house, if he might see her. The maid told him that she had not seen Amy in over a week, that she had been instructed to stay downstairs, so not to disturb the child while she was ill. And that now she had left, gone ahead to London while Bernard closes up the house. Dr Lydon is insisting he see Bernard, but Bernard is refusing. I am worried that the doctor will come here and question us. We must be completely as one and solid in our story: just that Amy is recovered and the family is moving. Are we agreed?'

Dismally, I nodded with the others, glancing beside me at Conor, who was staring blindly ahead.

'And for the present the meetings must stop,' Mairéad said. Noreen started to protest but Mairéad hushed her. 'No, Noreen, if the doctor calls here it is best he sees as few of us as possible. Less chance for each of us to be questioned. We must do this for now.'

I certainly did not regret that the meetings were to stop. I had no intention of ever attending a meeting again and wished them not only to stop for now but for ever. I withered as I thought of it: *the Spring*. My previous zeal, my belief, seemed now a lethal numbing of my senses. Not only my special sense, but every good sense. A blindness, deafness to reason. The ringing crystals, dancing lights a hysteria. I could not fathom how Mairéad or the others could think differently. Conor rose. I watched as he left the room. A silence fell.

'It is Conor is the danger,' Noreen said.

I went to look for Conor, finding him standing in the hallway, hugging himself against the wall.

'Conor, dear, Conor.' I reached up to cup his face. 'I am sorry, so sorry.'

His lip trembled as he spoke. 'It's not your fault. It was all of us. You were only trying to heal. Only trying to do good.'

'No, Conor.' I shook my head at his words. For I had not been simply driven by the desire to do good but had been basking in the raptures of others, been swollen by the hysteria and worship. All wanting to be touched by the Rose. 'I thought *only* I could heal. *Only* I could do good. I was so consumed by my own power I could not see what was before me. A gravely sick child. A dying child. And I made you a part of that. I am so sorry.'

He raised his hands. 'But what *I* did with these hands.' He looked at them as if they belonged to another. 'I carried her little body. I walked her into the dark, saw her laid on the mud. I cannot forget the sounds. The digging in of the spade, the scatter of the sod . . .'

He sobbed, starting to shake violently, and I reached for him, held him in my arms as he choked it over and over: '*I cannot forget.*'

* * *

The meetings had stopped but each day I went to Mairéad's. You may ask why, Father. I can only tell you that it was a need not to be alone with my thoughts but to be with others who knew the stain on my heart.

Those with whom I shared this bitter bond. And Mairéad was, as always, gentle, pleading with me not to blame myself.

I tried to let her lies soothe me, even though it was clear Gus blamed no one but me. But I was bemused by her response to the tragedy. Although I could tell she was greatly shaken by it, that she felt the greatest need to protect Ciss, she did not seem to waver in her core beliefs. Nor did Noreen, who was also a constant visitor. In Noreen I sensed no true sorrow for Ciss and Bernard and little mourning for Amy; more a quiet glee at my downfall and vexation at our abandoned meetings. There were those who still called to the house, enquiring about healings, but Gus or Mairéad sent them away. Mairéad told the Fitzpatricks and our closer crowd that the Rose was resting, taking time to replenish her powers. Thankfully, they accepted this, seeming to believe that, indeed, one as in demand as the Rose would need time alone to reflect and restore.

I was on my own with Mairéad in her parlour when the day we feared came: when Dr Lydon called. Rising at the sound of the knocker, Mairéad returned with him, her face set. She was well prepared for this visit. I hoped I was also.

As he entered the parlour, Dr Lydon nodded a terse greeting to me. 'Rosaleen.' Mairéad bid him sit, which he did.

'Well, Dr Lydon, how can we help you?' Mairéad said, sitting herself.

I gauged him in no humour for pleasantries as he spoke quickly. 'I am calling about the Armstrongs. As you must know, tomorrow they are bound for London. It is a very sudden move and I can find no one else on the street who knew of it. However, what concerns me more is the whereabouts of Amy. I have been informed by their maid that the child has gone ahead to London. Do you know this to be the case?'

'Yes, indeed.' Mairéad's tone was even. 'Mr Armstrong has told me that Amy is already with her cousins in London.'

Dr Lydon shifted to the edge of his seat. 'But why on earth would they send the child ahead? She is so young. Why not simply travel with her? I don't understand it.'

He looked at each of us in turn. A nerve was trembling in my jaw, I was sure he would see it. Luckily, Mairéad spoke.

'I don't know. Perhaps they felt with all the upheaval of the move, the closing up of the house, that Amy would be unsettled. That she would be better with her cousins for a very short time.'

Dr Lydon looked doubtful. 'So, the child was well enough to make the long journey to London. Yet the last time I saw her, little more than a week ago, she was weak and sickly. So much so I suspected a serious illness. And now it seems she is miraculously recovered.'

'But you yourself said you could not be certain what ailed her. It seems it must not have been so serious,' Mairéad said.

Dr Lydon turned to me. 'And yet, Rosaleen, you asked me what would make me sure of what I suspected. Diphtheria. Why did you ask me that?'

I shrank under his stare. Mairéad did not know I had asked him this question, and I felt her eyes on me also. I had to think. Think quickly.

'I was simply interested,' I said. 'When Amy recovered I was curious to know what symptoms she might have had if it had been diphtheria. That's all.' It sounded feeble to my ears, but I could think of nothing better.

Dr Lydon looked between me and Mairéad. Then rose.

'If that is what you say, I must accept it,' he said. 'If the Armstrongs insist that the child has gone ahead safely to England, I cannot challenge them. But you should know that I will do my best to put a stop to your practices. I will warn everyone that this is a house not of miracles, but menace. That in the guise of healers you do the greatest harm.'

34

The Armstrongs were gone. Every day I would pass their empty, shuttered house, and that emptiness would feed my desolation. My aunt was no help. 'I see the Armstrongs have moved,' she said to me. 'Just up and away without a word to anyone, it seems. I didn't know them well but there's a lot of talk about it on the street. Do you know why they left?'

As she spoke I stayed busy with my chores. Mindless tasks that distracted me. 'Business,' I replied listlessly. 'Bernard Armstrong had business that called him away. That's all I know.'

I found my thoughts those days often returning to Lorcan. Sometimes I longed to see him. I knew I could simply call on him at the Roto, but much of what I yearned was to lay down my burden and confide in him. I knew that was impossible. Just as I knew that I would not be able to pretend with Lorcan, even if I wished it. That, as with my mother, those eyes would search mine and find what was hiding there. But mostly it was Conor who occupied my thoughts. My great worry for him. I was desperate to ease his torment and somehow lessen his grief. Lessen my own.

I was revisited those days too by the shadows. I saw them everywhere, fall on every shoulder. Plagued by them, I could not tell if they were portents of further catastrophe or simply the shadow of my own grief. It was only through my need to share that grief with Conor that I would even remember Rían. Through that time of great sorrow he did not occupy my mind at all.

* * *

Rían's mind, though, was greatly occupied with her. Occupied both with her and his brother. Since that night of horror at the monastery, Conor had spent endless hours in his room, not attending college but feigning some vague illness, taking his food on trays to satisfy his mother.

Rían knew how Conor must suffer over that abominable night, for he suffered just the same. He, too, longed to feign illness, hide from the world but, as he was employed by his father, it was impossible. He would sit in their Rathmines office, staring at his hands. In those first awful days after, the skin between his thumb and forefinger had been chafed from the wooden handle of the spade. The tender rawness of it would make him retch. It had healed now, but his mind was still under attack. The dark images only becoming more frequent, more invasive, he tried to think on the reasons he had carried out such an act. He had needed to get it clear in his mind.

In the week after the horror he had sought out his old law professor at University College. Professor MacGrath had been in the lecture hall, arranging heavy legal tomes upon the desk before the blackboard as Rían approached.

'Rían!' The professor had turned, clearly shocked but pleased to see him. 'What brings you here? Is the lure of my astounding wit and wisdom too strong?'

Rían had assured him that indeed that was so, and the two had settled on the row of seats before the desk. Rían had carefully rehearsed his piece. He told his former tutor that, passing the college, he'd had a hankering to walk its corridors again. And now here, he would like to take advantage of the professor's vast knowledge. He informed him that he was presently mentoring a young university graduate working at his father's practice. The boy hoped to join King's Inns and become a barrister, so to enhance his knowledge, Rían had been concocting legal scenarios for him. He laid out one such scenario and its cast of characters for the professor now and asked of him his questions.

'A faith healing? Faith in what?' Professor MacGrath said. 'No matter. It's all the same. Faith in some super-natural entity or other. So, you want to know who would be charged and with what. I suppose it could be argued that they were all so deluded that none amongst them was fit to stand trial. But, seriously – in your scenario the child dies. Is that correct?'

Rían's gut wrenched. He nodded.

'Well, you're surely thinking of the cases surrounding the Peculiar People, are you not?' He looked surprised as Rían, nonplussed, shook his head. 'The Peculiar People,' Professor MacGrath went on, 'a puritanical religious sect in Essex, England, founded sixty or seventy years ago, still active. They call themselves the Peculiar People after some line in the Bible, stating that God's chosen will be a peculiar people.' He laughed. 'That's for sure. They don't believe in science or medicine, think prayer and God's power is all that's required in healing. Is this the kind of thing you're talking about?'

'Similar,' Rían said.

The professor's words conjured up a vague memory of a newspaper article Rían had once read on this strange clan. One he'd paid very little mind to at the time.

The Professor went on. 'Well, it was this sect refusing medical treatment for their children, and some children's subsequent deaths, that brought about a change in the law about forty years ago. Made it illegal for parents to wilfully withhold medical treatment for a child. And there have been several successful prosecutions of parents within the sect for manslaughter since. In fact, I think there have been more convictions in the last year or so.'

Rían's stomach churned. He tried to settle it in his mind. 'So, in my scenario the parents of the child would be charged with manslaughter?'

'Almost definitely,' said Professor MacGrath.

Rían hesitated before asking his next question. 'And the others?'

'Well, in your scenario you have a leader who seems to be persuading the parents not to take the doctor's advice. And overseeing the so-called healing over many days while watching the child failing.' Professor MacGrath paused. 'In my view, this person would be seen to be acting recklessly in law and could well be open to a charge of involuntary manslaughter. With the others, the bystanders, so to speak, it's less clear. They certainly should have been able to foresee what the consequences of their actions or inaction might be, indeed you say they were aware of a warning by the doctor, so perhaps a case could be made, again, for involuntary manslaughter. But it's far from certain. It would really depend on whether the authorities thought they could make a case for each individual and how much they wanted to make an example of this "healer" and his or her cohorts. It's certainly an interesting case for your student to research and consider.'

Rían had smiled and thanked the professor but left the classroom with a heavy heart. He'd tried to absorb the information. Only one thing was certain: had they not concealed what had occurred that night, the Armstrongs would have faced a charge of manslaughter. And Rosaleen. She could well have been open to that charge. Charged or not, her ruination would be assured. But Conor. The professor's ambiguous opinion regarding his and the others' liability only played into his own doubt that with Conor, so young, the authorities would have pursued a charge. A wave of remorse came over him. He should have persuaded Conor to go to the police that night. They almost certainly would have treated him leniently. But Rosaleen. *Rosaleen.* He had needed to act for her. He had not needed to ask the professor what his own culpability was: he was all too aware. By not reporting the death he had made himself an accessory – an accessory after the fact to the crime he now knew to be manslaughter. And he himself was guilty of concealing the body. The unlawful burial of the child.

He tried to comfort himself. He had learned through Conor that the Armstrongs were gone, and with them, it seemed, all talk of the child. So they were gone and it was done. And she, Rosaleen, was saved. Except it was not done, not in his own mind. Nor his brother's.

And their mother was growing concerned for Conor. After yet another evening of trying to coax Conor from his room, she had stopped Rían on the stairs.

'What on earth is wrong with Conor?' She'd taken his arm. 'If this continues I will have to fetch a doctor.'

'No.' Rían's voice had been firm. He'd prepared for this inevitable questioning. 'It's a girl, Mamma,' he'd whispered. 'Some girl or other who has spurned him. He's heartsick. That's all.'

'A girl?' His mother had released his arm. 'Conor?' She'd looked surprised, somewhat pleased at the notion of her son being amorous. But quickly her eyes grew pained. 'The poor soul. I must talk to him.'

'No, don't, Mamma,' he'd said hastily. 'Let him keep his pride, at least. He has me to confide in.'

She'd nodded, let it be. She'd insisted though, from then on, that Conor come from his room to eat. Those mealtimes were torturous, he and Conor sitting opposite one another, avoiding one another's eyes, both so full with their secret they had little appetite for food. All this under the watchful gaze of their mother, a barrage of banter from their father. Conor would escape to his room afterwards while Rían sat and chatted with his parents, trying to maintain some show of normality. But it was hard. So hard.

Sometimes he would go to Conor and sit beside him as he lay on the bed. He would place his hand over his brother's.

'You didn't kill her,' he'd whisper but Conor would only moan and turn to face the wall, unable to hear any mention of Amy.

Unbearable, the sounding of it. Unbearable, the silence of it.

And through all of this he thought of Rosaleen. He wondered how she was bearing it. If she needed a friend to talk to. If she needed *him*. He thought too that Rosaleen might bring comfort to his brother. Perhaps by sharing in his sorrow she could soothe his soul. He told himself that it was principally for Conor that he must go to see her.

35

It was due to my worry over his brother that my heart leapt at the sight of Rían on the doorstep. The relief that I might hear something now of Conor was tainted, though, by fear. I had allowed myself to be close only to those who knew and shared my agony. I dreaded having to face Rían, having to pretend, for I could not know if Conor had confided in him. But, quickly, I settled it in my mind. I would be able to keep up my guard with Rían. He could not reach me in the way Lorcan would.

I hurried him in from the cold and sat with him at the parlour table. He had brought in the chill from the February day, and his face was nipped red. He seemed not as nervous around me, as if he had something he wanted and was ready to say. If it was news of Conor, I was eager to hear it.

'Well?' I said. 'How are you? Tell me. And tell me also, how is Conor?'

He looked at me, curiously, as if he were surprised by something in my voice. My manner. Then, slowly, he spoke.

'Conor is . . .'

He did not finish his sentence. His hesitancy concerned me, and I reached across the table for his hand.

'Is Conor all right?'

Again, he seemed puzzled but then his face cleared as if in some kind of understanding. He touched my hand lying over his.

'Rosaleen,' he said softly. 'I *know*.'

It was as if I'd been struck. My breath grew short, my chest tight. So Conor *had* told him. Of course. Of course. How could Conor possibly have borne this alone? Understanding now Rían's surprise at my casual manner, I dropped all pretence. I withdrew my hand.

'You know,' I said slowly, then paused. 'Who else . . .?'

'No one,' he assured me, quickly. 'Just Conor and I.'

I looked away with a swell of shame and sorrow, digging my fingernails into my palms.

'Please,' he said, reaching for my hand. 'Please do not feel ashamed before me. I could never think badly of you.' He hesitated a moment, looking towards the door. He lowered his voice. 'Do you feel able to tell me anything of what happened at the healing that night? Conor will not speak of it.'

'No.' I slid my fingers from his, placed my hands in my lap. 'I cannot talk of it. Just thinking of it is torment enough.' I looked up at him. 'Conor is the same?'

He nodded. 'He hardly leaves his room. I've tried many times to coax him out, to talk to him, but he's deaf to me, he just lies there in silence. That is why I have come, to ask if you will visit him. I think that he might speak to you. That you might be able to help him.'

I felt a tremor. I wanted to see Conor so much. Not only for his sake but for mine. I needed to share my burden with him. But the thought of those looming Tallaght Hills. The monastery, now menacing to me. The *bell tower*. I was not sure I could bear be near them.

'He will not come here? To me?' I asked.

He shook his head. 'I think not. He will not go anywhere.'

Thinking for a moment, I drew myself up. It was I who had inflicted this torture on Conor. Now I must be strong for him.

'Then I will come.'

*   *   *

Rían had left Eccles Street, heartened by their encounter. She knew now he was privy to her secret. Knew too that he intended to guard it and was her willing confidant. He had wanted to tell her he was so much more. Tell her what atrocity, for her sake, he had committed. But this was not the time. Her emotions were too raw, her mind too fragile. The day would come when he would tell her. For now, what he had seen in her eyes that afternoon was enough. A yearning, almost a pleading for someone. He would fulfil that need.

*   *   *

Next evening, beside Rían in the hansom cab, beneath the dull February sky, I watched the city fade away, the dim, blue mountains drawing closer. I shivered, knowing each roll of the wheel brought me closer to the monastery. Finally, up ahead, I spotted the lanterns at its gates, quickly turning my face from the window. Rían reached to touch my gloved hands on my lap. He understood.

Conor was expecting me. He was sitting, waiting for our arrival, on a chair in the hallway as I followed Rían through the arch of the front door. When Conor saw me, he leapt up.

'Rosaleen!' He rushed to me, throwing his arms around me. I held him tightly.

'Conor, dear, Conor.' I stepped back, gripping his shoulders to study his face. It was pale, shadows under his eyes. He had always been slight but now he seemed unbearably thin. 'How are you, my dearest?' I whispered. 'I must know.'

At my words, his eyes welled with tears and I embraced him again.

'Come into the drawing room.' Rían spoke behind us. 'Our parents are in town so we'll have privacy.'

Holding Conor's arm, I followed Rían into the drawing room, immediately recalling our tea there with Amy, how afterwards we three had taken her to walk in the monastery woodland. Had taken her to the bell tower. I felt wretched, my heart punched, but for Conor's sake I could not let it fell me. I sat beside him on the couch, Rían settling on a chair opposite.

'Conor.' I held both his hands in mine and searched his eyes. 'Rían tells me you are not sleeping properly and that he hears you wandering all hours of the night. That you are staying in your room and eating hardly enough. He tells me you will not talk. But you will talk to me now. You must.'

Conor's eyes cast down, his hands clutched mine. 'It's so hard. So *hard*. It's like I am a prisoner of that night. I can see nothing else. I might be walking into the hall or the garden, and I don't see the grass, the hedgerows, nothing before me, only . . .'

Only Amy. My mind finished the sentence for him. *Only Amy choking. Only Amy dying.* And one other vision he must bear that I did not. Amy buried. That child, that sweet child so full of light and life, silent now, beneath the sod. Where *I* had put her.

'I know.' I stroked his face. 'I see her too. Everywhere I look.'

He buried his head in my shoulder, and, holding him, I could feel his sobs through his ribs. 'But it was not you that harmed her,' I whispered to him. 'You were only doing my bidding. It was all my doing.'

'It doesn't feel that way to me,' he sobbed.

I looked over at Rían, his eyes so greatly pained at his brother's grief. I turned back to Conor, lifting his face.

'I will help you, Conor,' I said to him intently. '*We* will help you. Rían and I. We will help each other.'

I stayed with him some hours. Later, he seemed calmer for having talked and I left with a hope that he had found solace in unburdening himself to me. As I made my way to the courtyard, to the hansom cab Rían had summoned, I met his parents in the hall, just returned from their evening at the opera. His mother, removing her fur, recognised me from our previous encounter and greeted me warmly, but looked at me, I thought, curiously.

Conor had returned to his room, and Rían insisted on escorting me home in the cab. As the carriage passed by the monastery, I could not help but glance up and, emotion overwhelming me, let out a sob. Rían reached for me. I looked at him, then allowed myself to bury my head in his shoulder. And I cried.

*   *   *

That evening, before Rian had climbed into the cab with Rosaleen, his mother had stopped him in the doorway.

'Is that the girl?' she'd whispered to him. 'The girl that has my son lovestruck?'

He'd shaken his head, assured her no, but made silent whisper. *Yes, that is the girl. The girl that has your son lovestruck.*

*   *   *

That spring I spent much time with Rían and Conor. Rían had managed to persuade his parents that it was best if Conor withdrew for some months from college.

They were concerned, of course, but Rían assured them that Conor would return rested after the summer. Even though he was relieved by this, it remained hard to coax Conor outside, but as the weather grew warmer, the flowers coming into bloom, we enticed him into the garden, then further, to walk with us through the nearby fields.

Always looking for signs, I was certain he was growing more robust. I seemed to be on a mission to heal him. Not now through any immaculate mystical spring, but simply through the warmth of my imperfect human touch. My hand holding his. This helped me also, giving me purpose as I tried to make amends to this gentle soul I felt I had damaged. I could not undo the wrongs I had done Amy and the Armstrongs, but I was desperate to make reparation where I could.

Sometimes, as we wandered uphill to the meadows, we could see the monastery up ahead and we would fall silent, walking on, only resting when it was no longer in sight. One warm day we were sitting in the long grass, picking at daisies and wildflowers when Conor spoke.

'These are all the spring flowers she will never see.'

I sat rigid. Glancing at Rían, I was about to say something when Conor spoke again.

'I want to go to her. I want to bring her flowers. I don't want her lying there untended and alone. I want to mark her resting place, adorn it with beauty. And love.'

I locked eyes with Rían, then touched Conor's hand.

'You know we can make no mark there, Conor.'

His eyes were impassioned. 'But we can lay flowers nearby. Or scatter them. That would be enough.'

I searched his face. 'Is that what you want? That will bring you some peace?'

He nodded. My stomach gripped at the thought of going near the monastery, like a spectre in my mind. I could tell Rían felt the same. But I pressed Conor's hand.

'Then we will do it,' I said.

We gathered meadow flowers that day as we walked downhill, through the wild grass. My every step was sluggish, not only due to the balmy day, and it was clear that Rían, beside me, was just as reluctant to carry out this act. But Conor strode on ahead, almost buoyant, seeming galvanised by the prospect of paying tribute to Amy.

I was greatly nervous as we approached the monastery gates. Afraid we might be spotted by the Abbot, I wanted to climb the wall steps to the woodland, but Conor could not countenance climbing those steps again, as he had that dreadful night. Mercifully, though, we were undisturbed as we entered the gates and took the woodland path. Over scrub and brush, Conor led the way, Rían taking my hand to help me over the bridge where, just by the brook, we saw bluebells. We stopped to pick some, adding them to our posy. I did not want to look up at what I knew stood ahead: the bell tower.

When I finally lifted my eyes I was repelled by the sight of it. Looming over us, casting its shadow over the dried mud and fern. Conor had stopped. He stood staring at the tower. I looked at Rían; his eyes were fixed on the ground.

It seemed we stood there an age. At last, I went to Conor, touching his arm softly, gesturing to the flowers. It roused him from his trance and he took them, walking towards the tower. I had no wish to follow him, no wish to know precisely where she lay. I looked away but was aware when he came to stop just beside the bell tower, near the trees. I felt a cold white horror. But for Conor's sake, I made myself go to stand beside him. Conor knelt, laying the posy gently near some stray ferns before him. He whispered.

'We have brought you spring flowers, Amy. Bright as your smile.'

I could hardly bear to listen. Hardly bear to look at the pitiful posy on the barren ground.

'Scatter them.'

Rían's voice came from behind us, hoarse. 'Scatter them,' he repeated. 'So they don't look laid. They will still surround her.'

Conor picked up the posy and stood. He kissed the flowers, then in gentle sweeps, scattered them. He was silent a moment, looking down upon the red petals of one blowing gently in the breeze. Then he whispered, 'The next time we will bring you just one flower. The flower that is most sacred. Most beautiful.' He looked at me and smiled. 'The mystic Rose.'

It was from that day, Father, that Conor would pluck a single rose from his mother's garden and together we would walk with it to the woodland. There, Rían and I would stand while, before the bell tower, Conor knelt, and laid down the rose.

* * *

Rían would think on it, those days, as he watched his brother kneel: the mystic rose. Symbol of the Madonna, queen of heaven and earth, the rosary her devotion.

He would think too of the Graeco-Roman mysteries: of Eros gifting the rose to Harpocrates, the god of silence, so he would ever after keep the secrets of Aphrodite. Born from that myth the rose became a symbol of secrecy, engraved upon the ceilings of council chambers: *sub rosa*, under the rose. Binding all never to reveal what was talked of beneath the rose. Engraved too on the confessionals as a pledge that all told within would remain unspoken. He too would keep the secret of the Rose. Hold it for her in his heart. And make to her a pledge:

Never to be spoken of. Never to be revealed.

What lay beneath the rose.

36

The laying of those roses haunted me. I could not fathom why Conor would choose to pay homage to Amy with the very flower that had once been used to pay homage to me. I believed that lauded creature a foolish and dangerous creation that belonged to a naive past. No longer did I see myself as the Rose, touched by the Graces. I could not understand why Conor did not blame me as I blamed myself. That he had forgiven me only somehow deepened my wound. But the rose seemed to bring him comfort. As if by laying it, it brought us closer to Amy, our secret sign to her that we who had loved her were near.

Just as I no longer wished to be called the Rose, neither did I want dealings with anyone other than Conor who knew me as such. Since starting to visit him and Rían, I had stopped visiting Mairéad. I wanted nothing more to do with her or the mesmerists.

I knew Mairéad was still close to Noreen, that they were holding meetings again, with visitors to the house. I knew this, for one summer afternoon they called on me. As I admitted them, sitting rigid with them at my aunt's parlour table, they told me of their gatherings now. They said the meetings were once again hosted by Mairéad but their inner circle now comprised only Noreen and Gus. The rest of us had gone: Gerard, apparently, was also keeping his distance. This did not surprise me as, although his neighbour, Gerard had become a stranger to Conor too. Through those many months he had never once called on Conor to see how he fared.

Mairéad and Noreen entreated me to join them once more.

Mairéad reached across the table for my hand as I stiffened. 'Will you not come back to us?' she said softly. 'For now, we are telling our guests that you are taking time to reflect. But they are all asking when you will return.' Her eyes were doleful. 'We miss you.'

I stared at her, staggered that she thought I might return after all that had happened. I studied Noreen. The tragedy had hardly seemed to affect her at all. Her dogged belief had made her body a fortress, one that could fend off any arrows poisoned with bitter reality. I could tell she was tetchy beneath her smile – her dislike for me had not dimmed, but neither had her zeal. And that zeal drove her desire to have their celebrated Rose walk amongst them once more. Although I despised her for it, Noreen's resolve did not surprise me. But that Mairéad would wish to carry on with this reckless and lethal quackery astounded me. I wondered how she could justify it in her mind. I could only suppose that Noreen was ever in her ear, dispelling any doubts, persuading her to stay true to her faith.

I snatched my hand from Mairéad's. 'I will never return. I will never lay these hands upon anyone again. And if you have any conscience – if you have any wits at all – you will stop too.'

Mairéad looked desolate, but Noreen's eyes sparked with malice. Mairéad made some sorry attempt to cajole me but when it was clear I would not waver, they stood. I did not rise to see them out, and, at the parlour door, Noreen turned back to me.

'How is Conor?' she asked.

I was vexed at this. I knew she had no interest in his well-being. That she simply wanted to be assured of his state of mind, certain of his silence. I made some curt reply, watching with relief as they left. Whenever I stepped on to Eccles Street, I dreaded seeing them just as I dreaded seeing Dr Lydon.

Those times I did see him, I would lower my eyes under my hat and cross the road as if unaware of him. On the occasions he called to my aunt's I busied myself elsewhere in the house. But my guilt felt his cold eyes seeking me out wherever I might hide.

I only wanted to be with Conor. And Rían. For Rían, too, brought me comfort. Often, when he and I were alone, on his mother's garden seat, in the warmth of the sun, there, amongst the heady scent of flowers, I would find myself confiding in him what I would not in Conor, not wanting to add to Conor's burden. Never would I talk of the sights that haunted me. Amy's stricken face. Never the sounds. The choking. The *strangling*. Never could I talk of them. But I revealed whatever I was able. He would sit close by me on the seat, listening intently.

'Through my arrogance – my ignorance – I brought suffering, such great suffering to that dear sweet child,' I said one afternoon, letting his hand lie across mine in my lap. 'That she died is the greatest crime. But that she suffered so under my hand – that is so hard to bear. I can never forgive myself for it.'

'But you must try.' His voice was gentle. 'To hurt her was not your intention. Your actions – although you say they were ignorant – were pure. Your aim only to help. To heal. That is what you must think on.'

I appreciated his kindness. But no matter how he tried to banish my torment with tenderness, still it sat heavy over my heart. To have such a friend, though, one I could unburden myself to, meant much to me. Even through my despair, the shadows I constantly saw everywhere, my sense was strong enough to know that he continued to harbour a special affection for me. But I was sure he had it settled now in his mind that we were friends. True friends.

* * *

It was on one summer's afternoon that we next encountered the Abbot. On that afternoon Rían and I stood at the bell tower, watching Conor kneel to lay the rose. Since he had begun carrying out this tribute to Amy, Conor seemed lighter. As if the act rendered her resting place more beautiful, honoured and made sacred her memory. Conor had just risen when I heard footsteps on the bridge. We all turned to see the Abbot.

My stomach twisted with fear. I glanced at the rose upon the ground, then up at the Abbot. On each visit we removed the withered rose, replacing it with a fresh bloom so only ever one rose lay there. It was simply a rose. But the Abbot would surely wonder at it. He had almost certainly seen them before and now he witnessed us gathered near.

'Well, good afternoon.' The Abbot's tone was cordial. 'What a pleasant surprise to find you here. I have not seen you, Conor, Rían, in so long. How are you? And . . .' He looked at me as if trying to place me.

'Rosaleen,' I said. My mouth was dry.

'Rosaleen, of course, how could I not remember? You must forgive the memory of an old man.' He smiled around at us. 'It is so good to see you again. But, alas, not my little girl. Little Amy.'

My heart gripped. I looked quickly at Conor, who was staring as if he'd been struck. I felt Rían stiffen beside me.

'My little girl has been taken from me,' the Abbot went on. 'Gone to London, so Gerard Mallon tells me. I will be very sorry not to see her here any more. She brought me great joy.'

My legs threatened to buckle. Rían lightly touched my hand, I knew to assure and steady me, then stepped nearer the Abbot.

'Indeed,' he said to him. 'She is a great loss to us all. I'm afraid you'll have to make do with our slightly less vivacious company, Father Abbot.' He smiled.

I stared at Rían, unable to fathom his composure. He stood as a barrier between myself and Conor and the Abbot. He had placed himself there to protect us. I felt a rush of gratitude and shame.

'Perhaps less vivacious, but no less charming,' the Abbot said. His eye wandered to the ground. To the rose. I stiffened.

'The roses.' The Abbot looked up at us again. 'Is it you that is bringing them? I have often seen them there and wondered.'

I was terrified my legs would not hold me. Terrified, too, what this onslaught might cause Conor to say or do. I tried to meet his eyes to strengthen him but he was staring blindly ahead.

Again, Rían spoke. 'Yes. Rosaleen likes to bring them here. In memory of a much-cherished aunt in Clare who has sadly passed away. Her aunt had a great devotion to St Benedict, so it seems fitting to lay them here.'

Rían turned to hold my eyes. Dumbfounded, I nodded.

'Yes.' My throat was tight. 'I hope you don't mind, Father Abbot?'

'Oh my goodness, no, not at all, not at all.' The Abbot smiled. 'I not only do not mind, but welcome it. You are only adding to the bell tower's beauty. Long may you lay your roses here.'

The Abbot was gone. We were silent as we walked back. Treading over the bridge and brush I was still unsteady and Rían, aware of it, took my arm. Conor was deathly pale. I offered him my hand but he appeared too dazed to understand my gesture. Once home, Conor did not want to talk, but went immediately to his room. Rían and I sat on his mother's seat in the garden.

I turned to him. 'How did you do it? How did you think of what to say to the Abbot?'

'I've long thought on it,' he said quietly. 'What I might say if we were seen.'

'But how did you remain so calm? I couldn't speak.'

His eyes were cast down. 'I did what I must,' he said.

* * *

Conor was badly shaken by that encounter with the Abbot. From that day, any lightness Rían and I had witnessed in him disappeared and he withdrew once more to his room. Over the next weeks, we tried to coax him back into the garden, to the meadows, but all in vain. He no longer wanted to lay down the roses. It seemed we had tainted them with our lie. Had robbed them of their sanctity, their beauty.

At last, the summer dying, we persuaded him to walk with us one last time through the wild flowers in the meadow and sit for a while under the sun. As we sat, Conor picked at the long grass, his mood dark, presence heavy while I exchanged glances with Rían.

Finally, Conor lifted his eyes to speak.

'I want to confess.'

37

Only bird song broke the silence. Rían turned to stare at me, I at him.

At last, Rían spoke. 'What are you saying?' He stared at Conor. 'You can't mean it, Conor.'

'I do mean it.' Conor would not meet Rían's eyes. 'I can't bear it any longer. The guilt, the horror of it is eating me up inside.'

I looked to Rían, then to Conor. I reached for Conor's hand. 'But you know what will happen if you do,' I said to Conor desperately. Still he would not raise his eyes. 'Conor, you must think,' I went on. 'Think what would become of you. Of the Armstrongs. Of me and the others.' I hoped mention of consequences to others would sway him. 'And Rían. He knew what we did but did not report it. He would be in trouble too.'

Conor shook his head. 'I have thought it all through. I will go to the police and tell them it was I and I alone who carried it out. I who persuaded the Armstrongs to let me heal Amy. When it was done it was I who took her from their house and buried her here close to home. I will bring none of you into it.'

Rían gave a scornful laugh and Conor looked up. 'And how exactly did you carry the child from the Armstrongs' to here?' Rían said. 'On a magic carpet? You neither had nor can drive a car. And the Armstrongs would be implicated anyway for they would have had to have known their child had died and had been taken to be secretly buried. Your story makes no sense at all.'

Conor looked dazed, his mind so obviously fuddled. His eyes darted rapidly between us. 'Then I will say I attempted to heal her at our house. That I buried her nearby at the monastery without the Armstrongs' knowledge.'

My hand still on his arm, I gripped it. 'Conor, sweetheart, you must know that is impossible. Even if you had brought the child here to heal her, the Armstrongs would have to have known of it. They would know their child had died. That she had to be buried somewhere. Rían is right. It makes no sense,' I said gently, stroking his arm.

'Besides,' Rían said. 'Even if your story had any merit, if you brought our parents' home into such a sordid story it would be the ruin of them. Our father's career finished. That would probably be the case whatever tale you tell. The stain on them too great. You could not wish that upon them.'

Conor shut his eyes, dug his knuckles into his temples, so deeply confused.

'But I must tell.' He was mumbling, almost to himself. 'I *must*. I cannot stand it.' He let out a sob, a great choking sob. Distraught, Rían and I looked at one another. Rían leant to touch Conor's shoulder.

'Come,' he said softly to Conor. 'We'll go home now. We'll talk more of it there.'

My mind was in turmoil as I left them that day. As the tram rattled away from the hills, I stared blindly from the window. I was overwhelmed by emotion. Anguish over what I could hardly bear to name: the end I had brought to Amy; the agony I had caused the Armstrongs. I despaired over the pain I had caused Conor. But I was aware of another emotion. One rising in the pit of my stomach. One I had denied before. Fear. Yes, fear too.

Fear for myself.

* * *

Rían had counselled his brother long into the night. They had sat in Conor's room and he had held Conor's shoulders as the boy sobbed. Gently, Rían had tried to persuade him. Asked him to consider every implication of his confession. He had told Conor that he did not ask through concern for himself but for their family. The consequences for the Armstrongs. Conor's friends. And Rosaleen.

'It is she, Conor,' he said. 'She the world might hold most guilty.'

He asked him to think on all of this. As he'd left him in his room that night, he'd looked back on him, curled like a child on the bed. Sure he would sleep now, he felt satisfied that his brother had listened. Had heard. And understood.

That he must never tell.

* * *

That autumn day. It has stayed for ever etched on my mind. The minutiae of it before I knew. Those trivialities hold a fascination for me. The world as it was *before*. The breakfast of grapefruit and boiled egg I took with my aunt and uncle in the parlour. The ray of sun that shone into the hallway through the stained-glass arch above the front door. My aunt hurrying Uncle Noel out to the post office. All those moments before the note came.

I heard the door's brass knocker as I was going upstairs to fetch a cardigan for the chill. When Mary called to me I went back the few steps to take the note from her. I unfolded it curiously for it had come with a messenger and not in the morning post. I read it:

Please come. Come now.
Rían.

I could not fathom it. The brevity. The urgency. And then, with a bolt, I understood. Conor. This was it. He was going to expose us. He was going to confess. Those past two weeks, Rían had tried to allay my fear, assure me that Conor had come to understand and accept that he must remain silent. That the danger had passed. But now came this summons.

Swiftly I took my hat and coat from the coat stand, shouting to my aunt that I was leaving, not waiting for her reply. On the street I dithered over whether to hail a passing hansom cab or walk for the tram. Deciding it would save time I hailed a cab. As it rolled through the city, on to the hills, I willed that it move both quicker and slower. Quicker in case I could stop Conor. Slower, for I was loath to confront him.

The cab leaving me at the O'Lochlainns' gate, I hurried on to the tree-lined avenue, spying the rise of the house up ahead. I drew closer, then stopped. Stopped suddenly. For I was struck by a feeling. A sense as great as any I had ever had. Although nothing looked out of place I felt dread. The house seemed to wear a pall, its windows as if they were eyes cast down, the walls shoulders hunched. I felt my blood drain. For I knew then that I was too late. Rían had not been able to stop Conor. Conor had told all.

I dragged my feet on, pushing against the force driving me back, for I knew if I entered that house all would be over. I would learn my fate. I thought of running back down the leafy avenue, back to the city. But I made myself go on.

As I approached the pillars and steps I saw something peculiar: the front door slightly open as if someone had forgotten to close it. Gently, I pushed it and peered into the grand hallway. It was silent but I could hear murmurings coming from the direction of the drawing room. I called out softly to announce myself, but, no one coming, I stepped towards the drawing-room door, which was ajar.

Looking through the gap in the door, I could see Rían and Conor's father standing at the unlit fireplace. At Rían's face I drew back. It was ghastly grey and stricken, his father's the same, his mother sitting bent over on the couch, her head bowed. Looking for Conor, I searched further into the room and then saw them. Two men. I saw the helmets in their hands. Two policemen. Oh, God. Two policemen. So, truly it was done. I had been called to give account of my actions. But why would Rían summon me without warning me of it? I stood there, unsure what to do, but Rían must have sensed something. His eyes met mine at the doorway. He rushed from the fireplace, flinging open the door and into the hall.

'Oh, Rosaleen.' He gripped my shoulders, his eyes red-rimmed and wild. 'Rosaleen.' He sobbed, burying his face in my shoulder as, bewildered, I held him.

'What is it? What is it, Rían?' I pleaded.

'Conor.' His voice was a whisper. 'Conor.'

* * *

They had cut him down that morning. The police had sawn through the rope. Rían told me the alarm had been raised when his mother had gone to Conor's room to find him not there. But on his washstand was a note. She had unfolded it, read it, standing there a moment, unable to absorb its meaning. Then had dashed for the stairs, screaming over the banisters for her husband.

Rían's father had hurried to meet her at the foot of the stairs, Rían coming, at the noise, from the dining room. She had thrust the note into her husband's hand. He had clutched the banister as he read it, Rían snatching the note from him. He had read only a few words when he felt the bile stir in his stomach. Dropping the note, he'd sped to the front door, not waiting for his parents. He'd heard their shouts behind him, their footsteps chasing him as he raced towards the monastery.

'Where is it? Where is it?' His mother had been screeching, as they trampled over the brush and gnarled wood, Rían not replying, just stumbling on through the woodland.

At last, they stopped. Rían stood as if struck, hearing his father's breath in his ear before it turned into an unworldly moan. His own body was paralysed. His blood frozen. His mother's screams were making his sickened stomach retch.

'Take her away from here, for God's sake take her away!' he'd shouted at his father before he broke free from him and ran. Ran to where his brother was hanging.

At the bell tower.

* * *

I could not stay at the O'Lochlainns' house that day. Rían took me into the drawing room to his parents but his mother looked through me as if I were glass, his father hardly conscious as he acknowledged me. The police were talking to them gently about arrangements while Rían clutched my hand. I wanted to loosen his grip and run. At last, I told him he should be alone with his parents and he nodded before burying his head in my shoulder again, in the hallway, holding me so tightly I could not breathe. I needed to escape. Finally, he released me and I wandered stunned along the avenue, out through the gates and on to the road.

On I wandered. Along the hedgerows, below the hills, not caring or even aware of what direction I travelled. I don't know how long I wandered that day. At last, I sank down on a rock by the gate of a field, watching the wind blowing through the grass. It could bring me no solace as it once had.

As it blew against my face, I felt the tears come. What had happened to the gift I'd been born with? That knowing which had once coursed through my blood? It seemed now that every all-seeing Grace had deserted me. With Amy, swollen with arrogance, I had sensed nothing, but what of Conor? It was true I had seen shadows everywhere since Amy but I had not seen them settle heavy upon his shoulders. And now he was gone. Amy. Now Conor. Oh God, oh God, what had I done?

* * *

'She started to cry then.' Father Sheridan rose, going to the window, looking out upon the candlelit woodland, before turning back to Brother Thomas. 'I tried to comfort her, to assure her, "If you have true remorse your sins will be forgiven," but she shook her head.

'"I cannot be forgiven. I cannot."

'"And yet you have called me here," I said to her. "To make your peace. To confess yourself before God. You must believe there is forgiveness for you."

'"I do not know what I believe," she said. "I only know that I am afraid. Afraid for my mortal soul. And that I must cleanse myself of this lie before I die. I must tell you the truth both for my own peace and for him. The Abbot." Her eyes were desperate. "*Why* did he confess to the killing of Amy?"'

38

Tidings of a death usually speed on wings, but Conor's passing, if mentioned at all, was only spoken of in whispers. For to die by one's own hand was a mortal sin. It brought shame upon the sinner, shame upon his family. As it had happened so far away, in Tallaght, the night I returned from the O'Lochlainns' and for a long time afterwards, my aunt was not even aware of it. For this I was grateful as I did not have to suffer her scrutiny. But others in Eccles Street learned of it swiftly. Mairéad, Gus and Noreen. For, of course, Gerard, like all in Tallaght village, knew of it and brought them the news. Mairéad and Noreen arrived on my doorstep the following afternoon.

'Rosaleen.' Mairéad's face was agonised as she held out her arms but I did not step into them. I had no wish to be touched by her. By anyone. Noreen stood, grim, behind her. I did not want to let them enter but knew I must, showing them reluctantly into the parlour.

'What happened?' Mairéad asked, as she sat beside Noreen at the table but I shook my head. Knowing Gerard must have told them already more than they needed to know, I had no wish to relive the hellish scene

Rían had painted for me. I could not bear to feel the words in my mouth.

'He has died,' I said coldly. 'That is all.'

'That is all?' Noreen said incredulously. 'The poor, tragic boy has taken his own life and you say that is all?'

I wanted to strike her. *The poor, tragic boy has taken his own life because of what I did. What we did.*

'But why?' Mairéad moaned. 'Why?'

I gave her a hard look. 'You *know* why. We *all* know why.' In that moment I was burning with hatred for Noreen. I thought of her sending Conor, dear, gentle Conor, to carry out such a heinous act in the dead of night. Perhaps it had been the memory of that act which had finished him. Perhaps it was that memory he could not live with. If he had merely been at Amy's bedside that night, perhaps I could have persuaded him, as I'd tried so many times, that he had done no wrong. That he had been led astray by me and others older, professing wisdom. Perhaps Noreen was to blame.

'We must go to the funeral,' Noreen said.

I hissed at her. 'There will be no funeral. He has taken his own life, so has committed a mortal sin. There will be no funeral Mass. He will not be buried in consecrated ground. Wherever he is buried, the family will want no one there.'

Mairéad clutched her head in her hands. 'I will for ever blame myself. For ever.'

I observed her bitterly as Noreen placed her arm around Mairéad's shoulders. I had no interest in

Mairéad's remorse. I damned the day I had met her. Damned myself for listening to her. For falling under her spell.

'It is done.' I rose, wanting them to leave. 'Nothing we can say will change it.'

Mairéad looked stunned at me. 'How can you be so cold?' She let out a sob. 'Conor is *dead*.'

She wept as, rapidly, I sat back down to face her. 'I know all too well he is *dead*.' The word felt repugnant on my tongue but I spat it at her. 'And it was *we* who killed him. And never should you forget it. Never forget it as you feed people your fables, sermonise sorcery over science. Now get *out* of my house. And do not come back.'

Noreen stood quickly, holding the weeping Mairéad. 'You are evil,' Noreen said viciously. 'You are *not* and never were blessed.'

I turned my back on them, did not watch as they left. But as I heard the front door close, a swell of grief nearly felled me. In that moment I blamed no one but myself. *Yes. I am evil.*

* * *

Just as I had told Mairéad and Noreen, in punishment for his mortal sin, funeral rites and burial in consecrated ground were denied Conor. But then came the Abbot. The dear, sweet Abbot. Rían told me how he had called on them at their home, how in the drawing room, his face etched with pain, he had held out his arms to Rían's mother and embraced her. How he had gripped Rían's shoulders, his eyes a well of compassion. How he had spoken gently to his father.

'No church will take him, Father Abbot,' Rían's mother had wept as the Abbot sat beside her on the couch. 'There is no hallowed ground where we can bury him. What are we to do?'

The Abbot had laid his hand over hers. 'I too am bound and cannot offer a funeral Mass or our chapel's consecrated ground, but my brothers and I can offer up prayers in the chapel, and I hope you might think of all of our monastery lands as hallowed,' he said softly. 'I like to believe they have God's blessing. Perhaps you would consider letting us take Conor. Laying him to rest amongst us.'

Rían's mother had looked up to the Abbot, her eyes shining with hope through the tears. She gripped the Abbot's arm.

'You would do that for us?'

'Indeed I would,' the Abbot said. 'That and so much more if only I could. It would be my honour to take Conor. To allow him to rest in peace amongst us, close to home and, I pray, close to God. All I need is your blessing.'

Rían's mother had sobbed with relief, collapsed against the Abbot as he held her. Rían had watched them, his throat choked, he could see his father the same.

And so it was done. Quietly. Swiftly. That September morning, still unaware of what had happened, my aunt simply thought I was going, as I so often did, to visit my friend Rían. I walked alone through the monastery gates in the autumn sun. In agony I looked towards the woodland. There, where Amy lay. And now the earth lay in wait for Conor.

Uphill, I spied Rían with his parents and the Abbot at the chapel door. I had been worried at intruding on his parents' grief but Rían had assured me that, far from objecting, they would be glad of me, a friend of Conor's, there. I was told that no one else would be present. Yet as I grew closer the form of Gerard Mallon came clearly into view. I was dismayed. I did not want to see him. Although I held myself most guilty of all, I blamed Gerard for leaving Conor alone that dreadful night.

As Gerard saw me approach, he nodded slowly in greeting. I barely acknowledged him, but touched Rían's shoulder from behind as he talked to the Abbot.

Rían turned and I could see his eyes were red and sore, as if he had not slept or had been weeping. While his parents did not seem to mind Gerard there, I could sense an animosity in Rían towards him. I supposed that Conor had told him how Gerard had deserted him. I linked Rían's arm as his parents and the Abbot greeted me.

'It is so good to see you here,' the Abbot said to me. 'A true friend of Conor's.' I flinched, feeling far from worthy of the title, as he gestured inside. 'Shall we begin?'

Gerard stepped forward. 'I will not intrude any further,' he said to Rían's parents. 'I just wanted to offer you my most sincere condolences.'

They shook his hand gratefully, and I balked at it. They obviously thought him kind for coming, when perhaps no other neighbour would even speak of it. But I could only think what they might feel if they knew whose hand it was they shook. If they knew what he, what all of us, had brought upon Conor. And Gerard, supposedly a friend, had not been near Conor since the tragedy. Gerard leant to shake my hand but I turned away. Rían merely gave him a brisk nod. Then, mercifully, he was gone.

Inside, the tiny chapel was aglow with warm, golden candlelight. In the chancel by the altar the brothers, adorned in their habits, lined the pews. As I walked the aisle with Rían, before the altar, I saw Conor's coffin. I faltered. I could hardly believe it was possible that Conor, our own dear Conor, lay so still within. It seemed unnatural, perverse. That his youthful laughter, the warmth of his gentle heart, could be contained within the confines of that wooden box. I gripped Rían's arm and he clutched my hand as we took our seats in the front pew with his parents. The Abbot stood beside the coffin.

He raised his arms in welcome, speaking softly. 'Today we gather in memory of our dear, departed brother, Conor. This day we will offer prayers. Together, we will pray for our brother's soul. That the light of God will shine upon him and grant him eternal peace . . .'

Peace. Yes, peace. That is what I wished for him as I bowed my head, listened to the sweet song of the brothers, the mellow murmurings of their prayers. All the while

Rían's hand gripped mine as, by his side, his mother wept, his father coughing in an effort to stem his tears.

At last, the prayers done, Rían and his father walked to the coffin, four brothers coming sombrely to help them lift it. Rían's face was stricken as he took his place beside his father at the front of the coffin, lifting his brother on to his shoulder. Behind Conor's mother and the Abbot, I followed the coffin down the aisle.

From the dimness of the chapel we stepped into the bright autumn sunshine and walked to the shade of a beautiful aged oak tree where a plot had been prepared, the dug earth heaped beside it. As Rían began with his father and the brothers to lower the coffin, he stumbled, letting out a sob. His mother gasped, clinging to the Abbot. I thought Rían would be unable to go on, but quickly he recovered himself. I knew he was forcing himself to perform this one last service for his brother. When it was done he came to my side.

I stared down upon the coffin so deep in the ground and made silent whisper to it: *Is that a softer bed for you, more restful than the one you left behind? Will you have more peaceful slumber now in that cold pit?*

Along the grass I saw a black raven's feather dancing, blowing in the wind, calling to me of a freedom, that long-ago childhood freedom that my heart, leaden now, could no longer feel. But for Conor I wished it.

Two brothers came, carrying a spade each for Rían and his father. As I watched father and son toss in a scattering of earth, I looked towards the woodland, mindful of that other burial, that other soul who'd had no prayers over her grave. I felt myself waver, suddenly unsteady. Rían, too, the spade in his hand, was trembling. It was clear he could not carry on, and a brother came to gently touch his arm, taking the spade from him. As Rían returned to my side, another brother approached his father who gratefully relinquished his own spade.

The Abbot stood at the head of the grave, under the waving branches of the tree. He bowed his head, whispering over Conor an Irish blessing: '*Ar dheis Dé go raibh a anam.*'

'May his soul rest at the right hand of God,' Rían whispered to me.

'Amen,' I whispered, faithless, to the heavy sod.

It started to softly rain, the wind rushing through the leaves of the tree, and I rested my head against Rían's shoulder. I looked up at the bowing branches and leaves, the dancing sun, and felt it as Conor's smile. His sign to us that he was free. I closed my eyes and raised my face to the sun's warmth. And I knew in that moment that Conor did not lie below in the cold earth, but somewhere far beyond. Somewhere all around us. Somewhere in the sun's light, the softness of the gentle rain. Somewhere in the wind. And as I felt it touch my face I smiled. *Fly free, sweet boy.*

* * *

Father Sheridan sat silent. At last he spoke. 'I told her that was my greatest regret. That I could not say Mass for Conor, perform the funeral rites. I learned of his passing through the university. I had no grounds to bury him at my small city church, but anyway I would not have been permitted. She talked of that. Of Conor's Mortal Sin. She feared for him.

'"Is his soul really damned, Father?" she said to me. "I beg you to pray for him. Sometimes I hear him whisper to me in the night. A soul not at rest. Or perhaps his soul is easy and it is my own soul not at peace. But now you know the truth – now you know it was only due to me that he had any hand in Amy's death – that it was his great remorse that caused him to take his own life. Will you pray for his mortal soul now?"

'I knew the Church teaching but I tried to reassure her. "I believe he died with his soul graced. With a heart washed innocent by true remorse. You have no need to fear for him." That seemed to give her comfort.' Father Sheridan stared into the flames. 'Yes, that seemed to give her some peace.'

* * *

When they'd returned home from the burial, Rían's father had arranged a cab for Rosaleen. Rían had embraced her before she'd climbed into the carriage, loath to let her go. This woman with whom he and his brother had shared the deepest of secrets. Only with her now could he be true. He wanted to keep her close for his brother was gone. *Gone.* He needed her as he had never needed another before.

Bereft as the carriage rolled away, he went to the drawing room where his father stood by the mantlepiece, his mother sitting staring into the empty hearth. He stepped into the silence. The awful, smothering silence that had descended upon them since his brother's death. There seemed nothing to say. No words that could bring comfort. It was only in small gestures that each could reveal to the other what lay in their hearts. Compassion. Love. He went to make such a gesture now to his mother. Lifting her shawl from the arm of the couch, he started to put it around her shoulders. He stepped back in alarm as she snatched it from him, flung it to the floor.

'You told me he would be all right.' Her voice was low, unnatural, almost a hiss. 'You told me it was *nothing.* That you were counselling him. You stopped me fetching a doctor. You stopped me from talking to him. Every time I tried, you stopped me. It is your fault. All *your* fault!'

Blindly he stared at the fallen shawl. Stunned. Stung by her words. For he knew the truth of them. Yes. It was his fault. All his fault.

39

My mind was in turmoil, a tangle of thoughts. I was tortured now not only by what fate I had dealt Amy, by what we had made Conor do, but by a fresh torment: what if Rían and I had allowed Conor to confess? Almost certainly if we had, he would not lie cold in the ground today. He would surely have found relief in unburdening himself; he could have tried to make atonement. But my own fear had made me convince him to keep close that secret he found impossible to bear. I had trapped him in the lie. But then came another thought: what would have become of the Armstrongs if we'd let him confess? These thoughts hounded me, allowing me no peace.

My aunt still mercifully unaware of the tragedy in those faraway hills, I at least found some sanctuary in my home. I would walk the city streets if only to feel the Liffey breeze on my face or hear the gulls screech. But no once-beloved wind could bring me solace. It could not sweep away the agony in my mind or the anguish in my heart.

After the funeral, I received many notes from Rían asking if I would come or if he might visit me. Although feeling guilty at deserting him in his sorrow, I would always reply with a reason why a meeting was not possible. The truth was I could not face him. To see him would remind me too much of my pain. And I had a fear. Often it felt that the disharmony in my mind would drive me to madness. To see Rían would only compound my confusion. I did not want to pick over the bones of this tragedy. I wanted no one near me that could stir my emotions. I came to dread seeing Rían again.

It was on an October morning that what I feared came to pass. While on the upstairs landing I heard the brass knocker below, the rush of carriage traffic as Mary pulled open the front door. I heard his voice. A surge of panic made me want to run for the loft, hide in Mary's room, but she was calling to me.

'Rosaleen, a visitor for you.'

It was no good. He knew I was there. My steps leaden, I rounded the landing and started down the stairs. As I saw him there in the hallway, I did what I must. I gave a wan smile.

'Rían.' I stepped into the hall. 'It is good to see you.'

The sight of him shocked me. Although his clothes were as ever pristine, they seemed to hang on his thin frame. His face was gaunt, eyes darting. He was haunted, I could see that. Every bit as haunted as I.

'Forgive me.' He spoke quickly, removing his hat. 'I felt I must come.'

My eyes warning him to hush before Mary, I ushered him into the parlour, closing the door, to sit with him at the table.

'Rosaleen.' He reached across the table to take my hands in his. 'I had to see you. You are the only person I can talk to. The only one who can help me.'

He started to weep, his head collapsing upon our joined hands on the table. I longed to take my hands away. His despair was stirring my own. The very emotions I so wanted to escape. I damned him for it, but kept a hand under his, reaching with the other to reluctantly touch his head.

'Hush, hush now. It will be all right.' The lie felt feeble in my mouth.

'It will never be all right.' He looked up at me desperately, still clinging to my hand. 'He is gone. And *I* killed him.'

'No, *no*.' This time I spoke truly. 'Don't say that. Never say that. It was nothing to do with you, Rían. Never anything to do with you. If anyone is guilty it is me. You know that. It is with me the blame for every part of this lies.'

'But if I had let him confess.' He looked desolate. He had voiced the very thought that so taunted me. I had no answer to it, just looked at him hopelessly.

'But then what would have become of the Armstrongs?'

He shook his head. 'No. My duty was to *him*. I should have let him confess. And I should never have let him carry on with it that night. I should have stopped him.'

I was confused. 'What do you mean? Carry on with what? What night?'

He stared at me. '*That* night. The night of . . .' He faltered, looking towards the door, listening for any sound beyond it. 'The night of *Amy*. The night of her burial.'

I could not fathom his meaning. 'What do you mean, stopped him? You were not there that night. How could you have stopped him?'

'I *was* there.' His voice caught on a sob. 'I was there with him in the woodland. After Gerard Mallon abandoned him he came for me. I went with him to the monastery. It was not Conor buried the child, but I.'

He started to sob so loudly I feared he would be heard. I put my hand over his mouth, urging him to be quiet. He clung to it, starting to kiss it and I felt repelled. It made no sense but his mouth on my hand, his hand on mine, now revolted me. The hand, the hands, that had buried Amy. I did not want them touching me.

'I did it for you,' he sobbed. 'For Conor. And for you.'

'For me?' I bent down, almost hissed into his face. 'What do you mean, for me? What did you owe *me*?'

His eyes were deep and welling. 'My love. My protection.' He lifted my hand. 'And I would do it again. God help me, I would do it all again.' He continued to kiss my hand, over and over as I stared at him in horror. I snatched away my hand, pushed myself backwards on my chair and stood quickly. I looked down on him. His pitiful devotion I found only sickening. That he should carry out such an abominable act for my sake, in my name, appalled and disgusted me.

'Get up,' I said to him sharply. 'Get *up*.'

He looked at me, shocked, his sobs stopping. I could see bewilderment in his eyes.

'Get up, Rían.' My voice was ice. 'And get out. I do not want to see you any more.' My stomach was awash with a terrible mix of anguish and revulsion. I wanted him gone. And with him every reminder of Amy and Conor and what I had wrought upon them. I did not want his odious adoration. I wanted rid of him.

Still, he sat, looking stunned at me. 'What do you mean?' He stood quickly to face me, as I turned away from his gaze. He grasped my shoulders. 'I did it for you, Rosaleen. For *you*. I *love* you. I have always loved you. You must know that.'

I shook my shoulders free. 'I do not *want* your love,' I spat. 'I never have. I want nothing from you. *Nothing*. I only want that you should leave me.'

'I cannot believe that.' His voice was weak. 'I cannot believe that you could be so cruel.'

'Well, you should believe it.' My voice was like a blade. 'I have killed a child. And I killed your brother. You *should* believe it.'

His eyes were wild. He shook his head. 'No, I will not believe it.' He was firm. 'This is not you . . .'

'This *is* me,' I said fiercely. 'And you would do well to remember that. Perhaps I am not the woman you thought me. Perhaps you fell in love with another. A mythical creature, known as the Rose. But I am not that woman, Rían. I never was. I am mere flesh and blood. Natural and impure. Imperfect. Cruel.'

'No.' Still, he shook his head, his eyes disbelieving.

'*Go!*' I shouted, turning my back to him. He tried once more to take my shoulders, to turn me to him, but I lashed out with my arm and struck him across the face. Tears sprang into his startled eyes as I shouted again, 'Get out!'

I turned from him so I did not see him leave. But I heard him tread slowly, heavily across the wooden floor. Heard also the opening and closing of the parlour door. Then, at last, the sound I prayed for, his footsteps walking down the hall.

* * *

Rían had stumbled out on to the street. Through blurry, unseeing eyes, he'd looked up, then down the road. He'd had no notion which way to go. There seemed nowhere he could go now. The shock was too great. There was no refuge for him, no place to carry this pain or lay it down. He staggered downwards towards Sackville Street, every building and thoroughfare, every passing carriage or pedestrian seeming unreal to him. He could not comprehend what had just happened.

Who had been that banshee in the place of his Rose? How could those gracious lips have uttered words so vile? He shook his head in disbelief, mumbling as if crazed while he walked. To think he had once thought that demonic creature a vision. For *her* he had risked all. His livelihood, his liberty, it seemed his very life. A rage began to rise through the anguish, ghastly images of the unspeakable things he had done, what he had endured for her. Every atrocity he had performed on that horrific night.

He remembered now. How, once alone, in the monastery woodland he'd stood, paralysed, staring down at the grotesque bundle lying sodden amongst the ferns. How at last he'd bent, reaching for a spade with shaking hands. How he'd driven it deep into the mud, the sting of tears and bile in his throat as he'd tossed aside the soil. On and on went this torture. Finally, his hands raw, he had looked down into the pit.

As he'd stepped towards the bundle – the child – he'd wept. For he was cursed now by an awful clarity at what – who – he must take into his arms. Sobbing, he'd lifted the blanket, but those sobs had sounded loud in the silent night, and he'd realised he must be quiet. Gently, he had knelt with her. Had whispered, 'Forgive me, please. Forgive me.'

He had tried to lower her softly, with dignity into the ground, but her body had tumbled and rolled the last inches, making him retch. As he rose, the physically lighter task of covering her, replacing the earth, had felt the most heavy. The violence of the sod battering her body. As the first scattering had hit, he'd tasted vomit. But he'd forced himself on. With every strike, thinking of Conor. Thinking of *her*. His Rosaleen.

This he did for him. For her. It was this he must keep at the forefront of his mind. As the pit had filled, his sobs had lessened. With the spade he'd evened the ground, roughening it with his foot, scrambling for brush and deadened winter leaves to cover it. He would return next morning to make sure. To ensure this tiny grave lay hidden. That this earth would keep its secret. Conor's secret.

He walked amongst the crowds and bustle of Sackville Street, the trams, the flower sellers' cries, a melodeon playing. He lifted his face to the cold autumn air, trying to stem a rage so pure.

Her secret.

40

You will think me cruel, Father. For what I inflicted on Rían. But you must understand my mind was slipping from me. Every natural human sense soon to be lost.

For it was then the sickness came. Sickness such as I had never known before. It came upon me with such savagery, such force as if I were under attack. Mairéad had always talked as if sickness were our spirits not at ease, not aligned truly with nature. Almost something gentle, over which we had dominion. But when my own illness struck I knew that Mairéad must never have truly been sick. That those women who claimed themselves healed by me had never been sick. Not like I was now. For the violence of it was ungodly. Inhuman.

It began as a thousand questions; a thousand conflicting answers in my mind. A rock that crushed my heart as if burying beneath it a deep, dark well of tears. But soon those unspilled tears had morphed into the greatest terror. And I remembered Ciss's words: *I am trying to see through eyes that are two dark tunnels in a mind no more solid than a rolling sea.*

Truly now, I understood how she felt. Except this was no feeling, but an absence of all human feeling.

I was trying to navigate the world robbed of every power of reason, stripped of all heart and soul. In their place a void. I was petrified. All softness and warmth disappeared from my body. I felt constantly cold and would shiver endlessly.

And yet, even through this torment, with shaking limbs and unsteady steps, I was able in some way to function, to carry out my chores as if I were not living this horror within. But something in my manner or sluggish speech must have betrayed me, for my aunt quizzed me on it. She stopped me one morning on the stairs.

'Rosaleen, are you all right?' Her face was concerned. 'You have seemed strange lately. Distant. You don't seem yourself.'

I hesitated a moment. 'No. I'm all right. Just tired.' I yearned to tell her. Yearned for someone to help me. But how could I describe this hell? Whilst in its clutches I did not have the words. I feared my aunt would think me mad.

My answer did not satisfy her, though. She sent for my mother. When Mammy came and I saw her gentle face, her familiar frame there in the hallway, I broke down. I ran to her, buried myself in her.

'Oh, Mammy, Mammy,' I sobbed.

She held on to me tightly, like she would never let me go. I clung to her, as if to a buoy that would save me from drowning. At last, we went into the parlour, sitting alone in the two chairs at the window.

Mammy leaned into me, gripping my hands. 'You're to tell me what's wrong. Tell me what has happened that has you in this state. Tell me now, Rosaleen, and whatever it is I will help you. God help me, I will.'

I longed to tell her. Oh, how I longed to. To lay in her lap everything that had happened, to have her soothe it all away, just as she had when I was a child. But, of course, I could never tell her. Never tell anyone. At this thought I started to sob again.

She came to my chair, cradling my head at her breast as she stroked my hair. At last I spoke the only truth I could.

'I think I am ill, Mammy.'

My mother begged me to return home with her. Home, to where she could watch over me, nurse me back to health. So much of me ached for the trees, the fields, the wind rushing from the hills; the comfort of my mother and the comfort of home. But I knew I could never again sit peacefully in the kitchen with my aunts and uncle. No more could I belong to that innocent world, nor could I deny what had made me leave it.

Mammy insisted then, if I would not return with her, that I must see a doctor. I was greatly alarmed at the thought of seeing Dr Lydon again, knowing he thought me guilty of colluding with my former friends to keep Amy, a sick child, from him. He had no notion, I was sure, of how abominable was the actual truth but I was certain he suspected me of some duplicity. But although I tried to dissuade my mother from calling for him, she was adamant.

He came that very evening. As he walked through the parlour door to where I sat at the window, expecting him,

I could hardly look up to greet him, fearing he would be able to read my crime on my face. He took the chair opposite me and waited. Waited for me to look at him. At last I did, and he held my eyes.

'Your mother and aunt are worried you are not well, Rosaleen,' he said softly. 'Will you tell me what is wrong?'

I could not fathom his kindly manner. His gentleness. I had thought he despised my past comrades, despised me as I despised myself. I was frightened to open my mouth. Afraid my words would betray me. That he would know from every symptom I described, the evil in me that had caused them. Finally, he spoke again.

'Your aunt says you have been very low in mood. Very silent. That you have not been eating properly. And that you have little energy. Will you try to tell me how you are feeling?'

The urge to confide in him, confide in someone this hell, was strong. Strong enough to override my fear. At last, I found the words tumbling from me. I told him of the vile black tunnel, my mind not solid but streaming like a river before my eyes. He listened carefully until my torrent of words was finished. Then he spoke gently.

'I think you are suffering from melancholia, Rosaleen. A disturbance of your emotions, your nerves, your senses. The result of a long-held anxiety. Or a deep sadness.'

The disturbance of my emotions, nerves and senses I recognised. I recognised too the crucifying anxiety. But the sadness I did not. I wished I could feel sadness.

Could feel anything. What I suffered felt a lack of all natural human feeling.

'I don't feel sad,' I said. 'I hardly feel anything any more. I have no emotion. I have been swallowed whole by the black mist.'

'Nevertheless, the symptoms you describe are what we call melancholia. Perhaps it has been caused by some deep trauma.' He looked at me then, and even in my dull spirit I felt a spark of fear. I was sure he was going to mention Amy. But he only said, 'I know what happened to your friend Conor. Do you think, perhaps, it is shock and bereavement that are at the root of your trouble?'

Yes. Yes, indeed I thought that. But I knew it was not only the tragedy of Conor that had caused this affliction but the tragedy of Amy too. The secret that festered in the core of my heart. But I was able to answer truthfully, at least.

'Yes. It started when he died.'

He leaned forward to emphasise his words. 'There is little medicine I can prescribe you to restore your balance. Our science is not yet advanced enough. I could give you a bromide to sedate you. But I do not think it is sedation you need. There is a school of thought that talking to someone of what troubles you, perhaps a psychiatrist, might help. Would you consider this?'

I was seized by terror. Being probed on the cause of my trouble was the very last thing I wanted. Besides, I knew no amount of talking would shift this black shroud smothering my mind. I answered quickly.

'I don't think so, Doctor. But perhaps I will talk to my mother. Yes. Perhaps that will help me.'

He studied me, then nodded. 'And if you ever want to talk to me I am just a few doors away. You must not feel alone.'

I was so grateful for his kindness. A kindness that pierced through the black shroud to touch me. I felt I would cry. But I did not. When Dr Lydon left that day, no matter what he had said, I knew that no one could help me. I was alone.

Truly alone.

41

I spent a year or more trapped in that hell, Father. I had
satisfied my mother, and Dr Lydon had assured her, that
I was better keeping busy and the distractions of city life
might help me, so, reluctantly, Mammy left me in the
care of my aunt. My aunt scolded me for not telling her
about Conor. Now she had good reason for my dismal
mood she let me be, allowing me to go quietly about my
chores. The mindless tasks and chatter of the boarders
did indeed help distract me from that great silence,
yet turmoil, I endured within.

Four seasons came and went. Seasons that saw Dublin
rupture every bit as much as my mind. That first summer
Uncle Noel would sit with the newspaper in the parlour,
shaking his head.

'I can hardly reach the quays to get to work any more.
Sackville Street and everywhere is full of them, spitting,
shouting, raging at one another. It's bloody dangerous
out there. I've told Ellen and I'll tell you, Rosaleen. I
don't want you going out during the day.'

The lockout. It had started in August, employers
blacklisting and locking out – dismissing – any worker
who they suspected of joining Jim Larkin's union and

there were hundreds of them. Jim Larkin, who'd come from the Liverpool docks and gone about organising both skilled and unskilled workers, many from the tenements, who were fighting each other for jobs, always awarded to the man or woman willing to work for the lowest wage.

'I don't blame them joining the union,' Aunt Ellen said, 'the conditions in those tenements – slums – are brutal. They're riddled with disease. The children are dying daily, the poor *créatúrs*. And the men are fighting each other for work, then labouring up to seventeen hours a day, they say, for a pitiful sum. They need some protection. A fair wage.'

'Thank God for Guinness,' Uncle Noel said. 'They've always been good employers but they've warned the workers they don't want them going out on sympathy strikes. There's very few have done that, because the bosses have refused to lock out any workers who've joined the union.'

The summer sun powerless against my mind's black pall, I had no wish to walk in it, which was just as well because the streets were indeed dangerous. With the strikes came mass pickets and when they brought in the strike-breakers, the blacklegs, there were riots. The police charged a massive rally on Sackville Street, killing two men, injuring three hundred more. That day they called Bloody Sunday. Then came the death of sixteen-year-old Alice Brady who, carrying a food parcel from the union offices, walked into a crowd of women shouting at the blacklegs, one of the blacklegs shooting into the crowd, hitting Alice in the hand. She died from tetanus in hospital two weeks later.

The battle lasted into autumn and winter. In all it lasted nearly five months until January saw starvation force the strikers back to work and to sign a pledge they would not join the union. It had damaged businesses too. Many declared bankruptcy.

As Dublin in some way seemed to regain its senses so did I regain mine. That spring, the spring of 1914, I felt myself emerge from the pit. Walking out, I began to notice the breeze on my upturned face, for the first time in an age felt it penetrate my skin. The freshness of the Liffey in the air, the scent of breads and buns wafting from the bakeries brought me a rush of pleasure. My deadened senses once more came alive, starting to sing sweetly like a bird.

I was so thankful, so ecstatic at this rebirth. I revelled again in the sights and sounds of the city: the hawkers' cries and flower sellers' cheeky young faces; the scruffy boys at the barrel organ, the rattle of the trams and clatter of horses. The sunlight, the soft rain touching my face; all life once more bringing me joy. And I felt such relief within my soul. By enduring that terrible darkness it truly felt I had done penance for my great wrongs. For what had been visited upon me had seemed worse to me than death.

Nature and the terror it could wreak had taught me undeniably who was master. I understood now that if

Mother Nature chose to assail me I was no match for her. *Not everything in nature is benign.* Dr Lydon's words returned to me. I had once thought him so arrogant. Now I understood he had been only too aware that mankind was no ruler of nature, but her subject. And he was merely attempting to remedy whatever damage she was minded to inflict. No, it was I as diviner who had placed myself above nature's laws. I who avowed I was bowing to nature while, in truth, I was trying to command it. Now I felt myself truly touched by the graces. The grace of humility.

My sickness had taught me that I was mortal and fragile. Hardly a single note in nature's symphony. A minuscule player in her monumental orchestra, not her conductor. I could not wave my baton and sweep away all ills. And once so set against science, I believed now so fervently the contrary: that the doctors were virtuous in their attempts to tame the forces of nature. If there had been a pill or potion for my condition, I would have devoured it.

And yet it was nature I craved now. With my senses once more alive, I yearned to feel the rush of my beloved wind. To be surrounded by cooling hills and woods, sparkling streams and rivers. To breathe them in. No longer to try harness and wield nature's power but to root me solid to the earth. And I felt another yearning. A deep need in my heart. To go to Conor. To Amy. To carry for Conor what he had thought most beautiful. To carry for him a rose.

On a May day I cut two blooms from Aunt Ellen's garden. I was anxious as I rode the tram to Tallaght, but my longing was greater than my anxiety as the hills came into sight. The tram leaving me near the monastery, I walked hesitantly to the gates. The last time I had passed through them had been to attend Conor's funeral. Now, I took a breath before stepping through them again. Walking uphill, I glanced up at the cloisters, the chapel, the great stone walls of the monastery. But no longer did they seem malevolent, witness to Amy's hidden grave, but benevolent, for they had proven a sanctuary. Had welcomed Conor as no other would. I climbed until I reached the oak. There, below its boughs, at Conor's grave, a cross with his name had been mounted. The sun was warm as I knelt, the grass rippling in the hill wind. I kissed the rose in my hand.

'A rose for you, Conor,' I whispered to him as I laid it down. Laid it down for him as he had once done for Amy. 'A rose as beautiful as you were. As you *are*. For you will ever live in every heart you touched.'

Lulled by the warm breeze, I felt serenity. Thinking so often of Conor, I realised then that I hardly ever thought of his brother. Of Rían. Now I wondered how he fared. I hoped he, too, had found a little ease. Had forgotten me. Had made some peace with Conor's passing. I did not want to think on this or linger at Conor's grave too long, for I did not want to attract the attention of the Abbot. Rising, I bade a silent farewell to my friend, then started to walk downhill. Towards the woodland.

Reaching the pathway, I no longer felt easy, my breath growing short as I made my way through the trees, past the bluebells, over the bridge and trickling brook. I stood there then and looked upon it. The bell tower. This place where Amy lay. Where Conor had died. It seemed to rise over me, almost demonic, to stare down at me accusingly. I could feel no peace here, as I had at Conor's side. I gripped the rose in my hand. There was no need to worry who might see it; now it could be supposed that I offered it in memory of my aunt, and Conor also.

And there I knelt and laid down my rose. For Conor, yes. And for Amy. In my own name. And in his. I laid it down just as he had done. Just as I now would ever do.

*　　*　　*

That past year, Rían had suffered his own stifled hell. The silence at home was suffocating, although his father did his best to mask it. His mother sat hushed, barely able to hide her condemnation of Rían, her bitter blame. In the refuge of the office, his father, distressed by his wife's coldness, was kind to Rían, never chiding him for the mistakes he now made frequently or the fact that it was obvious his son had little heart for his work.

Rían would often visit his brother's grave. He would never kneel, but stand, tortured, above it, staring down upon the waving grass. His mother's recriminations could not match his own. She was right to condemn him. He had persuaded her not to approach Conor in those dark times, afraid that under her scrutiny his brother would break. Now, he wished so desperately he had not kept her from him. Perhaps, by confiding in his mother, his life would have been saved.

Still he berated himself for denying Conor the chance to confess, the chance to clear his conscience and soothe his soul. But it was Amy's brutal burial that hounded him most. It was on that night he should have saved his brother. If Rían had insisted they go immediately to the police, confess what tragedy had occurred at the healing and what heinous act he'd been instructed to carry out in the wood, Conor would have done his bidding.

But Rían had not advised him so. He had not, because he had been so in Rosaleen's thrall. So blinded by the fear of the consequences for her. And yet now he saw, with an awful clarity, he had sacrificed his brother for her. For a creature so unworthy of his loyalty and love, who had bewitched both him and his brother, who had led his brother so badly astray. She had taken what she needed from Rían, then cast him aside.

And now he stood at his brother's graveside and saw lying there a rose. He stared at it, willing it away, not wanting to believe it real. His mind raced through the possibilities. Perhaps it had not been left by her but another. But he knew it a vain hope. It was only he and his family came here.

And so he forced himself go where he never went. To a place abhorrent to him. The place his brother had last breathed. He must go, for he would know then for sure. He walked hesitantly through the woodland, barely raising his eyes, sickened by vicious visions of the last time he had taken this path. At last, he reached the bell tower. He kept his eyes lowered. He could not look upon it. But there was no need. For, there, in its shadow, he saw it: the rose.

He stared at it for an age. Then he slowly bent to pick it up. In his palm he curled his fingers around it, closed his eyes. Making a fist he crushed it in his hand. As the thorns pierced him, he felt the springing of blood. Good. The pain felt as great as the rage in his heart.

He ground the petals until they were pulp, digging his fingers hard into the thorns until the blood ran down his palm. Until the rose was stained red with his blood. Until it lay lifeless in his hand.

42

I felt my sickness, that time of darkness had purged me: rid me of every twisted uttering of Mairéad, Noreen and the others and cleared my mind. I felt restored to myself, much simpler, as I had been when I was a girl, free of the outlandish expectations of others. No longer the Rose. Although my heart still bore the scar of Amy and Conor, with a cleansed mind I felt my true gifts, those I'd been born with, breathe once more within me.

So much more the girl I'd been that first spring I'd met Lorcan, I felt a yearning to see him again. I did not fear his sensing what I kept hidden, for that horror I no longer carried at the forefront of my mind but deep within me. It was my burden, mine alone to bear. I would not inflict it on another.

I sought him out at the Roto. When I entered and enquired after him at the ticket office, I was both nervous and relieved when the girl nodded recognition at his name. I waited anxiously, rubbing my gloved hands as she went to fetch him. At last, as he entered the foyer I flushed, but my anxiety eased, for his eyes lit up at seeing me.

'Rosaleen!' As he hurried towards me, I felt a rush of pleasure, my face breaking into a smile, just like his.

He held my eyes a moment, then pulled me into a tight embrace. It felt so comforting to be in his arms. I stayed there, breathing in his scent, until he stepped back to hold me by the shoulders.

'I can't believe you're here. It's so good to see you.' He was still smiling, looking deep into my eyes. Then his smile faded. 'But what brings you here? Not trouble, I hope?'

I was sure then that he had not heard of Conor's passing. I did not want those dark tidings to be the first words between us, so I assured him all was well.

'Well, then we must go for tea – immediately!' he joked. 'Or not quite immediately, but in an hour. After the matinee. Will you meet me? At Wynn's?'

I nodded gladly. There was nothing I would rather do.

* * *

Later, in Wynn's lounge, Lorcan sat across from me at the white-clothed table, leaning forward, eager to hear my news.

'Tell me of everyone. Of Ellen and Noel. And Mairéad and the others. Even spiky old Noreen. And Conor. Tell me all.'

As he took a sip of his tea, my heart wrenched. He had mentioned Conor. I knew now I must tell him.

'Aunt Ellen and Uncle Noel are well. Aunt Ellen has forced Tidy Tony to play bridge with her because he always loses. But as to the others on Eccles Street –' I hesitated – 'I don't see them any more.'

He frowned, clearly puzzled. 'But why not? You don't go to the meetings now?' As I shook my head he smiled, saying, 'But you are their Rose. What will they do without you?'

I did not return his smile. 'Something has happened, Lorcan.' I spoke slowly, loath to say what I must. I kept my eyes lowered. 'Conor died.'

When he made no reply I looked up to meet his eyes. They were wide, stunned. He seemed unable to make sense of what I was saying. He shook his head in disbelief. 'Died? How? When?'

Little by little, I told him what I could of it. That Conor had become withdrawn, had left college. That Rían and I had spent much time with him but had been unable to reach him. That Conor had seemed haunted. I did not tell him that I knew only too well what haunted him. I felt treacherous, sure that Lorcan would sense it. But he was too shocked. He listened without saying a word. I could see his distress and confusion and reached out to touch his hand.

'Where is he?' he said at last. 'Where is he buried?'

'At the monastery,' I replied.

'Please,' he said. 'Take me there.'

*　*　*

The day I took Lorcan to the monastery, once more I carried two roses. The sun was warm as we climbed the hill to the oak; Lorcan stared at the mound of earth as we came to stand under the tree. He was mute at the sight.

'It's so hard to believe,' he said finally, 'that he lies there beneath the ground. So young. Such a sweet, gentle soul. Perhaps too sweet, too gentle for this world.'

I crouched to lay a rose upon the grave.

'I bring him roses,' I said, 'for he loved them.'

Lorcan looked down at me and smiled. 'And he loved the Rose.'

His words stung me. That he should still be thinking of me as the Rose, as one revered when I felt so unworthy, wounded me. I stood and touched his arm. 'Will you come somewhere else with me?'

He nodded and, linking his arm, I led him downhill towards the woodland. He understood where we were going.

'We're going to the bell tower?' He hesitated. 'Where he died?'

I pressed his arm in answer as we walked on into the woodland. At last, as he let me go ahead across the bridge I looked back at him. I could see the sight of the bell tower was hurting him. I walked slowly towards it to lay down my rose.

Lorcan came to stand over me. 'You lay roses for him,' he said gently. He looked at me softly and smiled. 'The Rose lays down her rose. Here at the bell tower. The Rose Bell.'

43

I saw Lorcan often last summer. The summer the war broke. The British at war with Germany. The world at war with itself. It was then I knew my sense had returned, for although those battles raged on distant fields, my nerves were taut, every shelling, gunfire and blast seeming to shudder in my blood. I felt it then as I feel it still, Father: a malevolence in the air. It is as if the earth has tilted, is off-kilter. And all the while its children are screaming, flailing and falling into the deep, black unknown. In that blackness I hear the screams of sons calling for their mothers. Mothers crying for their sons.

I knew those cries to be echoes from far away, but, as summer turned to autumn, I could also feel the tension on the Dublin streets. Droves of young Irishmen began to appear in uniform. Some passers-by would stop to slap their shoulders in congratulation. Others confronted them, condemning them for going to join a British fight.

'It's a bloody imperialistic, capitalistic war and they're using our Irish boys first as a feast for the Germans,' Lorcan lamented to me, over the table, at Wynn's. 'Some of them are just idiots. Signing up for certain death, fighting for a country that has only wronged them. But others were blacklisted by employers during the lockout and can't get work now. They've had to sign up to get a living wage.'

I nodded, pouring him some more tea. 'Yes, Uncle Noel says that many of them are from the tenements. They're seeing this as a chance, at last, to earn some money. People shouldn't judge them too harshly.'

Lorcan lit a cigarette. A new habit. 'Meanwhile some of us are busy with armies of our own,' he said, almost under his breath.

I looked at him. 'What armies?'

He lowered his voice. 'The Irish Volunteers. An army we've formed in response to the Ulster Volunteers, the Ulster Unionists who are threatening violence if Home Rule goes ahead. You know they've passed the Bill?' He blew some smoke. 'Home Rule was due to be enacted but then the war started. It's been postponed for now because of it.'

I did know. Uncle Noel and Aunt Ellen often talked of it. They were both in favour of Home Rule. 'Sensible,' Uncle Noel said. Lorcan, of course, didn't think so.

'The Ulster Unionists don't want it because they won't accept anything less than being fully subject to the Crown and we won't accept anything less than being a true and independent nation – a Republic.' He leaned in to me. 'And there's another army. The Irish Citizen Army. Formed by Jim Larkin and James Connolly during the lockout to protect the workers from the police. Made up of both men and women. Constance Markievicz has joined them.' His eyes lit up. 'And Saoirse too.'

My heart was sore. Saoirse. When I had first seen Lorcan smoking, remembering him lighting her cigarette, I'd been glumly aware of why he might have taken up the habit. Soon after our reunion I had enquired after her. I had asked in trepidation, hardly wanting to hear the answer, although I'd harboured a hope that his admiration of her had faded, their courtship come to nothing. But I had hoped in vain. They were still very much a couple.

He'd grown animated now. 'And just this spring, in this very hotel, the Daughters of Ireland merged with others to form a solely female army, Cumann na mBan, to aid the Irish Volunteers if needed. These are exciting times, Rosaleen. I want you to meet Saoirse soon again.'

And meet her I did. Not long after that conversation, Saoirse joined us in Wynn's for tea, from then on doing so often. Always she was amiable, seeming to bear no rancour at the time I spent with Lorcan. Rather, she appeared pleased by our friendship, frequently leaving us to talk alone. I wondered at her. This honourable creature. One so generous of spirit. She was noble, so much more noble than I could ever be.

I tried to be glad for Lorcan, for they were happy, that was clear. But, as I left them there in Wynn's one summer afternoon, I turned back to look at them as they smiled at me from the table, their hands raised to wave. And for a moment I stopped where I stood. For I saw it. The shadow settling around them.

*　*　*

Brother Thomas sat with Father Sheridan in the silence. He stared on, into the fire. Finally, Father Sheridan spoke.

'She saw the shadow. You see, she knew. Knew what was to come.' He paused. 'Yet it seems she had no sense of her own shadow.'

*　*　*

Perhaps I yearned to be worthy like Saoirse. Perhaps I was driven by guilt. But in the summer's light evenings I took to wandering in the fervid stink of the city's backstreets. I took food and treats to the filthy children who were gathered barefoot outside the squalid buildings; they scrambled and fought for the bits I brought, either devouring them or running with their haul to their mothers. I did not tell my aunt, or any other, of my visits there. I did not want them to worry, but, more, I did not want to be lauded for my charity. For, in truth, I knew what it was that drove me to those slums. That, having taken the life of one child, I longed to save another.

I think it was in that hot grime it found me, Father, but it made itself known in the autumn chill. At first, I thought it only the change of season, an early winter malady: the scratchy cough, the hint of wheezing as I walked home uphill from Sackville Street with groceries from Findlater's. The climb felt harder than ever it had before.

I thought it would pass but by late October what fatigue I'd suffered had worsened, my cough become hacking. Even before that, my aunt had remarked on my waning appetite, and I'd noticed the skirts loosen around my waist. Aunt Ellen insisted we call for Dr Lydon.

I was not bed-bound, but sitting on the armchair by the parlour window when Dr Lydon came that after-noon. He smiled as he crossed the room, his manner warm, all tension once between us seeming forgot-ten, faded in the year's melancholia he'd witnessed me endure. He sat on the armchair opposite me, placing his bag on the floor.

'You're feeling a little poorly, I hear,' he said kindly, then asked that I describe my symptoms. As I did, he nodded. 'And chills? Do you have chills?'

I thought on it and realised that I did suffer shudders but had thought them nerve shudders due to the war, or the autumn cold in the air. Dr Lydon took a stethoscope from his bag, placing it on my chest, then on my back, as I breathed heavily. At last, he removed the stetho-scope and looked at me.

'I need you to rest, Rosaleen. Do only what you find easy. No chores for now. And take as much fresh air as you can. Gentle exercise. Will you do that?'

I nodded up at him. 'Will it pass, Doctor?'

He smiled, gently. 'Rest, fresh air and exercise, Rosaleen,' he said. And did not answer my question.

They did not tell me immediately the nature of my affliction. But Dr Lydon told my aunt at once, for it was vital that all in the house were informed: that they hold a scarf or a handkerchief to their noses and mouths when around me. That my wash cloths and towels be kept separate. I was told that when I coughed it should always be into a handkerchief, which Mary would take away to be boil-washed.

'It's like a plague,' I later learned Dr Lydon had told my aunt. 'It's rife out there. And there is no cure.'

No. There was no cure. No remedy for this curse. Tuberculosis: the graveyard cough. When, at last, my aunt and mother, who had come straight away from Clare, sat with me to gently tell me in the parlour, somehow, after the first shock, I did not cry or rail against it. Rather, it seemed to settle easy upon me. I felt a certain calm. It seemed, somehow, just as it should be. For I had abandoned Amy to the Strangling Angel. Now I was visited by my own.

It was my aunt and mother who seemed more heart-sick, suffered more than I in those early days. And Lorcan. Lorcan who came seeking me when I did not arrive for our usual Tuesday morning meeting at Wynn's. As I sat in the parlour, I heard my aunt whispering to him in the hallway. When, at last, he appeared at the parlour door, he rushed towards me at the window, crouched down before me, took both my hands in his.

'My love.' His eyes were desperate. 'My dear, dear Rosaleen. My own beautiful Rose.'

To hear him call me his love – how I had longed to hear those words. I allowed myself for one precious moment to pretend that I was indeed his love. Just as he had always been mine. Then I met his eyes.

'Lorcan. I need you to take me somewhere.'

*   *   *

I asked him to take me to the monastery that day. That day and many after. From winter into spring, it was there I yearned to be. To spend whatever was left of my strength in carrying my gift to those who lay there: a winter rose. And the first bloom of spring. With Lorcan silent by my side, I would lay down my rose on Conor's grave. And at the bell tower. By Amy's.

One spring afternoon we stood over Conor's grave, the hill breeze gentle enough to feed me air, rather than snatching away my breath. Sensing a presence, I looked up to see the Abbot walking downhill towards us.

'Rosaleen.' He said my name softly as he reached us. As I introduced him to Lorcan, he smiled, vaguely recognising him from their previous brief encounter in the woodland.

The Abbot turned back to me. 'I have often watched you out here from my study but have not wanted to disturb you. I hope you will forgive me doing so now.'

'I am glad of it.' I spoke truly, for his kindly manner I found comforting. I could feel his scrutiny and understood it, for I was aware of my appearance. My pale, gaunt face, my frail frame. He surely also noticed the way Lorcan supported me with his arm. My laboured breathing. But he made no mention of any of it. Instead, he looked down upon Conor's grave.

'Dear Conor. We must believe he is at peace now. And you, Rosaleen.' The Abbot looked up to meet my eyes. 'I pray you have made your own peace with it.'

I smiled at him. Since I had learned my fate, indeed I had felt a certain sense of peace. For there was justice in it. And as I stood there in the flitting spring sunshine, like Conor's spirit dancing over the bough of the oak; as I looked upon the grave, the red beauty of the rose as if it were my own heart laid upon his – for those moments, at least, I had peace.

44

And now, Father, I must tell you. Must tell you while I still have breath to speak. Warn you, as I have tried to warn them: my mother, Aunt Ellen and Uncle Noel, Dr Lydon. And Lorcan. But they will not listen. They insist it is only the fevers. No longer can I leave my bed. But in early summer I was still able to walk with Lorcan in the cooler morning air, savouring the fresh mountain and sea breeze, the screech of the gulls as they swooped and settled on roofs, the rush of the horses and trams. Every sight and sound of my dear, beloved Dublin. But it was then, Father. Then they came.

They came fleeting at first. Like a blemish in my vision. But one morning as we neared the Gresham Hotel I faltered. I stopped, stunned, to stare at its windows. For, in that second, I saw there no elegant sheen but a row of cavernous dragons' mouths, spitting angry sparks and orange fire. I said nothing to Lorcan, who assumed I had only stopped to rest, but steadied myself to walk on.

But there came more visions. One morning soon after, passing Clerys' grand façade, I saw its walls shimmering as if melting under a merciless sun, set to crumble in a ferocious white heat. I was terrified. I judged this an unsettling of my senses, just as I'd suffered at the coming of war, but this felt an onslaught, much closer, as if the heat would scorch me. I feared, too, that my eyes might be failing but still said nothing to Lorcan.

One morning, unable to walk, I travelled with Lorcan in a cab to Wynn's. As we approached our destination, I gripped his arm suddenly. For as I looked at the hotel through the carriage window, a black mist lowered over my eyes, a smothering like a thick smoke rising through my chest. I gasped, truly frightened that this was the plague come to take me. I begged Lorcan to turn the cab and take me home. Urgently, he rapped the roof, shouting at the driver. But once home in my parlour armchair I felt revived, the mist and smoke disappeared, the smothering eased.

But from then, when walking with Lorcan, no longer did I see those buildings on Sackville Street as majestic. They had become malevolent. Looming over me as if, without warning, their walls might moan and tumble, bury me under their stone. Through my feet upon the paving I could feel a rumble, the earth beneath not at rest. I knew then.

'Lorcan,' I said. 'Something is coming.'

* * *

As the fevers have taken hold, I have woken screaming in the night, deafened by crashings and whinings in my head, as if something mighty has been felled, my nightdress and sheets drenched. One night my cries brought my mother running from her room.

'Flames!' I shouted, clutching her arm. 'The night sky is red, alive with fire. Can you see it, Mammy?'

She tried to soothe me. 'Hush, my love, hush. It is you that is on fire. Let me dry you, my darling.'

I long to cling to Lorcan when he comes to sit for short times at my bedside but to embrace him is too great a risk. Instead, I beg him to listen.

'Fire, everywhere *fire*. Everywhere flames. I see them, Lorcan. And I see you. *You* amongst them.'

Always he tries to comfort me.

'No, dear Rosaleen, there are no flames or fire here. It is the war beyond that is disturbing your senses. Please, sweet thing, try to rest.'

I have tried to tell them, Father. And I will try to tell you now.

* * *

Father Sheridan looked at Brother Thomas. 'The night she confessed herself to me was shortly before she died. An August night, 1915.'

Brother Thomas met his eyes. 'Eight months before it happened.'

* * *

Listen to me, Father. The day it will come, all will be still. Even nearing the noon warmth of day, the city as if sleeping. Veiled in a golden hush.

* * *

Father Sheridan's voice was a whisper. 'The city so still. Bathed in golden sunlight. Easter. Easter Monday.'

* * *

As if from beneath the earth will come a tremor. From every hidden alley, every narrow street they will come. Shadows sweeping over the city. And without warning will come a sound. Shattering every peace of that blue, blue sky . . .

* * *

Father Sheridan spoke softly. 'The crack of a single shot. Dealt by Sean Connolly an Abbey Theatre actor, scheduled to appear on stage that very day. Instead he led a company of the Irish Citizen Army to where a policeman stood on guard at Dublin Castle. The rebels come to seize the castle . . .'

* * *

And I see those shadows rise. Rise. Rise. Until they are shadows no more but a swell of flesh of blood, a crashing wave pouring through every building, washing over every street. I hear their roar. I see every paving stone I have ever loved shudder, every majestic column quake . . .

* * *

'The Brotherhood. The Irish Volunteers and the Irish Citizen Army. Rebels many more than a thousand strong,' Father Sheridan said. 'Storming Liberty Hall, City Hall, the Four Courts, factories and mills. Barricading the bridges. Seizing St Stephen's Green. Laying siege to the heart of the city.'

Brother Thomas nodded. 'I spoke to a nurse afterwards who'd escaped the mayhem in Sackville Street; she went running up to Temple Street Hospital, to spread the news that the rebels had taken over the GPO. And a doctor who was coming from Mass at the Pro-Cathedral, who could make no sense of the shots until he saw a child writhing on the ground, his leg torn by a bullet . . .'

* * *

And everywhere I hear panicked, confused shouts and roars. I hear dashing feet. Legions unleashed to chase down the risen. I hear the screams of onlooking women, the wails of children. Terror and bewilderment in men's eyes: *What is happening?*

* * *

Father Sheridan gazed upon the sparking logs. 'The British troops stormed the streets, climbing to the rooftops to open fire on the rebels. Their soldiers were firing from the roof of my own church. Down from the University Church and the Shelbourne Hotel, into St Stephen's Green where the rebels had dug trenches. The Irish Citizen Army hunkered down in the mud, firing back at them, beside them their commander . . .'

The two men held eyes as Brother Thomas spoke. 'The Countess Constance Markievicz.'

* * *

And come from that swell of flesh and blood I see them: an army, a formidable army, hundreds strong. A sea of green.

A sea of warrior women.

* * *

'The Cumann na mBan.' Father Sheridan turned back to the fire. 'The Countess was aided by another sniper, a schoolteacher, Margaret Skinnider, who was shot three times, trying to burn down houses to cut off British access to the rebel-held Royal College of Surgeons. Another, a Labour activist, Helena Molony, was firing from City Hall down into Dublin Castle. They say the British got confused when they realised women might be involved in the combat – women putting themselves in mortal danger, delivering guns and messages in plain dress, then changing back into uniform to join the firing squads. It seemed they'd heeded the Countess's rallying cry years before. When she'd urged them to cast aside their feminine shackles.

'*Dress suitably in short skirts and strong boots, leave your jewels and gold wands in the bank, and buy a revolver.*'

Her message to the Daughters of Ireland.

* * *

Father Sheridan gazed upon the gently licking logs as the two men fell silent, Brother Thomas lost to his thoughts.

Five full days and nights. Dublin under a barrage of fire and counter-fire. Bombardment. The British trying to crush the rebels and drive them from their strongholds. The deafening racket of machine guns, the blast of shells. Musketry and cannonfire. Sackville Street and its surrounds a raging inferno, canopies alight, buildings devastated, swallowed whole by the blaze. The British taking up command at the Gresham Hotel, firing on the rebels' own headquarters, the General Post Office. Its stately walls ravaged under the onslaught. A roaring sea of flames from the Gresham's windows . . .

A row of cavernous dragon's mouths, spitting angry sparks and orange fire . . .

Father Sheridan spoke. 'So many buildings destroyed. Clerys' vast windows melted in the heat of the flames.'

Shimmering as if melting under a merciless sun, set to crumble in a ferocious white heat . . .

'Men, women and children caught in the crossfire,' Father Sheridan said. 'Dying, clutching white flags in their hands.'

Brother Thomas thought on. Doctors and nurses tending to the wounded in churches, the Jesuits from Belvedere College risking their lives to come and offer them comfort, the nearby Capuchin friars tending to the wounded on both sides. The chaos and mayhem. The desperation. Food running short. Black smoke choking the air. The sky lit in a sickly glow.

'It was just as she had said.' Father Sheridan's voice broke through his thoughts. '*The night sky is red, alive with fire.* And she had seen something long before. Remember? At the party with the poet. As she laid hands upon his gentle friend.'

Brother Thomas recalled what had happened that Easter Monday. The rebels had raised the green flag of Ireland upon the GPO's regal roof. And they had raised another. The Tricolour. Green, white and orange. Signifying a white bridge of peace between the Orange loyalists to the Crown and the green of the Irish nationalists.

And a single figure had come to stand before the grand columns and proclaimed from his charter. He had declared Ireland free. With Easter, reborn. A new nation. A Republic. He had promised this land would grant to each of its citizens religious and civil liberty. That it would cherish all the children of the nation equally.

Father Sheridan spoke softly. 'The gentle schoolteacher, Padraig Pearse. Fated to become just as she had seen. Consumed by fire. Blood and fire.'

* * *

And the battle done, Father, I see in its wake a smouldering wasteland of embers, ashes and stark stacks of rubble reaching to the sky. The stench of burning. Dublin, my Dublin, those places I have so dearly loved, felled, become only a city of skeleton buildings and ghostly shells.

And I think of Lorcan. And I know now, as I look upon my ghost city, that it was no woman I had lost him to. But long ago to another who bore my name. His own Dark Rosaleen.

I had lost him to Ireland.

* * *

Father Sheridan looked up from the fire to Brother Thomas. 'She would not live to know what became of Lorcan. But, you see, she already knew. After what she'd told me came to pass I made enquiries at the Rotundo

Rooms. With so much of the city in ruins, it was one of the buildings to survive the Rising. They told me Lorcan had been lost. Had died in the fighting.'

Brother Thomas nodded. 'And Saoirse?'

Father Sheridan shook his head. 'I don't know. But I can only guess from what Rosaleen said of the shadow, that she was involved in the fighting and died also, possibly in the crossfire.'

The two were silent for a moment. Brother Thomas shifted to stoke the fire.

'And do you think that Pearse and the others will be proven right?' Brother Thomas asked. 'That from that Easter, Ireland will be reborn? Become a nation? A republic?'

'I don't know.' Father Sheridan mused on the glowing logs. 'At first, most Dubliners, like me, were devastated at the destruction of their city. Wynn's Hotel, where they say much of the Rising was plotted, was destroyed, the rebels defeated, Pearse and many of his comrades executed. As you know, the Countess was jailed, saved from the gallows by virtue of her gender. But after the grim slaughter of those executions, I felt a shift. When they executed James Connolly, the man who was such a champion for the workers in the lockout, a founder of the Labour Party – when they carried him, so badly wounded, on a stretcher to be shot and had to tie his body to a chair; when Joseph Plunkett married his sweetheart in his cell, only hours before facing the firing squad – it was then I sensed a change, sympathy towards the rebels.

Since then there has been a great stirring. A thirst for freedom. Where it will lead, I do not know. I don't know if I dare believe we can truly become one nation. That the Tricolour can achieve its vision: that the Crown's Orange loyalists and green Irish nationalists walk that white bridge of peace to one another.'

Brother Thomas nodded. 'Only time will tell.'

'Time she did not have.' Father Sheridan still stared at the fire. 'With the evening drawing in, she was growing weary. Even so, when Dr Lydon looked in, she assured him she was able to continue. When he left, she spoke of him.'

45

Dr Lydon has been so kind. I find it strange to think I once made him my enemy. Often he sits as near as is prudent by my bed and I talk with him, as I do now with you, through a handkerchief; take care, when I cough, to turn from him. I have told him I am sorry that in the past I scorned both him and science. At my contrition, he shook his head.

'Don't fret, Rosaleen. I don't pretend doctors have all the answers. But we are trying. And it is my great hope that, in the future, science will find the means to fight many of the diseases that afflict us today.'

'Like the disease I have now?' I said. 'You think that, one day, there might be a remedy for it?'

'I hope so,' he said gently. 'Perhaps we might even be able to prevent it and other illnesses through vaccination, like we have with smallpox and cholera.'

It was never far from my mind. I could not help but think of Amy and the Strangling Angel. 'If such illnesses are prevented, perhaps people will forget they ever existed,' I said.

'That, I hope too.'

'I hope they don't. Hope they don't forget.' Thinking still of Amy, I thought too of the medicine that might have saved her. 'If they do, they might forget also what a miracle they have in medicine. It is my great wish that you find your answers.'

He smiled ruefully, speaking of Aunt Ellen's lamented lost neighbour. 'No more death with the mere prick of a rose.'

Lorcan also comes to sit by my side. I see his torture in his eyes; he cannot hide it. I have been desperate. Begged him many times to heed my warning of the fire and shadows but he has no wish to hear. He thinks only of my suffering. I have tried to comfort him, assure him I have made my peace with my fate. It is evident, though, he has no peace with it. One evening I entrusted my love with my dearest wish.

'Lorcan.' I held his eyes. 'When I die I do not want you to lay flowers wherever I rest, but instead carry two single roses to the monastery. Carry them for me. Lay one upon Conor's grave. And one at the foot of the bell tower. Please. Do this in my name.'

It was plain he found it hard to bear such talk. But I entreated him. 'Please, Lorcan. Do this for me.'

At that, he nodded, his eyes welling.

'I will. I promise. I will lay down your roses. There, beneath the oak. And at the Rose Bell.'

What I told Lorcan was true. I had found peace. But then Dr Lydon brought me news. I could sense he was troubled that afternoon when he entered the room, as if there were something he was loath yet compelled to say. I urged him to tell me what was wrong. At last he sat by my side.

'Rosaleen.' He faltered before he spoke, then met my eyes. 'They have found Amy Armstrong.' He hesitated. 'The body of Amy Armstrong. Buried up in the Tallaght Hills at the Benedictine monastery.' He looked as if he could not fathom what he was saying. 'The Abbot has confessed to killing her.'

It was as if he'd struck me. I sat rigid against my pillows, stunned and senseless. Tremors flooding my blood, I could hardly see before me. Dr Lydon touched my arm; in his eyes I saw concern that he should deliver such devastating news when I was in so fragile a condition. But I also saw questions in those eyes.

Stupefied, in that moment I nearly confessed myself to him, told him all. I could not understand how this had happened. How had the child been found? Why now? And why, *why*, would the Abbot claim himself her murderer? But, somehow, even in my shocked state I thought of the Armstrongs. What the words I spoke now might cost them. I stuttered something.

'I don't understand.' My throat was raw. 'It can't be true. The Abbot knew and loved Amy. Why would he confess to such a thing? No. It cannot be true.'

Dr Lydon spoke slowly. 'And yet it is true that they have found the child's body there at the monastery.' He hesitated, I sensed not wishing to further upset me, yet needing to ask. 'You told me the Armstrongs said she had gone to London.'

To lie, to sully my soul, as I lay so close to death felt the greatest wrong. Yet I could not think what else to do.

'Yes,' I said. 'That is what they told me.'

I turned away my head to escape his scrutiny. I knew he would think me too distressed to talk. And, judging me too weak, would question me no more. To my shame, I was right.

With Lorcan the deception was even more torturous. When he came later that afternoon, it was clear he had heard the news. That he, too, was agonised, bewildered.

'You've heard?' he said, sitting hastily by my side. 'They have found little Amy, dear, sweet Amy Armstrong at the monastery. *Buried* at the monastery.' He wavered as if his next words might wound me. 'At the *bell tower*, Rosaleen. I cannot believe, as we laid roses for Conor, we stood so unknowing over her grave. I don't understand it, any of it.' He shook his head. 'They're saying that everybody thought Bernard and Ciss had taken her to London. And now . . .' He looked at me, anguished. 'The Abbot seemed such a kind, gentle man. But it seems we have been deceived by a *monster*.'

Seeing his anguish, his confusion, with every heartbeat left to me I longed to tell him the truth. As he spoke, I thought surely he must guess at my guilt. By my rose-laying at the bell tower. By the tower being also where Conor had met his death. But, no. Lorcan would never suspect either myself or Conor capable of such grievous wrongdoing. And I could not enlighten him now. Not even in my dying. Especially in my dying.

I thought again of what consequences any confession might bring to the Armstrongs, but, in truth, I thought more of Lorcan's final thoughts of me. I could not bear to see the recrimination in his eyes, to have such horror poison our last moments together, our last words. I felt too weak for the onslaught it would bring and I was a coward. As he took my hand and clasped it, the words he spoke next made me even more ashamed. He looked deep into my eyes.

'Now when I lay roses at the bell tower, I will lay them, too, for Amy. In your name.'

* * *

And so you have heard my story, Father. You have heard my confession. Since the news of Amy came, I have known no peace. I feel a stain on my soul for the lies I am telling those I love as I prepare to leave them. I know I must confess. For the sake of my soul, yes, but for the sake of the Abbot most of all. For his sake I can no longer think of what might befall any other. I can only think of him, a true innocent held guilty.

And now I have laid down my secret before you, I leave it in your care. I only ask that you keep it close, await my death before you reveal it. After that, the truth is yours to tell.

Do with it what you will.

*　*　*

'*Do with it what you will.*' Father Sheridan paused. 'She died soon after. On this very August night, three years ago. I returned to her to administer the last rites. Lorcan, her mother, aunt and uncle were gathered by her bed. She struggled that night, but I hear that at the end she was peaceful. Mercifully, her last breaths were easy. Her mother took her home to be buried in Clare.' He gazed quietly for a moment into the fire. 'Where I pray she is touched by the greatest grace – the grace of God. And the wind blows gentle around her.'

46

For a short while, the two sat in silence.

At last, Father Sheridan spoke. 'After she died, what she'd told me haunted me. I did not know whether to believe it. She'd been suffering from fevers, so I thought she might be confused, her mind disturbed. Perhaps all she'd confessed was merely the consequence of a delirium. Yet she'd seemed so clear. I thought above all else of the Abbot in jail. I was hounded by the notion that he might not be guilty.'

Brother Thomas thought back to the morning they had come for the Abbot. There would be no trial, for he'd confessed his guilt. The two policemen had come to take him into custody to await sentencing, keeping a respectful distance as he'd bid his farewells. The Abbot had walked solemnly around the great hall, nodding silently as he touched the hands of his disbelieving sons. Reaching Brother Thomas, he'd gently laid his hand on his. Brother Thomas's heart had been broken as he'd looked into the Abbot's eyes.

Father Sheridan's voice interrupted his thoughts. 'I could not forget Rosaleen's words and the possibility of the Abbot's innocence. I knew I must see him.'

Brother Thomas looked up. 'You saw the Abbot?'

Father Sheridan nodded. 'Yes. At Mountjoy Jail, so close to Eccles Street. As I walked there, I passed Rosaleen's house, looked up at the window of the very room where I had heard her confession.

'It pained me to see the Abbot in that place. Perhaps because of his age or his once revered position – perhaps because of my own – they allowed me to see him alone in a private room. It was grim – grey slabbed walls, a heavily bolted iron door – but at least it was somewhere we could talk undisturbed. When he appeared at the door, aided by two guards, I was shocked to see him so frail. I could see the tremor in his arms as he pulled out a chair and rested his hands on the table between us. But he tried to smile.

'"It is good to see you, Declan," he said.

'"And so good to see you," I replied.

'Waiting for the guards to leave, I studied him for a moment, then, not wanting to waste what little time we had, I told him what I must. I repeated all Rosaleen had told me. I observed his face as I talked, watching it for signs. I thought I saw an initial flinch but he steadied his gaze, eyes not leaving mine as I talked. When I had finished he spoke:

'"You say the poor girl was dying, had been suffering from fevers." His voice was weak but even. "Well, there you have your explanation. I'm sure she was greatly fond of the child. Perhaps when she heard the news of her death it unsettled her mind. Perhaps memories of healings became confused, one with another. It could be that some other sickly child had died naturally, one she had previously tried to heal, and she blamed herself. There might have been tortures in her mind we cannot guess at. Whatever her troubles, the truth of the situation we know. I have confessed it."

'His words made some sense to me. But I could not forget her clarity. Yet, even though fragile, he was firm. I began to speak but he stopped me.

'"It is finished, Declan; it is done. I am to blame for the death of the child. I and no other." He held my eyes. "Please. Let it be."'

Brother Thomas watched Father Sheridan's face. The priest spoke slowly. 'You remember when the child was raised from the bell tower?'

Brother Thomas nodded, then looked away. He remembered all too well that horror. The brothers had been huddled at the windows, murmuring prayers as they looked out over the woodland. But he could not bear to watch.

Father Sheridan went on. 'And then the day of her funeral. Rosaleen had died by the time they laid the child to rest in consecrated ground. I went to Amy's funeral. I saw many of your brothers there, but not you, Thomas.'

Brother Thomas thought back to that awful day. He shook his head. He had not been able to endure it. 'No. I spent the day in prayer.'

'There were so many there; the community was in shock,' Father Sheridan said. 'I saw Dr Lydon and

Rosaleen's aunt and uncle with Lorcan, who introduced me to the Dr Mallon Rosaleen had spoken of.
I searched his face but the man was stoic. If there was
any truth in her story I did not find it in his eyes. If any
of the other mesmerists were there I did not meet them.
Lorcan introduced me to no one else. Amy's parents
were not there. The word was that they had sold up
their London house and left for a life in the missions.
No one knew if they had gone to India, the Orient or
Africa. They could not be found.'

Father Sheridan rose, going to the window to look
out over the woodland in near darkness now. Only faint
flickers of candlelight weaving downhill with the last of
the pilgrims. Father Sheridan mused on them.

'The first year they came, the first anniversary of her
death, the embers were barely cooled on the ruins of
Dublin. Tonight is her third anniversary. Now it seems
that every year on this night, they will come. Come to
walk the Way of the Rose. Come to lay roses at the
Rose Bell.'

'Yes.' Brother Thomas still gazed into the hearth.

Father Sheridan turned from the window. 'It appears
that after she died Lorcan told his old friends, the mesmerists, what Rosaleen had seen in her last vision. Told
them too of her dying wish that roses should be laid
upon Conor's grave and at the bell tower. When what
she had seen came to pass, the mesmerists hailed her
as a prophet. A great prophet. And healer. All began
to talk once more of how the passing of her hands had

cured them. A mania grew around her name. The Rose. The legend was born.'

'A myth.' Brother Thomas whispered into the fire.

'And it is Noreen who leads the vigil,' Father Sheridan said. 'The same Noreen who once called Rosaleen evil. It is she who now claims the Rose immaculate.'

Brother Thomas lifted his eyes. 'It suits her purpose. Her mission. Her zeal.'

Brother Thomas looked back to the fire. He thought of how he had once had zeal. Belief in an ideal. How he made of flesh and blood an idol. It was a zeal he derided now. Zeal was dangerous. Robbed you of your senses. Made you blind to all else but your mission, the object of your adulation. Made you do inhuman, inhumane things. He recalled the Abbot's guidance: *We must think on love more than zeal.* He remembered again the Abbot's words: *The imperfect human. The fragile human. There is beauty in that.*

He thought of the fallible and imperfect Rosaleen, now held immaculate. A symbol of near divinity and grace. The Rose. But from that rose had sprung vain and callous thorns. He thought of the cross that stood in the monastery grounds. Much good had been done in its name. He witnessed it every day here amongst his brothers. But he thought too of the Christian zealots, so fired by belief, who had wielded the cross like a weapon in their desert crusades, shedding the blood of the unfaithful. He thought of the differing symbols of each and every religion, their disciples believing themselves bearers of the one true creed, therefore righteous in imposing their will. He thought of the revolution just passed in Russia. The Bolsheviks' symbol of hammer and sickle. Romanov blood was still fresh on the paving. He wondered where those idealists' vision would end. What tortures would ensure their countrymen bowed to their word. He wondered if all ideals were destined to become tyrannies.

'Noreen's zeal. The same zeal some hold for God.' Father Sheridan's words came as if reading his mind.

He looked up at the priest still standing at the window. Father Sheridan was silent for a moment, then took a step towards the fire. 'But it was no zeal for God that brought you here, Thomas.' He stepped closer to the hearth. 'Not love of God, but the love and loss of a man. And so now you know what I must ask you.'

His eye was steady as he looked down upon Brother Thomas.

'Is what Rosaleen confessed to me true?'

47

Rían had stood many misty, early mornings at his brother's grave. Those endless days after his death had somehow become weeks. Months become a year. Beneath the bough of the tree, he would stare down upon the silent mound, sometimes weary with self-recrimination, sometimes merely numb. One morning he had sensed a gentle approach. He had looked up to see the Abbot.

The Abbot had not spoken, just placed his hand softly on Rían's shoulder, his eyes deep with understanding. Rían had looked again to the grave. He'd felt a certain solace at the Abbot's touch. Appreciation at his silence. His knowing there were no words.

From that time on, the Abbot would often come to stand beside him. Sometimes words were spoken, but mostly they simply stood together quietly. One morning, as Rían turned to leave, the Abbot said gently, 'Rían, you must know. If ever you need to talk, I am here.'

Rían had nodded in gratitude, but later, working at his desk, he'd been sure he would not avail himself of the Abbot's kindness. What good was there in talking? When all you longed to speak, but dare not, was the truth. That truth must remain buried with Conor.

With Amy. Yet, as time passed, as he mindlessly shuffled papers regarding matters that meant little to him now, he found growing within him a yearning. A need for the tender compassion he had felt from the Abbot. A tenderness, a compassion absent in his silent house, no longer a home. His mother still sat stiff with blame, his father kinder but remote, behind a barricade which allowed no mention of Conor.

Finally, one evening, Rían had found his usual stroll leading him to the monastery. He had hesitated at the gates, then passed through, climbing the hill to Conor's grave. There, he had stared at the monastery's grand arched door, at last finding himself moving towards it. Tentatively, he had looked though the doorway, stepping into an echoing hallway, alcoves adorned with statues, candles and flowers surrounding him. He studied the graceful and sorrowful face of the Madonna set upon a plinth, amongst a row of serene saints. The scent of incense was heady and soothing. When a passing brother enquired how he could help, Rían had asked if he might see the Abbot. The brother had led him down an oak-panelled passageway towards an arched wooden door, disappearing through it. Soon, the brother reappeared to beckon him.

Rían had stepped into a beautiful room with ochre colouring and wooden rafters. Imposing bookshelves lined the walls, and before the window stood a mahogany desk piled with books, beside them a honey-coloured candle. From the vast, latticed, arch of the windows he could see the oak and Conor's grave. The Abbot rose from his desk and smiled.

'Rían. I am glad to see you.'

* * *

That first evening, in the Abbot's study, they had talked of many things. The Abbot had not talked directly of Conor; Rían sensed him not wishing to aggravate the wound. But he had asked how Rían was finding the world. Rían knew what he had meant. He meant this world without his brother.

'I am finding it . . .' Rían had hesitated. 'Meaningless.'

The Abbot had nodded in understanding. 'The loss of a loved one can rob life, the world, of its meaning, at least for a while. Until we find a way to go on. To travel with grief. But I hope you can draw comfort from knowing that grief is an experience we all share. The whole human family. We all come to know what it is to love, to lose. Everyone is your brother or sister in grief.'

Rían thought on it. Everyone would come to know what it was to grieve. But not all knew what it was to kill. To be to blame for the death of your loved one. In that moment, he longed to lay down his burden. Lay down the heavy weight of his guilt, his sorrow, but he had not the courage. Still, his knotted mind was somewhat eased at the Abbot's calm counsel.

Over that first winter of war and spring he came, gradually becoming familiar with the brothers, feeling comforted by their peaceful air, their gentle humour. At first he watched, then found himself closely observing their way of life. He was struck by its simplicity. They prayed, they read and studied, they worked the land. He watched them making jam and cordials from the garden berries, digging vegetables for their own kitchen and boxing them for the poor.

And over time the thought took hold: in this simple life, this life of service, he might find meaning. To live here, by Conor's grave, and stand watch over his brother. To live close to him and amongst those who, in turn, would become his brothers. To escape from the world but be not alone. Yes, perhaps in this way he might find peace.

When at last in spring, he confided his thoughts in the Abbot, the Abbot smiled as if perhaps he had expected it. He had risen from his study desk, holding out his arms to him. Rían had stepped into his embrace.

'Brother, dear brother,' the Abbot said. 'You are welcome.'

He had become a postulant. Come to live in the monastery amongst the brothers to afford him time to ensure the path he had chosen was the right one. Joining the monks at prayer, he was conscious that he did not share their faith. But since Conor's death he had believed in nothing, either Divine or worldly, and in some way the brothers' mellow mantra filled the void. The austere room, the cell, he slept in served as a penance for his wrongs. But there was also solace. For in the evening at Vespers as he listened to the monks' chant and sweet song it lulled him to another place, a place of peace and harmony. He enjoyed the brothers' warm companionship at the refectory meals and the times he sat with them in reflective silence. As they worked the land and he helped gather food for the needy, he'd felt surer of this calling than anything else in life.

It had been during this time that his conversations with the Abbot had grown deeper. As the Abbot prepared him for his first vows, the taking of the habit, he had counselled him in monastic life. Together they would sit at the Abbot's study desk.

'The rule of St Benedict, the monastic life, petitions us to seek not only God, to know him better and truly, but also asks us to seek and know the truth of ourselves,' the Abbot had said, one evening. 'It asks us to uncover the truth of our own hearts and minds.'

He'd been stunned. Suspected somehow that the Abbot had seen the stain on his soul. Knew the truth of him and was asking him to reveal it. He'd searched the Abbot's eyes but they were merely steady and kind. No. He was not testing him. But even as Rían recoiled from the truth, everything in him longed for it. He longed to unburden himself to the Abbot who was now like a kindly father to him.

The Abbot's words had stayed with him as he went to stand at Conor's grave. He thought much those days of his part in his brother's death. The terrible night at the bell tower. How he should have demanded that they halt the madness, go to the police before the wrong-doing became too great, before Conor became trapped in the lie. He had not done so because his thoughts had been of her. The Rose.

He had made of her an idol. He had thought he loved her, but it had not been love but obsession. Desire. Desire was not love. Desire was a coveting of the prized object for yourself; love was wishing all that was good for the other. He had not wanted to protect her but to possess her. He had not cared for her but craved her. Every deed had not been for her sake but to make her indebted to him, that she might come to love him, need him. It had not been love, for love was unbreakable, even by death. And he had no love for her now. That desire had withered away, lay dead on the ground, like every rose they had laid.

Each day, facing the Abbot's probing eyes, his heart would swell. With every day the need to unburden himself grew stronger. At last, he realised he could never hope for any meaningful life, any peace, until he had confessed himself.

One afternoon he had gone to the Abbot's study, knocked only briefly before entering. The Abbot had looked up from his reading, surprised at Rían's haste. He had sat before the Abbot.

'I must tell you something,' he'd said.

48

That day he had confessed all. He'd wept as at last it came: truth, blessed truth, his heart releasing like an unclenching fist. He had told of the ill-fated healing, of the gruesome task imposed on Conor, of what he had done in his brother's place at the bell tower. And what had become of Conor because of it.

The Abbot had listened, stunned. He had asked questions, urgent questions, as Rían stuttered through sobs. With head bowed, at last Rían was done. In the silence, Rían had lifted his welling eyes to see the Abbot's face tight and white with shock.

'And the child is buried there, at the bell tower?' the Abbot had said finally.

Rían had nodded with a flood of shame. The Abbot shook his head.

'This cannot be. Cannot be,' he'd mumbled as if to himself. 'It must be undone.' He was silent for a moment, then eyed Rían. 'And the parents, Amy's parents. Where are they now?'

Rían knew what had become of the Armstrongs. A year or more ago, worried that guilt might loosen their tongues, wishing to at least know their whereabouts, he had used his position as a solicitor to his advantage. Under the guise of needing to contact them on a legal matter he had managed to obtain their London address from Bernard Armstrong's former employer. When he'd enquired there, he'd learned that the house had been sold, the Armstrongs sailed for the missions with no plan to return. They had not left word where they might be reached. Rían was certain of why they had gone. Like him, they were unable to cope with their grief, their guilt. Like him, they needed to live a life of service. He told the Abbot what he knew.

The Abbot was silent a while, then spoke. 'Rían, I want you to go to the chapel. I want you to lay down this burden before God as you have laid it down before me. Then, I want you to go to your room and stay there until I call for you. I must think.'

* * *

The Abbot had not called for him that evening but sent word that he should take his meal in the refectory with his brothers then return to his room. It was the next morning that the Abbot summoned him.

For a moment they sat silently facing one another at the Abbot's desk, the sun through the arched window, streaming warm between them. Then, the Abbot spoke.

'Rían, I have thought through the night on what you have told me. I have thought and I have prayed.

And of one thing I am sure: the child must be raised from the bell tower. She must receive the funeral rites, a proper Christian burial and be laid to rest in consecrated ground. Of this there can be no doubt.'

Rían had bowed his head in accordance. So, the day was come. When finally he must go to the authorities. He replied almost in relief. 'With your blessing, then, Father Abbot, I will go to the police. Then the child can be raised.'

'No.' The Abbot's voice was gentle but firm. 'Not you, but I. I will go to the police. I will tell them that it was I who buried the poor child there. That it is I who was to blame for her death.'

Rían looked up, not comprehending. He uttered in confusion but the Abbot stopped him.

'I will tell them that when Amy was ill I persuaded the Armstrongs to bring her here,' the Abbot said. 'That it was I who convinced them I could cure the child through the healing power of God. That I insisted they leave the child to me and she was under my care. That after the child died under my hands and mine alone, I assured them that I would arrange a Christian burial. That instead of keeping that promise to them, fearing for myself, wanting no investigation, no shame brought upon the monastery, I secretly buried the child at the bell tower. It is plausible. The police will believe me.'

Rían stared in shock. He could hardly form the words: 'But why?'

The Abbot softly smiled. 'I am old, Rían. My life is nearly done. Yours is before you. And it is not only you we must consider, but your family. If you confess, not only will your already bereft parents have to contend with their son going to prison but also learn that their other beloved son was involved in a crime, one that caused him to take his own life. It would add so greatly to their pain. There would for ever be rumour around it. They would have to suffer a lifetime of shame for both their sons. And if you tell the truth there is more danger for the Armstrongs. If it is known the child died under their watch in their home, that they let her be taken for secret burial, if they ever return or are found, the consequences for them would be great. If I confess, I will be able to persuade the police that the Armstrongs were blameless, leaving their daughter to my care in a holy place, trusting me, a man of God, to do right by their child. I will say I forced them to stay silent afterwards, threatened them into submission. I am sure I can persuade the police that they were greatly deceived and are grieving. I believe that even if the authorities could find them, they might not be inclined to try.'

Rían stared at the Abbot. He was shocked but the Abbot's words made sense. He thought of his parents – their grief and shame should their son be convicted of such a heinous crime; their anguish if they came to know Conor's part in it and the abominable reason behind his death. And if they followed the Abbot's plan, the

Armstrongs would also be protected. For a moment he sat speechless, then reached for the Abbot's hands.

'No, please, Father Abbot,' he begged. 'Speak first to the Abbot Primate in Rome. Ask him what you should do.'

The Abbot shook his head. 'If I go to the Abbot Primate I will either have to incriminate you by telling the truth or lie to him. Neither of these am I prepared to do. I also fear the Abbot Primate might be minded to try to conceal this. I want, above all, the vile subterfuge around the child's death and burial place to end. I want her raised once more into the light. I do not want to be counselled to keep this hidden.'

Rían fell silent. The Abbot gripped his hands.

'Allow me to do this for you, Rían. I am the confessor but even though I am an ordained priest I have never given absolution, for I do not consider myself a vessel of divine power. I will not place myself above my brother or sister. This is my choice because I am master within my own monastery. But my hope is that I have humanity. That I listen. I hear. I have made myself the keeper of sins. One who takes sins and makes them his own. Let me carry yours.'

*   *   *

And so it had been. One summer morning the Abbot had left for the city. That day in Dublin Castle he had made his confession before the attending officers, pleading that they attach no blame to the Armstrongs. He insisted that they had been betrayed by him and in their shock and grief had not known what to do or where to turn. The Abbot told the police he confessed now, for he could no longer live, nor did he want to die, with this horror on his conscience. The police, greatly shocked at this extraordinary confession from an eminent member of the clergy, had not taken a statement or charged him immediately but said they must speak first to their superiors. The Abbot learned through his conversations with them that his confession had reached the highest echelons, the Chief Secretary and the Viceroy himself before his claim was investigated and he was charged with manslaughter and the unlawful burial of the child.

The Abbot had suspected this might be so. The administration did not like to disturb the status quo that existed between themselves and the Catholic Church, fearing a backlash from the nationalists but, in this case, they had little choice. The crime was too outlandish and, more pertinently, with the child having to be raised, too prone to discovery. It would fall to the police to remove the child from her secret grave and, after examination, deliver her to the proper authorities for burial. With so many people involved, too many would know of it, and if it was learned that the administration had tried to conceal it they would be held complicit in a crime. The probable consequences of suppressing this were too great.

Dublin Castle had hoped to keep the proceedings against the Abbot himself as quiet as possible. It seemed they were not minded to bring a charge against the Armstrongs, even if they could be found. Possibly through some sympathy for the couple, more likely because to pursue others would only make the fuss greater. But however they hoped to contain the situation, they must have known it a vain hope. For, once the recovery of the child at the Rose Bell began, it was not long before the *Irish Times* and *Daily Express* had the story and the scandal was mighty, the fodder on every tongue. The judge then had no option but to impose what must be seen as an appropriate sentence. Five years. Shorter than it could have been. Too long for a man of the Abbot's advancing years.

The morning the Abbot had left the monastery to make his confession, he had called Rían to his study. They had stood close together before the desk. Rían was barely able to look into the Abbot's eyes – filled with such goodness when his own were filled with shame. Seeing this, the Abbot spoke.

'Do not be ashamed, Rían. My greatest wish is that your soul be renewed. Soon you will take your first vows. And take the habit. I have acts I must perform before I finally leave the monastery. Two last acts. Let the first of those be that, from this day, you will be known as Thomas. The Apostle Thomas was known as Didymus, 'the twin'. So now I see before me the twin. One who looks the same as another but is not. You are reborn. A new man, free of the sin I carry for you. Innocent before God.'

*   *   *

Father Sheridan's eyes remained on Brother Thomas. In the silence, the priest sat down before him once more.

'So is it true, Thomas?' he asked again, softly. 'That it is you – you who I once knew so well at the university as Rían – who buried the child at the bell tower? You who kept the secrets of the Rose? Is the Abbot innocent?'

Brother Thomas said nothing, his eyes cast downwards.

'I ask you now, for I have been again to visit the Abbot in jail.' Father Sheridan tried in vain to meet Brother Thomas's eyes. 'He is frail and failing, Thomas. He is dying. I do not want him to die in that place, surrounded by violence and hatred. I wish him to spend his dying days surrounded by love. If he is innocent I want to bring him home. Home to the brothers.'

Thomas felt his heart grip. The Abbot had instructed him he must never visit him in jail. He did not want Thomas's mind disturbed by witnessing him in captivity. Instead, he wished his sacrifice, his gift, to allow the reborn Thomas to walk lightly in the world, dedicated without distraction to a life of service. In this way he could atone. In this way he would honour the Abbot. And Thomas had made the Abbot's wish his mission. But the thought now of the Abbot alone, fragile and dying tortured him.

Yet there was so much at stake. Revealing the truth would have consequences. Not merely for himself but others. Too much depended on his answer. He must think before acting. He remembered the Abbot's words. He spoke them:

'I am innocent before God.'

49

Mountjoy Jail, Dublin, September 1918

Brother Thomas waited to be admitted to Mountjoy Jail at the grim, grey gatehouse. Soon a prison guard escorted him across a stony courtyard into a vast, echoing hall. Leading him through a myriad of bleak passageways and iron gates, the guard finally showed him into a rough stone-walled room, bare apart from a table and two chairs. Left alone, Thomas took a seat at the table, listening to the shouts and clanging of doors beyond. At last, he heard the whine of the heavy door beside him.

He was shocked to see the bent man being aided by two guards. This man looked old, too old, too frail to be the Abbot. His feet shuffled over the flagstone floor, yet as he looked up, even though his face was sunken, his eyes shadowed, at seeing Thomas his dry lips parted in a smile.

'Thomas.' His voice was a croak.

'Father Abbot.' Thomas stood hastily, wanting to assist the Abbot, but the guards waved him down. Thomas sat again as they lowered the Abbot into the chair opposite him. Once the Abbot was seated, the guards hovered.

'Please.' The Abbot looked up to his jailers. 'Would you allow us some moments alone?'

Eyeing one another, each guard silently nodded, clearly yielding to the Abbot's fragility and age. As they left, the Abbot studied Thomas through weakly smiling eyes. Thomas remained silent, still shocked by the Abbot's appearance.

'It is so good to see you, Thomas.' There was a tremor in the Abbot's voice. 'I welcome the sight of my brothers whenever they come. And many do. They are so good.'

Thomas started, distressed. 'But you told me you did not want me to come.'

The Abbot nodded. 'That is true. Yet now I see you I cannot help but be pleased. But I must ask you: what is it that brings you here now? I hope nothing troubles you?'

At the Abbot's concern, Thomas wavered, his eyes cast down. He knew the question he had come to ask and had no difficulty asking it. But he hesitated at what reason to give. The Abbot guessed at it.

'You have come because I am dying?' he said softly.

Thomas looked up. The Abbot held his eyes.

'I have no fear of it, Thomas. And neither must you fear for me.'

'You have no fear of dying *here*?' Thomas shook his head, incredulous. 'Alone?'

The Abbot smiled. 'I am never alone. The guards make sure of that. And I believe my maker will receive me just as well from this place as any other.'

Thomas shifted in his chair, leaned closer to the Abbot. 'But if you *could* come home?'

The Abbot frowned. 'But I cannot. I must serve my sentence.' He observed Thomas a moment. 'We have long settled this. Why must you raise it now?'

Thomas told him then. Of Father Sheridan's visit. Of the confession of the Rose. He told him in what manner he had replied when Father Sheridan had asked him directly of his own guilt: that he was innocent before God. The Abbot smiled again.

'That is good, that is good.' He met Thomas's eyes. 'And there you must leave it. Let it be.'

Thomas was agonised. 'But I cannot leave you here. I can no longer do it. My conscience, my soul –' he faltered – 'my *heart* will not allow it.'

The Abbot reached across the table to touch his hand. 'That is because your heart is good, Thomas. Just as I have always known. But you must understand, nothing has changed. If you confess now, your parents will still suffer. The Armstrongs too. You will bring great trouble down upon them all. And that, *my* conscience, my soul and heart, will not allow.'

Thomas stared at him, bereft.

The Abbot spoke again. 'Do not allow what time I have already served here to be in vain, Thomas.' He gripped Thomas's hand. 'Return to your brothers. Go with my blessing. Go with this, my dying wish.'

50

Mount St Kilian Abbey, Dublin, September 1919

From high in his chamber, Brother Thomas gazed through the arched window, over the lush grass and sweep of the hill. His eye roamed over the cloisters to the chapel roof, beneath it the monastery graveyard. Where the Abbot now lay.

They had brought him home. After Thomas had visited the Abbot that day, he had gone immediately to the prison governor. Put his case before him. Pleaded with him for clemency for the Abbot. He had told him that, truly remorseful, the Abbot was old, frail and dying. He had called upon the governor's mercy. The governor had been easily persuaded. Thomas guessed it was because the fuss around the Abbot's conviction had now faded. If the Abbot were to die in jail it might once again reach the ears of the journalists and reignite their interest. Far better that he die beyond the scrutiny of the prison guards and inmates, quietly at home. The governor's reply had not come immediately but soon enough that the Abbot had not languished much longer in a cold prison cell, but had returned to be surrounded by the warmth of his brothers.

Thomas's eye settled on the great oak standing watch over Conor's grave. Conor. *Gone.* The Abbot. *Gone.* Their absence had dimmed the light in his heart. Yet he basked still in their own hearts' warmth. Their love dwelling within him. He thought of the eulogy he had written for the Abbot: *Our love travels with you. Your love remains here with us.* Loved, lost, loved. Love so untouched by death. This must sustain him. His eye strayed towards the woodland and lingered there. There upon the leaves turning golden, concealing what lay within. The Rose Bell.

Going to sit in the armchair by the hearth, he leaned back his head, listening to the ever-blowing wind from the hills.

'*I hear it whispering to me now at the window. It carried me into this world, now it comes to carry me away . . .*'

And, she, the Rose, gone too. But in the wind he heard her voice. He searched himself for feeling. He harboured no love for her – what had passed for love – now. Nor the malice and rage he once bore. Now his heart was numb. But regret. Yes, regret. For what had happened at the bell tower, for whatever part he and she together had played in Conor's death. That regret he would carry with him through this world and to any world beyond. Never would he be free of it.

And another regret. For now the Rose was adored. An idol. Myth masking her mortal form. She had been elevated to the divine while the Abbot, he of the greatest humanity, had been cast a devil. The wind blew stronger at the window. He remembered its rattle at the window on the night the Abbot had died. To the world beyond he was the fallen angel, Lucifer, but to the brothers, he was beloved.

The brothers had never thought their Abbot guilty. They had known of no time when the child had stayed in the monastery and, furthermore, could not believe him capable of such an act. But even if they did not understand, they had accepted their Father Abbot's word, believing the reason known only to him. When they had brought him home the brothers had laid him in his bedchamber to tend him, Brother Thomas constantly by his side. The night before he died, the Abbot had looked up from his pillow at Thomas. His voice was weak.

'I have been anointed. Given the last rites. And I have made my confession.' Thomas took his hand, bending to listen. 'But perhaps I should make my confession to *you*. To you, the confessor.' He smiled, his eyes closing at the effort of speaking.

Thomas gripped his hand. 'You have nothing to confess. There is no stain on your soul.'

'Nor yours.' The Abbot opened his eyes. 'You must believe that.'

Thomas had been silent, looking down upon the Abbot's fragile hand, its silky, pale skin marked by liver spots.

The Abbot spoke again. 'I am human, Thomas. I have not been free of sin. That is the truth of it. But perhaps it is not only truth that brings atonement. Perhaps through my false confession I have redeemed myself. Perhaps my mortal soul has been saved by a lie.' He smiled again, closing his eyes, giving in to slumber.

Thomas had been with his brothers at the Abbot's side when he died. He had held the Abbot's hand as he took his last breath. He had leaned down to kiss his fingers, whispering to him silently: *Go. Go gently now. My love goes with you.*

A knocking disturbed his thoughts. He looked up from his chair to see young Dominic, now a novitiate, in the doorway.

'Brother Thomas. There is a woman here; she is asking for the confessor. Will you see her?'

Brother Thomas straightened in his chair. 'Yes. Of course.'

A woman, perhaps forty, entered the room, in a plain black coat and hat, bringing the chill of the day in with her. Beneath her hat, the wind had tossed her hair, tendrils falling loose. Clutching her small bag, her eyes darted around the room until they came to settle on him. She had a look he had seen many times. In the eyes of others. In his own. Haunted.

He stood to welcome her. 'Please.' He gestured to the second chair at the hearth. 'Please, sit.'

The woman sat stiffly. She seemed unable to meet his eyes, fiddling with the handle of her bag. He watched her a moment before speaking, recalling the morning he had stood facing the Abbot in his study. The morning the Abbot had left to make his confession. He remembered how the Abbot had looked into his eyes, a deep smile in his own.

'And now my last act. When I depart the monastery I will leave you under the care of a newly appointed Abbot. To him I will pass my mantle. But to you, Thomas, I pass another. I decree that at your final vows you will become the confessor.'

Brother Thomas had not questioned it. The two had looked at one another in silent understanding. They both knew the words the Abbot did not speak:

For you know what it is to sin.

Brother Thomas leaned closer to the woman, her eyes lowered. His voice was gentle.

'I can see you are troubled. Whatever your burden is, please lay it down here with me.' He reached to touch her hand. 'I am the confessor. The keeper of sins. One who takes sins and makes them his own.'

He smiled at her raised eyes. 'Let me carry yours.'

Acknowledgements

Firstly, a big thank you to all the Welbeck team for bringing this book to fruition. Special thanks to my editor, Jennifer Edgecombe, for her hard work and diligence, and also to Rosa Schierenberg, for initially embracing The Rose. Great thanks as always to the indefatigable Cat Camacho for the cast of her steely eye. Thank you to Simon Michele for the beautiful cover. A big thank you to my agent, Sara O'Keeffe at Aevitas Creative, for her faith, work, and ever patient ear. For guidance on legal matters pertaining to plot, I thank District Court Judge Elizabeth MacGrath (who manifests on these pages as Professor MacGrath). Any errors are entirely my own. I am grateful, too, to our Irish jewel, author, Donal Ryan, for his support and generosity with his time.

The Graces is set in the era when my youthful paternal grandparents courted in Dublin. Thank you to them, my father and my beloved late mother (initially a country girl) for the many stories that inspired not only much of this book, but also stirred in me a desire to live myself in that city, which I did in my early adult life. There, the magic of Dublin town and magic of youth intertwined to create a heady mix. A corner of my heart will always beat for Dublin. To my brother and sister-in-law and those of my family in Dublin, Tipperary, and England, however far, I always feel you near. Thank you to my dear friends of old for your love and loyalty. And to my husband, who I am thankful for every day.

Grá mór to you all.